PRAISE FOR THE NOVE

Winner of the National Readers Choice
of the Daphne du Maurier Award fo

A KISS TO KILL

"Rich with dialogue and filled with tight suspense, Bruhns's latest holds true to the excellence readers have come to expect from this author." —*Romantic Times*

"Greg and Gina are one of the hottest couples I've read lately . . . There's not one thing I didn't like about this book. It's fast paced. It's got an intriguing and complex story and mystery. It's got fascinating characters on every page. It's sexy and sensual and then some." —*The Good, The Bad, and The Unread*

"A thrill ride of fast action and hot sex in the steamy Louisiana bayous, Nina Bruhns's latest delivers it all!" —*CJ Lyons, bestselling author of Warning Signs*

IF LOOKS COULD CHILL

"This is a fast-paced action adventure with a steamy romance . . . a keeper." —*Night Owl Romance*

"Nonstop, edge-of-your-seat action that never lets you down . . . the relationship between Marc and Yankee Tara was H-O-T . . . There was never a moment that I wanted to put it down." —*Joyfully Reviewed*

"I loved *If Looks Could Chill* . . . I can't wait to read what will happen in the third book of this marvelous series!" —*Manic Readers*

continued . . .

"Anything but chilly—the sexual action is as hot and steamy as the action in the field . . . If you like a thrill a minute, you will enjoy *If Looks Could Chill*. The gripping tale is well written and filled with intrigue and passion."

—*Romance Reviews Today*

"Suspense just got a whole lot hotter with Nina Bruhns's dynamite romantic thriller. A hero to die for and a heroine to cheer for . . . an awesome, sexy story."

—Allison Brennan, *New York Times* bestselling author

SHOOT TO THRILL

"Bruhns makes a successful move from category romance with this fast-paced thriller . . . powerful chemistry."

—*Publishers Weekly*

"A wonderful, suspense-filled, nonstop action thriller. The chemistry between Kick and Rainie is explosive."

—*Fallen Angel Reviews*

"Sexy, suspenseful, and so gritty you'll taste the desert sand. A thrill ride from start to finish!"

—Rebecca York, *USA Today* bestselling author

"A provocative, sexy thriller that will get your adrenaline pumping on all levels. A riveting breakout novel that will shoot Ms. Bruhns straight to bestsellerdom. Move over, boys, and see how it's really done!"

—Tamar Myers, award-winning mystery author

"Intense pacing . . . powerful characters . . . searing emotions and explosive sexual tension! Once I started reading *Shoot to Thrill*, I couldn't stop! This is high-action suspense at its very best!" —Debra Webb, bestselling author

MORE PRAISE FOR NINA BRUHNS

"The stuff legends are made out of." —*Midwest Book Review*

"Shocking discoveries, revenge, humor, and passion fill the pages . . . An interesting and exciting story with twists and turns." —*Joyfully Reviewed*

"[A] delightfully whimsical tale that enchants the reader from beginning to end. Yo ho ho and a bottle of fun!"
—Deborah MacGillivray

"This is one you will definitely not want to miss!"
—*In the Library Reviews*

"Nina Bruhns . . . imbues complex characters with a great sense of setting in a fast-paced suspense story overladen with steamy sex." —*The Romance Reader*

"Gifted new author Nina Bruhns makes quite a splash in her debut . . . Ms. Bruhns's keen eye for vivid, unforgettable scenes and a wonderful romantic sensibility bode well for a long and successful career." —*Romantic Times* (4 stars)

"The intricate and believable plots crafted by Nina Bruhns prove she is a master of any genre. Her talent shines from every word of her books." —*CataRomance.com*

"The kind of story that really gets your adrenaline flowing. It's action-packed and sizzling hot, with some intensely emotional moments." —*Romance Junkies*

"Nina Bruhns writes beautifully and poetically and made me a complete believer." —*Once Upon A Romance*

"Tells a very rich tale of love . . . a book you are going to want to add to your collection." —*Romance at Heart*

RED HEAT

NINA BRUHNS

BERKLEY SENSATION, NEW YORK

THE BERKLEY PUBLISHING GROUP
Published by the Penguin Group
Penguin Group (USA) Inc.
375 Hudson Street, New York, New York 10014, USA

Penguin Group (Canada), 90 Eglinton Avenue East, Suite 700, Toronto, Ontario M4P 2Y3, Canada
(a division of Pearson Penguin Canada Inc.)
Penguin Books Ltd., 80 Strand, London WC2R 0RL, England
Penguin Group Ireland, 25 St. Stephen's Green, Dublin 2, Ireland (a division of Penguin Books Ltd.)
Penguin Group (Australia), 250 Camberwell Road, Camberwell, Victoria 3124, Australia
(a division of Pearson Australia Group Pty. Ltd.)
Penguin Books India Pvt. Ltd., 11 Community Centre, Panchsheel Park, New Delhi—110 017, India
Penguin Group (NZ), 67 Apollo Drive, Rosedale, Auckland 0632, New Zealand
(a division of Pearson New Zealand Ltd.)
Penguin Books (South Africa) (Pty.) Ltd., 24 Sturdee Avenue, Rosebank, Johannesburg 2196,
South Africa

Penguin Books Ltd., Registered Offices: 80 Strand, London WC2R 0RL, England

This is a work of fiction. Names, characters, places, and incidents either are the product of the author's imagination or are used fictitiously, and any resemblance to actual persons, living or dead, business establishments, events, or locales is entirely coincidental. The publisher does not have any control over and does not assume any responsibility for author or third-party websites or their content.

RED HEAT

A Berkley Sensation Book / published by arrangement with the author

PRINTING HISTORY
Berkley Sensation mass-market edition / June 2011

Copyright © 2011 by Nina Bruhns.
Excerpt from *White Hot* copyright © by Nina Bruhns.
Cover art by Kris Keller.
Cover design by Annette Fiore DeFex.
Interior text design by Laura K. Corless.

All rights reserved.
No part of this book may be reproduced, scanned, or distributed in any printed or electronic form without permission. Please do not participate in or encourage piracy of copyrighted materials in violation of the author's rights. Purchase only authorized editions.
For information, address: The Berkley Publishing Group,
a division of Penguin Group (USA) Inc.,
375 Hudson Street, New York, New York 10014.

ISBN: 978-0-425-24185-1

BERKLEY® SENSATION
Berkley Sensation Books are published by The Berkley Publishing Group,
a division of Penguin Group (USA) Inc.,
375 Hudson Street, New York, New York 10014.
BERKLEY® SENSATION and the "B" design are trademarks of Penguin Group (USA) Inc.

PRINTED IN THE UNITED STATES OF AMERICA

10 9 8 7 6 5 4 3 2 1

If you purchased this book without a cover, you should be aware that this book is stolen property. It was reported as "unsold and destroyed" to the publisher, and neither the author nor the publisher has received any payment for this "stripped book."

This book is dedicated to all the men (and now women, yay!)
past, present, and future who serve this country
so proudly in the Silent Service.

ACKNOWLEDGMENTS

My grateful thanks to STSCS (SS) Sid Busch, Senior Chief Sonar Technician, Submarines, proud veteran U.S. submariner, and knowledgeable source of much invaluable information on all things submarine. And thanks as well to Kapitan First Rank Vladimir Aleksandrovich Pelevin, decorated commander of the Soviet navy, for all his helpful insights into the Russian Kilo-class submarines.

1

\\\\\\\\\\////////

Goddamn KGB.

Captain First Rank Nikolai Kirillovich Romanov of the Russian navy marched into the Hotel Kursk and stalked through the vestibule, cutting an irate swath through a throng of startled hotel guests.

The notorious KGB had gone the way of the dinosaur two decades ago, but its successor, the Russian Federal Security Bureau, or FSB, was *still* trying to yank his goddamn chain.

Well, fuck them! He was a decorated naval officer now, a goddamn submarine commander, and the FSB had no right to issue him orders anymore!

Noticing the rash of speculative looks he was receiving, Nikolai forced himself to halt in the hotel lobby. He took a deep breath and let it out slowly—*very* slowly—wrestling his anger into submission.

It wasn't easy; he'd been so damn angry for the entire accursed, humiliating year. But this topped everything. The biggest mistake of his inglorious youth had decided to give him one last swift kick in the balls, and at the worst possible time in his life.

And didn't *that* just goddamn figure.

He jerked on the collar of his dark blue fitted navy sweater and smoothed back his already neat hair. It felt wrong to be out of his dress uniform in such a public place. But his old FSB handler had told him to blend in with the rank and file when coming to this meeting. A captain's uniform would attract too much attention, even in this navy town.

He didn't dare disobey. The KGB might be officially dead and gone, but the old men who used to run the sinister, secretive intelligence service were not. They'd merely changed the acronym to FSB and gained even more power under the new "democratic" government, doing their dirty business as usual.

Unfortunately, chain of command notwithstanding, a man in Nikolai's precarious position careerwise could not afford to piss off such powerful men.

He spotted Leonid Cherenkov crossing the lobby toward him, looking as dour as he had fifteen years ago. Comrade Cherenkov's nondescript brown hair was now gray, his nondescript pudgy features now florid, no doubt thanks to a fifteen-year flow of strong Russian vodka across those unsmiling lips.

"Kirillych," the man greeted him, using the familiar form of Nikolai's middle name, which had been his FSB code name back when he was young and stupid.

"Comrade," Nikolai returned. He didn't extend his hand, and neither did Cherenkov.

An old-school hard-line communist, Cherenkov had never approved of Nikolai, due to his remote connection with the old czarist Romanov family. The relationship had been distant enough that his father's grandfather had not been assassinated during the Revolution, but he had stubbornly refused to change the family name, which had been a constant source of difficulty for his descendants ever since.

"It's been a long time, Kirillych," Comrade Cherenkov said with false affability. "You've done well for yourself." He paused for effect. "Up until recently." The old man gave him a smug smile, one that implied he could have predicted Nikolai's fall from grace. "Blood will always tell" had been one of the bastard's favorite maxims, turning the original Western meaning on its head.

Nikolai didn't have the patience to play games. "What do you want?"

Cherenkov tutted. "In case you've forgotten, you still work for us, Kirillych."

"I work for the Russian navy," Nikolai retorted tightly.

Cherenkov shrugged, apparently as unconcerned with such technicalities now as he had been in the old days. "From what I've heard, you may be looking for a new job soon. Frankly, I'm surprised you haven't resigned your commission. Your present command"—he spread his hands for emphasis— "well, not up to your usual elitist standards, *nyet*?"

Nikolai ground his jaw. A month ago, following a near-disaster collision between two nuclear submarines for which he'd been held responsible, Nikolai had been demoted to commanding *podvodnaya lodka* B-403 *Ostrov*, the most pathetic, broken-down submarine in the entire notoriously neglected Russian Pacific fleet—a nearly mothballed Project 636 Kilo-class diesel-electric sub. This, after commanding the newest, most advanced nuclear submarine on the planet. Yeah, the one he'd nearly sunk.

"*Ostrov* is doing important work," Nikolai responded curtly, chagrined at the not-so-subtle insult. Even if it was all true.

"Playing water taxi to a multinational scientific expedition studying whales and polar bears?" Cherenkov chided.

"Not whales and polar bears. Urgent climate and environmental studies," he corrected stiffly.

Cherenkov shrugged again. "Still. A bit of a comedown for a decorated hero of the Russian navy, once considered the golden boy of the whole Northern Fleet. Eh?"

Nikolai'd had enough. "I'm leaving now," he clipped out and turned on a heel.

"There's a spy on your boat," Cherenkov said loudly enough to make Nikolai halt in his tracks.

He turned back to glare. "What did you say?"

"*Shpion.* A spy. One of the expedition team boarding *Ostrov* tomorrow is a CIA officer."

The news hit Nikolai like a punch in the gut. A foreign agent on his submarine? It was bad enough he still had to put up with the *zampolit* the FSB still always planted among the crew as its own damn *shpion*. But a real one? An American? Hell, no. Not on *his* goddamn watch!

"If you know this, revoke his visa!" Nikolai said hotly. "Send him back to Langley where he belongs."

"Not him. *Her*. The spy is a woman," Cherenkov said.

Nikolai's mind reeled. He was still getting used to the idea of women on his boat to begin with, as two of the international scientists were female. But now *this*? He didn't *think* so.

"Woman, man, I don't give a damn! If she's a spy, get rid of her."

"The thing is, I *do* give a damn. The FSB would very much like to know what she's doing here."

"Then arrest her and question her," Nikolai exploded. "I don't need a goddamn spy on board! I'll have enough problems just making sure the goddamned rust bucket doesn't spring a leak and sink in the middle of the goddamn Bering Sea!"

Cherenkov looked even more smug at this outburst.

"Which," the intelligence officer said calmly, "is exactly why we want her there. Why, I ask you, is CIA sending someone on a routine, unclassified scientific expedition aboard a forty-year-old diesel boat that barely floats?"

Nikolai assumed it was a rhetorical question. He ground his jaw even harder.

"*Nyet*. There is something going on here. Right under our noses. We want to know what it is."

"I am still *Ostrov*'s commander," Nikolai argued, "and I refuse—"

"You have no choice," Cherenkov interrupted flatly. "Unless, of course, you want certain buried information about your background to come to the navy's attention . . . ?"

Nikolai barely hung on to his temper. "I'm sure the admiralty knows I'm a Romanov, comrade. Even they couldn't have failed to notice the name stitched on my uniform."

"I'm not talking about your father's name," Cherenkov said menacingly. "I mean your mother."

Outrage swept through Nikolai. Did the man think he was a total idiot? This threat was an old one. His long-deceased mother had supposedly committed some terrible, treasonous— though conveniently undisclosed and top-secret—political offense. Bad enough to taint Nikolai's entire future, according to Cherenkov. Nikolai had bought into the lie when he was an ambitious eighteen-year-old from a politically suspect family who'd wanted nothing more than to get into the highly competitive, restricted, and elite submarine service. Cherenkov had offered to bury the information on his mother—for a price. Thus had been born Nikolai's intense, but thankfully brief, stint with the FSB.

He had wanted to believe that the collapse of the Soviet Union happening later that same year was somehow meaningful. A sign that his own new, independent life and future, away from his father and blessedly free of the harsh, restricting fetters of his past, would be joyfully reflected in that of his beloved country.

How wrong he had been. On both counts.

"Really? That old ploy?" he retorted and moved to leave.

"Perhaps this will convince you," Cherenkov said, handing him an envelope.

He halted and, with a tersely jetted breath, he opened the envelope. In it were orders signed by the navy *diviziya* commander, giving Cherenkov authority over Nikolai and *Ostrov* in all matters of national security. *Talk about shades of the past.*

Nikolai's hands were effectively tied. He had no choice but to obey.

Сволочь. Bastard!

"I see," Nikolai ground out, swallowing down his burning frustration. Cherenkov could have just given him the damn orders to begin with, instead of attempting to humiliate him first. Of course, that wouldn't have been nearly as fun. "What do you expect me to do?" he growled.

"Watch every move she makes," Cherenkov said, handing him a photo of a mid-thirtyish redheaded woman who might have been pretty except for her tight and unflattering hairstyle. "Her name is Julie Elizabeth Severin. She flew in on the morning Bering Air charter from Alaska, posing as a reporter. I want to know exactly what she's up to. What she's looking for. Who she's trying to contact, or recruit." The older man's eyes narrowed. "It could even be you she's after, Kirillych."

"Me?" Nikolai asked incredulously. "What would the Americans possibly want with me?" A man so out of favor with his government that his own petty official father hadn't spoken to him since the unfortunate incident for fear of his stench rubbing off. Besides, the Americans had had ample opportunity to recruit him during the year he'd spent there as an exchange student. They hadn't even tried.

Cherenkov's eyes revealed nothing. "Whatever it is they want, I trust you will not give it to them."

Nikolai straightened like a shot. "I love my country, Comrade Cherenkov, even if my country doesn't seem to return the sentiment. If you have so little faith in me, assign someone else to deal with her. Or send the woman packing as I requested."

Cherenkov ignored him. "Find out why she's here. And Kirillych, you are to use *any* means necessary." His lips thinned. "Understood?"

Nikolai was so appalled he couldn't even answer. Seriously? They expected him to pimp himself out to the bitch?

"She's in the hotel bar," Cherenkov said. "I'll expect daily reports."

With that final order, the FSB *apparatchik* strode away, blending into the crowd like the slimy weasel he was.

Чёрт возьми! Devil take it!

Nikolai couldn't *believe* he'd been roped back into the shady world of espionage. That was bad enough . . . but that he was also being forced to play demeaning undercover games, that was even more infuriating.

Damn, he hated the lies, the deception, the subterfuge. The compromises of his personal integrity. All he wanted was to live a normal, peaceful life in a place with people who gave a damn about him, and to do the job he loved above all else. But did he have an option here?

Nyet.

Not if he wanted to salvage the crash dive that had become his career ever since the disastrous collision that had landed him in his present state of disgrace.

But Nikolai had learned through long and bitter experience that moaning and groaning about things wouldn't help. He had a submarine to command, an expedition to protect, and a *shpion* to catch. The sooner that last thing was accomplished, the sooner he could get back to salvaging his career, and hopefully rebuilding the life he wanted.

Resolved, Nikolai headed straight for the hotel bar. In this whole mess, at least he'd had one small piece of luck, even if he didn't like it. The American spy was a woman.

Women he could do.

Entering the dim, smoky room, he stepped sideways and stood against the wall to orient himself. The bone-jarring blare of music and din of voices shouting over it was earsplitting. But the interior of the generous lounge was briskly cool and the pungent haze of cigarette smoke smelled relatively pleasant compared to the pervasive furnacelike heat and acrid petrol-fume stink of the diesel-fueled *Ostrov*.

With a practiced eye used to making the three hundred sixty degrees of a periscope circle scan, Nikolai took in the space before him. The Hotel Kursk lounge was large, starkly utilitarian, and packed with people sitting at a litter of stained linoleum bar tables. Mostly the occupants were men wearing various permutations of the distinctive black or blue and gold uniform of the Russian navy. There were a few small tables of men with their wives having a last night out together before leaving on patrol. And several tables occupied by groups of men seated with lone females wearing far too much makeup. But one table—two tables pushed together, actually—was surrounded by a half dozen foreigners.

They were easy to spot. Petropavlovsk-Kamchatskiya was normally closed to noncitizens, due to the highly military nature of the area, and they stuck out like a sore thumb.

The decibel level precluded hearing what language they spoke, but even from this distance it was obvious they did not belong. Their clothes, their choices of drinks, their very demeanors marked them as foreign.

These would be the scientists. The ones *Ostrov* would be ferrying through the polar ice for the coming twenty-one days.

Nikolai searched each of the women's faces for his target, mentally measuring them against the redhead in the photo he'd tucked into his shirt pocket.

She wasn't sitting at the table.

As a conscientious Western reporter, she should be down

here in the bar soaking in the "exotic" atmosphere, meeting the scientists on the research team she was covering, gathering background for the articles she'd be writing about the expedition.

But of course, Julie Severin wasn't a real reporter.

Where *was* the damned woman? Annoyed, he scanned over the lounge again. And finally spotted her. It was impossible to miss that neat auburn bun at the back of her neck. The color was nice, but the style was ug-ly. He slid farther from the door, blending into the shadows.

She'd just walked into the bar. Dressed in an elegantly cut business suit, she couldn't look more out of place if she tried.

As he had, she'd stopped right inside the door and was looking around. He saw when she spotted the table of scientists, but she didn't immediately head over to join them. She hesitated, watching them impassively for a full minute without moving. Then to his surprise she straightened and walked briskly in the opposite direction, to the bar.

Interesting. Perhaps she was seeking a more intimate encounter with the Russian navy than a mere ride on a submarine. Which would make his job easier, if even less appealing.

Unsurprisingly, the ranks of men lined up three deep at the bar parted to let her through. A young rating jumped from his stool and offered it to her. Chivalry was not quite dead in Russia, Nikolai was gratified to see. Or maybe the kid thought he had a snowball's chance in hell with her.

She thanked the rating politely, sat, and ordered from the attentive bartender. Men pressed in around her. She proceeded to ignore the lot of them, the scientists and the youthful rating included.

Even more interesting, if a bit puzzling. What was she up to?

As Nikolai watched, the short, bald bartender set a full shot glass of clear liquid in front of her with a flourish. She downed it in one gulp and ordered another.

Nikolai almost snorted. Who was she trying to impress, anyway? No one could outdrink a Russian. Especially in a roomful of Russian sailors.

Enough of this nonsense. Time to make a move.

He pushed off the wall and ambled up to the bar, elbowing aside the ratings to sidle in next to her stool. He turned toward her. And got another surprise. No wonder the men were flocking around her. The photo had not done her justice. Not remotely. Even with the unflattering hairdo, up close the woman was gorgeous.

She was much younger than he'd thought, with vibrant red-gold hair fighting to escape its tight confines. Her body appeared lithe and curvy beneath her tailored gray business suit; her legs were long and provocatively crossed under a skirt that barely flirted with the tops of her knees. A sophisticated red high heel dangled casually from the toes of her shapely foot. Against his will, his body stirred. Хуйня. He wondered if her toenails were painted to match.

Perhaps he'd find out.

Okay, so this spy thing might not be so bad after all.

He did a quick mental shift and opened his mouth to deliver one of the many pickup lines that had served him so well in the past. He didn't get the chance to utter a syllable.

"Fuck off, sailor," she cut him off in almost flawless Russian and tossed back her shot. She did not even bother to glance his way.

Shock speared through him. Still, he had to stop himself from grinning. Beautiful, sassy, and she wasn't afraid to drink. His favorite feminine combination. Too bad she was a spy.

He gestured to the bartender to set up two more shots and casually said to her, "American?"

She looked briefly irritated, then switched to English—probably hoping he didn't speak it. "You have a problem with that?"

"Not really," he returned in near-perfect American English. "But some of the men in this room might."

She glanced around. "I'm terrified," she drawled.

The bartender placed the two brimming glasses between them. Nikolai picked up one and gave her his best winsome smile, a smile that usually had women falling all over him. "An American woman alone in a place like this . . . you really should have a protector."

She looked positively bored. "And that would be you, I suppose." Her tone oozed disinterest.

He shrugged and threw down his shot. "Sure. Why not?"

When she finally glanced at him, her eyes were a cool gray-green. The exact color of the sea on a cold, rough morning in the icy north. The kind of morning that reminded a man he was alive. He almost shivered.

Anticipation surged through him. Hell, she'd had him at "Fuck off."

"No, thanks. I can protect myself," she stated. Her chilly gaze cut to the second shot glass, then back up to him. "And you can keep your damn drink."

He feigned a brief confusion, then picked up the glass. "Oh, this wasn't for you." He tossed it back and wiped his mouth with the back of his hand. "Me, I'm a two-shot man." He leveled her a look. "One is just never enough. Don't you agree?"

She stared at him. A tinge of red flushed across the apples of her cheeks.

He felt a coil of hunger tighten deep in his belly. Or maybe it was the vodka.

Abruptly, she stood. Without a word, she turned on her sophisticated city-girl toe and strode like an arrow through the crowd toward the lounge exit. An invitation? He sure as hell hoped so. He slapped an appropriate ruble note onto the bar and followed her. She moved with confidence, a subtle hint of sexuality in the sway of her hips. A stray lock of her auburn hair had sprung loose and lay curled over her shoulder, looking silky and touchable. He suddenly had a vision of loosening that tight bun and letting the freed waves of red cascade over *his* shoulders.

Damn, he *wanted* her.

He wanted her in his bed, naked. Under him.

Which was all the more unbelievable because that was exactly what Cherenkov had asked him to do.

Using any means necessary.

It hadn't taken a genius to know what *that* meant. He was to sacrifice his body for the good of his country. Of course, at the time he'd had absolutely no intention of doing so. He wasn't a damn gigolo. Besides, there were other ways of learning the secrets of a *shpion.*

But a man could change his mind, couldn't he?

He pursued Julie Severin through the lounge and into the hotel lobby, feeling the same familiar thrum of excitement he always felt when chasing an enemy sub through the dark waters of some deep Arctic trench.

He decided to corner her at the elevators. But she must have sensed his intent, and she bypassed the lift alcove, quickening her stride to elude him. *So much for the invitation.* She hurried into a dingy corridor and swung open a door marked Emergency Exit. The stairwell.

Her red spiked heels clacked furiously as she sped up the stairs. Nice try. A woman in heels didn't stand a chance against a naval officer in the best shape of his life.

He caught her at the first landing.

Bracketing his arms to either side of her body, he pushed her back against the wall and stepped in close.

"Don't worry," he said. "I won't hurt you."

She didn't scream. Didn't struggle against him. *Much.*

Her storm green eyes met his. Wide, with a shade of fear. But more of . . . defiance. She was breathing hard, her breasts rapidly rising and falling, her pebbled nipples grazing his chest with each ragged breath. The two rapid shots hit his bloodstream, and for a second he was dizzy with desire.

He stood there for a long moment, drinking in the excitement of her, savoring the predatory urges twisting in his groin and the blatant sexual tension arcing between them.

Then her tongue peeked out and wetted her lower lip.

And he lost it.

He wrapped his fingers around her waist, pulled her to him, and leaned down to capture her mouth with his.

He took ruthless advantage of her gasp of surprise. As he invaded the hot, wet depths of her, a soft moan worked through her throat. And turned into a moan of surrender.

Of their own accord, his fingers sought the two long pins holding her bun in place and yanked them out. Her hair tumbled down around her face and he drilled his fingers into the soft waves.

"Open," he ordered.

With a shiver, she did. Fully. He plunged his tongue deep. The kiss was bruisingly hard and ferociously intense. Her arms came around his neck and her body pressed into him, center to center. She moaned again. Or he did. Or both. He couldn't tell.

This was not what he'd expected.

Suddenly a loud mechanical *clank* ratcheted through the stairwell. She yelped in fright and jumped back from him, hitting the wall again. He grabbed her shoulders and steadied her as the metallic clink morphed into the familiar screech of a cable pulley.

"It's okay," he reassured her. "Just a noisy elevator."

She struggled to quell her physical reaction to her fear, looking acutely embarrassed. "Sorry. It startled me. I'm not used to . . ." She let the sentence hang.

To what? *Loud noises? Poor Russian machinery? Kissing strangers in dark stairwells . . . ?*

It was probably a good thing they'd been interrupted. The way he was feeling, without a doubt she'd have ended up plastered against the dingy wall, her skirt around her waist, with him inside her.

But he wanted more privacy for this. And a lot more time.

He tugged her back against his chest. "Why don't we go to your room, where we won't be interrupted?"

She licked her lips, and her gaze dropped to his mouth for a brief second. She started to shake her head. "I don't—"

Чёрт возьми. Really?

He grasped her jaw and kissed her again, preempting her refusal. She stiffened at first, but he kept at it, making the kiss hot and long and very persuasive, until once again she was moaning and melting into him.

"Come," he urged, backing her toward the stairs. "What is your room number?"

"This is crazy," she protested halfheartedly between the amazing kisses. "I don't even know your name."

"Nikolai," he murmured. "And yours?"

"Julie," she said after a short hesitation.

He smiled. "Good. Now we've been introduced." He lifted her off her feet and started up the stairs, still engrossed in kissing her. Thankfully, she was as into it as he was. He could see the rapid beat of her pulse in the vein above her collarbone and felt it in the mad pounding of her heart against his chest. It matched the hammer of his own heartbeat. "Room number?"

"Two fifty-seven. But Nikolai, this really isn't—," she started to object.

"You want me. I want you," he whispered into her mouth as he kissed her. "What else matters?"

She let him kiss her to the door of her room on the second floor, but when he set her down and put his hand out for her key card, she took a few nervous steps backward. She looked . . . regretful.

За ебис.

"I'm sorry," she said. "I can't do this."

The taste of her swirled on his tongue. He drew in a steadying breath. "You're not afraid of me, are you? I'm sorry if I've been too rough . . ."

She shook her head. "No. It's not that. It's just, you're Russian. And . . . and I'm leaving in the morning."

Well . . . duh, he was Russian. That was the whole point of this. Right . . . ?

For a split second he wondered if Cherenkov had pegged her all wrong. Maybe she really *was* just a reporter. A seasoned undercover agent would not be this skittish about a one-night stand with the other side. Quite the opposite.

Or perhaps she was just very good at her job, and this was merely part of her usual blushing flower routine.

He hiked a brow. "I'm leaving in the morning, too. And as for being Russian, the Cold War is over, *milaya moya*—my sweet. You won't be sleeping with the enemy, I promise."

That earned him a little smile. The sight of her full, curved lips made him a little lightheaded.

She took a few more steps backward. "I'm sorry if I led you on, Nikolai. Honestly I didn't mean— You're very attractive, and . . . a wonderful kisser. Believe me, if I did this sort of thing, you'd be on top of my list."

His body wanted to roar in protest, but he knew when he was being given the heave-ho. So he did the gentlemanly thing. For now.

With a feigned sigh of defeat, a few words of regret, and a traditional Russian kiss on both cheeks plus one for good measure, he let her go.

For now.

This was frustrating, but he wasn't too worried. Next time,

they'd both be trapped in the confines of a two-thousand-square-foot submarine with nowhere to go. She wouldn't get away from him then. He'd make damn sure of that. And she would give him everything he wanted. *Everything*.

Because he knew something she didn't.

He really *was* the enemy.

Ostrov might be a broken-down wreck of a submarine, but she was *his* broken-down wreck of a submarine. He had no intention of letting a CIA operative—no matter how sweet and tantalizingly sexy—wreak havoc on or upon his boat.

Oh, yeah. He would definitely be getting up close and personal with the recalcitrant Ms. Severin, whether she liked it or not. For the next three weeks he'd be stuck to her like a barnacle on a hull. He might despise the FSB for dragging him back into their sordid world of lies and intrigue, but if they were right about this woman, he was grateful for the heads-up. Hell, she was attractive enough that he just might have tried his luck with her anyway. And fallen right into her trap.

He had to find out what she was up to and prevent whatever bit of sabotage or espionage she had been sent to carry out against his boat or his men . . . and against his country.

If that involved finishing what they'd started tonight, so much the better. He had his orders. And for once, he had no intention of rebelling against them.

Hell, there was a solid door on the captain's stateroom, and it had a lock.

He narrowed his eyes speculatively as an idea formed in his mind. Well, what the hell. Why not? It would be against every regulation in the book . . . but seriously, what could his navy superiors do to him if they found out? Demote him? He snorted. *Too late*. At least this time he'd have earned it.

As he walked away, he turned one last time to look back at her on his way down the corridor. She waved uncertainly and sent him a regretful smile.

Slowly he smiled back.

A hot tangle of conflicting emotions churned through his body.

But regret? *Nyet*. Not one of those warring emotions was regret.

2

''''''''''/''''''''

"*Gospozhá* Severin?"

Central Intelligence Agency analyst Julie Elizabeth Severin stood at the end of a very long pier jutting into Petropavlovsk Harbor, and did her best to steady her rocketing heartbeat. How the hell had this happened?

She was in Russia—*Russia*, of all places—at the far edge of the Pacific Ocean just a few hundred miles shy of the Arctic Circle, about to embark on the worst nightmare of her life. It was raining cats and dogs, and she was already soaked to the bone, not to mention freezing her butt off. The end of June, and it felt like freaking December.

Not that she noticed. She was too busy being terrified of other things to care about the crappy weather. She squeezed her eyes tightly shut and again tried to calm her racing pulse. It was no use.

She groaned inwardly.

I need someone on this mission who is smart, her boss had said. *Someone confident, who can think on her feet and outside the box. Are you that person, Miss Severin?* James Thurman had peered at her with a stern frown.

At the time she'd answered yes, absolutely she was that

person. But that was before she'd known what the mission was. And where.

Now, confidence was the last thing she felt.

Oh, God. What was she *doing* here? She was a *China* specialist, a freaking desk analyst, not some undercover Jason Bourne–type spy! What had Thurman been *thinking*?

And then there was her other little problem . . . the irrational fear of water she'd been plagued with since early childhood when she'd fallen in a lake on a family vacation and nearly drowned.

Terror gripped her belly with sickly fingers as she looked past the harbor and out over Avachinskaya Bay with its deep, frigid water . . . and then back at the sinister gray submarine, B-403 *Ostrov*, lurking like a shark in the cold, churning waves before her. The cylindrical steel monster rose and fell, rose and fell, the long cement pier shaking and squealing like a banshee every time the curved hull rubbed up against its rubber bumpers. Lord, the mere *words* "submarine" and "ocean" sent chills of dread running down her spine. Thinking about going *under* those ominous waves in that floating death trap was likely to put her into a blind panic if she wasn't careful.

There were only two things she truly hated in this world: large bodies of water . . . and Russians.

This mission involved both. In a big way.

"Miss?" the Russian sailor waiting to help her onto the ugly, bobbing submarine asked in heavily accented English.

She jolted back to the present. She felt the impatience of the gang of Russian submariners behind her, waiting for her to move forward so they could get on with their duties. The entire flat deck of the sub was a beehive of activity, men loading last-minute supplies, unfastening safety lines, and disconnecting heavy electrical cables. Julie was the last of the scientific expedition team to go on board, having used every possible excuse to delay her arrival at the pier. Unfortunately, there was no way to put it off any longer.

She had to find a way to get past her fears. Or she'd let down her boss, her country, and most of all herself.

The sour acid of fear bit into her insides as she steeled herself for what she must do.

"*Ty v poryadke?* Everything okay?" the Russian sailor asked.

It had to be.

Julie would do anything in her power to protect her country from its enemies.

Then again, she sure as hell didn't have to like it.

"Yes. I'm fine," Julie lied, straining not to let her teeth chatter from the freezing rain that continued to soak her to the bone. Or from the fear that clawed at her gut.

She forced her eyes open, but looked down at her high heels instead of out over the bay or at the submarine that was about to carry her down into the terrifying depths of all that horrible, horrible water.

Oh, God.

Russians and the deep blue sea.

Fabulous.

She pushed out a steadying breath and wrapped her frozen fingers around the handle of her bright red rolling carry-on, gripping her matching laptop case firmly in her other hand. If she could just get onto the boat and down inside its belly, she would no longer be able to see the suffocating expanse of water lapping at its sides like a hungry monster waiting to swallow her whole. She'd still know the sea was out there, lurking dangerously on the other side of the hull, but at least she wouldn't have to stare it in the face.

Then she'd only have to deal with the Russian thing. Not that she hated the actual Russian people. No, of course not. It was the country she hated. The government. And most of all, the FSB.

Because they'd killed her father.

But now was not the time to think about her father's death. The anger would wait . . . it wasn't going anywhere anytime soon. It hadn't for nearly twenty years.

Just get on the damn submarine. She took a soggy but determined step toward the gangway.

"Please," the sailor said and indicated her suitcase. "I take for you."

Grateful, she nodded and passed him the handle, wiping the icy rain from her face and shivering as it ran down her neck, soaking her silk blouse. "Thanks."

He jerked his chin at the laptop. "I take that, too?"

She shook her head. "No. I'll hang on to this one." Her

pint-sized notebook computer contained all her briefing files, plus the special software that would help complete her mission on board. Inside the case was also her precious satellite phone. No way was she letting go of either. Even if getting across that narrow, lurching gangplank alive clutching anything but the handrails would be a pure damn miracle.

"Okay," the sailor invited politely. "You go first."

Visions of walking the plank on a pirate ship flashed unnervingly through her mind.

Swallowing heavily, she took an unsteady step onto the gangway, striving not to think about the fact that if she lost her footing and fell off the flimsy thing she'd land in the water. Which, she thought with a certain macabre resignation, wouldn't really matter because with the constant rocking of the sea, she'd almost certainly be squashed flat as a pancake between the solid concrete side of the pier and the heaving bulk of the submarine.

She sent up a silent prayer. The flimsy metal bridge swayed, and she wobbled precariously in her inappropriate footwear, silently cursing her decision to dress professionally rather than in more practical pants, sweater, and boots. The skirted suit and high heels had been a bad idea.

Suddenly a wave hit and the submarine pitched and rolled, causing the gangway to twist slightly, just enough to throw her off balance. She yelped, clutching her laptop case to her chest as the sailor grabbed for her arm and held her steady. "Have care!"

The splash barely registered. But from the corner of her eye she'd seen the flash of red go past. Ah *hell*!

"My suitcase!" she cried.

Too late.

She and seven submariners gawped down at the churning waters of the quickly closing gap between the sub and the pier. She winced as the soft-sided carry-on was ground to shreds.

"Oh, no! My clothes!" she groaned.

Her escort's face reddened in dismay. "I am so sorry, miss! Come. Quickly! Before—"

He didn't finish his admonition, but hustled her onto the deck of the submarine before any more mishaps occurred. Rain was sheeting over the rocking deck, making it slippery underfoot, especially in her heels. He led her over to a big hole. She peeked gingerly over the edge, careful not to get too close.

He motioned her toward it. "Here is to get in."

"You've got to be kidding," she muttered when she realized what he meant for her to do. There was a vertical ladder attached to the side of the gaping hole, which disappeared down into the stygian depths of the submarine.

This was the entry hatch? Why didn't this floating sardine can have a civilized door like an airplane or a subway car?

The skirt and heels had been a *really* bad idea.

With another mental groan, she added it to her ever-lengthening list of Stupid Things I've Done Lately. Principal among which was not to quit her damn job rather than accept this last-minute assignment from hell.

Her boss knew very well about her issues, her background, and her father's fate, the bastard. And yet, Thurman had picked her to do this. Why?

This is the kind of assignment that comes once a lifetime. It can make or break a career, Miss Severin.

Yeah. *Fuck you very much, Mr. Thurman.*

Clamping her chattering teeth, she grabbed the slick metal rails of the ladder and swung onto it. Descending down through the round hatch felt like descending straight into the seventh circle of her own personal hell. Despite the frigid rain and chilly outside temperature, her palms were clammy with sweat.

Making her day complete, a clutch of grinning Russian submariners in dark blue coveralls peered up at her as she endeavored to maintain a modicum of decorum on her way down. Between the skirt and the heels, it wasn't easy.

Suddenly an order was barked in a deep, authoritative voice and the men snapped to, scattering like balls on a pool table. *Thank God for small favors.*

She reached the bottom of the ladder and felt a strong hand grasp her elbow, supporting her as her high heels found balance on the rocking deck.

"Steady on, there. Are you okay?"

"Yes, thank you. I'm just—"

She turned to her rescuer. And almost fell over. Her words froze in her throat.

Oh. My. *God*.

It was *him*.

Tall, chisel jawed, blue eyed, with hair the color of golden honey peeking out from under his wide, distinctive black officer's hat, killer handsome in his uniform of black and gold.

Smiling down at her was the *other* Stupid Thing She'd Done Lately.

Well, almost done.

The man holding her elbow was the sexy, arrogant hunk from the hotel last night. The one with the ego as vast as Siberia, but who'd been such an amazing kisser she'd nearly overlooked that slight character flaw—and his bigger sin of being a Russian.

She gaped in shock, clutching her laptop case to her sodden chest. Despite the welcome warmth of the air inside the submarine, she shivered violently. This was *so* not good.

"Miss Severin," he said, peeling one of her hands from its grip on the case. He bowed over it formally. "Welcome aboard *podvodnaya lodka Ostrov*. I am *Kapitan* Nikolai Kirillovich Romanov."

Kapitan.

Ho-boy.

The man she'd almost slept with last night was the *commander* of the vessel she'd been sent to covertly search for top-secret material. The same commander who, if he caught her at it, would without hesitation have her arrested for espionage. And probably shot.

This could be . . . interesting.

Especially since the knowing smile presently creasing his lips and his unprompted use of her last name told her he'd known exactly who she was last night when he'd tried to seduce her. The *bastard*. She'd *known* she shouldn't trust a damned Russian.

But did he know he couldn't trust *her*? Had her mission already been compromised? She felt a knot tighten in her stomach. How could it not be? Not if he knew who she was. . . .

"Captain," she managed, striving desperately to sound a whole lot cooler and calmer than she felt inside. *Please, God, let me wake up from this nightmare.* "You should have introduced yourself properly last night."

He looked down at her from under the brim of his uniform hat through distractingly thick and tawny lashes. The sexy little crinkles at the corners of his eyes nearly sabotaged her concentration. "Would it have changed your mind about me?" he asked, as though they were discussing what to have for breakfast.

She thinned her lips. "No."

"Well, then. No harm, no foul."

Only to her equilibrium. And possibly to her mission. She'd really have to watch herself around the good captain.

Speaking of which. The submariners at their posts were starting to stare at them speculatively. Nikolai—Captain Romanov, she corrected herself—was still holding her hand.

She yanked it back.

He just smiled. Then his eyes narrowed as he took note of her rain-streaked face and sodden hair and clothes. "Good God, you're soaked. You must be freezing," he said with concern. "I'll have you taken to your quarters so you can change out of those wet things immediately."

"Yeah, well. That could be a problem," she murmured, just as the man who'd escorted her on board stepped forward and spoke to him in rapid Russian accompanied by much gesturing.

For a second Nikolai looked taken aback. "He dropped your suitcase?"

She nodded. "It was me or it. He made the right choice."

Without taking his eyes off her, Nikolai spoke to her escort in Russian. The man's expression froze and his gaze darted to her, then back to his commander. A young officer standing next to them scowled and said something to Nikolai in staccato Russian. Nikolai responded coolly to the officer, then snapped another order at her escort, who came to attention and said, *"Da, Kapitan."*

Nikolai gestured him over to Julie. "This is the boat's quartermaster, *Kvartirmyeister* Misha Kresney. He will show you to your quarters and find you a hair dryer. No doubt one of the lady scientists has brought one along. I'm afraid that's the best I can do at the moment. We are running behind schedule and must get under way. When we're clear of the bay, I'll attend to this matter."

"Thank you," she said, grateful for his impersonal demeanor, and for his promise of help.

"And we can continue our other discussion," he added in a low voice for her ears only.

So much for impersonal.

Before she could set him straight, Romanov touched the brim of his uniform hat, turned, and strode away. He disappeared through a narrow opening in the seemingly solid maze of hanging pipes and crowded instrument panels that filled nearly every square inch of the claustrophobic space. It was as though the escape hatch ladder had deposited her in a closet cluttered with the debris of a hundred years.

Escape. Now there was a good idea. She gazed up at the hatch and thought longingly of her pristine desk back at Langley.

A half second later Nikolai's head reappeared amid the pipes. He gave one more unintelligible order to *Kvartirmyeister* Kresney, then vanished again, this time for good.

For a brief moment she really wished she spoke Russian. Understanding the enemy always gave one an advantage. In *The Art of War*, the ancient Chinese strategist Sun Tzu said, "If you know the enemy and know yourself, you need not fear the result of a hundred battles." She was fluent in three other languages. How hard would it be to learn one more? Then again, no way did she want those words in her head. She wanted nothing to do with the country that had killed her father. Not its language. Not its secrets. And *certainly* not one of its navy captains . . . no matter how sexy or awesome a kisser he was. Thank goodness she'd had the sense and fortitude to turn him down last night.

Sun Tzu had also said, "Do not swallow bait offered by the enemy."

No damn kidding.

Already this mission was turning into a battle—of knowledge, of wits, of temptation. The lines had been clearly drawn between her and the attractive Russian navy captain. She just hoped to God she could keep up her resistance to him. Because as bait went, Captain Nikolai Kirillovich Romanov was far too enticing—and far too dangerous.

3

‖‖‖‖‖‖‖⟍⟍⟋⟋⟋⟋⟋⟋

Julie followed Kresney's stout, compact form into the same narrow passageway where Nikolai had vanished. The quartermaster slipped easily through a round opening that punctuated the end of the passage. She'd seen enough World War II movies to know this was one of the watertight doors that sealed off one compartment from the next in case of flooding. *Or sinking.*

The door was wide open, but seeing it was a rude reminder she was now several meters underwater, two thin, rusting husks of metal the only thing separating her from certain death.

Her chest squeezed, and she had to grab the hard edge of the watertight door to keep from sprinting back to the exit ladder and out of this nightmare.

When she didn't follow right away, *Kvartirmyeister* Kresney peered back at her through the opening. Her panic must have shown in her face.

"*Eto horosho,*" he told her in a thick accent. "Is okay. She is not pretty, but *Ostrov* is good boat. We do not sink, I promise." He grinned. A young sailor hurried past, eyeing her skirt.

Jetting out a breath, she hunched down and stepped gracelessly over the shin-high threshold of the round opening. The top of the door ended at her chin. She was only five foot six, but she felt like an afghan hound climbing through an agility hoop—all long limbs and ten kinds of awkward. *Kvartirmyeister* Kresney was a gentleman and pretended not to notice. She decided she liked him.

They went through two more watertight doors, passing several instrument-filled side compartments, a galley with attached open dining room, and a dozen coverall-clad submariners busy at various tasks, before slip-sliding down another vertical ladder to the deck below.

"Three decks," Misha explained. "Control room is on main deck. Now we are on lower deck, where are living quarters. Small deck below has batteries and such things. Not so nice." He made a face.

Here they traversed a very narrow section of passage, the wall of which was punctuated by three real doors. The doors were made of metal, as was everything else on board the submarine, and painted yellow, which seemed to be the *Ostrov* designer's favorite color besides dingy or rusty beige. Metal signs labeled each of the three doors in red Cyrillic lettering.

"Officer country," Kresney explained. He opened the last door and gestured her in. "Here. Where you sleep."

She stepped into the compartment. *Good Lord.* She'd seen bathrooms that were bigger! Into the microscopic room they'd somehow crammed a narrow bunk, a row of built-in cupboards above it, two tall lockers, a fold-down desk, and a pulldown aluminum sink, along with a wall safe and several communication devices attached to the scant inches of bare wall space left over.

On the plus side, most of the furnishings were done in honey-colored wood instead of metal. It was tiny, but nice. Nothing like what she'd expected.

"You make comfortable," the quartermaster said, his *r*'s and *l*'s rolling like thick ocean swells, punctuated by the dip of throaty extra *y* sounds. "Officers' head is down passage." He pointed back the way they'd come. "We serve welcome lunch after two hours, but coffee always in mess for everyone. Okay. I go now to find . . ." He made blow-dryer motions with two fingers. "You need anything, you ask me," he said. *"Da?"*

She nodded. "Yes. Thank you, *Kvartirmyeister* Kresney."

She must have mangled the pronunciation of his rank because his grin popped out again. "Please. Call me Misha. You most welcome, *Gospozhá* Syev'ryin."

"Julie," she said with an answering smile at his two-syllable-with-extra-*y*'s-stuck-in-there pronunciation of her name. She kind of liked it.

"Julie," he repeated, his hazel eyes merry. "Beautiful name for beautiful lady. *Kapitan* very lucky man."

She blinked. What?

Before she could correct any mistaken notions the quartermaster might have gotten about her relationship with his commander, he was gone, closing the door behind him.

Whatever. She let out a sigh and looked around the mini-cabin. Nice that she'd have it all to herself. She'd been warned how cramped submarines were, and to expect to share a cabin with two or three others, possibly sleeping in shifts. Maybe the crew had been instructed to give the best cabins to the passengers.

Last night she'd still been too shell-shocked about being sent on an actual field mission to meet with the scientific expedition team she was supposed to be covering as a reporter. She'd seen them gathered at a table in the hotel bar. She'd gone down there thinking a shot or two would calm her frazzled nerves and allow her to get some much-needed sleep . . . instead of staring at the ceiling all night struggling to get her irrational terror of the ocean in check before having to face it in the living, breathing flesh. But the only thing the alcohol had effectively deadened was her judgment—proven by her imprudent behavior with Nikolai Romanov. It hadn't done a damn thing for her jittery sense of impending doom. Nor her ability to get to sleep.

At breakfast this morning she'd finally introduced herself to the others on the team and established her cover. They were an eclectic bunch, a mix of young and old, five men and two women, formidable academics and environmental scientists from a half dozen countries. There were even two retired U.S. military men among them. Several knew each other already, from previous expeditions, she presumed. They'd treated her with casual politeness but no real interest. She was merely there to observe their important work and inform the world of their findings.

Or so they believed.

And boy, did she ever wish that were true. But no. Julie's presence on *Ostrov* was a bit more complicated than that.

Two days ago she'd been innocently delivering a report to James Thurman, her section chief at Langley, along with his boss, when he'd gotten a phone call about the undercover officer who'd originally been assigned to this mission. A car accident had put the man in the hospital. Thurman's boss had taken one look at Julie and pointed his finger at her, and less than twenty-four hours later she'd been on a terrifyingly small charter plane taking off from Nome, Alaska, to some godforsaken place on the Russian coast across the Bering Sea, posing as a reporter writing about the international scientific team that was studying the effects of global warming on the Pacific Arctic. On a Russian submarine.

Wrong place, wrong time. Insanely wrong mission.

She'd never been to the Arctic, knew nothing about global warming other than what Al Gore had taught her, and hell, she'd never even *seen* a real submarine before now, let alone ridden in one. Okay, yeah, she'd had the standard CIA field ops training for undercover case work, but she'd opted out of that end of things after being sent on her first mission. Hel-*lo*? They'd started *shooting* at her! Didn't matter that it had only been warning shots aimed over her head. Okay, over the head of the guy she was supposed to be meeting. Who could blame her for skipping the meet?

Nope. Everyone agreed, she just wasn't cut out for the danger of case work. Or the subterfuge. Good grief, she even blushed every time she told a lie. Some 007 she'd make. Not.

Unfortunately, as her boss had pointed out when she'd balked at this assignment, she *had* been a reporter in her former life as a civilian. Her beat had been Asia, as it still was. It had been her insightful, in-depth articles that had caught the attention of the CIA and prompted them to invite her to join the China desk a few years back.

Which meant she also knew how vital it was to U.S. national security to recover the tiny data storage, or SD, card that, through an unlikely series of events, had been stashed somewhere on *Ostrov* by a desperate, now-deceased Russian double agent—a Rybachiy submarine naval yard worker based in Petropavlovsk-Kamchatskiy—leaving only a one-word clue: *crown*. The SD card held top-secret plans for a breakthrough long-range guidance system for China's newest unmanned underwater vehicle, or UUV. Information that was crucial the United States acquire, for the protection of the North American coastlines. UUVs were fast becoming the new submarines out there in the world's coastal waters—except they were smaller, cheaper, more maneuverable than their big manned brothers, and therefore much deadlier. The government didn't like talking about it, but they were becoming a huge security threat. This guidance system would put China in the front lines.

To find the miniature storage card hidden on *Ostrov*, all she had to do was figure out what this mysterious "crown" was. Something on the sub. Maybe even part of it. It *should* be close by. But good grief. She'd had no idea what a chaotic maze of confusing equipment, pipes, wires, and control panels made up the interior of a submarine. Finding the microcard would be like seeking out a particular, small seashell at the bottom of the vast ocean.

Talk about mission impossible.

She puffed out a breath and turned her attention back to the cozy cabin she found herself in. At least this part wouldn't be so bad. The inside of the sub was surprisingly warm and toasty, so she'd finally stopped shivering. But she was still freezing in her wet clothes. And dripping all over the floor.

Kicking off her heels, she removed her sopping raincoat and hung it up to dry on a hook she found on the back of the door. Thank God she wouldn't be needing a coat anytime soon. After securing the door lock so Misha wouldn't accidentally walk in on her when he returned with the hair dryer, she slipped off her skirt and peeled her blouse off, looking around for a clothes hanger. She opened one of the tall lockers, figuring that was what passed for a closet.

She was right. Several dark uniforms hung neatly from the rod. Okay. That was weird. Had she taken someone's room?

Behind her, the door handle rattled. Damn. It must be the *kvartirmyeister* returning already. "Hang on, Misha," she called, casting about for a towel, or anything to cover herself with.

She heard a click, and the door opened. She swung around
with a startled gasp. She felt her face go instantly hot. It wasn't
Misha.

"Nikolai! How did you—?"

The handsome captain stepped into the compartment, his
large frame filling the space. "Miss Severin." His gaze
brushed over her nearly bare body, raising a whole different
kind of goose bumps on top of the goose bumps she already
had from the cold. He held up a key.

She jolted out of her inertia, grabbed the first uniform
jacket she touched in the locker, and jerked it in front of her
body. "What are you doing here? Get out!"

At the sound of approaching footsteps, he leaned his head
backward to check who it was, then shut the door, locked it,
and propped a negligent shoulder against the door frame. "I'm
afraid I can't do that. You see, this is my stateroom."

"What?"

He tossed his large black captain's hat, along with a small
hair dryer, onto the bunk. "And this is my bunk. However"—he
lifted a shoulder—"I am happy to share both with you." When
she opened her mouth to protest, he held up a hand. "It's called
hot-bunking. You sleep while I'm awake, and vice versa. Not
together. Unless, of course . . ." This time his brow lifted.

Her jaw dropped. Was he *serious*? Suddenly his easy ca-
pitulation last night—and the stir his orders to Misha had
caused earlier—made perfect sense. It was obvious what he
had in mind.

Outrage swept through her. "You're crazy if you think
I'll— *Hell*, no! Give me a different cabin. *Now.*"

"Stateroom," he corrected, stepping away from the door
and opening one of the cupboards above the bunk. "This is
not a cruise ship."

"Cabin, stateroom, I don't care what you call it. I need to
be somewhere else." *Pronto.* She started to shiver again.

He pulled out a towel and handed it to her, then slid his uniform jacket from her fingers. "Well, we only have half a crew, so
there are several empty racks around the boat," he said, inspecting
the jacket and brushing stray drops of water from the front of it.

The towel was too small to cover her whole body, but she
did her best. "Good. Now please leave while I—"

"In the forward torpedo room, for instance," he continued as though she hadn't ordered him out, "since we're not carrying any live ordnance on this patrol. Of course, you'd have to share the space with two of the male scientists."

She scowled. "There has to be somewhere else."

He pursed his lips. "Sure. Several racks on the lower deck—but, again, with the crew. And the engines." He wrinkled his nose. "Not very pleasant down there. Diesel fumes."

"I meant another *stateroom*," she gritted out.

"Yes, well, that poses a bit of a problem," he said. "There are only three other staterooms, and they're all full." He ticked off on his fingers. "My senior officers have one, the male expedition leaders another, and the last is assigned to the two scientist ladies. Everyone else is in general berthing."

"Why wasn't I put in with the other women?" she demanded, starting to worry.

"Only two bunks in that one. Until yesterday we were expecting a male reporter. I'm still not sure why he was replaced. Not that I'm complaining, mind you. But this is the only remaining bunk on the boat appropriate for a lady."

She ground her teeth. *Of course.* She hadn't thought about the injured field officer being a man. Irritated, she wondered if her boss had made the switch deliberately . . .

She didn't know what to do. She certainly didn't want to bunk in an open area with a gang of Russian sailors. But *this* arrangement was unacceptable. "You'll have to sleep somewhere else, then," she told him briskly.

Instead of answering, he reached for another towel from the overhead cupboard. "Turn around," he said. When she didn't react, he did it for her with a firm hand to her upper arm.

"What on earth do you think—"

From behind, he toweled up the cold rivulets of water from her shoulders. The protest died on her lips. His hands were strong and gentle as they moved up and started to rub her hair dry. It felt . . . really nice.

So nice, she almost forgot she was standing there practically naked.

Almost.

When he started on her back, she said, "Nikolai, I'm serious. I'm not sleeping in your bed, with or without you."

"We'll see," he murmured. She could feel his warm breath on her neck. It raised the fine hairs on her nape to attention. His fingers began to push her damp bra straps off her shoulders.

Frustration swept through her. Why wouldn't he listen? "Stop! This is not some pirate ship where the captain can do as he pleases with his female passengers!" she said in exasperation, turning to face him. She clutched the towel to her breasts, determined to keep him at bay.

He looked down at her, his expression unreadable. Her pulse jumped madly. Unfortunately, her own body wasn't listening, either.

"You are welcome to make other sleeping arrangements, and I will undoubtedly rack out elsewhere for the most part," he said evenly. "But . . . isn't being in my stateroom an ideal situation for completing your assignment? Always knowing what the boat's commander is up to?" He tilted his head. "Perhaps I'll forget to lock up some important documents. Who can tell what state secrets you might discover?"

Her heart nearly stalled at the implication of his statement. Oh, God. He *did* know about her! But how?

She gathered her wits, praying she was just being paranoid. "My *assignment* is to write articles about the expedition," she said as forcefully as she could, "*not* about you or the secrets of the Russian navy."

His gaze met hers, lit with subtle challenge. "But what *else* are you here for, *dorogaya moya*?"

"I don't know what you mean," she insisted. What had he just called her?

His icy blue eyes seemed to pierce right through her. "I have been a submariner for many years," he said. "On every patrol without exception there has been a *zampolit*, an FSB political officer, hidden among the crew. Not to spout doctrine, as in the old days, but to spy on navy missions." He stepped closer to her. Their bodies were brushing now, the fine wool of his uniform scraping erotically against her bare skin. "Trust me, I know a *shpion* when I see one."

Shock went through her. Even she didn't need a translation for that word. Her heart pounded in her throat.

She forced a scoff. "Are you really accusing me of being a

spy, Captain Romanov?" Lord, she didn't know what she'd do if he actually said yes.

He leaned in, putting his lips to her ear. "Think about it. Stay here and seduce me. No one has to know. With such an incentive, I might voluntarily tell you everything you've been sent to find out. Hell, I may even want to defect to your country. Imagine what a coup that would be for you, back at Langley."

So much for any doubts that he knew exactly what she was and who had sent her.

For a second she was too stunned to speak. *More bait.* Obviously for a trap. But cripes. Talk about getting nailed! And not in the good way, either.

Somehow she found her voice, and she picked the easiest part of his dangled bait to address. "Defect? Don't be absurd. Russia is a democracy now. If you want to move to the United States, just get yourself a passport."

He chuckled, his breath caressing her cheek, stirring stray hairs against her skin. "Ah, *milaya moya.* You seem to be a worthy opponent. I believe I shall enjoy our upcoming game of matching wits." His jacket grazed the tips of her breasts, zinging them to painful attention. "And I especially look forward to the part where you seduce me."

She swallowed.

Ho-boy. This was *so* not good.

"But, in the meantime . . ." He reached behind her, opened the tall locker, and pulled out a dark blue coverall. He pushed it into her hands. "Get dressed." He gave her a drowning look. "Or I may forget that I am not a pirate captain after all."

Unable to form a comeback—for any of it—she watched him grab an old, *Hogan's Heroes*–style pilot's cap from a peg on the wall, tug it on, and leave the stateroom.

The door snicked shut.

With a long, unsteady exhale, she fought a sinking feeling in the pit of her stomach.

Oh. Mygod.

She was in such big trouble.

4

//////////////////

There was much to do to steer *podvodnaya lodka* B-403 *Ostrov* safely out of Petropavlovsk Harbor, through Avachinskaya Bay and past the Three Brothers rock formation that guarded the narrow mouth of the bay, and into the open waters of the North Pacific. But Nikolai did it all with a smile on his face.

He could see his men wondering at the change in him. For the past month, since being assigned as *Ostrov*'s commander, Nikolai's behavior had been reminiscent of the snarling Russian wolves that stalked the family's winter dacha. He resented his demotion, was mortified by the charges of negligence and rogue hotheadedness that had landed him here, and frustrated by a political system that condemned good, loyal men without a fair hearing. Чёрт возьми. *Devil take it.* With no hearing at *all*.

But the arrival on his very doorstep of an enemy *shpion* had given him new hope to redeem a career that had just yesterday seemed more than a shade beyond salvage. And what a *shpion!*

There was no doubt in his mind that Julie Severin worked for U.S. intelligence. Though shocked by his accusation, she'd never actually denied it. Was it mere coincidence that she was tantalizingly beautiful and seemed as attracted to him as he was to her? Nikolai did not think so. But it didn't matter whether her attraction was real or fabricated as part of her covert mission. Either way, he could turn it to his advantage.

He'd whispered in her ear what benefit she might gain over him if she remained in his stateroom, if she used her body to tempt him into treason, but in reality he planned to turn the tables on her. He would use their sizzling connection to find out what she was up to, all right. And then he would do his damnedest to coax her into becoming an agent for Russia— using whatever means necessary, just as Cherenkov had ordered. If he succeeded, even the navy *diviziya* admirals would be forced to reconsider their unjust treatment of him. And reinstate his rightful command.

Da. Things were definitely looking up.

Both figuratively and literally.

Standing in the central command post on *Ostrov*'s main deck, Nikolai glanced skyward through the conning tower's barrel trunk to the round patch of misty gray that sat heavily above the open hatch. The chilly bite of the northern summer air blasted through the opening, and he could see the mad flutter of his *starpom*'s long black coattails snap back and forth across the narrow cockpit. Nikolai grabbed his greatcoat from a rating who rushed up with it, along with his wolf fur *ushanka*, which only came out for trips up top. It wasn't really that cold, but wearing the fur hat was his private tradition.

"Permission to come up to the bridge," Nikolai called to the *starpom*—his executive officer, Captain Third Rank Stefan Mikhailovich Varnas, who was currently serving as officer of the deck. As OOD, Varnas held the conn as well. After clearing Avachinskaya Bay, Nikolai had gone below to make sure his passengers were comfortable and his crew was settling into the routine. This was their first real patrol together.

With a severely reduced contingent of less than two dozen of the usual fifty-two men, and being a strictly scientific expedition rather than a military one and carrying no weapons on board, he'd had to do some shuffling of assigned duties. In the Russian navy, men stayed at one post for life. But not on this patrol.

There'd been grumbling. Until, that is, Nikolai had given orders allowing everyone four hours on duty followed by a full ten hours off. Unconventional, yes, but it had immediately and dramatically improved morale and ensured the men's loyalty.

If that made him a rogue, so be it.

"Come on up," *Starpom* Varnas called down. "Hope you brought your *ushanka*, *Kapitan*. The wind from the north is a screaming bitch today!"

With a grin, Nikolai checked that his coat was buttoned up and fur hat was snug on his head before he ascended the ladder. Stefan Mikhailovich had been transferred from a cushy post on the Black Sea, and he hated the cold breezes of the Arctic latitudes. He'd ended up here because he, too, was on the Main Naval Command's shit list.

Of course, so were nearly all the others among *Ostrov*'s crew—the three other officers and five senior enlisted and petty officers, and all but a few of the ten ratings. Official Disfavor was the running theme, the reason they'd all been mustered onto this assignment. It reminded him of an old American war film he'd once seen where a platoon of navy misfits was sent out on a garbage scow to deliver a spy to a remote outpost in the Pacific. The parallels were ironic. He only hoped his own ending was as good as Jack Lemmon's.

Passing the midpoint landing and bypassing the small flying bridge compartment, Nikolai climbed up the ladder and into the cockpit at the top of the sail. He braced himself against a hard gust of wind as he clipped his safety harness to an attachment point at the rear of the bridge. The storm was still active, making the sea choppy and unpredictable. Normally on the sail they didn't bother with the harnesses, but during a storm he had given orders that safety procedures be strictly observed.

He made a quick scan around the horizon, nodding to the rear lookout posted at the aft of the sail, then asked the *starpom*, "Anything to report?"

There shouldn't be, not just an hour out of their sheltered home bay, but with this old tub he figured it was best to ask. After the fall of the Soviet Union, everything run by the government had descended into chaos and disrepair, nothing more so than the navy. Rusting, rotting ships and submarines littered every naval yard in the country, abandoned for lack of funds for upkeep or even proper disposal. The ships and boats left in service were hard-pressed to obtain needed spare parts or even the most rudimentary of required instrumentation. It had been getting better over the past few years, but not by much. It was a damned good thing the foreign scientists had brought a ton of modern equipment along with them. This obviously wasn't their first ride on a Russian submarine.

"So far, so good," Stefan Mikhailovich replied. "Just the usual noisy wingmen." He jerked a grin at a persistent flock of seabirds swooping and dipping over the sub's wake. "Oh, and a TU-142 Bear heading north," he casually added, avoiding Nikolai's gaze.

Great. Thanks to the Internet and Google, the whole damn universe knew the juicy details of Nikolai's fall from naval grace.

He glanced northward with a frown. The TU-142 Bear was a Russian anti-sub-warfare plane loaded with all the bells and whistles needed to track the ultrastealthy U.S. nuclear submarines that regularly plied the northern seas. Unfortunately, the Bears were in as bad repair as the navy subs. It had been a TU-142 that provided the faulty positioning information that had caused the collision in Norwegian waters that was ultimately blamed on Nikolai. He was now a fervent Bear hater. Give him a rocket-propelled grenade launcher and he'd be tempted to shoot the damned thing out of the sky.

Псина чертова. *Fucking dogmeat.*

He didn't comment on Stefan's observation, just clamped his jaw and turned his face into the wind, gazing back toward the distant snow-covered slopes of Mount Koryakskaya. The icy slap of sea spray managed to cool his simmering temper. Somewhat.

He turned back to the *starpom*. "So, why are *you* here, Stefan Mikhailovich?" he asked, just to level the playing field. "What did you do to anger Naval Command so much they assigned you to this delightful joyride?"

The *starpom*'s mouth twisted wryly. "An affair with the wrong woman."

That was a new one. Usually their superiors were not nearly so sentimental. Unless . . . "The wife of an admiral, I presume?"

"Daughter," Stefan Mikhailovich admitted with a dramatic sigh.

Nikolai winced. "Ouch."

"The woman has complicated my life considerably."

An understatement, no doubt. "Women do have a tendency to do that." One of the many reasons Nikolai had avoided involving himself with the creatures, other than for the occasional indulgence of mutual pleasure.

Until now, of course. But this was different. This was a job. And a means to an end.

"With any luck," Stefan said, "I can distinguish myself enough on this patrol that the admiral will accept me as a suitable son-in-law."

Somehow Nikolai doubted there'd be opportunity for anything close to that. But who was he to dash a young man's hopes? "With any luck," he replied neutrally, scanning the horizon again.

They were heading due east, in order to get out to deep water as soon as possible. The storm seemed to be drifting toward the west in the opposite direction, the black clouds already less angry than when they'd departed. The pouring rain had stopped, at least temporarily. He could even see a big patch of blue ahead. Good news for those who were feeling seasick—which included most of the new men on the crew, who refused to take the antinausea meds for fear of being labeled sissies, and the scientists who weren't used to being out on the open water.

"Do you think the weather will remain decent for us all week?" Nikolai asked, tactfully changing the subject. Traversing the Bering Sea to the Arctic Circle was always a tricky endeavor, let alone with half a crew and a bunch of civilian passengers.

The *starpom* shrugged. "If I could predict the weather, I'd be a rich man, *Kapitan*. The ice pack is pretty far north this year, and the forecast says only a slight possibility of a storm over the Arctic for the coming week . . . but I wouldn't even place my nonexistent government paycheck on that bet."

Nikolai gave a humorless chuckle. Both on account of their oft-delinquent salaries and his *starpom*'s pessimistic weather forecast. At the moment, the latter was of most concern.

Contrary to popular belief, not all submarines were below-surface dwellers. Diesel-electric boats such as *Ostrov* stayed on the roof most of the time. While a nuclear sub could—and usually did—spend months on end hiding in the ocean depths without surfacing, a diesel boat could only go down for quick dives of four or five days max before having to come up again to recharge its electric batteries. To charge the batteries, the diesel engines needed to run, and for that they needed air. The sub was also forced to ride out storms on top of the waves, for fear the batteries would be depleted below and the sub would be unable to surface again. A submarine was at its most vulnerable during a dive or surfacing maneuver. One big wave hitting at the wrong time at the wrong angle could easily send it to the bottom—a fatal experience Nikolai would just as soon forgo.

"Still," Stefan Mikhailovich mused, "these crazy scientists, they are probably praying for a big storm. More data for their damned spreadsheets."

Nikolai grunted in agreement. It was bad enough dodging icebergs and sea ice without taking unnecessary risks. He'd heard rumblings about the hair-raising exploits of the last expedition. An annual event, these research trips were sponsored and paid for by some international circumpolar academic institute that wanted to get the maximum bang for its buck. He wondered idly who at the Russian Naval Command had been bribed—or fucked—into lending it a submarine once a year.

"The Admiralty," Stefan Mikhailovich said with a sardonic smile, "is surely praying a cyclone will come and swallow us all. That would conveniently rid them in one fell swoop of about two dozen problematical thorns in their sides."

Nikolai turned to Stefan with a little smile. How right he was. "Then we must try to disappoint them, mustn't we, *Starpom* Varnas?"

Stefan Mikhailovich gave him a wicked grin. "*Da, Kapitan.* Typhoon or no, we will show them we submariners are not so easy to get rid of."

Julie smoothed a hand down the thigh of the navy coveralls she'd put on over, well, over nothing. She was not comfortable wearing the coveralls. And not only because her underwear was still too damp to put on and she was forced to go commando. The coveralls were too large, and she'd had to roll up the long sleeves and pants into thick cuffs. Unfortunately, she'd had no option in the shoe department. She had to wear her red dress heels. She felt truly ridiculous.

Her outfit, however, was a big hit with the crew, causing grins, thumbs up, and comments all along her wobbly pinball walk to the expedition's welcome-and-strategy luncheon. Which was far more attention than she'd wanted to attract. *Blend, Julie,* the boss had instructed her. *Blend.*

Right. Try doing *that* wearing coveralls and high heels.

A few minutes ago, *Kvartirmyeister* Misha had come to fetch her from the stateroom. She almost hadn't answered the door. Except, oh yeah, Nikolai wouldn't bother to knock. He had a key.

Tucking her trusty notebook computer into one of the coverall's roomy cargo pockets—luckily it was one of those really small ones and just fit—she tried not to stumble or trip as Misha led her through the pitching and rolling submarine. At least keeping her balance gave her something to worry about . . . besides seeing Nikolai again. With any luck, the captain would be far too busy running his boat to attend the scientists' luncheon.

But naturally, when she arrived at the dining area he was already lounging casually against the wall—or the bulkhead, as she'd learned from her briefing file on submarine lingo. She'd read the entire file twice, in an attempt to blot out her hovering anxiety. Anxiety over the deep ocean surrounding the boat, over the unnerving idea of sharing a bedroom with a high-ranking Russian military officer—just the *term* "hot-bunking" made her blush—but especially over the überdisconcerting thought of what might happen the next time she actually found herself alone with the man.

Nikolai stood next to one of the six small rectangular tables that had been squeezed into the open-sided dining compartment. When he saw her, his eyes swept over her outfit, then he gave her a neutral smile—without so much as a hint that he'd just accused her of being a spy . . . or seen her practically nude. He shifted aside, gesturing for her to take a seat at the table. She didn't want to be this close to him, but once again she seemed to be the last team member to arrive, and there were no other seats open.

She sat down on the narrow bench and did her best to ignore the sexy captain. Which wasn't easy. If not impossible, what with his firm thigh brushing her arm every time the boat rocked up and down. Which was constantly. Thank goodness she hadn't gotten seasick. The motion's perpetual reminder that the dark, fathomless ocean was just inches away was sickening enough.

She took a fortifying breath as a tall, white-blond man stood up at the front of the dining compartment, which was called the mess hall—a grand name for such a tiny room. The guy was so tall—or the space so short—that the top of his head nearly grazed the tangle of yellow pipes crowding the ceiling.

"Good afternoon, everyone," he said in a melodic accent, loud enough to be heard above the constant background hum of the diesel engines. "For those few who don't know me, I am Professor Björn Sundesvall from Umeå University, your team leader."

He went on to thank the captain and crew for their efforts on behalf of the expedition. Nikolai nodded graciously and introduced the few submariners in attendance for the meal, though most, like him, had to stand along the perimeter.

As he spoke, he beckoned to two noncom sailors—called ratings on a submarine—who proceeded to pass out plates of food. To Julie's vague surprise, it smelled delicious. She noticed that one or two of the scientists looked a little green around the gills and declined the food. But she was ravenous. Being in a state of constant panic took a lot of energy.

"Please, dig in," Nikolai invited everyone, as his leg brushed her arm again.

She eased away. Surely he was doing it on purpose!

"Thank you, Captain," the professor said, catching the subtle touch between them. He narrowed his eyes briefly at her. She endeavored to look completely innocent. Which she was. The Swede wasn't fooled, but mercifully, he looked away. "After we eat," Professor Sundesvall continued, "we will go around the room and everyone should stand and introduce yourself. Tell a little about your project and the type of data you'll be gathering on the voyage."

She had already gotten all that information in the project briefing files. Which was a good thing, because she could barely concentrate with the warmth of Nikolai's muscular thigh blazing through her coveralls like the heat of the sun. She picked up her fork, determined to ignore him.

"Hey, there," said the guy sitting next to her, startling her attention back to the room. He extended his hand. His face was handsome in an older, well-lived-in kind of way, and he sported a long silver ponytail and twinkling eyes. "I'm Rufus Edwards. How you doin'?"

She shook his hand. "As well as can be expected for someone who seriously hates the ocean," she returned with a crooked smile. "I'm Julie Severin."

He chuckled. "Ah. The reporter."

"Yeah. And you're the DAMOCLES guy, right?"

Master Chief Rufus Edwards was one of the retired U.S. Navy men on the team, an old-school sonar operator who'd gotten bored sitting around his Florida pool sipping umbrella drinks and started volunteering his expertise to various ocean conservation groups. DAMOCLES was a much-lauded ice-atmosphere-ocean monitoring and forecasting system that used sophisticated instrument buoys attached to drifting sea ice to collect weather and water data. No doubt his years of working with the navy's SOSUS network didn't hurt his expertise in the field.

"Done your homework, I see," Edwards said with a pleased expression.

"A little," she said. "This assignment was a bit last minute, so I'm still catching up on details. Looking forward to hearing more about your project."

He smiled. "So, you really hate the ocean?"

She grimaced. "Yeah. Almost drowned as a child. Never quite got over it. Being on a submarine is kinda testing the limits of my psychosis."

He laughed. "Well, sugar, the good news is, if anything goes wrong on this tub, trust me, swimmin'll be the least of your worries."

Wow. "Gee, thanks. Ree-ally needed to hear that."

Still laughing, he caught sight of Nikolai, who was silently following their conversation as he ate standing up behind her. Edwards slid over to the very end of the two-person bench and motioned for her to scoot in closer. "Have a seat, Skipper. We can squeeze in one more. I'm sure Miss Severin won't mind the close quarters."

Nikolai's eyes met and lingered on hers for a nanosecond before he smiled at Edwards and shook his head. "Very kind. But I'm sure Miss Severin will have enough close quarters with me before too long."

The master chief's brows hiked. Julie's suddenly queasy stomach did a somersault.

"We ran out of staterooms," Nikolai explained, "so I've invited her to share mine."

She couldn't *believe* he'd made their arrangement public. She was sorely tempted to pack up and move to the torpedo room just to spite him.

Edwards blinked twice, then grinned. "I see."

No. He didn't.

Okay, fine. Maybe he did.

God help her.

"I'm afraid I must get back to my duties now," Nikolai said, scraping the last bite from his plate. "I'll see you later, Julie. Master Chief."

"*Julie*, eh?" Edwards said with eyebrow still cocked. "Interesting development."

"No. It's not." She glared at Nikolai's retreating back. "The captain assured me he'll be a perfect gentleman."

Edwards's gaze slid to the front of her coveralls, pausing on the gold Cyrillic lettering on its left side. His steady grin didn't fade one iota. "Yes, I can see he already is."

It was her turn to blink. "Excuse me?"

"The name on your poopie suit."

Poopie suit? She creased her brow, then realized he meant her coveralls. She glanced down at her chest. "What about it?"

"Has anyone on the crew seen it?"

"Sure. Probably all of them. Why?"

"It says 'Commander Nikolai Romanov.' You're wearing his uniform. Therefore, there isn't a man on this boat who doesn't know he's your . . . protector."

She felt her face flood with heat. He had *got* to be *kidding*. Her hand went instinctively to her chest to cover up the name. Then she realized the futility of the gesture and dropped it.

Awkward. "My suitcase was . . . uh, lost . . . when I came aboard."

"So I heard." He gave her a lopsided smile. "Tough break."

"No freaking kidding."

"I'm sure we can scrounge up some more duds for you. Meanwhile, it's not such a bad thing to be under the skipper's protection."

She made a face. "Are submariners really so dangerous that a woman on board needs protecting from them?" she asked jokingly.

"Submar-*ee*-ners," he said, correcting her pronunciation. Right. She'd forgotten about that quirk of pride. Something about them not being "sub" to anything, especially not marines. "And yeah, I guess we do have a bit of a reputation with the ladies," Edwards admitted with another laugh. He leaned in conspiratorially. "But it's the scientists you really gotta watch out for. They might look like nerds, but they're Euro-*pe*-uns," he said, drawing out the last word, "if you know what I mean." He winked.

"I'll keep that in mind," she drawled.

Just then she noticed that the two men sitting across the table from them were listening with interest to the exchange. Wonderful. So now *everyone* knew her business.

"Hi," said the one with short black hair, bronze skin, and an exotic look to his dark eyes. He stuck out his hand. Around his wrist was a woven leather thong with something carved in ivory hanging from it. Native American? "Clint Walker. I'm the UUV driver."

She shook it and introduced herself, recalling him from her briefing papers. He was the other ex-navy man, in his late thirties—much too young to be retired. The file was silent on his current occupation, but on this expedition he'd be running the two remote undersea vehicles the team members would be using to gather various types of samples. Not unlike the kind of UUV that utilized the Chinese guidance system contained on the hidden SD card.

"Nice to meet you, Mr. Walker," she said.

"Clint, please."

The second man also put out his hand. "I'm Dr. Joshua Stedman. Call me Josh." Josh of the ice sheet melt, sea ice, and ice floes specialty. He looked very young, maybe mid-twenties. Canadian. And a bit . . . awestruck?

She gave his hand a firm shake. "Julie Severin."

"Girl," he declared, leaning in dramatically, his eyes wide, "how did you manage *that* so fast? That man is to *die* for. I am *to*tally jealous."

Clint and Edwards exchanged a look. Clint edged a fraction away from Josh.

Julie almost choked. "No need. I'm just sharing Captain Romanov's stateroom. I believe it's called hot-bunking. And it's *not* what you're thinking."

Josh made a solemn face. "And I *to*tally believe that."

She wanted to groan.

"Who cares if it is?" Edwards said with a good-natured shrug. "It happens. No one's business but your own."

Good grief. Just kill her now. Please.

Luckily she didn't have to respond further because Professor Sundesvall stood again and started the team in on their intros. Julie pulled out her notebook laptop and started typing away as each one spoke, taking down the details that weren't included in the briefing files she'd been given. No one looked twice. Being a reporter truly was the perfect cover for this operation.

Now all she had to do was come up with a plan for how to locate a piece of the submarine called the "crown" so she could locate the hidden data storage card. Good thing she had a clue. Otherwise it would be nearly impossible to find it among the insane conglomeration of pipes and instruments.

The size of a thumbnail, the microcard would be harder to find than a needle in a haystack. A task made even harder because people would be occupying every available inch of space on the sub as they worked on their projects, and therefore able to observe every move she made. Especially now that she and the captain would be the topic of rampant speculation and shipboard gossip, she'd be under intense scrutiny. But somehow, she had to find that SD card without anyone becoming suspicious. Except that Nikolai already was. More than suspicious. He knew she'd been sent here and by whom.

But did he know exactly what she'd come looking for? Guessing—or even being certain—she was a spy was a far cry from knowing her actual mission.

Damn it! She had to find out how much he really knew about what was hidden on board his boat.

But how? It wasn't like she could just walk up and ask him. Even though he'd already confronted her, she could never admit what she was or why she was here. Not aloud. Not ever.

She knew better than anyone what happened to American spies caught operating in Russia. They were killed. Murdered by the notorious FSB security service. Cut down on the street, brutally and without pity.

As her father had been.

Julie's heart squeezed painfully at the memory of her father's death when she was just twelve. She stopped typing for a moment, closed her stinging eyes, and took a deep, steadying breath. Pushed the memory back where it belonged . . . as the inspiration for her fierce dedication to her job. *Not* as the source of her life's biggest sorrow.

"You okay?" Rufus Edwards whispered.

She popped her eyes open. "Yeah," she said. She plastered a wry smile on her lips and lied. "Just a touch of seasickness. The whole ocean thing . . ."

He nodded, but his concern didn't entirely melt away. "If you ever, you know, need anything . . . to talk or whatnot . . . just give me a holler."

"Thanks. I appreciate that," she returned gratefully, suspecting a deeper, fatherly message in his offer. "But I'll be okay. Honest. And thanks."

"We Americans got to stick together," he stage-whispered with another disarming wink. "All these darn foreigners around."

Young Dr. Josh pretended to bristle. "Hey!"

"Shit, not you, Doc," Edwards told him with a laid-back grin. "Hell, y'all up in the Great White North are as American as we are."

"God forbid," the Canadian said with only half-mocked horror, and everyone laughed.

Everyone except Clint. His dark eyes searched Julie's for a moment, then slid away to the female scientist at the next table who was beginning to speak about her project.

A sudden chill trickled down Julie's spine. She wondered what the UUV pilot had been thinking about to cause such a harsh expression.

Probably nothing relevant, she told herself. How could it be? No one on the submarine knew her true reason for being there. Even Nikolai was only guessing.

She hoped.

Maybe Clint Walker just didn't like her fraternizing with the Russian commander. Though why he'd think it was any of his damn business, she couldn't guess.

Not that she disagreed. *She* didn't like it, either. None of it . . . Not that Nikolai suspected her of being a spy. Not that he'd essentially blackmailed her into sharing his stateroom—for purposes she suspected ran far deeper than just wanting to get lucky. And not that Nikolai was Russian—the one nationality she would never, could never, accept as a friend, let alone anything more.

But she especially hated the fact that, despite all the very compelling reasons to doubt and despise Nikolai Kirillovich Romanov, she was still attracted to him. More than she wanted to admit. To herself. Certainly to him.

It was exactly the kind of dangerous, insidious attraction for the enemy that her CIA training had warned her about, over and over. An attraction that could easily cost her the mission and jeopardize her country's security.

An attraction that could threaten her very life.

Somehow she had to fight it. And win.

If only she knew how. . . .

5

She was taking photos.

Or was it videos? Nikolai couldn't tell what kind of camera Julie was using. They all looked the same these days. But whatever it was, the images she was capturing were fairly puzzling.

He'd been observing her for the past half hour, hanging well back as she wandered through the rabbit warren of the motor and engineering spaces at the rear of the submarine pretending to take pictures of the scientists and crew. In reality, she was aiming her lens at every piece of *Ostrov*'s pipes, instruments, and hardware, as well as the small metal plates that labeled them.

The entire boat had been stripped of any sensitive or classified equipment, so it didn't really matter what she was taking pictures of. But labels? Surely, after forty years the Americans had plenty of detailed photos and schematics of Project 636 Kilo-class submarines and all the equipment on board. As vessels went, *Ostrov* was a limping dinosaur. What could possibly be Julie's purpose in photographing these things?

"Shall I take one of you?" he asked, coming up behind her and grasping the camera.

She spun, surprise letting it slide from her grip. "What? Oh, no, I—"

Too late. He'd already started shooting. "Smile, *dorogaya*. No, *smile*, love. Not a frown. Yes, like that."

"Nik—"

"I love your outfit, by the way. The blue coveralls with those red high heels, very fetching. You must e-mail me your photograph so I can put it on my Facebook page."

Her eyes widened incredulously. "You have a Facebook page?"

He took another photo and gave her a dry look, murmuring, "For an intelligence officer, you are very gullible, *dorogaya*."

"Why do you keep calling me that?" she asked. "What does it mean?"

"Surely you know what an intelligence officer is."

"No. *Dorogaya*," she ground out, trying to snatch her camera back.

He blocked her hand. "Just a term of affection. It means darling, sweetheart." He pressed the button on the camera to change the setting to "view" as she grabbed at it again. "Stop. First I want to see. Is this still or video?"

"Both," she muttered. "And I'm *not* your—"

"Ah. I get it now." He flipped through several of the photos she'd taken. Nothing looked of any interest whatsoever. Just jumbles of pipes and stretches of metal equipment housing, with the name of each clearly visible. He shook his head. "You have a very peculiar sense of subject matter, *milaya*."

Her cheeks flushed. "You need to use my name, not terms of— People will get the wrong idea." This time she succeeded in snatching the camera away from him. "And for your information, I'm taking pictures for a friend of mine. She's an art photographer and thought it would be cool to mix Russian and Ameri—" She saw the look on his face and abruptly snapped her mouth shut.

He weighed her answer. *Art* photos? It was just dumb enough to be the truth. However, the U.S. government would hardly have sent her here for that.

"Really?" he queried skeptically, pleased that he was flustering her. "That's the story you're going with?"

Her jaw set. "What do you want, Captain Romanov?"

"I want you to call me Nikolai."

She glanced around. Several of the crew had turned at

their lengthy conversation and were now watching with avid curiosity. "That would be inappropriate."

He lifted a shoulder. "You are wearing my clothes and sharing my bed. I think calling me by my first name will not make much difference to anyone's opinion."

Her pretty lips pressed together. "Don't you have a submarine to run or something?"

He tutted. "Always trying to be rid of me."

"Shame you don't seem to take a hint."

He suppressed a smile. She liked him. He could tell.

"Actually, I've come to find you," he said, seizing on an impromptu idea. "To ask if you'd like to come up on the bridge with me."

"The bridge? You mean the room where you steer the ship?"

"Boat."

"Whatever."

"But no, that is the central post, on the main deck. The bridge is up on top of the sail."

There was that incredulous look again. "Submarines have sails?"

He grinned and shook his head. "*Nyet*. The sail. The fairwater. The conning tower." When she still looked blank, he drew the profile of a sub in the air with his finger. "The big thing that sticks out of the top."

"Oh." Comprehension dawned. She perked up. "It's also called the crown, right?"

He shook his head. "Not that I know of. There are actually two bridges, the bridge and the flying bridge. The bridge is on the very top, up in the open. The flying bridge is a small compartment in the conning tower just below, with windows for a lookout to be posted. No crown."

"Oh." For some reason that seemed to disappoint her.

"So how about it?"

"What?"

"The bridge. With me."

"Wait. You're asking me to go *up* there?" She shook her head vigorously. "Good God, no. Thank you."

"It's still a bit windy, but the sun is finally out and shining off the ice. It's a beautiful sight no one should miss," he tempted.

"I'm sure it is, but . . ." She couldn't finish her excuse.

"You're afraid of the ocean," he completed for her with a solemn nod. "I heard you tell the master chief."

"Yeah. Silly, I know." Her cheeks colored again. It was charming how she kept blushing. Not at all like a hardened *shpion*.

"I understand," he said. "Still. Eventually you will have to forget your fears and go up there."

She snorted softly. "Hell, no. Not gonna happen."

He regarded her curiously. "Then how are you going to file your stories?"

Her forehead twitched. "What stories?"

"To your newspaper, or magazine, or whatever it is. You *are* a reporter, *da*?"

She blinked. "Yes, of course I am." She cleared her throat, looking peeved. "But, um, freelance."

There. He'd caught her. A transparent lie. Obviously she hadn't considered that little detail. "I assume you didn't lose your satellite phone with your suitcase?"

Hesitantly, she shook her head. "No. I still have it."

"Well, the only place it will work is up on the bridge. The rest of the boat is too well shielded to get any kind of signal." He shrugged.

She said a bad word under her breath.

He smiled. "Change your mind?"

She tipped her face heavenward. "God, give me strength."

"It's not so bad," he assured her. "You'll have a safety harness. And me. I'll hold you tight."

She glared at him. "Are you always this persistent, Captain Romanov?"

"Nikolai. And yes. At least, regarding a woman I want. And my career, which I wish to keep."

She huffed out a breath. "And which category do I fall under?" she asked tightly.

He suddenly felt a lot more in control of this whole situation. Finally, a battle he was winning.

He smiled benignly and answered, "Both."

Unfortunately, that sense of control did not last long.

"I'm sorry, Nikolai," Julie said. "I'm just not up to it."

Nikolai wasn't sure to which part of the equation she was referring, personal or professional, or if she was back to the invitation. Before he could ask, the 1MC came on with a squeal of static.

"This is Dr. Sundesvall," the main overhead loudspeakers announced scratchily. "Mr. Edwards has received a hail he thought you might all enjoy hearing."

Nikolai frowned at the breach of protocol. "What the—"

Of course, why should this be any different? This whole *poganaya* patrol was one giant breach of protocol as far as he was concerned.

The air was suddenly filled with the eerie sound of a plaintive, foghornlike call. Instantly Julie broke out in a huge smile.

"Whales!" she exclaimed. Her entire face transformed with pleasure. It had been pretty before, but now it was glowing. So beautiful!

All along the length of the submarine, cries of delight were heard from the scientists and crew alike.

Earlier, when the American master chief had requested to launch his towed sonar array, Nikolai hadn't realized it was in order to listen in on wildlife. On his previous commands, the sonar techs had been too busy tracking U.S. and Chinese submarines to bother listening to cetaceans. He had to say, it made for a nice change. He'd always liked the mysterious-sounding love songs of the whales. Protocol be damned.

Nikolai grinned. "Humpbacks."

Julie glanced at him, looking impressed. "You can tell?"

"One can't be a submariner and not have heard whalesong. Humpback calls are fairly easy to recognize. Although unusual this time of year . . ."

"Yeah?"

"Fall and winter are more common. The males sing when they want to mate." He waggled his brows.

She rolled her eyes. "Lord, you have a one-track mind."

More like two-track. But who was counting? "Hey, it's just what I've read," he protested with a laugh. "At least you needn't worry about going up on the bridge," he added. "It's probably overflowing with folks trying to catch a glimpse of him."

They stood and listened for a few minutes, then made their

way forward to the sonar shack for a peek at the monitor. Nikolai followed her, trying not to get distracted by those sexy red high heels.

He was curious to see how his crew's young Russian sonar tech, *Starshina* First Class Anton Gavrikov, was getting along with the American master chief. Nikolai would have liked to get a look at the equipment Edwards had brought along to monitor the sound signals, before he'd launched the array. Obviously none of the stuff would be classified—even if Edwards weren't now a civilian—but you never knew what could prove interesting.

They found the two sonarmen sitting head to head, twin pairs of big black headsets covering their ears; both were leaning into the massive console, avidly watching the conglomeration of screens. To one side, a separate monitor sat jammed onto the crowded console. Huge, brand-new, and high-tech, its screen flashed all the colors of the rainbow. The master chief's fingertips tapped lightly on a space-age touch-keyboard, bringing up different patterns on the monitor.

The two men were deep in conversation, using a higgledy-piggledy mix of English and Russian with a generous dose of hand gestures thrown in. Nikolai was somewhat surprised Edwards spoke Russian and, from what he could hear, not too badly.

"Kapitan!" Starshina Gavrikov exclaimed when he and Julie entered. "You must see this! *Praporshchik* Edwards has the most astounding collection of underwater sounds I have ever heard . . . or seen. He has recordings of everything. From drum fish to a Type VII German U-boat." The young sonar tech looked enthralled.

The master chief waved a hand dismissively but smiled with pride as he hit a few more buttons on his keyboard and a snowy digital silhouette of a humpback appeared on the monitor. "Just a hobby of mine. In between the real work. And no, I didn't filch any from the U.S. Navy, so don't get your hopes up."

"Impressive," Nikolai said with a chuckle, eyeing the sophisticated equipment with more than a twinge of envy. It reminded him of his last command, a Project 971 Shchuka nuclear sub. Now *there* was a boat.

He tamped down on the useless wistfulness and added,

"We shall put you to the test if we run into any vessels *Starshina* Gavrikov is unable to identify."

Edwards winked. "I look forward to the challenge." He cocked an ear. "Speaking of which . . ."

"Picking up a contact, sir," Gavrikov said.

Both sonar men turned to their monitors, listening and watching intently. Behind the whalesong and the usual mishmash of ice and ocean background noise came a distinct buzzing.

"Another aircraft," Gavrikov said and fiddled with his dials. "I'll bring up the EW."

The radar output sprang into view on the center screen. Both men said, "Chinese," at the same time.

"Y-8MPA," added Gavrikov quickly.

Edwards nodded. "I concur."

Looked like international cooperation was going strong. "You two carry on the exemplary teamwork," Nikolai told them. "And feel free to broadcast any other amusing noises you run across, Master Chief."

"Thanks, Skipper. Will do."

Nikolai turned to Julie to suggest they—

But she was gone.

Irritation trickled through him. Did she really think she could lose him on a two-thousand-square-foot submarine?

As soon as he left the sonar shack, one of the female scientists approached. She was short and dark haired, and she spoke with a strong French accent. "*Capitaine*, Dr. Matilde Juneaux."

"Yes, of course I remember," he said, casting an eye down the passageway to see if he could spot Julie. There was no sign of her. "How can I help you, Dr. Juneaux?"

"I was hoping to have a word with you about setting up the measuring devices on the sail for my project." Which he recalled had something to do with air pollution and volcanic ash.

"Just let me know what you need," he told her.

"How long will we be running on the surface?" she asked.

As she spoke they were joined by Professor Sundesvall. "Yes, I was wondering the same thing, Captain."

Nikolai hesitated. "Given the condition of the boat, I would prefer to stay on top as much as possible. However, it's about five hundred nautical miles to the first scheduled stop, at Attu Island, with a thousand more to the Arctic Circle—assuming the pack ice will allow us passage that far north. Transiting on the surface, it will take us a full two days to reach Attu. Submerged, it would cut our underway down to thirty hours or so, but also prevent taking any outside measurements other than through the towed arrays. At least until we reach the Aleutians. Your call, Professor."

Sundesvall glanced at Dr. Juneaux. "What do you think, Matilde?"

"To take continuous air samples, it would be invaluable," she said hopefully.

Sundesvall nodded. "There's your answer, Captain. Let's stay on the surface."

"Very well, I'll give the order," Nikolai said with some relief. In the month since he'd been transferred to Rybachiy Naval Base, *Ostrov*'s home port, he'd been so busy scrounging much-needed spare parts, and fixing what they couldn't get, that he hadn't taken the boat through more than a few limited safety evolutions in the Sea of Okhotsk, testing the new instruments, and newly welded seams, and fittings. The resulting leaks had been fairly easily repaired, but that didn't mean there weren't more serious issues waiting to spring on them at greater depths . . . so to speak. They hadn't had time to dive to *Ostrov*'s maximum operational depth of two hundred forty meters to test the hull integrity.

Though technically, they shouldn't be diving any lower than a very safe and cozy ninety meters—indeed, for more than half their journey the maximum depth of the Bering Sea floor would be less than fifty meters—one never knew. Salt water was notorious for eating away at the welds that held the steel hull plates in place and corroding the plates themselves. Project 636 subs had a life expectancy of about thirty years under the best of conditions. This one was at twenty years and counting, under some of the worst maintenance ever. He'd actually seen wooden timbers being used in the frames of a few hapless submarines being repaired that were surely destined for future disaster. It made his hair raise.

He'd informed his superiors of his grave misgivings about

Ostrov's readiness, but they hadn't wanted to hear it. The practice runs had gone fine, hadn't they? The international expedition was leaving as scheduled. Period.

And they'd called *him* negligent.

"Frankly," he admitted now, "I'm far happier transiting on the surface until we've completed a deep-water fitness dive, which I plan to do while you are all ashore on Attu Island. God knows the last time this vessel was tested at any real depth. The Arctic is not the place to have an emergency."

Dr. Juneaux paled, but the professor gave a half smile. "Trust me, we're all grateful for your caution, Captain. And your cooperation. The CO on our last expedition was . . . let's just say he was not interested in either."

"Happy to oblige," Nikolai said. "Dr. Juneaux, I'll summon *Kvartirmyeister* Kresney to help set up your gear."

"*Merci, Capitaine.*"

An hour later the whalesong had faded, the air sampling instruments were mounted on the sail, and Nikolai had made his tour of the central post and popped up to the conning tower bridge to be sure the underway was proceeding as it should.

Then he was once again free to devote a few minutes to tracking down his favorite *shpion*. Best check on what she was doing now.

He found her in the torpedo room chatting and peering at a laptop computer with Trent Griff, a tanned surfer-type from New Zealand whose specialty was coral reefs.

That's when Nikolai made an unexpected, and uncomfortable, discovery.

He did not like the other man's roving eyes on Julie, nor did he like the clear interest radiating from them.

Nyet. Not one damn bit.

What the hell? Surely he hadn't started liking the woman. He couldn't possibly be *jealous*. But his uncharacteristic reaction told him loud and clear. He did. And he was.

За ебис. When had *that* happened? He had to be out of his fucking mind.

6

〃〃〃〃〃〃〃／／／／／／／

"These are incredible."

Julie finished scrolling through the two dozen colorful photos of delicate corals and sponges on Trent Griff's laptop computer for the second time. Every bit as gorgeous as more familiar tropical varieties, the formations were lavish orange, purple, green, and blue, in a multitude of fanciful shapes and sizes.

"I had no idea coral even grew in the Arctic."

"Yep," Griff said in his distinctive Kiwi accent, resting his ankle casually across his knee and playing with the end of his shoelace. "Pretty amazing stuff. Takes centuries to grow. And now bottom-trawling fishing boats are coming along and systematically destroying it all. These fishermen's livelihoods depend on the fish, but what they don't understand is that the fish are dependent on the coral gardens for their habitat." He shook his shaggy head. "Kill the coral, kill the fish, starve the fishermen."

Julie took more notes, seriously getting into her role as a reporter doing an exposé on the burgeoning environmental disasters of the Arctic. The public really should know about this stuff. "Sucks for everyone," she said with a sigh.

"Yep."

She returned the laptop to Trent. "So what specifically is your project here?"

"Taking more photos, basically. To support further research funding. You can talk yourself blue in the nose about these things and write a hundred scholarly papers, but two good pictures projected in living color are worth two million words. Show the magical coral gardens, get some oohs and aahs, then show the same garden the next year bulldozed by a trawler. Very effective."

She winced. "Yeah. I'll bet it is."

"I can get you some before-and-after pix if you like. For your newspaper article."

"That would be great," she said, feeling uncomfortable for her semi-deception. What was her boss thinking, putting her in this position? He'd arranged to print the articles she sent him, but until this moment writing them had seemed more like an annoyance than anything. Suddenly this had become more than a cover to her. "So how on earth do you take photos that deep in the ocean? Surely you don't intend to scuba dive in these frigid waters?"

Griff grimaced. "Nah, not quite *that* cold-blooded. I'll be using the UUVs. One has a built-in digital camera that's pretty fab, with cool filters and a special spotlight to shine things up down there."

"Of course." She glanced over at the torpedo racks where Clint Walker's two UUVs were resting. They looked just like torpedoes, designed to be launched from the same tubes. Nikolai had said there weren't any real torpedoes on board. Was that true? She didn't see any, but they could be stashed away—

All at once she remembered she should be searching for the hidden SD card, or at least for the mysterious crown of the clue. She'd gotten too caught up in Griff's photos. She stood and went over to the UUVs, touching the end of one gingerly. "Is this called the crown?"

"The cone, I think."

"Do you happen to know where the crown of a submarine is?" she asked nonchalantly.

"Never heard of it. But then, I'm not a submariner. Strictly a passenger. Why?"

"Just ran into the term in my research. Wondered what the heck it was. Even Google doesn't know."

"Ask Rufus Edwards. He's an old salt."

"Yeah. Good idea." If she could ever get him alone. The master chief always seemed to be in the middle of a crowd.

"Or Captain Romanov . . ."

"I'm sure the commander's got better things to do than answer my stupid questions."

"I wouldn't be so sure," Griff ventured, jiggling his foot as he spoke. "So. You and the captain . . ."

"Not you, too," she muttered and pulled out her camera. Obviously *nothing* was going to make these rumors go away.

"Heard you and he are hot-bunking it."

Especially when they were true. Technically. "Yes, well," she said, "I haven't gotten in his pants yet, if that's what you're asking. So go for it. He's all yours."

Griff's eyes bugged out. "*Hell*, no. That's *not* what I mean—"

She *so* did not want to know what he *had* meant. She interrupted, "Can you tell me how these things work?" She pointed at the UUVs.

"Hey, that's *my* job," Clint said, stepping through the watertight door into the compartment.

Griff glanced at him and summoned a smile that appeared almost genuine. "Be my guest, mate," he said.

Walker gave him an assessing look, but smiled cordially back.

Julie started snapping pictures of the UUVs and the labels around them. It had been her idea to load special software into her notebook computer that would be able to digitally analyze the photographs and detect and identify the tiny SD card in the mass of unfamiliar pipes and instruments much more efficiently than she could with her own eyes. Her boss had been impressed with the idea and given the okay. Frankly she didn't know how she would have been able to pull this off without it.

"So how *do* the UUVs work?" she asked Clint.

"Mind if I listen in?" Nikolai's voice sounded from the doorway as he, too, ducked in through it.

The two Russian crewmen standing at their posts moved aside and cleared a space for their captain when he entered.

Damn, it was getting crowded in here. Julie could practically smell the testosterone flying around the cramped compartment.

"Sure thing, Skip," Clint answered. "The more the merrier."

Nikolai sauntered closer, nodding to his two men and to Trent Griff before propping himself against the torpedo rack.

"Well, to answer your question, Miss Severin," Clint began, "UUV stands for 'unmanned underwater vehicle,' and these two are controlled remotely, from this console here, sort of like a wireless robot." He indicated a setup that looked similar to the sonar station, with monitors and keyboards, plus several joysticks.

She listened attentively to his explanations as she casually continued to snap photos, squeezing in between and behind the racks and pipes, pretending to get interestingly angled shots of Walker as he demonstrated the controls.

Nikolai had chosen to stand in a place with a better view of her than of Walker. He watched her every move with a half-lidded gaze that made his interest seem very personal. But she knew better. He was carefully observing what she was photographing. To her, his suspicion was crystal clear.

But not to the others. Griff was giving them both the eye, a slight smirk curving his lips. It was crystal clear what *he* was thinking, too.

Damn it! She might as well just give up and sleep with the captain. Everyone thought she was doing it anyway. The way he followed her around playing the role of possessive lover to perfection didn't help matters any.

At the thought, a frisson of unwilling arousal shuddered through her body.

Wait.

That wasn't her, it was the *boat* shuddering!

All at once the deck tilted sharply to the left, throwing everyone off balance. She wheeled to keep from falling on her stupid high heels. In less than a second, Nikolai was there with his strong hands wrapped around her upper arms, holding her upright from behind. She opened her mouth to protest, but was cut off by what sounded like a giant sledgehammer striking the hull. A big ca-*lunk* reverberated through the deck right up into her bones.

Oh, my God. What was that?

She and Griff both froze in alarm. Clint paused and looked up but didn't appear worried. The two crewmen didn't even seem to notice. Behind her, Nikolai murmured, "Hold on. There may be more."

"More what?" she croaked, fighting her instinct to wriggle free of his grasp. This was one time she didn't mind his hands on her.

"Sea ice," he said.

Another giant *clunk* resounded through the deck.

"Icebergs?" she squeaked, looking over her shoulder at him, her pulse jumping madly. "This far south?" Visions of the *Titanic* sinking flashed through her mind. Good Lord, she hadn't thought of *that* possibility. Great. Yet *another* danger to be paranoid about.

He squeezed her gently. "We're on our way to the Arctic Circle, *dorogaya*," he reminded her. "Just a few weeks ago this whole area was frozen over. Quite a few lingering ice chunks are still floating around on the surface."

She shivered. And no, it *wasn't* because his body was brushing up against hers. Well. Not completely, anyway.

A series of lighter bumps and clangs pinged through the sub. Panic started zinging in her veins, growing with every noise.

The overhead speaker came on and a voice announced something in Russian, then said in broken English, "Not to worry, everyone. Just little ice. Small pieces. We are past in minute."

"See? Not icebergs," Nikolai said. "And not dangerous."

He loosened his hold on her and she quickly extricated herself. "But still," she countered worriedly, "couldn't one of them rip a hole in our side?" She turned to face him. He was watching her with a gentle smile. Like he understood how terrified she was of all this.

"It would take a very big piece indeed to put even a dent in our pressure hull," he said reassuringly. "And a very careless lookout." He reached out and tucked an errant lock of her hair behind an ear. "And if that did happen, which it won't, there are two hulls, an inner and an outer one. *And* on top of that, this sub is made up of six watertight compartments. If the breach pierced both hulls and we couldn't fix it, we could just seal it off. We'd be fine."

She rubbed behind her ear where her skin still tingled from his touch. It all sounded so matter-of-fact when he said it. But the idea of all that freezing seawater rushing into the submarine and suffocating everything in its path terrified her. "Please promise me you won't let that happen," she pleaded. She had to work at not allowing her voice to shake.

"I promise," he said, looking so sincere she actually believed him. And for a second, as she met his warm blue eyes, all her fears just melted away. He *would* keep her safe. Somehow she knew he would.

Which . . . upon closer reflection, was a patently absurd notion to have about a man bent on exposing her as an enemy spy.

Feeling flustered and chagrined, she glanced away and turned back to Clint Walker. "Okay, then," she managed, determined to get hold of herself. "What were you saying about the UUV?"

One look at his disapproving face and she knew the former navy man had missed nothing that had just passed between her and Nikolai. What was his problem?

"I was pretty much done," he said.

"Oh. Okay." She regrouped, making a note to ask her boss to run a check on him when she called in. "So what project are you working on?"

Clint spread his hands. "This is it."

"You don't have a project of your own?"

"I wouldn't have time to do one," he replied. "I'll be spending every minute either flying or prepping the two UUVs for the scientists. It's a full-time job."

All right. That made sense. "I'd love to watch one of the launches," she said. "Would you mind?"

"Sure, anytime." Clint glanced at Griff. "You're scheduled for the first run in the morning, right?"

Trent Griff nodded. "Yep. First me, then Arja."

Dr. Arja Lautenen from Finland, Julie recalled, was working on mapping solid pollution migrating into Arctic waters from the south. Things like plastic water bottles and foam coffee cups.

"We'll be firing up right after breakfast," Clint told Julie.

"Thanks," she said. "I'll be there. Now I think I better go find Dr. Lautenen and get the details of her project."

"Then I'll be getting back to work," he said. "There's a ton to do before tomorrow's launches." He glanced over her head at Nikolai. "Skipper." His expression was neutral, but she could feel the tension stretch taut between the two men as he turned away. What was going on?

Nikolai was still standing behind her shoulder. She felt his warm breath stir in her hair and wished it didn't make her want so desperately to lean back against his chest. She had chosen her solitary lifestyle, deliberately avoiding romantic entanglements because of the nature of her work and her dislike of deception. Men who didn't work for the Agency didn't understand her reticence to talk about her job. And her male colleagues at CIA were either total geeks or men who had no problem lying to a woman's face. No, thanks. She was pretty sure her mom had found the last honorable spy. And look where *that* had gotten her. And him.

Still. The loneliness was hard sometimes.

"Have you taken all the photos you need here?" Nikolai asked her.

"Yeah."

But being lonely was better than the alternative.

She turned to leave, but he didn't move. He blocked her path, and for a long moment he just stood there, an indecipherable look in his eyes as he gazed down at her. Almost like he wanted to say something.

But he didn't. At length, he stepped aside and let her pass, then followed her out the watertight door. She walked past the control room, kicked off her heels and stuck them in her coverall's pocket opposite her notebook, then climbed down the ladder barefoot to the deck below—praying she didn't lose her grip and fall off. Nikolai was right behind her.

Putting her shoes back on, she went forward through another watertight door and into the narrow passageway that held the officers' staterooms. When they were finally alone, she stopped and whirled around to face him.

"Do you plan on following me all day?"

He smiled. "Perhaps."

"I want you to leave me alone," she said.

"Yes, I know."

"Good. Then I'll see you later. *Much* later."

He folded his arms across his broad chest. "Julie. On what planet do you live to imagine that I would let a spy roam freely around my boat without at least trying to ascertain what she is up to?"

He'd made no overt move. Hadn't loomed over her or even darkened the tone of his voice. But he was so damn tall. And his crisp black captain's uniform trimmed in gold with its row of ribbons marching across his chest suddenly made him seem less like a sexy hunk and far more like a formidable authority figure. The rest of the crew was all dressed in coveralls like the ones she had on. She was sure he'd deliberately kept his uniform on, to let everyone on board know in no uncertain terms who was in command of *Ostrov*.

He was big and broad and handsome as the devil. And intimidating as hell.

In an attempt to counter his aura of power, she pulled herself up to her full height . . . such as it was. Her show of defiance was only marred by the fact that his name was plastered across her chest in bold letters like she belonged to him. And by the completely irrational wish, insinuating itself into her mind—and her body—to know what it might feel like to belong to a man like Nikolai Kirillovich Romanov.

"I am not up to anything," she insisted, studiously avoiding his gaze lest he see her embarrassing thoughts pooled in her eyes. "Have you seen me do anything other than shoot photos? You saw the pictures yourself. Anything suspicious about them?" she demanded, finally able to make eye contact. "If I had anything to hide, would I have consented to stay in your stateroom, where you can easily search the few belongings I have left?" She held up a palm. "And don't tell me it's so I can seduce you or try to get you to come over to our side. That's completely ridiculous."

His gaze narrowed and drilled into hers. "Let's say I go along with that. Okay, if I'm not your target, then who is?" he shot back.

"No one!" she returned.

He moved in on her. She could almost see his mind whirring with alternatives. "Are you here for a drop? Is that it? Someone on board is passing you Russian state secrets?"

"No!"

"Then it must be something in those photos you keep taking. There's no other explanation."

She struggled not to blanch. "You're wrong."

"I swear to you I'll find out. What have you been sent here for, Julie Severin?"

She gathered herself for the lie. "Nothing! I've already told you, Captain Romanov. I'm just a journalist. That's it. Nothing more."

"Prove it," he said, his voice dark and gritty.

"How?"

He glowered down at her. "File your story."

Taken aback, she blurted, "I haven't written one yet! I'm still talking to people about their projects!"

"Fine. You have one hour. That's plenty of time for a seasoned journalist to have something written. And it better be good."

"But—"

"One hour, *dorogaya*. Meet me on the bridge. And bring your satellite phone." He lowered his voice to a velvet growl. "Or I'll be forced to find more creative ways to get the truth from you. And don't think I won't."

7

ıllılılv/ıllıll

Nikolai swore under his breath as he ducked back through the watertight door. Чёрт возьми.

The little *shpion* could deny it all she wanted, but Julie Severin was lying. It was written all over her pretty, blushing face. How could CIA have sent someone as transparent and inept at prevarication as her? It was almost insulting.

And another thing. There was definitely something going on with those photos. She'd practically fainted when he'd mentioned them.

Suddenly the answer hit him.

She was *searching* for something.

It all fell neatly into place—her going through every square inch of the submarine taking photos, and her ridiculous explanation. Art? He didn't think so. There was only one possibility that fit her behavior.

Something very small or very well disguised must have been hidden on board *Ostrov*. Something hard to spot in a casual search with the naked eye. An enlarged digital photo would reveal something anomalous tucked away among the pipes and instruments. Something like a tiny computer memory card, for instance. Microdots for the new age, with enough power to store the entire plans for a battleship. Or a nuclear submarine.

He didn't know why it had taken him so long to figure it out. Her method of searching was ingenious.

But not quite ingenious enough. Because he would know exactly when she found it—as soon as she stopped taking those photos. It would be a simple matter then to go through the stateroom and find whatever it was, wherever she'd hidden it. Or had tried to. Unlike her, he knew every inch of that stateroom. And far more of the insides of the submarine than she could ever hope to learn. In the worst case he could simply confiscate her camera and computer and turn them over to Comrade Cherenkov and the FSB. *They* could deal with it.

And her.

Pressing his lips together, he grabbed the rails of the ladder and started up to the central post. What happened to Julie Severin after that was not his concern.

She was a spy. Spies knew the price of being caught.

Nothing to do with him.

He ascended two rungs at a time and stormed into central command. "Captain on deck," *Starshina* Dmitry Borovsky announced quickly—and waited expectantly for Nikolai to take over the conn and the deck. But he had no intention of doing so. There was some kind of problem reported in engineering that the chief engineer wanted him to take a look at.

Since they were transiting on the surface, the OOD was currently up on the bridge, with Borovsky down here in the central post as junior OOD. *Kvartirmyeister* Kresney stood lookout up in the flying bridge, with a rating posted in the conning tower as his and the OOD's talker. They were perfectly capable of dodging whales and sea ice without Nikolai looking over their shoulders. The problem in engineering was more important for him to deal with.

First, however, he wanted to go over the plans for tomorrow. Spy or no spy aboard, the scientific expedition had to run smoothly or his career would end up in deeper shit than it already was.

"Dispatches, *Kapitan*," *Starshina* Borovsky said crisply, handing him a single piece of paper.

"Thank you," Nikolai said just a shade sardonically. "Dispatches" was a rather glorious word for the routine two-line weather report *diviziya* command deigned to send them each day. It wasn't like they were on an autonomous military patrol, forbidden to contact headquarters except for rare encrypted radio bursts. As long as they were transiting, the scientists were free to use their satellite phones and laptops, and even the crew was allowed to e-mail home whenever they liked. No, officially, *Ostrov* was simply being ignored. Which actually suited Nikolai just fine. It worked both ways.

He approached the chart table and greeted the navigator, a man he hadn't sailed with before. "How goes our progress, *Praporshchik* Zubkin?"

"Cold, straight, and normal, *Kapitan*," Konstantin Zubkin reported with a crooked grin.

Nikolai chuckled at the reference. Obviously Zubkin had spent time on a torpedo post. Or possibly he'd heard Nikolai was a film buff who'd seen every submarine movie ever made at least five times. "Hot, straight, and normal" was American sub-speak for a torpedo running true to its target. But today, the open hatch to the top of the sail was keeping the central post temps more Arctic than tropical—thus the paraphrase.

"When do we reach the first study area?" he asked.

"Just before oh-eight-hundred tomorrow, sir."

Zubkin produced a set of detailed maps of the ocean floor—rather, as detailed as it got, which was to say filled with masses of blank spots—proceeding from their current position along their charted course going east then north to Attu Island.

Their projected route would take them over the edge—metaphorically speaking—of the Asian continental shelf and the Kuril-Kamchatka Trench into the topmost corner of the Pacific, then over the Miezi Seamount and past the international date line, and finally to Attu. Attu was the last American island on the very tip of the Aleutian chain, the westernmost official bit of American soil, or the easternmost, depending on whom you asked and whether they took a traditional view of the international date line as 180° longitude or acknowledged the zig and zag imposed upon it to keep the Aleutians all on the same day.

Zubkin spread the charts on the light table, then brought out a transparent overlay and put it over the chart. "These are the research stops proposed by Professor Sundesvall for tomorrow."

Nikolai knew there was a strong southward drift in the ocean current to compensate against, so hitting such small targets was not quite as simple as it sounded. It took constant adjusting by the helmsman. "Foresee any problems with getting to them?"

"*Nyet, Kapitan.*" Zubkin indicated a red *X* marking the last stop. "There are some large rock outcroppings and natural obstructions here as we approach Attu, but if we stay on the surface we should be fine. The UUVs should have smooth flying both days. No bad weather or rough currents predicted for tomorrow."

"Very well, *Praporshchik* Zubkin, plot a course for tomorrow's evolution and run it past Professor Sundesvall before reporting to me."

"*Da, Kapitan.*" A hesitant look shadowed his face.

"Was there something else?"

"Well, we were just wondering, sir. Will there be a ceremony?"

Nikolai blinked. "Ceremony?"

"We'll be crossing the Arctic Circle on this patrol. And the international date line as well, *nyet*?"

"Ah." *That* ceremony. With all his other, more immediate concerns, Nikolai had totally forgotten about the traditional crossing-of-the-line festivities. For centuries, the rare event of passing north of the Arctic Circle had been marked by initiating the first-timers—pollywogs, as they were known—into the Royal Order of the Bluenose. But first they were put through a series of trials . . . to test their worthiness to enter the frigid realm of the northern sea gods. These trials were usually amusing—to those watching, anyway—often disgusting, and always freezing cold. The date line ceremonies were generally far less elaborate, and often skipped altogether because crossing it had become so routine in these days of easy global travel.

"A few of the men," Zubkin continued, "it is their first time crossing either. And one of the expedition members, too. Miss Severin."

The entire command post watch had looked up at the mention of the ceremony and were now following the conversation with avid interest. All but *Starpom* Varnas, whose face had suddenly lost much of the color it had gained from the morning's watch.

"Because it jogs around Attu, we'll actually be crossing the international date line several times," Nikolai corrected, then grimaced. "It has made writing down the watch schedule ridiculously complicated."

The nav nodded. "Our first crossing of the date line will be tomorrow. On Midsummer's Eve." He emphasized the last two words.

"Quite a coincidence," Nikolai said cautiously, sensing there was more coming.

"A very auspicious coincidence," Zubkin said gravely, but with a twinkle in his eye.

Slowly, Nikolai smiled. Okay, he'd play along. "Indeed. And how would you suggest we mark this momentous occasion, *Praporshchik* Zubkin?" he asked.

"Well, sir"—Zubkin leaned in, feigning conspiracy, but spoke loudly enough for all to hear—"we have received a missive from Boreas Rex, Ruler of the North Wind and Sovereign of All the Frozen Reaches It Touches. He wishes to send an emissary to prescreen the warm bodies who wish to enter his Icy Realm as Bluenoses."

Nikolai lifted a brow. "Doesn't that usually happen when actually passing the Arctic Circle?"

Zubkin pretended to frown. The rest of the men's grins grew even wider. "Not the actual trials, *Kapitan*. Just a quick assessment. King Boreas says he's extremely busy this week, sir. An unprecedented number of pollywogs headed for the Great North. Quite a traffic jam."

"Okaa-ay . . ." Nikolai had a hard time imagining a traffic pileup at the Arctic Circle.

Zubkin continued, "Boreas would like his emissary to assess each initiate's worthiness, in preparation for the physical trials the king himself will conduct when we reach the Arctic Circle."

Nikolai was beginning to see where this was going. Any excuse for a party. "And when exactly would this assessment take place . . . ?" Like he didn't know.

"Tomorrow, sir. On Midsummer's Eve. When we cross the international date line."

Nikolai felt his lip twitch. "I see. And who, may I ask, has Boreas appointed as his emissary for this unusual visit? King Neptune, perhaps?"

Zubkin shook his head. "Unfortunately, Neptune is also very busy this week. At the equator, sir."

Now Nikolai was really curious. Neptune and Boreas were the only two gods who could officially preside over Arctic Circle–crossing Bluenose ceremonies, as far as he knew. Of course, this wasn't the actual ceremony they were talking about. . . .

Again he played along. "All right. Then which god will Boreas send in his place to assess our lowly pollywogs?"

"In honor of Midsummer," Zubkin said with a barely maintained aura of sagacity, "Lord Ægir has graciously consented to officiate, sir. The mighty Nordic God of the Sea."

It took a second to understand why Zubkin and the others looked ready to burst their seams. Then Nikolai got it and laughed out loud.

Ægir was also the god in charge of brewing beer.

Normally on military evolutions no consumption of alcohol was allowed on board. But as had been repeatedly drummed into him, this was not a military patrol, but a civilian expedition that was merely using military transport.

So why the hell not?

"How fortuitous for us," he said with a grin.

"Doubly fortuitous, *Kapitan*," Zubkin said slyly, "because we will be crossing the date line into yesterday, and therefore we are able to celebrate Midsummer twice!"

Nikolai chuckled. Or at least able to have a do-over with no alcohol involved. "Has the galley secured provisions fit for such an illustrious celebration?" he asked.

"Absolutely, sir. A steel beach barbecue is planned— weather permitting—with American-style ribs courtesy of *Praporshchik* Edwards, and liquid refreshments provided by the Swedish professor." Zubkin waggled his eyebrows.

This had obviously been planned well in advance. "Sounds like you have everything in hand, *Praporshchik* Zubkin. Keep me informed."

"You can count on me, sir."

Of that, Nikolai had no doubt.

He handed back the charts, checked the control room clock, then turned to the JOOD. "*Starshina* Borovsky, I am expecting Miss Severin shortly. I'll be taking her up to the bridge to use her satellite phone. Call me when she arrives, will you? I'll be in engineering."

Borovsky nodded vigorously. *"Da, Kapitan."*

As soon as Nikolai was through the watertight door to the neighboring compartment, excited conversation erupted behind him. It carried an edge of gleeful anticipation.

He was in fact pleased with his men's initiative. Whatever the plan was, it would be good for camaraderie on board. And an excellent idea to have the barbecue at the beginning of the voyage instead of waiting nearly a week. Scientists and crew would form an early bond, forged in ritual and celebration. Afterward, they would be transformed from a disparate conglomeration of different people from different countries, with vastly different backgrounds, into members of a single tribe sharing a rare and unique common experience.

Even his little *shpion*.

Which was not a bad thing when he thought about it. Forcing her to take part in such a bonding ceremony would try her growing friendship and allegiance to the scientists and crew. And hopefully make her feel good and guilty as she prepared to betray them all. . . .

With a flourish, Julie finished typing the last sentence of her feature article, read it over, and saved it to the satellite phone's micro storage card—coincidentally the same type of SD card as the one she was searching for. If Nikolai thought he was being clever making her prove her reporter chops, he was in for a real disappointment.

She'd started out working as a journalist after college and had been a damn good one. On top of that, she was interested in and passionate about the expedition projects—at least the ones she'd learned about so far. It was no hardship at all to write about them in glowing terms. Plus, as part of her cover her boss had arranged for anything she sent in to be published by the newspaper she used to work for—minus a few prearranged code words carefully included in the text.

Yeah, *that* proved she wasn't a spy.

Along with the news story, she would upload a zip file of the photos she'd taken so far. They'd be run past an expert in case the word-and-object-recognition program on her laptop had missed something important. She didn't have a lot of hope that would be the case. So far, the software had seemed to recognize everything in the photos. But it had discerned no SD card. And nothing called a crown, or anything remotely close to that word.

In her news article, she'd highlighted the CO, Captain First Rank Nikolai Kirillovich Romanov, with a coded alert, letting her boss know he'd been tipped off to her from day one. Which still worried her. Where had he gotten his information? Was there a mole at CIA who had leaked her mission to them? How long could she continue to deny she was a spy when it was obvious he knew better and didn't believe a word she said?

More important, what would happen when she finally *did* find the hidden SD card with the stolen Chinese UUV guidance system plans?

What she'd told Nikolai earlier was true—he really could search her few belongings anytime he pleased, including her computer if he was conversant with hacking skills. Too bad for him he'd find nothing incriminating. No hidden files. No gun. No disguises. No secret spy gadgets designed by a modern-day Q. Just one totally-out-of-her-element China analyst, a bunch of meaningless photos, and a so far useless one-word clue—which he wouldn't find because she hadn't written it down. All completely innocent . . . until she found that elusive SD card. *That* would be fairly incriminating.

Still, maybe she wouldn't ever find the damn thing, so she wouldn't have to worry about being exposed as a spy and shot on the spot when he discovered it in her possession.

With a groan, she stuck her satellite phone in her pocket, then did a double take at her shoes. She should really try to find some sneakers somewhere to change into. Maybe one of the women scientists had an extra pair she could borrow. Or Josh—Dr. Stedman. He was skinny enough he might be her size.

Oh, what the hell. Why bother? Who knew, maybe wearing the high heels with Nikolai's coveralls gave her a slight psychological advantage over the man. He'd noticed for sure. He'd said she looked . . . fetching. Whatever that meant.

Maybe the sexy shoes would distract him by reminding him of their undeniable physical attraction—and the implied sexual meaning of her wearing his name on her chest—so maybe he'd pay less attention to his suspicions about her.

Hadn't Sun Tzu said, "The opportunity of defeating the enemy is provided by the enemy himself?"

It could happen.

Yeah. Maybe in an alternate universe.

Stifling another groan, she pulled in a deep breath, checked her watch for the dozenth time, and reluctantly headed for the control room. Time to face the music. Or more precisely, the ocean.

God, was she ever dreading this.

Almost more than she dreaded being shot as a spy.

Almost.

8

~~~~~~~~~~~~~~~~~

Nikolai made her wait, of course. The power play was so cliché it bordered on being humorous. But Julie was in no mood for laughing. In fact, as she stood at the foot of the barrel ladder leading up to the top of the sail, she was insanely grateful for the delay. It gave her a chance to gather her badly flagging courage.

Stupid.

Stupid, stupid, *stupid*.

Who was afraid of water?

Wimps.

Certainly not competent officers of the Central Intelligence Agency. Imagine if the enemy found out about her weakness and used it against her. Her training had warned her about techniques like that.

Except, of course, the enemy already *did* know about it.

It suddenly struck her. Good Lord. Was *that* what this was? Nikolai trying to break her down, not with the reporter thing, but through her fear of the ocean? Sex hadn't worked, so now he was using psychological tactics?

Damn. The bastard!

Anger and indignation swept through her in equal measure. And this should surprise her? Not.

What did surprise her was the spike of hurt she felt. *Talk about stupid.* That's what she got for wanting to think of him as a man instead of the enemy.

No. She'd be *damned* if she'd let him get to her. Either as a man *or* the enemy.

She turned to the officer who seemed to be in charge of watching over her while she was waiting. "The captain has obviously been delayed," she clipped out. "Can you take me up to the bridge, please?" When he didn't seem to understand she pointed at herself, then up the ladder.

The guy peered back at her like a deer caught in head-lights.

"That's not a problem, is it?" she asked, softening her tone.

"N-*nyet*," he said on a cough. "No p-problem." But the ex-pression on his face told a very different story.

He shuffled a little and glanced behind her for help from the other men in the command center. None was forthcoming. Only shrugs. She smiled sweetly at him, and batted her eyelashes for good measure, then grasped the handrail of the ladder.

"I . . . Please to wait." He hurriedly said something to one of the men in the room, who ducked through a door at the rear and a moment later emerged and held out a pair of thick woolen socks to her.

"Take," the officer said in his heavy accent and pointed at her high heels. "Is danger."

She accepted the socks with some relief. "Thank you." She quickly made the change in footwear.

"Okay," he said and gestured upward. "Is good."

She took a steadying breath, clinging to her anger at Niko-lai like a life preserver against her rising panic.

She could do this.

She started to climb. The rungs ended abruptly above a sturdy but open hatch, not outside as she'd expected, but in a dark, wet, tiny room. It had open steel doors leading both left and right. To the right was a small area choked by three long, thick metal columns. Probably the periscope housing or maybe the radar. Past those was an even smaller compartment with a row of clear, stubby windows overlooking the front end of the submarine. This must be the flying bridge Nikolai had mentioned.

Two of the windows were also wide open, and she could feel a stinging ocean wind hit her face. It smelled thickly of salt. And lots and lots of water.

She quickly started to turn away.

"Miz Syev'ryin? Come in, come in!" a man exclaimed from inside the room. "You want tour?"

With a start she recognized the *kvartirmyeister*, Misha. She'd been so intent on the disturbing view through the windows that she hadn't even seen him standing there. Another man, much younger, stood at his side.

Even if she'd wanted to go in, the compartment was so small it would be a very tight fit. And she didn't particularly want to go in. Even from here she could see the pewter sea wash over the round nose of the submarine in huge waves, spraying the sides of the sail with bullets of white. A rolling wake churned outward in an inverted vee as the sub sliced steadily through the water.

Nausea bloomed instantly in her stomach.

And yet, it suddenly occurred to her that having those windows positioned firmly between her and the sea would be a great improvement over nothing but the thin air. Maybe she could get satellite reception in here. . . .

Swallowing sharply, she told herself not to be a baby.

"Hi, Misha," she said in greeting. "I'm on my way up to the bridge. The other bridge."

"In English can call top bridge cockpit. Less confusing." He smiled.

"What are you doing up here?" she asked curiously, glancing around. There didn't seem to be any equipment in the tiny space.

"Lookout. I watch for big ice and other boats," he said with a wink. "Oleg is talker. He yell down to control room if we hit something." He grinned. "Sometimes even before."

She winced and made herself focus on Misha instead of scanning the disturbing expanse of water behind him for large white chunks of ice. "Mind if I take a picture?" she asked, to distract herself. The SD card could be hidden in here, too.

"Yes! Take many photos!" Misha urged, and he hammed it up for the camera, pulling a series of muscleman poses with his binoculars as a prop.

She laughed and snapped several of him and the young rating, Oleg, who was busy rolling his eyes and flashing his cute dimples. For a few minutes she actually forgot to be afraid. Then it was back to reality, and she could no longer delay the coming ordeal.

"Well, I better let you get back to your watch. I wouldn't want to be responsible for us hitting an iceberg," she said.

"I keep telling you there are no icebergs around here," said a deep, familiar rumble behind her.

She spun to the sound, swaying out of the compartment as another wave rolled the deck. The door swung closed behind her, smacking her butt.

"Nikolai!"

"Ready to go up?"

"Yes, I— Yes."

Despite the scowl on his face, he looked more handsome than ever in his rakishly tilted cap that reminded her a little of a Greek seaman's cap, and a long black greatcoat. He had another coat in his hands. He held it up for her. "Here. Put this on. It's chilly up there."

She wanted to say no just on principle, but she really hated being cold. She stifled her mulishness and slid it on. "Thank you," she said politely.

His narrowed gaze dipped to her feet. "I see you found some better footwear."

"Thank goodness. One of your men gave them to me."

He pulled a similar pair from his coat pocket. "I also brought you a pair. I promised to take care of you, *dorogaya*."

She met his eyes defiantly. "No need. I can take care of myself."

He reached out and fixed the collar of her coat. "Why do you fight me so, Julie Yelizaveta?"

Her pulse quickened. He was too close. Being too nice. Smelling too good. She swallowed. "You know why, Nikolai Kirillovich."

The corner of his lip curved. He slowly smoothed his hands over her shoulders and down the arms of the coat, then pulled the front edges together, as though he was about to button it. "Because you want me. But you are afraid."

"I don't want you. And you threatened me." She stepped back and started to button her coat herself.

"Wait." He stopped her with a hand on hers. Her heartbeat skyrocketed. He put his other hand to her waist, gently tugging her closer.

She sucked in a breath, her body instantly reacting to the warm touch of his fingers on her skin.

"Nikolai, no—"

"Don't worry," he said, and from somewhere he produced a webbed belt and slid it around her waist. He expertly cinched it. Attached to the belt was a sturdy nylon line with a carabiner at the end. "Just putting on your safety harness. I told you I'd take care of you."

For a second she couldn't move. Confusion surged through her. Sharp disappointment that his touch hadn't been for more personal reasons . . . along with intense relief that it hadn't.

"Why?" she managed to ask, taming the urge to press her body into his and *make* it personal. God, she was so confused!

"So you don't fall off the bridge into the water," he said, catapulting her back to reality.

Her panic and fear flooded back instantly, and she stared at the lifeline, paralyzed. "Oh, God," she whispered.

She didn't even protest when he buttoned her coat for her. "Ready?" he asked when he was done.

"No!" she choked out. All her anger, frustration, and attraction dissolved into an adrenaline rush of dread. She stabbed her hand into her pocket. "I have a better idea. You go up and make the call for me." She stuck out her phone to him. "It's all set up to send. I'll wait here for you."

She'd managed to surprise him. After a moment of astonishment, he hiked his brows and actually looked tempted to take it. But then he shook his head. "No, Julie. You need to do this. And sooner rather than later. Trust me, you'll kick yourself if you wait until the last day to conquer this useless phobia and miss all the incredible sights along the way."

She was taken aback. Was that *concern* she detected in his statement? Surely not.

"What makes you so certain I'll conquer my phobia?" she asked. "Maybe it'll conquer me instead."

He snapped up the collar of her coat and buttoned the top button for her. "*Nyet*. You will."

She searched his expression. There was little doubt he meant it. It was the strangest thing. The man had faith in her when she didn't have faith in herself. Could it be this trip up to the bridge *wasn't* about torture and intimidation, after all?

But if not . . . what—?

Her musings were interrupted when he plopped a hat on her head. A big, round furry one that was much too large and covered her entire head from her eyebrows to her nape. It was thick and silky and utterly gorgeous. "I don't wear fur," she protested, at once feeling guilty for wanting to luxuriate in its amazing soft warmth. "I don't believe in killing wild animals."

"Neither do I," he said.

"This hat isn't yours?"

"It is." He looked at her for several moments, as if debating how to explain. "When I was a boy," he said at length, "my family was at our dacha one winter, and I found a wounded wolf out in the forest. Two of its legs had been badly hurt in a trap and it was very weak. I was young, and didn't know any better, so I wrapped it in a blanket and brought it home. Hid it in the sleigh barn, and tried to nurse it back to health in secret. Almost succeeded, too."

He raised his fingers and stroked them gently over the long fur with a sad little smile.

"What happened?" she asked, quietly bespelled by the poignant look in his clear blue eyes.

"My father shot it," he said and dropped his hand.

She was so shocked she didn't know how to react. "My God," she said. "That's . . ."

He straightened the hat on her head, his fingers lingering in the fur, his eyes gazing at something far in the past. "My mother skinned the wolf and made this *ushanka* for me from its pelt, as a Christmas gift. But she died in November, and my father . . . he doesn't believe in Christmas. Or in giving. I discovered it in a chest of her belongings years later, just before I left for university. It was still wrapped in bright red paper."

At the infinite hurt lurking deep in his words, the last of her anger fell away. She wanted to put her arms around him and kiss the sadness from his lips. "Oh, Nikolai. I'm so sorry."

His face shuttered and his voice cooled. "I keep it with me so I'll always have a reminder."

Julie waited, but the silence just stretched. "A reminder of your mother?" she asked softly.

He came back to the present and his eyes focused on her. He smiled, but it wasn't a nice kind of smile. Instead of answering, he said, "So, Julie Yelizaveta Severina. Are you ready to go up now and face your worst fear?"

And suddenly she realized that seeing the vast ocean spread out before her was not her worst fear. Not by a long shot.

Far worse was the genuine fear that what she was feeling for Nikolai Kirillovich Romanov was not simple sexual attraction for a handsome guy in a uniform. But that she was really, truly falling for this man . . . this Russian . . . this enemy of her family and her country. And that there was no way to stop it, nor a damn thing she could do about it.

Suddenly *that* was her worst fear.

"No," she said, shaking her head in dismay.

He tipped her chin up and looked into her eyes, reading her mind like a sea chart. "It would never work, you know," he said softly. After gazing at her regretfully for an endless moment, he straightened and turned her with his powerful hands so she was facing the ladder. "Now climb. Before I put you over my shoulder and carry you up."

She climbed.

"What do I do when I get to the top?" Julie asked, her limbs actually starting to shake. *From the torment up ahead,* she told herself. *Not because of the man climbing after her.*

"I sent *Starpom* Varnas ahead to clear the cockpit for us," he said. "He'll clip you to the rail and help you up."

She searched her memory and recalled the young executive officer from when she'd first come on board *Ostrov*. He'd been the one with the disapproving glare when Nikolai had ordered Misha to put her in the captain's quarters. *Great.*

Her life would be in the hands of one man bound and determined to expose her as a foreign intelligence officer, and another who thought she was the captain's bed warmer.

Or, God help her, maybe Nikolai had already told the XO of his suspicions about her being a spy. Wow. Even better.

She reached the top of the ladder and found an outstretched hand waiting for her. Behind it was a ruddy, smiling face. "Welcome to top of world, Miss Severin."

"Thanks. I think." Had he changed his mind about her? Or was that a spider-to-the-fly kind of smile . . . ?

She took his hand and her pulse pounded madly. She barely resisted squeezing her eyes shut as he helped her up into a postage stamp–sized observation well sunk into the forward sail. Right behind her, Nikolai passed him the end of her harness and he clipped it to a toe-rail. A breath of relief whooshed out of her lungs.

Even in socks she had to fight to keep her balance at the more pronounced pitch and roll of the vessel at this higher point of gravity. She kept her gaze firmly on the ribbed metal floor that was digging into her feet through the socks. The cockpit floor was awash, and she felt the cold, wet bite of seawater soaking into the soft wool.

She sucked down several deep, calming breaths. The briny scent of the wide open sea filled her lungs and slapped her senses awake after the dull, cloying diesel smell inside the confines of the submarine. In that sense, it was refreshing to be up here.

Nikolai climbed up, and his arm banded around her middle. "Okay?" he asked.

She nodded, still not daring to peel her gaze from the deck below her feet. Not daring to be reassured by his protective gesture. "Yeah."

The wind clawed viciously through her coat, cold as stinging icicles, and the waves kept her off balance, although she'd thought she'd grown used to the boat's rocking motion by now. Sea legs, the submariners called it. Apparently she didn't have them.

The prow hit a big wave, and she reeled as the cigar-shaped submarine heaved up over it, then down again like a child's seesaw. Thankfully, the solid steel walls of the cockpit came up to her waist, and she reached out to grab on to the edge with desperate fingers. She noticed that neither of the men were clipped onto safety harnesses. Did they feel that secure, or were they just being macho?

Nikolai tightened his hold on her, impervious to the motion. "Easy," he said in her ear. "You're okay. I've got you. Just a little swell."

She nodded again, steadied her stance, and blew out the breath she was holding. In front of her, the *starpom*'s boots adjusted position, reminding her of his presence. She forced her gaze up the XO's legs to his chest, then made the leap to his eyes.

He was still smiling, his dark brown hair whipping in the wind beneath a black Persian lamb *ushanka*. She managed to smile back. Sort of.

"Nice day for phone call," he said in a cheerful, unspider-like voice.

"If you say so." She cleared her throat. Some freaking spy she was. Being so wimpy was downright embarrassing. But not enough to tell Nikolai to let go of her.

None of this had been her idea, she reminded herself in her own defense. She was good at her job. Very good. But field ops *wasn't* her job. She was an analyst. Not a case officer.

She scrabbled in the deep pocket of the long coat to get her satellite phone. She wanted to make this quick.

"Nyet." Once again, Nikolai's hand stopped her. "Not yet," he told her. "You must look first. Really look, down into the depths of the sea, and show her you are not afraid."

Julie made a desperate noise of protest. "But I *am* afraid" slipped out before she could stop it.

Nikolai's voice in her ear was deep and low. "The sea is our mother, *dorogaya*. She is our father. The place where all life was born." He put his cheek against the soft fur of the hat his own mother had made for him. The one he'd placed on Julie's head like a halo of protection. "How can you fear your mother, *milaya moya*?" he murmured. "Come. Be brave and she will reward you. I promise."

Julie thought about her own mother, how brave she'd been when Dad hadn't come back from his last Company "business trip." How she'd found a shit job so they wouldn't lose the house and had silently, heroically, kept a heartbroken little girl's world from falling apart when her own had been shattered in a million pieces. *That* was brave. Opening one's eyes and facing a bunch of stupid water, that was child's play.

She groped for Nikolai's hand. It found hers and squeezed. Swallowing, she nodded at *Starpom* Varnas. He stepped aside so his body no longer blocked her view.

The vast ocean spread out before her in an endless, undulating expanse of frigid, ugly gray. There wasn't a sliver of land in sight.

The old panic instantly hit, sucking the breath from her lungs. The choking, the nausea, the helplessness of nearly drowning flooded back over her as vividly as when she was a child going under the water certain she was about to die. Her fingernails dug into Nikolai's palm.

He didn't seem to notice. "Say it," he said. "Aloud."

"What?" she croaked.

"Tell her you are not afraid."

She shook her head. It would be a lie.

"Tell her," he ordered firmly.

She hesitated. "I'm not afraid," she mumbled. It sounded pathetic even to her own ears. She let out a laugh of embarrassment. But . . . amazingly, the nausea was ebbing.

"Again," he said.

She squeezed her eyes shut and opened them again. And saw nothing but deadly water all around. *Oh, God.*

"I'm not afraid!" she said, louder this time, and clearer, though still not convincing.

"Better. Again," he ordered.

The water isn't *deadly,* she told herself. She'd *survived* that childhood trauma. It hadn't gotten her then, and it wouldn't get her now, either.

"I am not afraid. I am *not* afraid," she shouted, each syllable more forceful than the last. Finally, the words sounded like she meant them. And felt like it, too.

She felt Nikolai smile as he hugged her, his broad chest pressed securely against her back. "Good," he praised. "Good!"

Miraculously, the feeling of helplessness dissolved. She couldn't believe it. She'd done it!

But it would never have happened without Nikolai's help.

She turned in his embrace, and before she knew what she was doing, she threw her arms around his neck and kissed him.

After a second of surprise, his throat rumbled, and then he

was kissing her back. His breath was warm and his lips were hot. One big hand slid behind her nape and held her with powerful fingers as his mouth covered hers and demanded she open to him. How could she refuse? She felt the deep stroke of his tongue down to her freezing toes . . . and all the places in between. *Especially* the places in between.

He kissed her and kissed her, until she was a mindless pool of need, swimming in the taste of him, caught in a whirlpool of desire. She was drowning in passion for a man she should never, ever want like this. But, oh, she couldn't stop if she tried.

He lifted his lips at last and murmured, "Still afraid of the ocean, *dorogaya*?"

"What ocean?" she asked on a shuddered sigh.

And from behind her, the *starpom* observed dryly, "*Kapitan*, I think you have surely cured her."

9

\\\\\\\\\\\\///////

Kissing Julie in front of Stefan Mikhailovich and the lookout posted at the rear of the sail was perhaps not the wisest of moves. Okay, it definitely was not. But Nikolai didn't regret it. Not for a single second. Not even as he saw the look of intense concern flash across his *starpom*'s face when the man thought he wasn't looking.

"Don't worry," Nikolai told him in Russian when he had released Julie to make her call, "I know what I'm doing."

"Do you?" Stefan Mikhailovich asked, skepticism ringing in his voice. "Perhaps when it comes to curing phobias. But you should not get personally involved with this woman, *Kapitan*."

"Believe me," he said. "It's not what you think."

"She's an American!" Stephan warned, as though Nikolai hadn't spoken. "Probably an intelligence officer sent to spy on us!"

Nikolai stifled a wince.

Julie glanced up at them as she waited for the satellite phone to connect, perhaps recognizing the word "American." Nikolai gave her a wink.

"All the more reason to keep her close," he returned, keeping his face pleasant so she wouldn't suspect they were talking about her. "Besides, why would CIA send an agent onto this

outdated diesel boat to spy on a scientific expedition where half
the members are already North American? Or maybe you think
she's here to contact someone on our crew, a traitor?"

They were questions Nikolai had asked himself more
than once since his meeting with Comrade Cherenkov back
at the Kursk Hotel. But he didn't think that was why she was
here. He had little doubt she was searching for something.
Why would a traitor hide something on board for her to find
if he could just hand it to her in person? Which meant the
traitor was no longer on board. Her search and the photographs would make no sense if he were. But Nikolai wasn't
about to share any of those insights. He needed to solve this
himself.

Stefan Mikhailovich looked uncomfortable, but he did not
have any answers. "The men will be resentful," he said forcefully, "that you so blatantly have a woman in your bed."

"Captain's privilege," Nikolai said with a smile and a
shrug. In a way it was flattering that everyone believed he was
flouting every navy regulation in existence and was actually
sleeping with her.

"You are a Russian naval officer!" the *starpom* exclaimed
reprovingly. "Not some high seas pirate!"

Nikolai barked out a laugh. "Funny, that's exactly what she
said. And yet, if you will recall, it was *she* who kissed *me* just
now, not the other way around." Stefan Mikhailovich looked
so horrified that he felt sorry for his *starpom* and said, "You
needn't worry. She hasn't seduced me and she won't get the
chance. I don't plan to sleep in my quarters."

Julie looked from Stefan to him, clearly unsure about the
intensifying exchange.

Stefan Mikhailovich looked downright skeptical.

"Well, don't say I didn't warn you," *Starpom* Varnas grumbled, "I see that my watch is over. If you no longer need me,
Kapitan, permission to quit the bridge?"

"Granted," Nikolai said. "Tell your relief to stand his
watch from the flying bridge."

"Yes, sir."

"And Stefan, thanks for your help."

"Anytime, sir. Miss Severin." He gave a stiff little bow and
disappeared down the ladder.

Nikolai was now alone in the cockpit with Julie.

"What was that all about?" she asked.

"Nothing," he said. He reached out and smoothed the unease from her brow with his thumb. "Are you getting a signal on the phone?" he asked.

"Mm-hm, finally," she said and started to press buttons. She made no attempt to hide the number. "Hello?" she said a few moments later. And she proceeded to hold a completely normal, noncryptic conversation with the person on the other end regarding the article she was uploading. The only possibly suspicious thing about the entire conversation was that she never used the other person's name.

This would not do at all.

Just as she was about to hang up, Nikolai whisked the phone from her hand.

"Hey!" Julie exclaimed and tried to grab it back.

Nikolai easily blocked her. "Hello?" he said into the unit.

Julie looked like she wanted to strangle him. "What are you doing?" she demanded furiously.

On the phone there was a pause, then, "Julie? Are you all right?" It was a man's voice. He sounded concerned.

Nikolai stifled a completely irrational spurt of something that felt dangerously close to jealousy. Which under the circumstances was patently absurd. The man was eight thousand kilometers away. "This is Captain Nikolai Kirillovich Romanov," he said in his most commanding voice. "With whom am I speaking?"

"James Thurman," the man said and indignantly rattled off a high-level position and the name of a well-known Washington, D.C., newspaper. "What's going on, Captain Romanov? What are you doing with—"

"Miss Severin is fine," he interrupted, holding up a warning finger at Julie, who was still trying to grab the phone. "I just wanted to express my appreciation for your newspaper's interest in this important scientific expedition. Having a reporter along to write about it will do much to raise public awareness of critical environmental issues in the Arctic."

Julie's expression relaxed somewhat.

"Ah. Well. You're very welcome," said James Thurman—if that was really his name. "Miss Severin is an excellent journalist. I'm sure she'll do a great job with the articles."

"I'm sure she will," Nikolai agreed amicably. "But my question is, what is she *really* doing on *Ostrov* for you? I mean, of course, for CIA."

Julie gasped. There was a pregnant silence on the other end of the phone. "I don't know what you mean, Captain. Miss Severin is a legitimate journalist working for—"

"Yes, yes, I'm sure her cover is impeccable. But you and I both know that's not why she's here. I'm giving you fair warning, she will *not* complete her mission. And if she does, she *will* be arrested."

"You speak English very well, Captain Romanov," Thurman said. A clear attempt at dissemblance. "Did you learn it as a spook with the FSB? Perhaps you're still on their payroll?"

"I spent my senior year at an American high school as an exchange student," Nikolai said smoothly. Which was the truth. Right after graduation and before being admitted into the navy as a candidate to the elite submarine service. His first assignment for the FSB had been to get to know the teen-aged children of influential Washington movers and shakers. It had paid off with several useful contacts, though his own ties with the kids involved had been severed long ago. Those were the days before social media and limitless e-mail. "As I'm sure you're already aware," he added. "Now if you'll excuse me, I must get back to interrogating your operative." He pushed the "off" button and handed the phone back to Julie.

She stuffed it in her pocket. "You are completely insane, you know that?" she ground out.

"I've been called worse," he said, slipping the micro storage card, which he'd surreptitiously ejected from its slot in the phone, into his own pocket.

"I can't believe you said those things to my boss!"

"Look on the bright side," Nikolai said with a crooked smile, as he tapped the end of her nose with a finger. "Even if this mission of yours is doomed to failure—and trust me, it is—at least you aren't afraid of the ocean anymore."

She snorted. "Says you," she muttered.

And from the look on her face, he knew she hadn't been referring to her fear of the sea.

Julie flushed at her own inane comeback. Wow. What was she, like, twelve?

Cripes. More like sixteen. Because that was exactly how old she felt whenever she was around the astonishingly insightful Captain Romanov.

"We'll see," he murmured with a knowing curve to his lips.

The way he was regarding her now made her heartbeat kick up. It was a very male look. Assessing. *Hungry.* He was remembering their kiss, she could tell. His lids had gone to a sexy half-mast and he was scorching her lips with his stormy gaze.

She couldn't believe she'd kissed him earlier. What had she been thinking? Unfortunately, she knew *just* what she'd been thinking.

It was like some obsessed hormonal teenager had taken over her body, making her think and do things that were totally crazy and out of character. She was *so* not this person she'd become after stepping onto this damned submarine! She didn't go around wanting to kill a man one minute, then wanting to rip off her clothes and drag him to bed the next. And then turn around and want to kill him all over again.

Oh. My. *God.*

She had to get *hold* of herself!

Though admittedly—and she really did hate to admit it—he was right about the ocean thing. She wasn't afraid anymore. Well. Not terrified, at any rate. She still didn't like it, but the sight of all that deep, lurking water no longer made her dissolve into a trembling puddle of abject panic. She could stand here and gaze out over the sea without being convinced she would die any second. Yes, she still felt an edge of unease that was too imbedded in her bones to exorcise quite so easily, but looking out over the undulating blue-gray expanse, she also had to admit that it possessed a beauty unlike anything else she'd ever seen. Powerful, savage, and unforgiving, but beautiful nonetheless.

That truly was progress.

She met Nikolai's gaze and couldn't decide which part of their increasingly complicated relationship to address first.

"What?" he asked, his voice dipping an octave, when she just stared at him for a long time.

His conversation with her boss had been even more upsetting than the kiss. Nikolai's parting threat had been like a dash of cold water, reminding her of their true relationship.

"Would you really arrest me?" she asked him.

"If you are a spy? Of course I would," he said; then, after a nanosecond's hesitation, he added, "I'd have no choice."

"So all these kisses, they really mean nothing? They're just part of your personal counterintelligence kit?"

His eyes narrowed. "There have been no kisses since the hotel, *dorogaya*. Not until you kissed me just now. So perhaps it is I who should be asking that question."

She felt a blush rip up her throat. *God, he's right.* After their passionate encounter last night in the hotel stairwell, any kissing between them had just been in her own vivid imagination. "You kissed me back," she defended herself, fighting the acute embarrassment.

"And I'd do a lot more if given the chance," he conceded. "But it would change nothing. I would still have to arrest you. I have my career to think of. Letting a spy go free . . . well, let's just say I would not be popular with my superiors."

Okay, then. At least she knew where she stood.

"Then it's a good thing I'm *not* a spy," she said and turned away to concentrate hard on the horizon, a focal point for her chaotic thoughts . . . and feelings.

What was going on with her? She didn't understand why she was so drawn to this man. It was totally unnerving. And nearly as terrifying as the sensation of drowning. In a way it *was* like drowning. She was floundering in a sea of unfamiliar emotions and desires. Wanting to know him, wanting him. No, it wasn't like she'd never fallen for a man before . . . but never one so screamingly wrong for her. And never so hopelessly.

Under a brooding bank of storm clouds, the late-afternoon light saturated the sea, turning it a deep, rich pewter, painting the crests of the choppy waves in liquid silver. It had a deadly, ominous power. No wonder it lured men to abandon hearth and home to taste the mysteries of its depths.

Sort of like a certain Russian sea captain.

But she would be a fool even to think of pursuing this any further. He'd said it himself—it would never work between them. Ever.

For God's sake, he'd just told her he'd have no qualms about arresting her for espionage!

"Milaya moya—," he began, apparently sensing the direction of her thoughts.

"Don't," she said, cutting him off, feeling foolishly, stupidly hurt by the brutal candor he'd just displayed. "Don't call me your sweetheart thirty seconds after you threaten to have me executed."

His fingers gripped her arm and swung her around. His expression was as stormy as the sea. "I would never do that!"

"Don't be naïve. What do you think happens to spies who are arrested?" she shot back. "You think they're sent to a country club on the Black Sea, perhaps?"

He blanched, his head snapping backward as though she'd slapped him.

She *should* have slapped him. "Well, *I* know *exactly* what happens to them," she spit out. "They killed my father, you know. Shot down on a street in Moscow in broad daylight. *Your* people. Your Russian FSB murderers. How fitting if the same should happen to me!"

He looked stricken.

She jerked her arm from his grip, fury pouring through her like salt on a fresh wound. She couldn't get past him to escape down the ladder, so she spun away, grabbing the cold metal edge of the cockpit with white-knuckled fingers, facing into the bitter wind.

He swore in Russian, then said, "I'm sorry," his voice oddly gritty. "I'm so sorry, Julie. I didn't know." She felt his hands alight almost convulsively on her shoulders.

She stiffened. "Don't touch me! *Please.*"

The feel of his hands melted away, leaving a stinging hurt where they'd been. Her cheeks hurt, too, from the icy wind. And her eyes—they swam and stung like someone had ripped them out. Along with her heart.

Why? Why did she give a damn?

"Julie," he said in that dark voice, and his body whispered gently against her back. "I would never let them hurt you. I swear."

Too late. Almost twenty years too late.

She felt the press of his face against the fur hat his mother had made for her grieving boy, a loving gesture that had become a constant reminder of a father's cruelty . . . and of an even greater grief. A parent gone forever.

She couldn't stop her tears.

For herself. For him.

Maybe even for them. They were so attracted to each other. But they were doomed from the start.

Blindly she turned and tried to push her way past him, to get to the ladder.

"Julie, wait. Talk to me. I need to—"

"No! Let me go," she said between soft sobs. "We can't be friends and we damn well shouldn't be lovers. Please, Nikolai. Let's just leave it alone. While we still can."

She tore his hat from her head and thrust it into his hands. She stumbled to the access trunk ladder and, almost against her will, glanced back at him.

But he didn't try to stop her.

Pain razored through her heart as his mute expression turned to one of shuttered acceptance.

Well, what the hell had she expected? A goddamn declaration of love?

10

It nearly killed Nikolai to let Julie go.

It was like someone was tearing him in two.

It made no sense. In one short day she had managed to get to him, to burrow under his skin—and into his soul—more thoroughly than any other human being on earth had done since the death of his mother. He was at a complete loss as to why. What had started out as an explosive sexual attraction had quickly burned into something far deeper.

How? They'd barely spoken. Barely kissed. And yet, every time they touched it felt like a depth charge had gone off in his chest and laid his heart bare. He felt raw. Exposed. And almost desperate. He wanted her so badly.

Чёрт возьми! How the devil had this happened? How had she managed, as guarded and unwilling as he had—to awaken every male instinct he had—sexual, possessive, protective?

He wanted nothing more than to stash her in his stateroom and keep her there until he could spirit her away to his dacha and keep her there, safe, forever. Except, she wouldn't be safe there. She'd never be safe with him.

How had he let himself become so . . . ensnared by her? She seemed so damned innocent, so defenseless, so . . . unlike the sort of hard, heartless woman the word "*shpion*" invoked. Was she for real? Or was it all just an act? Was she so skilled at her craft that she was able to convince him so thoroughly of her goodness that he'd fallen for it—and her—hook, line, and sinker?

Hell, he didn't think anyone could be so accomplished an actress. Those tears, the anguish in her eyes as she'd torn herself away from him, were genuine. He'd stake his life on it.

Which, he feared, he was already doing.

Stefan Mikhailovich had the right of it. Nikolai must force himself to steer clear of her on a personal level. Keep it professional. Trap her, turn her in, then forget her.

The question was, how? How to ignore the overwhelming need . . . *and the guilt* . . . gnawing at his gut, and feed her to the *politchik* wolves?

He looked down at the fur hat in his hands and shuddered out a long, agonized breath.

A flash of lightning lit up the sky, followed by a boom of thunder that shook the deck beneath him. Seconds later rain began to pelt his face.

A rating popped up from below holding a hooded slicker. "Foul-weather gear, *Kapitan*?"

Nikolai waved it off. "*Nyet*, I'll be down in a moment."

But forty-five minutes later he was still standing there on the bridge, soaked to the bone and nearly frozen solid. He hadn't noticed the discomfort, nor had he moved an inch. He'd been lost in an unwilling tumult of thoughts . . . and memories . . . stirred by the pretty American. He'd been thinking about his mother.

One memory in particular. Of a photo he'd also found among his mother's belongings after she died.

A single photograph, old and yellowed with age, it had been carefully concealed under a false bottom in a small cedar jewelry box. It showed a smiling young couple with a child of about six or seven, posing in front of a huge waterfall. The little girl, despite the small size of the photograph, had features uncannily like his mother's.

Which was impossible, he'd always told himself. What he'd suspected at the time was wrong. Dead wrong. Even though the paper the photo was printed on had a troubling word repeated in faded print diagonally across the back: *Kodak*. And regardless that the waterfall in the background looked an awful lot like Niagara Falls, which he'd visited that year he'd spent at an American high school.

Impossible. Utterly and definitively impossible.

Nikolai had replaced the photo that day and never taken it out again. But the image had been burned into his memory. Down through the years he had steadfastly ignored the niggling feeling that Cherenkov's blackmail may have something to do with that single, damning photograph.

He'd ignored it, because his mother was *not* American. She'd spoken flawless Russian. She'd had a whole documented family history, proving her pure Russian heritage. She was sweet and uninterested in anything much beyond her summer garden, her winter embroidery, and her only child. His father had been—and still was—an important provincial party official. Rostislav Ivanovich Romanov was handsome and charming on the outside, though viciously, ruthlessly ambitious under that thin veneer of charisma. He'd been especially fanatical in the old Soviet days because of the taint of aristocracy in his family blood. Rostislav Romanov would never, ever, have married a foreigner, risking his ever-tenuous position in the party.

Unless he hadn't known who she was.

Or what she was.

Nikolai's turbulent mind did not want to think about Julie's father's murder.

Shot down on a street in Moscow, she'd said.

Ruthlessly. Cold-bloodedly. *For being a spy . . .*

Was that a lie, too? Just part of her strategy to worm her way into his sympathy? Worse, was she trying to convince him to trust her by feeding on his own darkest fears about his mother?

But how could Julie know about the photograph? How could *anyone* know? And how in hell could she ever know his own mother had also been shot down on the streets of Moscow . . . ?

She couldn't, he told himself, shoving back at the sickening sense of foreboding rising in his heart.

Because his mother was *not* American. *Not* a spy. There was nothing more to say on the subject.

He resurrected himself from his disturbing thoughts and shook the cold rivulets of water from his hair. He looked up and saw that it had stopped raining. And realized the rest of his body was shaking like a dog.

Чертов ад. Fucking, fucking hell.

He stabbed his fingers through his icy, wet hair, snapped himself out of it, and climbed down the trunk ladder to the central post, where he stripped off his drenched greatcoat and tossed it and his mother's wolfskin hat to a rating.

"Captain on d—," *Starshina* Borovsky began to announce, but he halted as Nikolai swung around and headed in the opposite direction.

"Carry on," Nikolai called over his shoulder as he ducked into the radio room. He dug the SD card he'd taken from Julie's satellite phone and handed it to the surprised radio operator, *Lyeĭtenant* Danya Petrov. Petrov had a reputation for being a computer wiz. The kid also knew how to keep his mouth shut. "I want to know what's on this. Everything. My eyes only. Understood?"

"*Da, Kapitan.*"

Nikolai closed the door again and called to Borovsky, "I'll be in engineering if anything comes up."

He needed a major distraction, and this was the best one he could think of.

The engineering problem Nikolai had gone aft to investigate earlier in the day had actually turned out to be a malfunction in the atmosphere production equipment. Which, according to the chief engineer, *Praporshchik* Yasha Selnikov, was slowly strangling the boat's supply of oxygen. If Yasha hadn't caught it when he did, their breathable air would have slowly degraded. It could have been very bad news indeed if they'd submerged for any length of time.

Hypercapnia, or carbon dioxide poisoning, was an insidious thing; it started with headaches and fatigue, slithered quietly through hyperventilation and impaired judgment, and ended with painful convulsions and death. Chances were good that they would have noticed and surfaced in time—especially with all the scientists on board—but perhaps not before a tragedy had occurred, either medically or from a mistake resulting from the crew's mental erosion.

The chief engineer had been working to correct the problem all day. Nikolai wanted to make sure the cause was found and fixed, without fail. This was not something to be trifled with.

Before exiting the central post a second time, he turned back to call another order to Borovsky. "See that a drill is scheduled for tonight on the use of the IDAs. Everyone on board who's not on critical duty is to participate. Officers to supervise."

The IDA-59 was a personal breathing apparatus designed to provide ten to thirty minutes of good air in an emergency. Every Russian submariner was issued one and was required to have it on his person at all times. He'd planned to do the drill tomorrow, but in light of this development, the sooner the better.

"Scientists, too?" Borovsky asked, mildly surprised.

"Everyone," Nikolai repeated. "And see that they also carry them from now on." It was probably just spies on the brain, but the whole oxygen malfunction thing was bothering him. Better safe than sorry.

Nikolai ducked through the watertight door and headed aft. He really should go to the stateroom and change out of his soaked clothes first. But Julie might be there, and he wanted to keep his distance from her until he regained a more even mental keel. And if she was still upset, he didn't want to intrude on her.

Luckily, having the diesel motors running nonstop guaranteed that the aft compartments would be stiflingly hot. His clothes would dry quickly, and he'd soon stop shivering. On the outside, anyway.

When he got to engineering, a concerned *Praporshchik* Selnikov glanced up from amid the guts of the atmospheric equipment, some of which was in parts on the deck. He did not look happy.

"What's the word, Yasha?" Nikolai yelled over the ever-present mechanical noise of the engines.

He had served with the older man several times previously,

and for his money *Praporshchik* Selnikov was the best engineer, mechanic, and all-around fix-it man in the Russian navy.
On this patrol, Yasha was also chief of the boat, or COB, a
sort of intermediary between enlisted men and officers. There
wasn't a man on the crew whose judgment Nikolai trusted
more.

Yasha glanced around and waved the other crew members
off, to give them privacy.

Damn. Any discussion that required secrecy never delivered good news. Nikolai squatted down on his heels so they
didn't have to shout.

"It's not good, Comrade *Kapitan*."

"Tell me the worst. Can't you fix it?"

The *praporshchik* gave him a withering look. "Of course I
can fix it."

"Then what?"

"It is a very unusual break. One that happens very rarely."

Nikolai returned the older man's steady gaze, reading between the lines. За ебис. "Are you saying it may have had a
little help breaking?" he asked, not really wanting to know the
answer.

Yasha swiped his oily hands on a rag. "There's no way to
tell for sure. But yes, there's a fifty-fifty chance this malfunction did not happen on its own."

Sabotage?

Nikolai's first thought was of Julie. He scowled. "What
level of expertise are we talking?"

"High. If this was deliberate, the person who did it either
knows exactly what he is doing or has been given explicit di-
rections and knows enough to follow them."

Nikolai digested that with trepidation. Julie didn't strike
him as having an advanced engineering degree. True, looks
could be deceiving. He'd ask her what she had studied. But if
it wasn't her . . .

Чёрт возьми. Nikolai didn't want to think about the
possibilities.

"Again, it may not have been deliberate," Yasha said and
pursed his lips. "There were no overt signs of tampering. And
with the general run-down state of this vessel . . ." He let
Nikolai draw his own conclusions.

"If there was no outward indication, how did you find the break?" Nikolai asked.

Despite the serious subject, Yasha gave him a boyish grin, taking years off his weathered face. "I was testing a new piece of equipment. A kind of chemical sniffer I saw on an American TV show about crime scene investigators. Thought it would be fun to try to build one myself."

Nikolai gave him an incredulous look.

The COB winked. "Hulu. Gotta love the Internet."

"Shit," Nikolai said after a chuckle, then went back to the problem at hand. This was just what he needed. A spy, and now *this*? "What the hell do we do if there's a saboteur on board?"

Yasha pushed out a breath, the both of them once again going somber. "Pray we catch the bastard before he kills us all."

It wasn't easy to hide on a submarine. Every inch of space was filled, either with hardware, equipment, supplies, or people.

But tucked way in the rear of the sub, behind the aft hatch ladder where she'd originally climbed in, Julie had managed to find a small corner to be alone. Well, relatively speaking.

After leaving the confrontation with Nikolai on the freezing bridge, she'd taken a short but blessedly hot shower. There was no way she was putting that skirt back on, and the socks were too wet to wear, so she'd had to put the damp coverall back on, along with her red heels. Now she sat huddled there knees-to-chin on the floor behind the ladder.

Some of the crew knew she was sitting there. But they'd all taken one look at her puffy red eyes and tear-tracked cheeks, and let her be. Apparently men were the same the world over. None of them wanted to deal with a crying woman. Even now, two hours later, she was still sniffling and they were still avoiding her.

She hated that she couldn't stop crying.

She'd thought she'd cried herself out over her father's death long ago. But being in the country that had murdered him, and seeing the pain-mingled sympathy in Nikolai's gaze at her revelation . . . it had brought all the emotions boiling to the surface that she had managed to hold at bay for so many years.

Feelings of grief and anger, and the fierce need to avenge her father's death. The same need that had driven her to accept a job with CIA in the first place, and had kept her so dedicated to her work as an analyst.

Except now she no longer had the comfort of a finger to point blame. She genuinely liked the Russian people she'd met since her arrival. They were not the monsters she'd wanted to believe her whole life. They were ordinary laughing, loving people, just like her.

And she liked Nikolai so much, with a genuine depth of feeling. He was an enemy warrior, but he'd suffered as much as she had. Perhaps more. At least she still had one loving parent left, and a large and nurturing extended family. Who did he have to soothe his hurt and grief? A father who seemed worse than none at all.

So she'd cried for herself, and for him, and for the frustration that she could never be the person who would hold him in her arms to comfort.

Or to laugh with.

Or to love.

Goddamn mission. Why had she come here, anyway? Why did she have to meet a man like Nikolai? A man she could so easily see herself falling for in a big way? A man she could never have.

Because he was the one man who might well have to choose between his country . . . and her life. And she could never be sure which way he'd choose. Or be forced to choose.

It wasn't fair.

On either of them.

So she hid out, folding herself as small as possible, and fought her demons, hoping to come to some sort of mental resolution. Dinnertime arrived. A young rating stuck his head around the corner of the hatch barrel she was hiding behind and made eating motions. She gave him a watery smile and shook her head. She wasn't hungry, and the thought of facing anyone, let alone coming up with idle dinner chitchat, made her stomach hurt.

But the interruption did serve to bring her out of her funk. She had work she should be doing. She really should go to the stateroom and fetch her laptop, run some more photos, maybe even start another cover article to send to her boss, along with a progress report—or rather, *non*progress report.

Tomorrow would be a big day for the scientists—the start of their intensive sampling and data gathering. From now on, until the expedition reached the Arctic ice pack, *Ostrov* would halt each day to conduct several hours of research.

Clint Walker would be running UUV sorties practically nonstop. She was excited to see how the unmanned vehicles worked. And couldn't wait to see Trent Griff's coral gardens, as well as learn more about all the other interesting projects. Along with her real job of finding the hidden SD card, there would be plenty of things to keep her occupied on the voyage.

Which was good. Because then she wouldn't have time to think about other, more personal issues . . .

Like how on earth she was going to sleep in Nikolai's bed without wanting him there with her. Or asking him to join her, for however fleeting an affair. She bitterly regretted not taking him up on his proposition at the hotel, back when he was just an anonymous body. For now that she knew him, she wanted him all the more. But she also knew all the reasons she should leave him be.

Somehow she had to find the strength to resist her own desire.

And do her damn job.

With a sigh, she lowered her knees from under her chin, wiped her eyes, and shook out the cricks in her bones. Tears and feeling sorry for herself were not going to help the situation. She'd just have to learn to live with her aching heart.

Determinedly, she got up and headed forward. However, the last thing she wanted was to run into Nikolai while she was feeling this vulnerable. So she took the long way back to the stateroom, down the ladder to the lower deck and along the twisty length of the sub, passing under the mess hall where everyone was still gathered for dinner.

Massively relieved that she hadn't passed anyone but random crew members along the way, she swung open the state-room door.

And got the shock of her life.

Nikolai was standing in the middle of the tiny compartment, a towel draped around his neck.

Other than that, he was completely, delectably, mouthwateringly naked.

11

〟〟〟〟〟〟〟〟

Oh. My. God.

Water drops glistened on Nikolai's bare skin, catching the glow from the small green desk lamp. His honey-gold hair was dark and wet, rivulets dripping down his angled cheekbones onto his shoulders and chest, slick and shadowed in the dim light. On his right pec was an elaborate tattoo that looked like . . . eagles maybe? . . . and a double anchor. His legs were slightly spread, his feet planted against the motion of the boat.

Lord have *mercy*. There was no doubt, whatso*ever*, of his gender.

All that made her mouth water, but what got her in the end were his eyelashes. They were long and tawny and spiked with moisture, making him look like some kind of sultry, seductive demon.

Her own personal demon of temptation. Those dark bedroom eyes were enticing her to do something that every cell in her body told her would be a terrible, terrible mistake.

But she just couldn't help herself. She stepped into the stateroom.

And closed the door behind her.

He regarded her evenly, warily. His hands curled to fists, holding the ends of the towel that was slung around his neck.

She stepped closer.

His blue eyes turned dark as thunderclouds. He didn't move, but at once the air between them thickened with tension. The clean fragrance of his soap tickled her nose, masculine and no-nonsense. Beneath it lurked the more subtle, musky scent of his male body, delivering its potent subliminal message—*a call to mate.*

Her nipples tightened at the recognition. *Her* mate. Her belly zinged with crazy want. She wanted to touch him. She wanted to taste him. She wanted to feel his body pounding into hers.

She shouldn't. *Shouldn't, shouldn't, shouldn't.*

But before she could stop herself, she reached out, her palm pressing flat against the tattoo on his chest. His flesh felt hot and moist. Hard as granite. So amazingly good.

His cock began to stir. His fists slowly unfurled, and he started to let go of the towel.

Oh, God.

"Don't," she ordered, her voice catching on the conflicting emotions flooding through her. Knowing what he wanted. What she wanted. *But shouldn't.* "Don't move."

His hands halted. But his cock didn't obey orders. It kept right on rising. Long. Thick. Straight.

Those spiky lashes lowered to half mast, his demon eyes searching hers. Still wary. But growing bolder.

She licked her lips. And raised her other hand to his chest, next to the flat discs of his nipples. She ran her fingertips over them, and they hardened instantly.

A muscle jumped in his neck. He asked, his voice gritty and low, "*Dorogaya*, what are you doing?"

Good freaking question.

What?

Her job?

Going insane?

Sealing her fate?

Inexplicably, her eyes filled.

God, how she wanted him! But, oh, such a very bad idea.

"Let me touch you," she said in a hoarse whisper, the need raging within her. "Just touch."

His expression went hesitant, crossed by a shadow of raw vulnerability. As though he wanted to let her, but didn't quite trust his judgment of the situation. Or perhaps of her.

"Please," she whispered, a tear cresting. She lowered her eyes, afraid he'd see how desperate she was feeling.

"Julie," he whispered. A question. A plea. *A warning.*

She didn't wait for permission. She leaned in and kissed his throat, spreading her hands over the firm muscles of his pecs lightly dusted with springy hair. Her breath shuddered out as she ran the tip of her tongue down the corded muscle straining at the side of his neck. An erotic blend of masculine musks spilled over her tongue, spiced with the salt of tears she couldn't hold back. She dipped into the little hollow at the base of his throat, where his pulse beat hard and strong, and licked at the shower drops that were pooled there.

God, so good.

A soft noise of agony escaped her. *Too* good!

Anguish clambered up her insides. She didn't want to be doing this. Yet she didn't want to stop. Not ever.

But she must.

Soon.

She drew her tongue farther along his collarbone and felt his chest muscles tighten beneath her palms. Again she brushed her thumbs over his hard nipples, and a rash of goose bumps rippled under her fingers.

He let go of the towel and started to reach for her.

She grabbed his wrists. "No!"

If he touched her, she'd be lost. Even more so than she already was.

"Milaya," he half groaned. But he didn't fight her. Not yet, at least. He wrapped his hands back around the towel ends, his knuckles white. Then he looked up and saw her face. Concern swept across his. "Are those tears?" His brows flicked together. "Julie? What is it? Has something happened?" He dabbed them from her cheeks with his towel-wrapped fingers.

She gave her head a little shake. "No. It's just . . ."

She didn't know how to explain what she was feeling. Instead, she let her hands slide slowly down his torso. Felt the crisp curls of his bronze chest hair; the firm thump of his quick, even heartbeats; the solid bulge of each hard-earned muscle in his six-pack.

He watched her intently as she touched him. Seeming to understand without words. Did he feel it, too? The craving? The intense longing? The irresolvable conflict in his heart?

Her hands reached his waist, and she hesitated. Just for a moment. Then she splayed her fingers across the angles of his hip bones and turned her hands to brush the backs of her knuckles over the sensitive hollows just above. He inhaled sharply. His cock jerked.

His face changed. Got harder, darker, more . . . predatory. His lips parted a fraction. He was breathing faster now. His heartbeat was far less calm. So was hers. The seconds ticked past as he waited for her to move her hands inward. And touch him where he most wanted to be touched.

She didn't. Because she could see it in his eyes—if she touched him there, it was all over. There'd be no holding him back. No more towel. No stopping him from taking her.

Even now, it could be too late.

Oh, God, it was!

Because he'd brought the towel over their heads and it was now around the back of *her* neck. He was slowly reeling her in, closer and closer, like a fish caught in a net.

She didn't stand a chance against his strength. Or his magnetism. Or his pure animal appeal.

She was being a coward tormenting him like this. Provoking him to act so she didn't have a choice, when in fact she wanted this as much as he did. *More.*

He paused with his lips just a shadow away from hers. He said something in Russian. A low, growled command that sent an avalanche of shivers coursing down her spine. She didn't know his language, but there was no doubt whatsoever of his meaning.

She gathered her courage. And touched him. There.

He grunted, his eyes squeezing shut as her fingernails scraped up the silky steel of his erection. Swallowing heavily, he opened them again and murmured something else unintelligible. His lips brushed against hers. He left them there, their mouths just touching. But he didn't kiss her.

She felt the taut press of the towel pull away from her nape, replaced by the powerful grip of his hand. His fingers wrapped around the back of her skull, holding her head firmly in place.

She felt her limbs start to tremble. "No," she whispered.

"Yes," he refuted.

"This isn't how it's supposed to go," she said, her lips catching on his with every syllable. The sensation was impossibly erotic.

His response was to tighten his grip on her. "Tell me then." His expression was . . . fierce.

"You aren't supposed to touch me."

His cock flexed against her fingers. "That doesn't seem fair."

She jerked her hand away like he was on fire. Which he was. Velvet burning on an iron brand.

"Not to mention you're forgetting something." He raked her with that demon gaze.

It was her turn to swallow. "What?"

He grasped the tab of her coveralls zipper and slowly pulled it down. She was naked under it. But she didn't stop him. The sound of the zipper's rasp sent goose bumps cascading over her skin. A shiver sifted erotically through her flesh. His hand slid through the opening and covered her breast.

Finally he answered, though by now she'd forgotten her question. His voice low and rough as he whispered, "*I* am in command here, not you."

Oh, God. Suddenly she wasn't so sure about this. She attempted to back away, a last effort to save herself—to save *them*—from the certain consequences of what was about to happen.

Was it futile to resist the inevitable? Especially when she was the one who'd instigated it. . . .

In a single motion he slipped the coveralls over her shoulders and down her arms. "I'll show you how this is *supposed* to go, *dorogaya moya.*" He reached back and tore the pins from her bun, making her hair tumble wild and free.

"Nikolai, wait."

"*Nyet,*" he growled. "We've waited long enough." His eyes narrowed. "If you want to go, then do it now, Julie Severin. Because if you stay . . ."

Her pulse thundered. But her feet refused to move.

He tumbled her backward onto his bunk. Going down on his knees, he yanked off her coveralls. They hit the floor.

He angled her lower body toward him. And spread her legs apart. "*This* is how it's going to go."

His mouth came down on her, all hot tongue and savage suction. She gasped. Her back bowed. Desire and excitement exploded through her, narrowing down to one perfect point of impact. Instantly, she was on the scintillating brink of orgasm.

She cried out, grabbing his shoulders, his hair.

His fingers dug into her thighs, his thumbs opening her to the blinding pleasure. His mouth clamped harder. His tongue swirled.

She gasped again, sensation overtaking every sense.

Too fast.

Too much.

She couldn't stop. She froze, poised in an endless, incredible moment of sublime weightlessness as her body drew in on itself. Then she fell over the edge and shattered in a quivering, shuddering, agonizingly intense climax. He kept at it until she was limp and weak, dizzy from the mindless rush of pleasure. It was like nothing she'd ever experienced.

From far away she heard a snap of latex, then suddenly he was on top of her, bringing her with a moan of need from one nirvana to another. His body was big, hard, commanding. He levered himself between her thighs, spreading them wide with his powerful knees.

He fisted his cock. Nudged her open with its blunt, slick head. She held her breath.

"*This*," he growled, "is how it will be between us, Julie Yelizaveta Severina."

He plunged into her.

And that's when she knew she truly was lost.

12

She was like a beautiful siren of the old legends, luring a hapless sailor to certain doom and destruction.

And yet Nikolai couldn't turn away from Julie. He had to have her. Couldn't get enough of her. So he took her.

Then he took her again.

And like a siren, she sang for him. In sweet moans and soft cries she filled his solitary stateroom with the sounds of her pleasure. And filled him with the need to claim her as his own. To keep her under him. To touch her as she had touched him. Deep, deep inside, where flesh could never reach.

"Nikolai," she whispered as they floated down from the last intense climax. "Oh, Nikolai."

All he could manage was a groan of agreement. After long moments, he dragged himself up on an elbow and gazed down at her, his mind muzzy with satiety and satisfaction. He had well and truly conquered her, and she had surrendered to him.

Or . . . had he been the one to surrender?

"That," she said with a deep sigh, "was amazing. *You* are amazing."

He leaned down to kiss her, a thorough, drugging kiss of total possession. He *felt* amazing. And finally in control.

"And you," he murmured when he lifted from the kiss, "are mine now."

She opened her eyes, and her body stirred under his. She gazed up at him, her kiss-reddened lips parting. Her tongue peeked out and swiped over the lower one, making him want to lick the glistening moisture from it, as he had more intimate parts of her earlier.

Her expression became uneasy and she said, "Nikolai, this doesn't change anything."

He lifted his brows.

"Other than make things a lot more complicated," she amended softly.

He supposed that was a matter of opinion. Things seemed suddenly simple and straightforward. She'd given herself to him, and now she was in his power. If he was smart and planned carefully, he could win over the girl and keep his job. He'd have to coax her over to work for his side. But there was plenty of time for that. He had every confidence in his powers of persuasion.

And then . . .

What?

For the first time since being given this mission, it occurred to him to wonder what would happen after he'd completed his assignment of winning her affections and learning her objective, and had successfully turned her into an asset. What about their future? The future they might have together if she changed her allegiance . . . ?

He almost smiled. Why not? He did *not* want to give her up.

Wouldn't his dear comrade father love that? His disgraced son consorting with an American double agent. Ah, the shame of it.

Then he thought of his mother, and the photo in her cedar box.

And Julie's father.

Both shot on the streets of Moscow.

He banished the specious thoughts. That wasn't going to happen to Julie. She was his now and he would keep her safe. He'd make damn sure of that.

"You're wrong," he told her. "It's not complicated at all. Because this"—he moved between her thighs—"*does* change things between us. You're mine. *Mine.*"

She gave him a soft smile, sliding her hands down his back in a loose hug. "Yes. For now."

"For as long as we choose," he said.

She sighed. "No. That's not possible. I wish it were, Nikolai. I really do. But we have to face reality. This is just sex. Nothing more."

It *was* more. She just didn't see it yet. *But she would. Eventually.* He wasn't about to argue when there were much more pleasant diversions with which to occupy themselves in the meantime. He grasped her jaw and kissed her again.

All at once there was a loud rapping at the door. *"Kapitan!"*

He cursed under his breath. He loved being a submariner, but privacy on board was nonexistent. Not that it usually mattered. But this was not the usual underway. Not remotely.

He gave his lover a regretful kiss on the nose. "Talk to me!" he called out in Russian, already sliding off her and reaching for his discarded towel.

"The IDA-59 drill, sir," a voice called back. Borovsky. "It's scheduled to start in fifteen minutes, in the mess. And, uh . . ."

Nikolai swung the door partially open, the towel hastily wrapped around his middle. "And?" he prompted when the OOD's ears turned bright red.

"I-I'm truly sorry to i-interrupt, *Kapitan*."

"Don't be. I expect you to do your job. Was there anything else?"

"Miss, um, Severin should report to *Kvartirmyeister* Kresney to collect her breathing apparatus. As, um, soon as possible."

Nikolai nodded and combed his fingers through his mussed hair. "We'll be there shortly. Thank you, *Starshina* Borovsky."

He closed the door and turned to Julie. She'd sat up and was holding the blanket over her naked body. Her face was as red as Borovsky's ears.

"Drill?" she asked, mildly surprising him by not dissolving into mortified maidenly laments at being discovered together. He liked that about her. She wasn't given to drama like most other women he'd known. Besides, there wasn't much they could do about it. Nor did he want to. It was far more honorable to acknowledge their relationship than to try to deny it, leaving her to fend for herself. This way she was under his protection. The crew would treat her with respect.

As he got dressed, he explained about the IDA drill and the reason for it—Yasha finding a malfunction in the atmosphere production equipment. He observed her carefully as he talked, watching for any sign of guilt or recognition. He saw only alarm.

"Are you saying someone may have *sabotaged* our air supply?" she asked, clearly appalled.

He hadn't said it. But now that she had . . . "Are you saying you didn't?" he asked bluntly.

Her mouth dropped open. "Are you *kidding*? I'm pretty sure death by toxic asphyxiation isn't a whole lot better than death by drowning in icy water. And you know how I feel about *that* idea." She shivered violently.

He did up the buttons on his fresh uniform shirt. Call him a fool, but he believed her. "In that case, any clue who might have done it?"

She blinked. "Me? How would I know?"

He puffed out a breath. Her prevarication was really starting to grate on him. Okay, so she was a spy, and her job was to lie. But devil take it, now that they'd—

He cut off the thought.

Nothing.

They'd fucked. For now that was all it was. He'd wanted it to mean more—to him it *did* mean more—but she'd soundly rejected that idea, not five minutes ago. He had to remember that, and not be deluded into thinking she was on the same page with him.

Not yet, anyway. That would come later.

"Liesha," he said, unconsciously transforming her first name to its Russian diminutive, a token of affection and familiarity. To call her Julie after such intimacy would be an insult. He sat down on the disheveled bunk next to her and took her hand earnestly. "Can we not be honest with each other now? If indeed there is a saboteur on board that neither you nor I know of, he is surely an enemy to us both, *nyet*?"

She was silent for a moment, and he could see her weighing the situation's implications. "You said it might not be sabotage," she said at length, skirting the real issue.

Irritation flared within him. "True. But it would be folly to ignore the possibility. Why not work together to find out for certain?"

"How?"

He gave her a stern look. "You could start by confessing why you're here on *Ostrov*. Tell me why they sent you and what you're looking for."

Her gaze slid away. "You know I can't do that."

Well. Miracles. At least she'd finally admitted—if obliquely—she *was* looking for something. "You are determined to make my life difficult, aren't you?"

"You call this difficult?" With a curve of her lips, she slanted the bunk a glance.

And just like that, irritation or no, he wanted her again.

Difficult? Hell, he was maddeningly easy when it came to this woman.

"Get dressed," he ordered with a swallowed curse, checking the clock. He rose and snagged his cap from its hook by the door. "You are not excused from the IDA drill just because you're . . . making the captain's life difficult."

She grinned shyly, and for some unfathomable reason he was sure she thought they'd reached some kind of unspoken understanding. He wasn't sure why, or even about what, but even he felt the wall between them had become a little less solid. And not because of the incredible sex they'd just shared.

Da. Maybe it was a little about the sex.

Okay, a lot.

Or . . . maybe he'd simply lost all capacity for reason and gone completely delusional. *That* was not outside the realm of possibility, either.

He paused on the way out and looked over his shoulder at her. "You *will* tell me," he said by way of warning. "If you trust nothing else, trust me on this, *dorogaya moya*. Sooner or later, you will tell me what you're up to."

He left her staring after him, a look of consternation on her face. Because she must surely know he meant every word.

"Как дела?" Nikolai asked *Kvartirmyeister* Kresney.

Not that he needed to ask how the drill was going.

"Пиздец," came Kresney's quick reply. *Goatfuck.*

Yeah. That was pretty obvious.

Nikolai had left the *kvartirmyeister* and *Starpom* Stefan

Mikhailovich Varnas in charge here in the mess hall, and slipped out to check on things in the central post—which had been fine—then stepped into the radio room to see if there'd been any further dispatches—which there hadn't. *Ostrov* was still being ignored by fleet headquarters. Big shock.

"I looked at that microcard you dropped off earlier," *Lyeĭtenant* Danya Petrov had said then. "Not much on it."

"Really?" Nikolai said, somewhat surprised. "Are you sure you found everything?"

"*Da*. It's not really possible to conceal anything on a small device like this. Not like a packed mega-terabyte computer hard drive with plenty of nooks and crannies to hide things in."

Nikolai nodded. "Okay, so what did you find?"

"It looks like it was used for a phone of some sort."

"A satellite phone."

"Yeah. There was a directory of phone numbers stored on it, and an article written about one of the scientist's projects. On coral gardens. I checked, and the article has already appeared online, on an American newspaper's website. There were a few differences in some of the words and phrases." Petrov shrugged. "My English is not good enough to tell if they're anything important. I printed copies of both for you to compare."

Nikolai took the printouts. "Excellent."

"I assume the phone belongs to the woman reporter on board," the *lyeĭtenant* said leadingly. Had word already gotten around about them?

Nikolai didn't comment. "What else did you find?"

"A bunch of photos of the interior of the submarine. And that's it, sir. Nothing more."

"Anything unusual about the photos?" he asked.

"Not that I could tell. God knows why she wants them." The *lyeĭtenant* grabbed a thumb drive off his console. "However, I took the liberty of making a copy of the entire card for you, sir, photos and all."

Nikolai took it from him. "Well done. Perhaps I shall borrow Miss Severin's laptop to take a look at them."

Danya Petrov grinned at him. "*Da, Kapitan*. Very good idea."

As Nikolai had made his way back to check on the IDA drill, he considered the likelihood of whether or not she'd allow him to touch her precious notebook computer. It seldom left her possession. The only time he'd seen her without it was up on the bridge—no doubt due to the rain. But as he'd approached the mess hall, all thoughts of Julie's laptop had fled.

The place was in chaos. People shouting. IDA devices flying. Tempers flaring.

Thinking it would be a good way to get everyone mingling, initially he'd had the officers task the off-duty crewmen with teaching the scientists how to don the masks and work the IDA rebreathers. But the language barrier had turned the exercise into a circus. Apparently too few of his men spoke any English, and of the scientists, only Edwards, Professor Sundesvall, and the Finnish professor, Arja Lautenen, spoke Russian. It was unbelievable how many otherwise competent people thought merely shouting could make someone understand a foreign language.

Goatfuck? More like clusterfuck.

Nikolai now strode straight to the comm, grabbed the 1MC mike, and in a firm voice ordered the crew to stop what they were doing.

There was instant silence.

"I want everyone not on duty to report to damage control stations," he ordered his crew, then keyed off the mike. *"Starpom!"* Nikolai turned to Stefan Mikhailovich.

The *starpom*'s dark head swiveled from where he stood overseeing a rating who had been adjusting a mask strap for Julie. *"Da, Kapitan?"*

"Assign each of the scientists a post as his or her battle station. And make damn sure someone in that compartment can act as a competent interpreter. Quickly, before a war breaks out."

"Da, Kapitan." Stefan Mikhailovich hurried off to poll the men as to their language skills.

Then Nikolai gathered the scientists together and explained that they would each be assigned a place where they were supposed to go immediately in case of an emergency, any emergency. There would be one person at every station who spoke the other language.

"Is there a reason we're doing this?" Arja Lautenen demanded. "We've never had to put on these things before or keep them with us. Are you *expecting* an emergency, Captain?"

He was appalled to hear that previous captains had not required this kind of safety drill. "These northern waters can be dangerous," he said carefully, "and *Ostrov* is an older vessel. The safety of passengers and crew should always be a commander's prime concern."

"I understand that, but—"

"Every Russian submariner is required to carry an IDA at all times," he interrupted as politely as he could. "I only want you to be as safe as my men." He smiled benignly.

Professor Sundesvall nodded. "Yes, naturally we will all happily comply," he said, cutting off any further protest by his team.

"Excellent. My XO will be back shortly to give you your assignments. Please feel free to come to me personally if you have any questions or requests."

It took another ten minutes, but soon things were running smoothly, the IDAs were being correctly donned, and the scientists and crew were at least communicating without shouting. The war had been averted for now. Hopefully the date line–crossing celebration tomorrow would soothe any lingering ruffled feathers.

As he made a pass along the length of the sub to check on everyone's progress, he came to an abrupt halt back where he'd started, in the mess. Julie was sitting at a table with a rating, frowning at her IDA canister.

He strode over in annoyance and waved off the rating, who scooted away in a hurry. "What are you still doing here?" he asked her. "I thought you'd been assigned to the sonar shack with Gavrikov."

She pulled off the full black face mask that made her look like an insect, and bit her lip. "Sorry. He and Rufus—Chief Edwards—were heavily involved in listening to some sonar thing. A transmission? Transition? Anyway, I said I'd find someone out here to help with this alien space suit." With a grimace, she held up the mask and the bright orange inflatable collar with attached blue canisters dangling from it. It was hopelessly tangled.

Nikolai frowned as he took the assemblage from her, straightened it out, and started checking it over. "You mean a transient?" he asked, going back to Gavrikov.

She brightened. "Yeah. That was it."

A transient was a sudden noise picked up on sonar. It could be anything from a dropped wrench on board *Ostrov* to an airplane motor buzzing above to an enemy torpedo tube flooding miles away. "Was it something unusual?" he asked. It must have been *very* unusual to make both his chief sonar man and the American navy man ignore a safety drill. They knew better.

"They didn't say what it was," Julie said. "But when I left, they looked pretty . . . intense."

Nikolai wondered about that as he felt over her IDA hoses and checked its air canisters. *What the*— He held them up. One of the valves was missing.

Angrily, he grabbed the 1MC mike and called *Kvartirmyei-ster* Kresney, who was in charge of equipment distribution and was scurrying back and forth acting as translator when teams got stuck in the language barrier. "This IDA is defective," Nikolai growled when Kresney arrived, breathless. "How is that possible?"

"Sir, I don't understand." Kresney looked aghast as he checked the valve fitting. "I assure you, I inspected every one of these sets before issuing them."

A chill went through Nikolai. Inwardly he swore. First the primary atmospheric equipment broken, and now this? How many other IDAs had been tampered with? Or other vital equipment?

He lowered his voice. "I want you to recheck every one of them," he ordered. "Then check them again every day. I don't want any accidental malfunctions. And Misha, do it discreetly."

Watching the *kvartirmyeister* hurry away, visibly upset, Julie asked, "What is it, Nikolai? What's going on?"

He shook his head. "I'll explain later. For now, let's get you another of these. One that works."

There was a big box of the rebreather sets sitting on one of the six mess hall tables, easily accessible to anyone. This was an open compartment right off the main deck passageway. If there was a saboteur on board, he would have had no trouble fouling the whole lot if he'd wished.

Nikolai examined each one of them. All were intact and good to go. In one sense it was a huge relief. In another, it made his blood run even colder.

Was it just a coincidence that Julie had gotten the only one with a missing valve?

Or had someone targeted her specifically?

Unfortunately, the answer was all too clear. To Nikolai, anyway.

He was not the only one on board with a hidden agenda concerning the pretty CIA officer. *Another* spy was in their midst. One whose intent was far more deadly.

The question was . . . who or what was his target?

Only Julie?

Or should everyone aboard *Ostrov* be fearing for their lives?

13

//////////////

Nikolai was very upset. Which made Julie very nervous.

He wouldn't tell her what was bothering him. When she asked, he just kept saying, "We'll talk about it later."

Great.

He was trying to act all efficient and captainlike as he took it upon himself to show her how to put on and breathe through the emergency IDA gear, but she could tell his mind was elsewhere. And judging by the scowl on his face, it was *not* back in the stateroom, in his bunk. Which was where *her* mind had firmly stalled.

Oh, my God, she had really gone and done it. She'd ignored every personal edict, every professional directive, every dire warning from her training, and succumbed to sleeping with the enemy.

Although after what they'd shared together in his bed, he felt like anything but the enemy. He felt like her lover. And the man she was falling more for with every passing minute.

She had to be out of her mind.

She'd tried to stop herself. Really she had. She'd felt so overwhelmed by the emotional conflict of being with Nikolai that when she'd first touched him she'd given in to tears. Too bad the internal struggle had done her no good whatsoever. In the end she hadn't been able to deny the need raging within her any more than she could stop the tides.

Nikolai had been incredible. He was an incredible man and an even more incredible lover. He'd made her feel things she'd never known her body could feel.

Or her heart.

Which was the real problem. For how could she go on deceiving a man after she'd made such passionate love with him? But telling him the truth would only force him to act upon that truth. And where would she end up then?

In Siberia.

Or worse. Facedown on a street in Moscow.

He'd warned her more than once that he'd have no choice but to turn her in if he knew she was a spy. Better to keep her mouth firmly shut. Much safer that way.

"Julie!"

With a start, she shot out of her disturbing thoughts. Nikolai was standing over her with a frown. Her IDA-59 was neatly packed in its orange carry bag, and he was holding it out to her. Lord, how long had he been trying to get her attention? "Sorry. What?" She took the bag.

"I said, come with me to the sonar shack. I want to find out what Gavrikov and Edwards are listening to that is so damn interesting."

She rose and followed him out of the mess hall.

"Penny for your thoughts," he said, letting her go ahead of him down the narrow passageway.

"You'd be wasting your money," she replied.

"So you weren't thinking about something so intently that you didn't hear me call you five times?" A slight shade of sarcasm colored his words.

"Nope."

"You're a terrible liar, Liesha. How you ever got to be a *shpion*, I'll never fathom." The skepticism in his voice sounded more than sincere. Despite the fact that she *wasn't* a case officer, she felt insulted.

"I keep telling you, I'm not a spy," she repeated for the millionth time, an edge to her tone.

Damn it, she *wasn't*! She was just an unlucky China desk

analyst railroaded into a mission she was unprepared for and ill equipped to deal with. And pitted against an opponent she was even less prepared to deal with. The man was intelligent, irresistible, and completely relentless.

"Soon you'll tell me the truth," Nikolai muttered. He was starting to sound like a broken record.

She ground her jaw. Coming to a watertight door, she stopped with her hand on the round rim and swung around to face him, unable to bear the mocking any longer. "I *am* telling you the truth, Nikolai." She squeezed her eyes shut and opened them again. "I'm an *analyst*, okay? I sit at a computer all day reading and interpreting news and research. *That's* what I do. I'm *not* a spy."

He blinked at her owlishly.

Ho-boy.

She should *not* have told him that. Total breach.

Before he could react, she swung around again and climbed through the hatch, leaving him staring after her in pure astonishment. Which lasted for about two nanoseconds. Then he was flying through the door after her, and his hand was gripping her arm. He whirled her back around and opened his mouth to blast her.

"Don't," she said, cutting him off while she glanced around. There were at least a half dozen people occupying the compartment, in varying states of frustrated discussion over their IDA gear. She may suck at this, but even she knew better than to have this discussion here.

He snapped his mouth shut again, adjusted his grip on her, and instead hustled her toward the ladder that led to the lower deck where their stateroom was located. No doubt to give her the third degree in a more private setting.

What. Ever.

"Captain Romanov!" Rufus Edwards hailed him from the door to the sonar shack, which was tucked into a corner of the control room just ahead.

Nikolai halted, but didn't let go of her arm.

"There's something we think you should hear," Rufus said, his brows flickering as he noticed Nikolai's grasp on her.

"So I understand," Nikolai said. "We were just coming to see you."

Julie let out a breath of relief as he urged her—albeit none too gently—in front of him as he once again reversed direction back toward the shack.

Thank goodness. Now she'd have a bit of time to prepare a more careful explanation of her monumental fail.

Stepping into the teensy sonar shack, she backed herself against the wall, giving the men space. Between the equipment, two swivel chairs, occupied by the sonar guy and Rufus's bulk, and Nikolai's broad shoulders taking up the rest, there was hardly room to breathe.

The young sonar man, Gavrikov, immediately ripped off his giant headphones and launched into a mile-a-minute speech to Nikolai in Russian from his perch in front of the monitors.

Meanwhile, Rufus shot her a questioning gaze and mouthed, "You okay?"

She gave him a smile, nodded, and mouthed back, "I'm fine."

He jerked his chin minutely at Nikolai and arched one disapproving brow. So he'd heard. Wonderful.

She answered with a wry "what's a red-blooded woman to do?" shrug.

He grimaced unhappily, but dropped the silent inquisition. Thank God. She wasn't sure she could justify her actions to herself, let alone to anyone else.

Meanwhile, Nikolai was quizzing Gavrikov while studying the various sonar screens intently. He waved off a pair of headphones when they were offered, and asked Rufus in English, "Do you agree with *Starshina* Gavrikov's evaluation, Chief Edwards?"

Julie wondered why they all looked so grim.

Edwards swiped a hand over his mouth. "Like the kid said, it's most likely nothing to be too worried about. Maybe a new captain using us to test his skills, hiding in our baffles, practicing his angles and dangles."

Huh?

"Malicious or not," Nikolai said, "I sure as hell don't like being stalked. And I take it you're suspicious about something."

Rufus tapped a fingernail thoughtfully on the console.

"He's being too cagey. Doing his best to stay hidden behind the ambient noise. My question is, why bother hiding from us at all?"

Julie wasn't following any of this. But apparently Nikolai was.

"Yes. I see your point," he said to Rufus. "And you're sure you've ID'd the vessel correctly?"

"Absolutely. We've checked the signature with both your software and my personal archives, and there's no doubt about it, Skipper. She's a Chinese Type 093 attack sub, all right."

Julie came to abrupt attention. Wait. "A Shang-class submarine?" she asked in surprise . . . mixed with a little concern. "In the North Pacific?" The Chinese only had two attack subs of this class, and they were usually stationed in the Atlantic. Her gaze darted to the inscrutable sonar display. "Where? Is it close?"

Three sets of eyes snapped to her and held, even more startled than she'd been.

Double crap.

God, she sucked at this.

By way of explanation she said, "Um, I wrote an in-depth article about the PRC's navy a while back." Well. More like a sixty-page white paper for the director, with recommendations for intelligence strategies. But who was counting? "From what I remember, they don't usually venture into this neck of the woods."

Rufus broke the silence first. "Well, then. Since you're so up on the subject, maybe you can tell *us* why the damn thing is tailing us?"

It was her turn to be startled. "*Tailing* us? As in, deliberately? Why would it be doing that?"

"Exactly."

Oh. Now she got it.

Again, the two men regarded her levelly, Nikolai with a calculating mien, Rufus more circumspect. Anton Gavrikov glanced between them and her, puzzled by the sudden acute shift in tension.

"I have no idea," she said. "It's not like this international scientific expedition is top secret or anything. It's been mentioned on every news program, website, and newspaper in the world."

Then all at once it struck her. Sweet Lord. *The SD card she'd been sent to find.* Being tailed by a Chinese attack sub would make perfect sense if they'd learned someone aboard *Ostrov* was in possession of stolen Chinese military technology! Especially something as important as the UUV guidance system contained on the SD card.

Oh, *hell.* She swore silently.

Nikolai's eyes narrowed as he watched her expression change from perplexed to horrified before she could mask her reaction and bring it back to neutral.

"Is there something you'd like to share with us, *dorogaya*?" he asked.

"No." Her throat closed on the word and she had to clear it. "It just makes me nervous"—she cleared it again—"that they're following us."

"Julie," Rufus interrupted, seeing Nikolai about to lay into her, "if you know something about this situation . . . God knows how, but if you do, seriously, girl, you've got to tell us."

Guilt swamped over her. If a Chinese submarine was hunting them—*her*—the potential consequences of keeping silent could prove . . . awkward in the best case, disastrous in the worst.

On the other hand, deciding *who* to tell was another thing that could easily prove just as disastrous. If Nikolai's hunch was correct, there was very likely another foreign intelligence officer on board. Someone who'd possibly sabotaged the sub's air supply.

Rufus Edwards, maybe? Or Gavrikov?

And then there was the problem of Nikolai himself. Aside from the whole blowing-open-the-spy-thing issue. Which was bad enough. But . . .

Good Lord. Suddenly an awful thought struck her. What about *him*? It had never even occurred to her that he . . . She'd always assumed he was working for the Russians. But what if he was a Chinese double agent?

Her pulse took off at a gallop. What should she do? God, what should she *do*?

She realized they were all staring at her. Hard.

Abruptly, she straightened off the bulkhead. "I need to make a phone call," she said. Her boss had connections at the

Pentagon. They'd be able to— She faltered at the look that swept over Nikolai's face. Pure, unadulterated suspicion.

"To whom?" he asked.

"My newspaper," she said. "If we're being followed by a Chinese attack submarine, I want someone in the outside world to know about it."

"Don't bother. I'm radioing in to Russian Naval Command immediately."

"My boss might be able to call in some Pentagon sources and find out *why* it's tailing us," she argued. "It's worth a try."

Before he could stop her, she scooted out of the sonar shack and didn't stop power walking until she was inside their state-room with the door shut. She didn't have long. He'd be coming after her just as soon as he'd sent the dispatch to his superiors.

She retrieved her satellite phone from the desk, where she'd set it after returning from the bridge earlier, grabbed the heavy coat Nikolai had given her that morning, and headed right back up to the control room where the access hatch to the top of the sail was located. If her luck held, Nikolai would still be in the radio room sending off his report. She peeked around the corner. He was nowhere in sight.

A man she didn't recognize glanced at her in consternation when she strode across the room and reached for the ladder. The officer in charge, no doubt. He said something to her in Russian, looking very much like he wanted to stop her from going up to the bridge.

She held her phone out for him to see and pointed at it, then upward. "Just need to make a phone call from the cockpit," she explained, knowing full well he didn't understand a word. He looked pained and glanced around at the others manning the various control consoles. They all shook their heads amid a smattering of discussion in Russian.

Seizing the moment, she grabbed hold of the ladder's handrail and, taking a deep breath, started to climb up. The officer ran over and stopped her. She started to argue, but he just handed her a safety harness and gestured to her waist.

Ah. Right. She quickly belted it around herself and buttoned up her coat. The officer didn't look happy, but he motioned her to continue climbing. She lost no time scrambling up.

He shouted something past her to whomever was posted up

top. There was an answering shout. After a second, he shouted something else, a little longer this time, and there came a short, *"Da, Praporshchik,"* in reply.

She figured she had about five seconds before the deck officer was on the horn informing his captain of her movements. And maybe two minutes after that before Nikolai came storming up after her. She had to make every second count.

Bitter cold wind blew through the open top hatch, but at least no rain pelted her face when she looked upward. Above the round opening, the sky was still glowing a dull, luminescent gray.

Wait. It was nearly eleven p.m. How could it still be light out? Then she remembered. Tomorrow was Midsummer's Eve. At this time of year, and so close to the Arctic Circle, the sun would be up all night.

She puffed out a breath. This was *so* not the way she'd imagined seeing the midnight sun for the first time.

As she reached the top of the ladder and poked her head up through the hatch, she tried desperately to concentrate on handing her safety line to the man above, and *not* on peering out at the surrounding ocean that was still churning up whitecaps from the earlier storm. Spume crashed over the bow, sweeping across the flat deck of the sub in a wash of glittering foam. Her stomach did a somersault . . . and not only from the exaggerated up-and-down motion of the boat. A buzz of fear knifed through her veins.

She battled it back. She didn't have time to be nervous or panicked. She swallowed down the agonizing tightness in her throat and forced herself to climb up into the cockpit.

Another man she didn't know greeted her with a smile and a few words in Russian. She smiled back and waved her phone again, already punching up her boss's number while it was searching for a signal. She clamped the set to her ear, ready to launch into a hurried report as soon as it connected, a report she knew would be taped, so she needn't worry about going too fast.

She frowned.

She couldn't hear a damn thing from the receiver. No dialing. No search tones. No static. And no blue light to indicate the set was switched on.

Worriedly she held it up and pressed the "on" button again. Still nothing. In mounting desperation, she shook it. Again nothing. Madly punching random keys, she prayed for a connection, or at least some kind of noise to indicate it was working.

"God *damn* it!" she exclaimed in dismay.

Nikolai's angry voice rose behind her. "What's the matter, your boss not answering?"

Her time had run out.

She ground her jaw. And rounded on him. "*You* did this. Didn't you!"

His face didn't alter. Even in the dim, golden midnight sun his expression looked dark and forbidding. "What are you talking about?"

"My sat phone. It's not working."

At that, his brows beetled. "Let me see."

It wasn't as if he could do anything else to it. Other than maybe throw it overboard. So she let him take it. He went through the same ritual she had . . . with similar results. Then he flipped it over, fished a pocket knife from his trousers pocket, and popped the battery cover off.

For a second he just stared. Then his lips thinned.

"Well, here's your problem," he said and held it up for her to see. A half dozen colored wires protruded from inside the phone every which way into the battery compartment. Every one of the wires had been cut.

Her jaw dropped. "What the— Someone sabotaged my phone!"

He slowly nodded. "I'd say that's a certainty. And I assure you, it wasn't me."

Her pulse took off as she met his stony gaze. There was no way he was lying. He looked too grim. "What does this mean?" she asked hoarsely, though she knew exactly what it meant.

"It means," he said with jaw set, "that it's time we stop playing games, Liesha. You're going to tell me what you're doing here. And you're going to tell me right now."

14

~~~~~~~~~~~~~~~~

Nikolai could tell Julie did not want to reveal a damned thing to him. He supposed he didn't blame her. If what she'd told him was true and she was only an analyst, her spycraft would not be terribly sophisticated, but she'd know better than to confess her mission to the enemy. But then, he'd like to think they'd ceased being enemies when they'd joined their bodies together.

Before she could balk at his demand, he handed her back the ruined phone and said, "But to answer your question, it means this is proof there's a saboteur on board. And that he is targeting you specifically. Which means he must know exactly who you are and what you're doing here." Unable to help himself, he ground out, "Which is a hell of a lot more than I can say."

"Nikolai—"

He held up a hand. "I am not finished. It comes down to this, *dorogaya*. We can take our chances and continue working at cross-purposes, each trying to find this saboteur on our own. Or we can choose to trust one another and work together. You know which way I vote."

Her lips parted. The night wind was blowing several ends

of her hair out of her usually neat bun and whipping them madly about her face. His fingers itched to yank out the pins again as he'd done earlier and let the auburn locks go free to whip and tangle in the crazy breeze. She was so lovely when she wasn't trying so hard to be . . . well, hard.

He reached up and skimmed a knuckle over her cheek. It was smooth and cool, like porcelain. "What's it going to be, Liesha?"

Her eyes cut down to the useless sat phone. "Rufus could probably fix this."

"Probably," he allowed. There were a half dozen others on his crew who could, as well. Submariners tended to be a talented and resourceful bunch. Not the point.

He waited.

She met his gaze. "What do you know about China?" she asked.

His brows went up. "Other than the fact that one of their 093 attack subs is tailing us?"

She nodded, scrutinizing his face.

A gnawing started in the pit of his stomach. It had been a serious question. За ебис. *Fucking great.* He didn't bother hiding his trepidation. "You better tell me what the hell the Chinese want with you," he growled. "By God, if you've put my vessel and crew in danger—"

"It's not me they're after! Damn it, Nikolai, I told you—"

"Wait." He glanced over at the forward lookout and snapped a quick order at him to continue his watch from the flying bridge below. As soon as the man had disappeared down the ladder, Nikolai said, "Go on."

She bit her lip. "The Shang-class sub being here in the Pacific might mean nothing. And it could just be practicing on us, like Rufus said. Nothing sinister."

"Then why are you so damned worried about it?"

She looked downright distraught when she said, "You realize if I tell you what I know it will mean my job."

He took a breath. He was so close to breaking this wide open. But suddenly, learning her secrets seemed a whole lot less important than protecting his boat and his men from the potential danger that may be closing in on them. And after this afternoon, the thought of betraying her trust turned his stomach.

"I'll make you a deal," he told her, making a snap decision. "Read me in on your mission so I know what the hell is going on, and when we catch this saboteur, I'll turn him in as the spy instead of you. I'll make sure he doesn't talk until you are safely back in the States." That last part killed him. But he understood that was reality. The idea that they could be together, especially now, was just a pretty fantasy.

"You would do that?" she asked, shocked.

"This is too important."

She stared at him. "But surely it would be trading your career for mine. I thought—"

"My career is already over," he said, and for the first time he let himself see the painful truth of that, too. He was done. Maybe if Julie had been a major player in CIA, a field operative, an expert in espionage rather than just a junior analyst, and if he'd managed to turn her into a valued double agent, perhaps then the prestige involved might have been enough to salvage his career. But as it was . . . even Cherenkov couldn't resurrect what was already as dead as the Soviet Union. It would take a damn miracle. And this much he had in common with his atheist father: he didn't believe in miracles.

Not anymore.

"Last year I was in command of one of the most sophisticated nuclear submarines on the planet," he said evenly. "No offense to the scientific expedition, but demoting me to driving this sorry rust bucket is the Main Naval Command's not-so-subtle way of telling me I should retire," he said in disgust.

"But why?" she asked, her eyes filled with guileless incomprehension. God, she was sweet. "What happened?"

He shook his head, realizing he'd already said too much. He was a big boy. He didn't want her pity. "Some other time."

She tilted her head. "Nikolai, you asked me to tell you everything, but you constantly put me off until later. That's not mutual trust."

He gazed out over the darkened sea, a field of slate blue spangled with the silver glitter of a thousand pieces of floating ice sparkling in the midnight sun. He felt like one of those ice chunks, alone and suspended in a harsh, thankless environment not quite cold enough to freeze you into a block of emotionless apathy, but instead slowly ate away at your body and your soul, your very humanity, until there was nothing left of you.

"Okay," he said. "You're right."

It wasn't as if she couldn't just Google it anyway.

"My last command was a Project 971 Shchuka, a top-of-the-line nuclear submarine. While out on patrol we collided with a Norwegian submarine during a surfacing. The Norwegian's propeller was clipped clean off."

She winced. "Ouch," she said.

"Ouch, indeed. Our sonar had shorted out because of a faulty gasket that had been slated to be replaced but wasn't, and we were coming to the surface to avoid driving blind."

"Jesus."

"It happened in Varangerfjørd. In the very north of Norway. Right next to the Russian border, close to the Northern Fleet headquarters." Surely she'd heard of it. Every news service in the world had made a huge deal about the incident.

"It was obviously an accident," she said. "If your sonar wasn't working, they can't blame you for that. Was anyone hurt?"

Not unless you counted his career. "The Norwegian boat sank, but luckily the crew was able to escape onto inflatables before it went down," he said.

Suddenly her eyes popped. "Oh, my God! *That* accident? In that storm last fall? The Russian sub that stopped to pluck up the Norwegians from their life rafts?"

"A bad storm was brewing. If we hadn't, they would have died for sure," he said. He looked uncomfortable, but nodded.

"But the press hailed you as heroes!" she exclaimed. "Why would your navy want you to retire because of that?"

His gaze slid away. "The navy brass didn't see us as heroes. Ironically, it wasn't the collision but the rescue that got me in trouble."

"You're kidding me," she said, incredulous.

"Unfortunately, it happened just inside Norway's territorial waters. When I reported the collision to my superiors, I was given direct orders to leave the area immediately."

"And just leave the Norwegians stranded out there in the freezing water during a storm?" She looked horrified.

He nodded. "To avoid exactly the kind of international incident that resulted. The Norwegian government protested loudly. And Russia could hardly deny culpability, under the circumstances. The president was forced to give away some very expensive concessions in a contract my government was negotiating with Norway for the disposal of dozens of our derelict nuclear submarines that are endangering the Barents Sea coast with leaking nuclear materials."

"And as captain, you took the blame."

Nikolai spread his hands, indicating the *Ostrov*. "When the dust settled, this is where I landed."

They stood in silence for a moment, gazing out over the achingly lonely twilight seascape. In the distance, a whale broke the surface of the water, looking gray and ghostly.

"Oh, look!" Julie exclaimed as the whale spouted and flicked its tail up out of the water, then was joined by first one, then two, then three others, breaching and shooting up through the liquid gold of the pale reflected light. A calf appeared, hugging its mother's side as the pod danced in the water, a fitting homage to the midnight sun.

Nikolai put his arms around Julie and together they quietly watched until, all too soon, the whales disappeared.

"Beautiful," she whispered, and he kissed the top of her head.

"Yes." He'd miss sights like this when he was no longer in the navy. Maybe he could get a job on a fishing boat.

"You should come work for us," she said, shocking him out of his bleak thoughts.

"What?" he asked, not quite believing his ears. He turned her in his arms.

"Our navy would love to have a man like you."

It was his turn to stare incredulously. Then he let out a bark of laughter. Touché. Despite himself, he grinned. Perhaps she was not so innocent and guileless after all. She'd timed that to perfection, at exactly his most vulnerable moment.

"I'll keep that in mind," he said. "But now it's your turn to talk. And Julie, I want to know everything."

She nodded, stepped out of his arms, and started her explanation. "The thing I've been searching for on *Ostrov* is a micro storage card containing a new Chinese guidance system for their stealth UUVs."

He grew more and more alarmed as the story spilled out of

her. About the dead Chinese and Russian double agents, about the circuitous route from China to Rybachiy by which the stolen SD card had ended up on his submarine, and about how she'd been hastily plucked from her job as a China desk analyst at CIA to replace the injured field operative. Nikolai suspected Julie's knowledge of China at least in part explained why they'd chosen her, a complete neophyte when it came to the spy business, for this mission. She was an expert on all things Chinese.

That, and her gender and her looks.

Did CIA have files on Russian officers in which their preferences in women were duly recorded for just such opportunities? If so, he had to believe no one had informed Julie of her backup role as honey in the plan B trap.

At this point he didn't give a damn that he seemed to be going right along with that plan.

When she was done with her tale and fell silent, he blew out a long breath. Despite the buzz of unease over the potential implications and possible danger of the situation, a profound sense of relief sifted through him. Her mission could have been much worse. At least CIA wasn't targeting him or any of his men. And Comrade Cherenkov could stop worrying about Russian state secrets being compromised. This was all about China. Good to know.

"You should have come to me right away with this," he told her. "I could have helped you search for this card instead of threatening you every five minutes."

She sent him a withering look. "Right. Because you definitely would have believed I was on a Russian submarine looking for Chinese weapons technology."

"I would have." He smiled crookedly. "Eventually."

She rolled her eyes, but didn't protest when, with a sigh, he took her in his arms again, this time front to front, her soft breasts pillowing against his chest.

He was getting used to her being close like this. It felt right, like she belonged there, cradled protectively against his body. Especially now that he knew she didn't make her living from intrigue and deception. It made a difference. The knowledge lifted a weight from his heart that he hadn't realized had been burdening it. And he was gratified she trusted him enough to confide in him.

He vowed she wouldn't suffer because of telling him the truth. Not if he could help it.

Over her shoulder he noticed the rear lookout glancing forward toward them. He was too far away to see the man's expression, but he could just imagine. He knew his behavior with Julie was way out of line—even for a captain whose formerly distinguished career was now toast. The crew would speculate rampantly at his motives for his flagrant disregard for navy decorum, wondering if he was angling for a ticket to America or just thumbing his nose at his superiors. Consorting with their traditional enemy, regardless of the end of the Cold War, would hardly endear him to the Admiralty.

Except his FSB orders were to do exactly that. The Naval Command must be aware of his assignment. The envelope he'd received from Cherenkov had contained orders placing him under FSB command. Surely, the navy hadn't ordered him blind. . . . Did they know there was a CIA operative among the contingent of foreign scientists aboard *Ostrov*? And what about the saboteur? Could that saboteur have been sent by his own navy superiors to neutralize Julie because they hadn't been informed of Nikolai's specific mission?

Would his promise to her backfire and take them both down as traitors by both countries?

Possible scenarios did crazy Ivans through his mind.

Finally he shoved them aside with a growl of impatience. He would *not* second-guess himself. He knew he was doing the right thing joining forces with Julie, and that was all that mattered.

"Okay," he said to her, "we need to find that SD card. Give me a list of where you've already searched. Day after tomorrow while the scientists are on Attu Island, I'll check some of the more inaccessible places you haven't gotten to yet."

"Good. I'll stay on board and help," she said, looking up at him.

He shook his head. "*Nyet*. It will be too dangerous. I'm planning to take the boat through a deep-water test while we wait." He gave her a sinister smile. "Perhaps if the Chinese 093 is still around, I can teach that tenacious commander a lesson in good manners."

She grasped his arms. "Nikolai, no! Are you nuts? The

Shang class is a nuclear submarine carrying every piece of stealth technology available! That's hardly a fair fight."

"Which is why he won't be expecting a challenge from us."

She pressed her body into his. "Please don't do it," she pleaded softly. "I couldn't stand it if anything happened to you or the crew because of me."

He kissed her hair. "Don't worry, *milaya moya*. This isn't on you. It's what I do. This kind of opportunity is golden. It's what a submariner lives for."

"But *Ostrov*'s condition—"

"I won't take any unnecessary chances," he promised.

Her arms came tighter around him. "You better not."

"Besides," he reasoned, "their captain will probably get bored and be gone by then."

"Let's hope so." She laid her head on his shoulder and leaned against him. He could feel her muscles relax a little. Or maybe it was just exhaustion.

"You should get some rest," he said. "It's been a long day."

There was a pause before she murmured, "What about you? You need sleep, too."

He smiled into her hair, breathing deeply of its scent. A scent his senses had begun to crave. "Don't you know a submarine commander never sleeps?"

There was an even longer pause. "Maybe I wasn't really thinking of sleep."

He put his lips to her forehead, more tempted than he could say to take her back to his stateroom right now and show her how not tired he was. "I knew you were out to seduce me. It won't work, you know."

She tipped her face up. "No?"

"*Nyet.*"

"Sure?" She brushed her lips over his.

He groaned softly. "Okay, maybe."

Her lips curved in a smile more like the Mona Lisa than Mata Hari. "Good." The smile widened. "Then meet me in our stateroom in half an hour."

Julie gave Nikolai a little wave as he left her at the bottom of the ladder to get back to his duties. He strode off. She hadn't told him what she planned to do, but it was more important than ever to get hold of her boss and let him know what was happening. With the Chinese sub chasing them . . . and with Nikolai.

She should confess to having confided in him what she was searching for. But what about their personal involvement together? Should she tell her boss about that, too? She was in an agony of indecision.

Before she could do either, she had to find a working sat phone. Who else on the sub might be in possession of one?

She thought immediately of Rufus Edwards. And grimaced. She'd just as soon skip getting a grilling from the avuncular chief, which she was pretty sure would happen if she went back to the sonar shack. It was obvious he didn't approve of her relationship with Nikolai.

So, who else?

Trent Griff? Or maybe the young Canadian researcher, Josh Stedman? She remembered seeing Dr. Josh hanging with the XO and a few of the other Russian crew during the rebreather drill. Maybe he was still up and about.

After a short search she found him back in the engineering compartment, practicing his broken Russian language skills on the amused crew members.

"Hey, Julie, come learn some new words with me," he said with a grin, waving.

She laughed. "I don't think I dare," she said dryly and motioned him over.

He excused himself and they walked a few paces down the passageway. "What's up?"

She asked him if he had a sat phone and was relieved when he said he did.

"Thank goodness. Mine—" She suddenly thought better of telling him about the sabotage. "Mine died, and I need to call in my article for tomorrow or my editor will kill me. Can I borrow yours for a few minutes?"

"Sure. I forgot to charge it last night, but I think there's still some juice in the battery. It's with my stuff."

He took her down to general berthing, where he had his rack, and pulled it out of his backpack and handed it to her.

"You're a lifesaver," she said gratefully. "I'll bring it back in a jiff."

She wasn't forgetting she had an important appointment in less than half an hour.

By now they barely blinked in the central post when she was back after just ten minutes and indicated she wanted to go up on the sail. The same man as before fished the harness from a cupboard behind the ladder and handed it to her with a wide smile. She blushed when she realized the entire watch was peering at her with expressions ranging from amusement to admiration to vague disapproval. She zipped up the ladder to get away from them, pausing at the landing halfway up to fasten her harness. Her ears burned and she was glad for the icy breeze that whistled down from the sail.

She was not ashamed of her relationship with the captain, but she didn't like being the object of gossip, positive or negative. She'd always hated that. She'd had enough of idle speculation about her after her father died. Her family had meant well, but she'd just wanted to be left alone.

Shaking off the discomfort, she steeled herself to face the sail alone. She noticed the lookout was still down in the flying bridge in the conning tower, so she'd be on her own in the cockpit. She took a steadying breath and went up to make her phone call.

After clipping her harness to the toe-rail, she crouched down and knelt close to the deck. Partly to avoid the Arctic wind, but also so she didn't have to look at the sea. Funny how it could be so lovely while tucked safely in Nikolai's arms, and so menacing when facing it alone.

She planned to make her call short and sweet because of the low battery, but it took longer to get through to her boss because she was calling from an unknown phone.

"What happened to yours?" James Thurman asked when he finally came on the line.

"Sabotaged," she said, and she told him about the gutted wires.

"Romanov?"

"No. It wasn't him."

"How can you be sure?"

"He was as upset about it as I was."

Thurman digested that. "So there's someone else on board who doesn't want you calling in?"

"Worse," she said, and she related the incidents with the atmospheric equipment and her IDA as well.

Thurman cursed softly. "I don't like it."

"You think I do?"

"Any idea who?" he asked.

"I'm working on it." She was about to tell him about the Chinese sub following them, but Thurman wasn't done with the topic of Nikolai.

"Look, I'm sensing you don't want to think it's Captain Romanov," he said, "but be careful around him. He could be using you to get his career back. Romanov was one of the youngest Russian naval officers to achieve his rank, with several commands before his current less than desirable one. He had a brilliant career up until last year. From what I've read he'd do anything to get it back."

Which was exactly what Nikolai had said himself. "I'm telling you he's okay with me. We bonded over family." Among other things.

"What's that supposed to mean?" Thurman asked sharply.

She scrambled. "His mother died when he was a kid, just like my dad." Well, not exactly, but still. . . .

There was a brief silence. "He told you about his mother? What did he say?"

She wasn't about to go into the wolf story. It was none of Thurman's business. "Nothing much. Just that his father treated her badly and that she died young. He misses her. The way I miss my dad."

"That's all?" Thurman asked. She thought she heard papers rustling, but it could have been static on the line. It was hard to tell in the echoing connection and the several-second delay in their conversation as each side was being transmitted across the satellite.

"Yeah," she said, then gathered her courage. "Look, I'm not having a lot of luck finding this SD card on my own. Have you ever *seen* the inside of a submarine? Would you freak out if I asked him to cooperate with us?"

There was a long pause. Carefully Thurman said, "Romanov's father is an old-school local politician with a very nasty reputation. What makes you think the son is any better? Why would he cooperate with an American?"

She swallowed and blurted out, "Sir, Nikolai already knows why I'm here. I told him. And he hasn't blown my cover. What does that say to you?"

"Nikolai?" Thurman said, not missing a beat. She gave a mental groan. This was why they paid him the big bucks. "Miss Severin, have you slept with Captain Romanov?" he demanded.

Crap, crap, *crap*. She felt the blood rush to her cheeks. "I—"

"Jesus, Julie," he muttered. "You didn't have to— Listen, there's something else I need to tell you about Captain Romanov's background."

She stuttered out a breath. Ho-kay. He'd taken that pretty well. "What's that, sir?"

"It's about his mother. This is top secret, you understand. But you should know that she—"

Suddenly the line went dead. There was only silence from the other end. Her jaw dropped.

"You can't be serious!" she cried and began punching buttons to try to get Thurman back. But the phone wouldn't power up. The battery was dead.

A storm of frustration welled up within her. Of all the times to be cut off! Top secret? What the heck was that all about?

What on earth did CIA have hidden in its top-secret files about Nikolai's *mother*? And what did it have to do with *her*?

Nikolai checked the central post clock for the tenth time since following Julie down the ladder from the bridge. The past twenty minutes had been the longest of his entire life.

"Kapitan?" Lyeĭtenant Danya Petrov poked his head out of the radio room.

Nikolai snapped up guiltily from the Bering Sea chart he was pretending to peruse. The whole time he'd been debating with himself over whether or not to notify Cherenkov of the presence of a saboteur on board. His first instinct was to keep that information close to the chest for now. But if the operative was a friendly, Nikolai's failure to report it would be noted, and throw him directly under a klieg light of suspicion. Especially considering his involvement with Julie, which the *zam-*

polit had no doubt already reported. Not that he gave a flying fuck.

He straightened. *"Da, Lyeĭtenant?"*

The radioman held up a paper. "Dispatch, sir."

It was from fleet headquarters and reported that the Russian government had made official inquiries to the Chinese about the 093 supposedly trailing *Ostrov* and had been assured that both their Shang-class submarines were presently in the Atlantic. Must be a faulty identification.

Sure it was. He was shocked, *shocked*, at the order to ignore it and proceed with the evolution as planned.

Well, if the 093 was nine thousand kilometers away, it wouldn't upset its commander too much if Nikolai played a little practical joke on him.

"Thanks, Petrov," he said, tapping the rolled-up dispatch thoughtfully against his chin. Now to figure out how best to yank the enemy commander's chain. Not that Nikolai could do anything too outrageous. Julie was right, every news bureau on the planet was following the expedition's voyage—if fairly cursorily. And every spy satellite in the sky could see when *Ostrov*'s lookout picked his nose should they choose to. But nevertheless he could send a message to their stalker. Despite his recent setbacks, *Kapitan* Nikolai Kirillovich Romanov was not to be trifled with. His reputation for being a rule breaker and a rogue among Russian sub drivers was well earned. It had been his nerves of steel and his outrageous daring that had shot his career to the top and gained him his first full command before the age of thirty. That those same traits ended up biting him in the ass was a risk he had gladly taken. He just hadn't counted on someone else's sloppy error taking him down in the end.

But that wasn't going to happen this time.

This time he'd be in complete control.

And *he* wasn't the one going down.

No way.

15

▬▬▬▬▬▬

Julie had already fallen asleep when she felt Nikolai's warm, naked body slide into the bunk next to her.

Make that on top of her. The thin mattress was so narrow there was no way they would fit side by side.

She didn't mind.

"Are you sleeping?" he murmured as he nudged her thighs apart with a knee and lowered himself between them. She was naked, too. She'd gotten undressed when she'd slipped into his bed to wait for him. No sense pretending she didn't know what was going to happen when he got there. No sense pretending she didn't want it to happen. Desperately.

She sucked in a breath as his thick cock pushed into her. "Mmm," she said breathlessly. "Not anymore. What took you so long?"

"Dispatches. Then Professor Sundesvall showed up wanting to know what the schedule is for tomorrow."

"What is the schedule?" she asked on a gasp of pleasure as he began to move.

He wrapped his big hand around her jaw and touched his lips to hers. "Do you really want to talk right now?" he murmured, thrusting deep into her.

She moaned. "No," she managed, and she draped her legs around his waist.

"Good," he said.

And for a long while they didn't say a word.

Not a coherent one, anyway. He murmured guttural phrases in her ear that may have been Russian. Or not. She could only respond with inarticulate moans and vaguely English-sounding noises of pleasure and encouragement as he took total possession of her body and made it his in an even more fundamental way than he had before.

It felt even better this time, closer, more urgent, and at the same time more . . . real. They'd left behind their doubts and mistrust, as well as the purely physical lust they'd succumbed to the first time. This time the lust felt centered more in their heads . . . and in their hearts.

At least on Julie's part.

Which scared the hell out of her.

So when the tumult was over and Nikolai collapsed with a satisfied groan onto her, his hard chest sweaty and heaving, she wished it didn't feel quite so good to have his firm, hot weight crushing her into his woefully inadequate mattress.

"I'm sorry," he said, breathing hard, "I'll move off you. Just give me a minute to recover."

She tightened her arms around him. "Don't you dare go anywhere," she murmured between pants. "I'm going to lose you soon enough."

And just like that, reality crashed back onto her, a thousand times heavier than Nikolai could ever be.

He lifted up on an elbow and gazed down at her, his tawny lashes slumberous. He drew in a deep breath and let it shudder out slowly. "Don't remind me. I hate to think about that."

"Me, too," she whispered.

He kissed her then. A thorough, intense kiss that mirrored her own growing fear that leaving this man behind would likely be the hardest thing she'd ever have to do. And that the day would arrive much too soon.

"This is such a bad idea," she murmured when he lifted his lips.

"What is?"

"Us. This."

"Do you want me to stay away?" he asked, his eyes going dark . . . and oddly guarded for a man in his present position.

She let out a rushed sound of denial. "God, no," she said, lifting her mouth to his again. "Bite your tongue."

His expression eased and he touched his tongue to her lips. "I'd rather you did." A twinkle lit his eyes. "Or maybe . . . somewhere else . . . ?"

And she forgot all about how bad an idea this was.

For a little while, anyway.

When she awoke, he was gone.

She wasn't too surprised, as it would have been incredibly uncomfortable for them to actually sleep together in such a cramped bunk. More's the pity. But she also figured that even if they'd had a king-sized bed, he wouldn't linger in it for any length of time. Not here on board. In order to keep *Ostrov* running at full speed, the crew was on a four-hour-on, ten-hour-off rotation that kept them fresh and on top of their game. But she knew Nikolai, as commander, was doing the typical macho thing of being available around the clock and only catching catnaps of a few hours when he could. On a nonmilitary assignment like this it didn't matter so much; but nearly all of the other subs out there were armed to the teeth, a good percentage of them with nuclear weapons. It was a wonder there weren't more serious accidents, with sleep-deprived submarine commanders all over the world making life-and-death decisions. Good thing the oceans of the world were big enough to give them all wide berths to work in.

Well. Except if there was an enemy submarine dogging your tail. In such close quarters things might get hairy. Which was why, thinking about that Chinese 093 trailing them, she really hoped Nikolai had gotten some sleep last night somewhere.

She swung her legs off the bunk and started to rise. But she lost her balance and sat right down again. Which was strange, because the deck was barely rolling under her feet.

She frowned. In fact, the boat wasn't rocking at all. It was like there were no waves, or—

Good grief. They were barely moving! Were they getting close to the first study area? Jeez, how late *was* it?

Tentatively rising again, she steadied herself against the boat's *not* moving, hurried to the small desk, and snapped on the light to check her watch. Eight forty-five a.m. She'd slept for over seven hours! And missed breakfast as well as Clint Walker's first UUV launch. Damn!

She noticed a pile of neatly folded clothes on the foldout desk—jeans, black T-shirt, and a navy blue sweater—with a pair of sneakers sitting on top holding down a handwritten note. In beautiful lettering that looked almost like calligraphy, it said,

> *Julie, I'm sure these will look much better on you than on my men. Hope you had a good sleep. Come find me.*
> *Kisses, Nikolai.*

She smiled. The man was a saint. *And* a romantic.

She grabbed a one-minute shower and gratefully pulled on the wonderfully dry clothes and sneakers. The jeans weren't a perfect fit, but they were a whole lot better than Nikolai's large coveralls. Though . . . to be honest, she'd miss wearing those. It had been a secret guilty thrill having his name emblazoned on her chest as though she truly belonged to him.

With a sudden pang of wistfulness, she reached out and ran her fingertips over the gold Cyrillic lettering on the coveralls, which still hung neatly on the peg where she'd left them.

If only—

She swallowed and pulled back her hand, curling her fingers into her palm. She had to stop thinking like that. She knew they couldn't stay together, that she could never truly belong to him. She had to accept it and just enjoy the few days they had together. That would have to be enough. There was no other option.

Before she descended into self-pity, she decided to see to her coffee fix and maybe scrounge some breakfast before going to find him. She hadn't had any dinner last night and she was ravenous.

In the mess hall she ran into Dr. Stedman, the young Canadian genius.

"Hey, Josh," she said, inhaling half of her first cup of coffee in one gulp. "What did I miss this morning?"

His brow and his lips crooked wickedly. "Girl, not a damned thing, from what I hear," he said. He leaned in. "Captain Gorgeous has been whistling all morning, and you, sweetie, look like one *very* contented cat with golden feathers in her mouth."

Her hand went reflexively to her lips before she could stop it. She hid a grin. "He is pretty gorgeous, isn't he?" Not that it was in any way a question.

Josh wagged his finger. "And a very naughty boy. This kind of thing has to be against every navy regulation in the book, I imagine."

"Yeah, well," Julie reasoned, taking another sip, "I'm not on his crew, and he's not one of the scientists I'm writing about, so there's no conflict of interest or impropriety or anything." Other than the whole spy thing, of course. But that was a different subject. "Neither of us sexually harassed the other," she said. "I don't see the harm."

Josh gave her a sardonic smile. "You wouldn't. But I doubt his admirals would agree."

She finished her coffee and went back to the urn to pour another. "I did mention that to him. He claims it doesn't matter, he's on their shit list anyway."

Josh nodded. "Yeah, that would be because of the Varangerfjørd incident."

She blinked. "You know about that?"

"Sure. First thing I did when I got on board was look for his name on the Web. Curiosity is my fatal flaw." He grinned. "Seems the captain made quite the stir with that incident."

"Yeah, and not in a good way."

"Depends on who you ask," Josh said. "Personally, I think he did the right thing picking up those Norwegians. And so does most of the world."

"Everyone but the people who should. No wonder he doesn't care about their hypocritical regulations. He doesn't deserve to be babysitting scientists and listening to whale-song," she murmured.

"*And* meeting hot American chicks," Josh added with a grin. "I have a feeling this morning he might think his fall from grace was totally worth it."

"Somehow, I doubt that." She puffed out a breath, remembering Nikolai's earlier comments about how important his career was to him, that he'd do anything to keep it.

Which was also what James Thurman had warned her about.

Suddenly the coffee in her stomach turned to acid.

Had she made a huge mistake in trusting him? Was that what the incredible sex had been about? Was their attraction all on her part, and his was just . . .

No.

She didn't believe that.

"You okay?" Josh asked with a frown. "You went quiet. And your smile's gone."

"Sorry," she said, forcing it back to her lips. "I'm good. Just thinking about how unfair life can be sometimes."

He nodded. "Yeah. Too bad. The captain seems like a nice guy."

"He is," she agreed.

At least she hoped to hell he was.

"Well," Josh said, looking at his watch, "I better get cracking. Our first sampling stop is in just five minutes."

"Yeah? How does that work?" she asked.

"Oh, nothing too exciting. The sub hovers for an hour while everyone takes their project samples for testing. You know, air, water, currents, pollution. The UUV is sent out and takes a complete set of ocean readings. Edwards launches one of his DAMOCLES buoys."

"Quite a bit for an hour."

"It does get hectic. You should come up."

"Up?" she asked.

"Sure. We take our samples from up on the afterdeck. I hear the weather is great today for a change. You know, fresh air, lots of sunshine." He smiled. "It'll be fun."

Two days ago the thought of standing on the open-air deck of a submarine surrounded by hundreds of miles of nothing but ocean would have put her into a pure panic. Now, a shiver of unease went through her, but she was able to subdue it and think rationally. Thanks to Nikolai. And she also recalled his words about kicking herself if she missed the sights and sounds of this incredible place on top of the world that few people ever had the privilege of seeing.

"Okay," she said with a smile. "I'd like that."

"Good!" Josh said. "We'll see you up there in a few."

As soon as he left, a Russian rating dressed in chef's whites came strolling out of the galley carrying a plate, and with a flourish he set it down on the table before her. He said something in Russian and grinned. She looked down at the plate, which smelled heavenly. French toast? Something like that, with powdered sugar and red sauce drizzled over it. Her stomach growled and the submariner, who had to be the cook, grinned wider.

Suddenly she remembered she was famished. "Thank you," she said with a returning grin, and she took the fork and napkin he handed her. He gave a formal bow, then swaggered back into the galley.

Wow. That was sweet. The regular service? Or a perk of being the captain's lady?

"Must be nice," a voice said dryly.

She looked up to see Clint Walker's sardonic smile. It was obvious what *he* thought. "I missed breakfast," she said, feeling vaguely guilty. On second thought, nah.

"Uh-huh."

"Sorry I missed your UUV launch. I overslept."

His lips twitched downward. "I just have to ask. Do you have any fucking idea what you're doing?"

He didn't say it in a nasty way, but her fork halted halfway to her mouth at his bluntness. "Excuse me?"

He slid into the seat opposite, cradling a cup of coffee between both hands. "You're Company, right?"

Her eyes widened and her pulse took off. He knew she was CIA? "*Ex-cuse* me?" she stammered.

He took a sip of coffee. "It has to be you. There are only three Americans on board. It's not me, and it sure as hell isn't Edwards. That leaves you. Reporter? Perfect cover."

"It?" She stared at him, appalled that someone *else* knew about her job. Was it common freaking knowledge? Did everyone on the damn boat think she was a spy? "What 'it'? Cover for what?" Her mind took off a mile a minute. Who the hell *was* this guy? And how the hell did he know—

Or maybe he was just guessing. Trying to trick her.

He tilted his head, considering. "Rookie mission?"

She unparalyzed her arm and took the bite from her fork. "Honestly? I have no idea what you're talking about."

"Must be new. Or you'd know better than to try and work a Russian navy commander by sleeping with him."

She ducked her head to hide the heat she felt streak across her cheeks. "I can't imagine what you mean. I'm sleeping with Nikolai because I'm attracted to him. Not that it's any of your damn business," she added tartly.

He nodded slowly. "Okay. Whatever. So have you found it?"

She shot him a glance. Her heart pounded in her throat. Oh. My. God. "Found what?"

"What you're looking for."

She felt a spiral of fear. This was more than guesswork. How much *did* he know? And *how?* Had her boss sent another case officer to keep an eye on her? For backup, just in case? If so, why hadn't Thurman told her about him?

Damn! She needed to ask him. But she couldn't. Her phone was ruined.

By this man, perhaps?

Was Clint Walker not an ally at all, but the saboteur?

She swallowed. "If by that you mean have I found a handsome, sexy man to pass the time with on this less-than-luxurious cruise, then yes. I've found what I'm looking for."

Walker's dark eyes held hers for a moment longer. "I hope to hell you haven't told him anything," he said. "Romanov'll turn you over to the FSB in a hot minute if he even suspects what's going on. He's on their payroll, you know."

Her heart zoomed painfully to her throat. That couldn't be true! "He isn't," she refuted hoarsely. He would have told her. Hell. *Thurman* would have told her. Wouldn't he?

She realized too late she'd given herself away.

"He's in disgrace, Miz Severin. Done. Unless he hauls in a big catch to impress his government. Be careful. Don't let that catch be you."

With that, Clint Walker stood and walked away, heading forward, toward the torpedo room. Leaving Julie's mind in a chaos of confusion.

If his dire warning hadn't matched Thurman's—and Nikolai's own—so closely, it would have been a lot easier to dismiss. As it was, she was left with a sick feeling of doubt. One side of her conscience was telling her even if it was true, Nikolai had changed his mind about turning her in. He'd said so. He'd promised to turn over the saboteur instead of her. He was working *with* her now. Not against her. They had an agreement, a deal. More, they had a real connection.

Didn't they?

She forced herself to finish her breakfast, even though it now tasted like sand on her tongue, hoping she'd be able to think better if she got some food in her stomach.

It didn't help.

One thing was crystal clear, however. As much as she wanted to trust Nikolai, and didn't want to believe Clint Walker, she'd be a fool not to heed his advice. She needed to find that SD card before Nikolai did, and hide it somewhere herself—somewhere he'd never find it.

So after sitting there staring at her empty plate for several long minutes trying to decide what to do next, she finally gave up. She needed to take at least one bull by the horns.

So she'd go to find Nikolai. And confront him.

But first, she'd take advantage of the absence of the scientists from their usual posts.

Time to get back to her search in earnest.

16

///////////////

Up on deck, Nikolai pushed the brim of his cap up with a finger, tipping his face to the sun. The morning was absolutely stunning. A practically tropical ten degrees centigrade and wind still, the Pacific as calm as he'd ever seen it. A perfect Midsummer's Eve for a steel picnic—and whatever pre-Blue-nose mischief his officers had planned. He really hoped the weather held through this afternoon. They still had a few hours of transiting until they hit the date line and the festivities could begin.

Meanwhile they'd reached the first research area and there were samples to be taken. Many samples. *Ostrov* had come to a stop, and the crew had helped the scientists get their equipment up to the deck where they'd commenced dipping and scooping, filming, netting, and filtering. Nikolai insisted everyone up top be wearing life vests, and the passengers all be clipped to the low toe-rails that rimmed the flat portion of the deck. The last thing he needed was someone to be swept overboard by a rogue wave. Calm as the sea was, just five minutes in the frigid water could kill a person. Hypothermia was a real danger.

He glanced aft as another head emerged from the hatch, hoping it was Julie. Disappointment streaked through him when he saw it wasn't her. He hadn't seen her since she fell asleep after the last time they made love, and he was missing her like mad.

The memory of having her lush body there beneath him, cradling his hips with her thighs and joined with him as one, caused his body to quicken. Damn, where was she? He needed to have her in his arms. Needed to put his nose to her hair and breathe deeply of the scent he was craving like a drug.

As though she could feel his longing for her, she appeared, and climbed up through the hatch. Her expression when she spotted him, however, was more guarded than glad.

What was wrong?

Maybe she was still nervous about the ocean.

He threaded his way past the busy clutch of researchers to get to her. He took her tether from the rating helping her up and clipped the end of it to his own belt so they could find a place where it was less crowded to talk. Maybe steal a kiss.

"Hi," he said and reached out to brush his thumb gently across her cheek. He wanted badly to touch her more, but this was probably a bit too public for overt displays of affection. Everyone undoubtedly knew about them. But for some reason, the scientists were far more critical of their relationship than his own men, who seemed to view it as a coup for their side. The only passenger who appeared to wholeheartedly approve of the liaison was young Dr. Stedman.

"Where have you been?" Nikolai asked Julie.

"Hi," she returned, peering apprehensively out at the ocean rather than at him. "I was taking advantage of the science team being up here on deck to do some searching below," she answered.

Ah. Okay, that made sense. But before he could pursue it, he heard a call from the rear lookout high up on the sail.

"Kapitan!" The man shouted something Nikolai couldn't make out and pointed at a dot on the port horizon.

"What is it?" Julie asked, squinting in that direction.

Nikolai watched as the dot materialized into a sleek cutter, slicing through the water toward them. "U.S. Coast Guard would be my guess," he said at length, fairly certain he was right. He'd been expecting to see them somewhere along here.

"What do they want?" she asked. She grabbed his arm, but it was just to keep her balance on the rolling deck.

"The Coast Guard patrols the MLB, the Maritime Boundary Line between Russia and the United States. Making sure no unauthorized vessels try to sneak into American waters." He put his hand over hers, hoping his touch would breach the sudden emotional distance she seemed to be keeping from him.

"You mean like terrorists and pirates?" she asked, glancing up at him briefly.

He made a wry face. "More like Russian fishing trawlers poaching over the line. You Yanks are very touchy about your fishing rights being violated."

"You think they'll board us? Ask for letters of transit or something?"

Nikolai chuckled. "*Nyet.* All the customs formalities were taken care of by the Arctic Institute and our governments. I'd guess the patrol is just making a courtesy drive-by—probably out of curiosity. Not often they get to see a Russian submarine up close."

"No, I imagine not."

Okay, something was definitely bothering her, and it wasn't the Coast Guard. Had she found something in her search below?

As everyone on deck watched the big cutter approach, he snaked an arm around her. To hell with what anyone thought. But she didn't lean into him as he'd hoped she would. Across the water on the other vessel a handful of white-uniformed Coasties were lined up against its rail, watching them back. When they got within range, everyone smiled and waved to each other—everyone but Julie. The cutter's horn tooted a hail, then it came about, leaving a graceful arc of spray in its wake, and sailed off the way it had come.

After a moment of excited chatter the scientists all went back to their experiments, and Nikolai returned his attention to Julie.

"So," he said, taking up their previous conversation, "any luck finding the SD card?" Though by her expression he figured she hadn't.

She didn't answer his question. Instead she said, "Listen, can we talk?"

"Sure," he said. "What's going on? Are you okay?"

She finally dragged her gaze from the sea, glanced around

to see if anyone was observing them, then drilled him with a dagger look. In a low but intense voice she asked, "Are you on the FSB's payroll?"

He was so shocked, he completely forgot about masking his reaction. "Why do you think that?" he asked, taken aback.

"Someone told me you are."

That got his attention. "Who?"

"Nikolai, just answer the damn question."

"Why would it matter?" he deflected.

He felt her stiffen. "I'll take that as a yes." She pulled away from him. "God damn it, Nikolai. Why didn't you tell me?"

He gazed at her in disbelief. "Really? You're really asking me that?"

She ignored the barb. "And here I thought we were being honest with each other!"

"We are," he ground out, lowering his voice. People were starting to turn around and stare.

He grabbed her arm and tugged her along the narrow ledge that led past the sail to the forward deck, but he halted at the halfway point and turned to face her. He grasped her shoulders when he realized she was nervously focusing on the sharp drop-off to the sea and not on him.

"Julie, what's this all about?" he asked, trying to keep his temper in check.

Again she pulled her gaze from the slate gray water below and pinioned him with accusing eyes. "It's about you misleading me. I spilled my guts, risking my job, and told you everything yesterday. I thought I could trust you!"

"And now suddenly you think you can't?"

"No! Not if you work for—"

"I *don't* work for them," he said, cutting her off. "I'm a *naval* officer, not an intelligence officer."

"Then why are you on the FSB payroll?" she demanded.

He ground his teeth. "I did work for them, for a while, but it was a long time ago. I was young, and they made it seem like a good choice. I know better now. But once you're in, they never quite let you go."

She searched his face for a long moment. "That's how you knew I was CIA," she said at length. "They told you."

"Yes," he admitted.

"You knew that night, at the hotel when we met."

"Yes."

"You were sent there to pick me up and seduce me. Weren't you." It wasn't a question but an accusation.

He took a deep breath. "Yes. But—"

"My God," she said, half in disgust, half in lament.

He wrapped his fingers tighter around her arms and pulled her closer. "*Milaya.* Believe me, it's not like that. I didn't—I wouldn't—"

She put the heels of her palms to her eyes. "God. I am *such* a fool. I can't believe I—"

"Stop this!" He shook her lightly. "Do you really think the man who made love to you last night did it because he'd been ordered to?"

"I don't know!" Her eyes grew shiny. She looked away. "I don't know what to think."

За ебис.

"Liesha. Listen to me."

"No." She pulled away from him. "I need to think about this. On my own." She tugged at her safety harness, pulling at his belt. "Unclip me, Nikolai."

"No fucking way. I'll walk you to the hatch if you want to go back inside."

She glanced tautly toward the group of scientists scattered over the afterdeck working on their projects. "No. I should be watching and taking notes for my next article. Just clip me to the toe-rail like everyone else."

"But you're still afraid."

"I'm afraid of a lot of things, Nikolai. I'll get over it."

He thinned his lips. He wanted to argue, but he could see it was useless. She had that stubborn look again that he usually so admired . . . when it wasn't directed at him.

"This discussion isn't over, *milaya.* But I suppose it can wait until we're alone." They needed privacy to hash this out. Now wasn't the time. "Come and get me when you wish to talk."

She didn't respond other than to worry her lip and turn her head away.

He wanted to hit something.

He swallowed down the impulse to put his fist into the sail, which would hurt him a whole lot more than it would the solid steel wall. Instead he ushered her back to the scientists and clipped her to the rail. As he was doing so, he heard a shout from up on the bridge.

"Kapitan!" He turned and glanced up at the lookout again. *"Periskop!"*

Nikolai stilled. Pulling his cap down to shade his eyes, he watched the waves closely where the man had pointed. There! A flash. The reflection of the morning sun off of something small and shiny. He clamped his jaw. The utter gall! The Chinese captain was getting bolder, bringing the 093 within a half mile of them.

Nikolai's irritation streaked into the stratosphere. Where was the damn U.S. Coast Guard when you needed them? He didn't think *Ostrov* was in any real danger. Not with civilians on board, the world watching, and the authorities nearby. The Chinese wouldn't dare try anything. Not even to get back their stolen technology. Not when retrieving it would involve effectively hijacking and ransacking another country's military vessel. Wars had been declared over far less provocation.

But this close, there was always danger of collision. He of all people knew that.

The Chinese commander's impudence was really starting to bug him. This was deliberate harassment. Too bad he had no way of answering it—not with the scientists on board. And the fucker knew that.

He narrowed his eyes as the sun flashed off the periscope again.

Or . . . maybe he did.

Julie was sitting on a thick rubber fender one of the ratings had taken pity and brought up for her from the storage room in the conning tower. The bare metal submarine deck was like a wet block of ice. Even in June the water temps must be not much above freezing. By comparison the air was a temperate fifty or so. Warm enough even in the shelter of the sail to unbutton her coat, spread it open, and enjoy the rays of the midsummer sun. If she'd had a light sweatshirt like the others, she'd be able to dispense with the coat altogether. She wondered if Nikolai had one in his clothes locker she could borrow. Though, he didn't really seem like a sweatshirt kind of guy.

She looked up from her laptop as a string of angry exclamations rose from one of the women scientists. Julie didn't understand the words, but it didn't sound like Russian. Sure enough, Dr. Lautenen was standing at the side of the deck holding something and swearing in her native language. It was a satellite phone.

"Something wrong?" Professor Sundesvall called over from where he was pulling a contraption on a long rope up from the ocean, which he no doubt hoped was filled to the brim with singled-celled slimy ooze. His project had to do with plankton, Julie recalled. Species change or migration or some such thing. She hadn't gotten to interview him yet.

"My sat phone is kaput," Dr. Lautenen called back angrily. "This is most inconvenient. I wish to send my readings back to the university today."

Nikolai had disappeared below shortly after the periscope sighting, so his XO, *Starpom* Varnas, who'd been left in charge of things topside, went over to lend assistance. He took the phone, examined it, then immediately popped the battery cover off. He grimaced. Uh-oh. Someone else's phone had been sabotaged, too?

Dr. Lautenen let out a cry of dismay, followed by a few other words in Finnish that Julie was glad she didn't understand.

Okay. This was just bizarre. Julie wasn't the only one being targeted? But why? It made no sense. Unless the Finnish woman was also a spy. . . . Good grief. How many people on board weren't what they seemed to be?

Or maybe this particular phone sabotage had nothing to do with spies or the SD card hidden on *Ostrov*. Maybe this was instead about the theft of scientific research, or competition for a first announcement of an important breakthrough. She'd heard academics could be cutthroat.

Still, this was ridiculous.

Starpom Varnas surprised her by announcing in his silky accent, "Miss Severin's phone was also tampered. Who else has satellite phone?"

Two other hands went up, Professor Sundesvall's and Josh's. That was when she realized two of the team were missing. Rufus Edwards and Clint Walker were not on the deck. She hadn't thought about it before because they weren't actually scientists.

"Please to check phones," Varnas ordered briskly.

The professor and Josh obediently pulled them out and punched buttons. Immediately Sundesvall shook his set and tried again. "Mine doesn't work either," he said, visibly upset. "Dr. Stedman?"

Josh, standing close to Varnas, put his phone to his ear and listened, then gave a quick shoulder lift and held it to the *starpom*'s ear. "Nothing wrong with mine."

Varnas met his eyes and nodded. "Is good." Then he held out his hands to Dr. Lautenen and the professor. "Give phones to me. Chief engineer very good. Maybe he can fix."

"Can you take mine, too?" Julie asked hopefully.

"Yes, of course," Varnas said. "Come. We get."

"Great."

She let him unclip her safety harness and walk behind her to the hatch, which was situated on the deck just before it dropped off into the blue oblivion. One slip of the foot and she'd plunge into the frigid water. She was glad the *starpom* was there to make sure she didn't. And that she was no longer wearing those wobbly high heels.

When they got to the bottom of the ladder inside, she had to stop and blink her eyes, letting them adjust to the relative darkness of the interior after the bright sunlight above. She wrinkled her nose against the diesel smell.

They landed in the same compartment where she'd hidden herself away just the previous night to recover from her discussion with Nikolai. Since she wasn't crying now, the men didn't avoid her. They greeted her politely.

At a beckon from *Starpom* Varnas, an older man came up to them, apparently the chief engineer. A quick exchange in Russian followed, and Varnas held up the two ruined phones, said a few more words, then gestured to her.

The older man chuckled. Not the reaction she'd expected. He led them through a watertight door to the next compartment and pointed. There, lined up on a console, were three more sat phones, wires gutted and exposed.

Good Lord.

There was another quick exchange in Russian. Varnas looked at her and made a face. "Phone epidemic. Spread like bad flu."

This was crazy. "Whose are they?" she asked.

"Crew men's. Expensive, but some buy together. Submarine gone long time from families."

"Why would anyone want to sabotage *their* phones?" she muttered to no one in particular. That *really* didn't make any sense. She looked hopefully at the chief engineer. "Can you fix them?"

He looked to Varnas, who translated. "Sure," the *starpom* told her in turn, relaying the engineer's reply. "He just need time. But not today." Suddenly the *starpom* looked nervous. "*Praporshchik* Selnikov busy today. Must to rehearse."

Julie's brow beetled. He must have used the wrong word, but she came up blank. "Rehearse?"

Varnas cleared his throat. "For tonight. We cross international date line, and we have"—he searched for the word—"theater?"

She blinked. "A theater? You're putting on a play?" *A Midsummer Night's Dream*, perhaps, considering the day? In Russian? That should be . . . interesting. But what did a play have to do with the international date line?

The *starpom* looked pained. "Yes, well, um, no. Is like ceremony. Really for Arctic Circle crossing. In five days." He pointed to his nose. "Bluenoses. Everyone first time to do terrible cold tests. You know?"

She blinked again. "Uh, no." What the flipping heck was he talking about?

"Anyway, *Praporshchik* Selnikov is Lord Ægir, Norse god of sea. Special extra ceremony tonight. We just to answer embarrassed questions. Not too bad."

She was so confused.

"After, everyone eat and drink very much," Varnas added, smiling. "Lord Ægir also god of beer."

Finally, something she understood. Apparently Selnikov got the gist, too. He grinned widely and waggled his bushy eyebrows, lifting an imaginary pint in a toast.

"Can't wait," Julie said dubiously. Talk about being out to sea. "In the meantime, I better get back to work."

"Okay." *Starpom* Varnas nodded. "I see you later. Oh, and *praporshchik* ask if you have bath suit."

She was halfway through the watertight door, but halted dead in her tracks and turned. "What?"

He gestured to his torso. "Bikini, yes? For tonight. Maybe will to get wet." He made a pained face.

Her jaw dropped. "I, um"—*thank you, Jesus*—"didn't bring a bathing suit along." Was he *nuts*? Who swam in the Arctic? Besides, her suitcase was now swimming all on its own—heading for the South Seas if it was smart.

Varnas conferred briefly with the chief. Then, "He say no problem. You borrow shorts from Dr. Lautenen."

Obviously Julie was missing something big here. She needed to ask someone who spoke English and was familiar with weird navy rituals what in blazes was going on.

Someone like Rufus Edwards.

While she was at it, she'd ask him if he had a satellite phone. And whether or not it still worked.

But for her own peace of mind, she really hoped it didn't.

17

\\\\\\\/////////

Nikolai didn't have to turn; he felt the exact moment when Julie ducked into the torpedo room. The atmosphere changed. Became more charged with electricity. The air itself suddenly smelled different, the distinctive odor of diesel petrol, amines, and fuel oil at once tempered by a subtle hint of her perfume . . . though that part was possibly his imagination. His need for her may be messing with his mind.

So he didn't turn. No use wrecking his concentration even further. While the rest of the crew secured the boat to get under way again, Nikolai and Clint Walker were in the midst of putting together a rude surprise for their Chinese stalkers.

"UUV system checks completed, Skipper," Walker reported. "All systems go and ready to launch anytime you give the word."

Nikolai had requested Walker's help on this little off-book adventure. The man had reacted to his initial explanation first with hiked brows, then with a slow grin. Apparently at heart they were cut from the same cloth. Troublemakers to the core.

They'd been collaborating with Master Chief Edwards on sonar, the three of them speaking in rapid English so none of Nikolai's crew would be involved if he was called on the carpet by his superiors. Not that he saw that as a real possibility. He seriously doubted the Chinese commander would lodge a complaint. Oh, wait. The 093 Shang class wasn't even here in the Pacific. No problem, then, right?

"Excellent," Nikolai responded. "Now all we need is to figure out what to blast her with."

Back at the bulkhead there was a soft gasp and he heard Julie's footsteps hurry toward them. "You are surely not planning to *shoot* at the Chinese sub, are you?" She sounded aghast.

Nikolai finally turned to face her. Her reluctance to be there, to meet his eyes, was also apparent. He wondered idly why she'd come. Obviously she hadn't expected to see him.

"Submarines don't shoot," he corrected. "We use torpedoes."

When Walker realized Nikolai was talking to someone else, he turned in his console chair and lifted his headset from his ears. "Here to watch the fun, Miz Severin?" he drawled.

"What are you two up to?" she asked, radiating suspicion, especially when neither of them looked the least bit guilty.

"No good, of course," Nikolai answered, and Walker gave a low, villainous chuckle.

She scanned the room, taking in the console all lit up and two weps—weapons—techs manning the tubes where the torpedo-shaped UUVs sat recharging their batteries. It had taken a good forty-five minutes to hurriedly offload the morning's science samples from one of them and ready it for another sortie after the last research run. But the delay didn't matter. The activity topside was now finished and the scientists had hauled the last of their equipment back inside. *Ostrov* was ready to fire up as soon as Nikolai and Walker's mission of mischief had been implemented.

He just hoped the 093 would get the message and take off to harass some other unlucky sub commander. He had enough to deal with from all the other shit raining down on him at the moment.

"If not an outright attack, then . . . ," Julie ventured as she completed her suspicious scan of their preparations. He could practically hear the cogs turning in her head. "You're going to send a UUV out there and what? Make the Chinese sub think it's . . . an aircraft carrier or something? About to mow them down?"

She was one sharp lady, he'd give her that.

"Not a bad idea," he said, his grin widening as her eyes did likewise. "So you know about the UUV's simulator."

A simulator was a broadcast device used to emit decoy sounds for various purposes, for instance to trick the enemy's sonar into thinking the UUV was a bigger, more threatening contact, or to lead a hot torpedo away from the home sub.

In this case the emitted noise would be aimed at the Chinese sub, and hopefully it would annoy them enough to leave.

"Yes," she said. "I know about simulators. And guess what? I'll bet the Chinese do, too."

"Oh, we're not trying to fool them or anything," Nikolai said. "We just thought they might be bored over there following us around. So we're putting together a little serenade for their amusement."

She looked even more skeptical.

"I'll need some appropriate sounds to upload," Walker interjected with a smirk. "I wasn't expecting to run nonscientific sorties, so there are no ship mechanicals or standard countermeasures loaded into the UUV's simulator. And definitely no Britney Spears." His mouth twisted wryly. "Nothing but biologicals."

"Whales are not nearly irritating enough," Nikolai said. "Use our sonar library. Ask Gavrikov to pick out something really loud and obnoxious."

"Edwards offered us his private collection," Walker said.

Nikolai returned an evil smile. "And I happen to know our chief engineer has an iPod. He's particularly fond of Tchaikovsky and Ukrainian balalaika music."

Walker winced. "Perfect. I'll have the quartermaster run him down."

Julie was listening to their exchange with parted lips. "What exactly are you hoping to accomplish with this adolescent stunt?" she asked incredulously.

Nikolai's frustration peaked. "Annoy the crap out of them. With any luck, enough to get them off our ass for good. I don't like being stalked."

"Seriously? You think *this* will work?" She darted a glance at Walker, then gave Nikolai a meaningful look. "All things considered?"

By which she meant their stolen technology being on board *Ostrov*, no doubt.

"Got any other suggestions? I'm all ears," he said flatly.

He understood her point, however, and he didn't necessarily disagree. If they were being followed because the Chinese wanted back the SD card, the 093 commander was unlikely to let *Ostrov* out of his sight for long.

"Christ," Walker said, his expression falling into disgust, all amusement gone in an instant. "You *did* tell him."

Shock flashed through Nikolai at the implication of Walker's muttered statement. Walker also knew about her mission. He glanced at Julie, wondering if he should feel betrayed. A lightbulb went off in his mind. It was pretty obvious who had been her source of information on his FSB background.

But how had Walker gotten hold of that intel? If the former U.S. Navy man was the one who'd told her, it stood to reason he must be some flavor of intelligence operative himself. Which meant he must *also* be aboard *Ostrov* for the purpose of espionage.

Good God, the boat was crawling with spies!

Fat lot of good Nikolai's own connections were doing him—the FSB was clearly underinformed. Either that, or they were playing him. Neither would be a huge shock.

But what did shock Nikolai was that Julie hadn't told him about Walker. Okay. He *did* feel betrayed.

Angrily, he flayed her with an accusing look. "What the hell is going on?"

She shook her head, looking genuinely chagrined. "Ask him, not me. I didn't tell him anything. And I have no idea who he works for."

Nikolai rounded on the other man. "I think you'd better start talking, Walker. And fast."

Walker's gaze shifted between them. He sighed. "Look. It doesn't matter who any of us works for, or even if we're on different sides. If I'm reading this situation right, for now we all have the same goal. To make sure they"—Walker stabbed a finger beyond the hull in the direction of the Chinese 093—"don't get their hands on anything, or anyone, aboard *Ostrov*. Agreed?"

Nikolai clenched his jaw. The man was being too reasonable by half. He was up to something. "How do we know we can trust you?" Nikolai asked tightly.

Walker gave a low laugh. "Isn't that *my* line?" He flicked a look at Julie then back to Nikolai. "Hell, I'm the American here. Just because you're willing to sleep with the opposition doesn't mean you won't betray her when push comes to shove."

Nikolai saw red. "*Me?* What about her? It works both ways, my friend," he snapped before thinking.

He heard Julie suck in a breath and he shot out a hand to grasp her arm before she could vault away from him. Хуйня. That wasn't what he'd meant to say.

He glared furiously at Walker. "*I'm* trying to protect Julie. What are you doing besides creating suspicion?"

"Hey, I'm standing right here," she ground out, jerking her arm back from him. "And I don't need protection from *either* of you. I can take care of myself!" She banded her arms over her abdomen.

Walker observed them both without expression. "Okay. How about we just say we all have our secrets, and that for now we choose to trust each other, more or less, against a common enemy. And leave it at that."

Nikolai slashed his fingers through his hair. And realized he had no right to be angry with Julie for Walker's actions. At least Walker was being relatively up-front about having an agenda. Plus he was an official member of the expedition team, the only UUV pilot on board. Not someone Nikolai could kick off the boat even if he wanted to and there were a way to do so. And as much as Nikolai hated to admit it, what Walker had suggested was probably their best option.

He was about to agree to the truce when Julie asked, "Do you have a satellite phone, Mr. Walker?" The other man nodded, and she asked, "Can I borrow it?"

Walker said, "Sure, but it won't do you much good."

"Why not?"

"Because it doesn't work," he said, his voice gruff. "Someone gutted the insides. Any guess as to who?" He narrowed a glance at Nikolai.

Julie's breath eased out while Nikolai's caught at the not-so-veiled accusation. He took an angry step forward.

"If you find out, let me know. He got mine, too," she said, grabbing his wrist to hold him back. "Okay, Mr. Walker. I'll go along with your alliance. For now. But that doesn't mean I trust you."

Walker gave another wry laugh. "Whatever you say, rookie. Captain Romanov?"

Nikolai ground his teeth. "Fine. I'm in. Now, any chance we can get on with the task at hand? Sometime today?"

"Aye, Skipper," Walker said and turned back to his console. He slid his headset over his ears again and started to hail Edwards, who'd been standing by on the circuit. "Give me fifteen minutes to upload the sound signatures and we're good to go."

Nikolai stalked after Julie to wait over at the far side of the compartment, away from the others. She was holding her small laptop folded in her arms across her midriff as she leaned against the bulkhead.

"When did you talk to Walker about me?" he asked angrily before she could turn aside and ignore him.

"At breakfast," she said, her eyes roaming the jumble of pipes and torpedo tubes all around them. "But he did most of the talking. He guessed who I work for and warned me about sleeping with you."

"How thoughtful," Nikolai drawled.

"He thought I was trying to 'work' you," she said with disgust.

Smart man. So Walker had tried to work her instead. Just in a different way. "And . . . ?" Nikolai almost didn't want to know.

She finally looked at him. "And I told him I had sex with you because I find you attractive. No other reason."

His anger eased a bit. The attraction was definitely mutual. But so much more than mere attraction—at least on his part. Still, he wondered if she was telling the whole truth.

Did it matter?

Yeah, he realized. It did.

But that was a whole different conversation.

"Does he know about the SD card?"

"I don't know. I certainly didn't say anything, and he didn't mention it specifically. But he knows I'm looking for something."

"You didn't find it this morning?" Nikolai asked pointedly.

She shook her head. "I get the feeling I could search for a year and still not find it." She sounded disheartened.

"What will we do if we don't find it?" he asked, changing the pronoun to remind her he was also in the equation. And not just for sex.

She firmed her jaw. "That," she said, "is not an option."

He thought about the distinct possibility that they wouldn't find the hidden data card before the expedition was over. If he personally didn't have it in his possession by then, he was sure Cherenkov and his FSB minions were poised and ready to seize *Ostrov* the minute she returned to Rybachiy, and tear her apart if they had to.

Whereupon, an unpleasant thought crept through Nikolai's mind. *Unless the Chinese did it first.*

Чёрт возьми. Surely *that* wasn't why the nuclear sub was tailing them . . . because the Chinese were planning to retrieve their stolen technology the old-fashioned way—by force? He'd never heard of one submarine hijacking another, but there was a first time for everything.

The idea raised the hair on the back of his neck.

Walker interrupted his harrowing thoughts. "Skipper," he called, looking over from his chair at the console monitor, "should I also upload some random mechanicals and standard countermeasures to the UUV?"

Nikolai shook off his prickling unease. The idea that they would be attacked outright was too outrageous. He was just being paranoid. "Yeah," he answered Walker. "Good idea. You never know what might come in handy."

"Will do. Almost there."

Julie made an impatient sound, reminding him of her presence. "I still can't believe you're doing this," she muttered. "You can't possibly think it'll have any real effect."

"But it will," Nikolai refuted. Hoping like hell he was right. "If only a psychological one. I'm sending them a message."

"Don't tread on me," she murmured.

"Exactly." He met her frown with a tentative smile. "See? You and I think much alike, *dorogaya*."

She sent him a withering look. He waved a hand toward the torpedo tube where the weps techs had finished preparing the fully loaded UUV. "Staying for the launch?"

She hesitated only briefly before nodding. "Yeah. Since I missed the ones this morning. I'd like to see how it's done." She unbanded her arms and lifted her laptop. "I assume I can't write about this ridiculous auditory assault in my next article?"

Nikolai nearly choked. "*Nyet*. Please don't."

Just then, a young rating stuck his head through the water-tight door and said, "*Kapitan*, *Starshina* Borovsky would like permission to pull certain members of the crew from their duties as soon as we're under way. He said you would know why, sir."

Nikolai glanced at his watch. They must be getting ready for the festivities. He gave his permission and told the rating to have the OOD substitute men on the watch accordingly. Then he switched back to English and said to Julie, "Besides, I have just been reminded there will be more interesting things for you to write about later this evening."

"Yeah, about that," she said, her tone still guarded but at once less prickly. "What on earth *is* going on tonight? *Star-pom* Varnas tried to tell me, but I didn't understand a word he was saying. Something about bathing suits and blue noses?"

Nikolai laughed at her confounded expression, his own tension easing somewhat. "No, tonight is just a party to cele-brate Midsummer's Eve. Though I understand there'll be a special appearance by Lord Ægir in preparation for the Arctic Circle crossing. That's when the Bluenose ceremony he was talking about will take place."

Her expression became even more uncomprehending. "Bluenose ceremony?"

"You've not heard of the Royal Order of the Bluenose? The secret society only those who cross over the Arctic Circle may join?"

"Not really," she admitted. "What gives?"

As he explained the centuries-old tradition, about the ver-bal and physical trials she'd be put through, he realized how glad he was that she was opening up to him again, if only on an impersonal level. He didn't like it when they were at odds with each other. It had nothing to do with his diminished chances of getting her naked again. He just liked talking to her. She was smart, funny, curious, and genuine. He'd never met a woman who was so interested in the world around her, or had so much honest empathy for those she encountered.

He wished he could take her to his family's dacha and spend a whole month just lying on the bear rug talking with her. *Da.* All right, talking and making love. He could tell they had much to teach each other. In both areas.

Too bad there was no possibility of that ever happening.

After he'd told her how several of the officers would dress up as ancient gods and, in the name of the King of the Northern Seas, put the warm-blooded pollywog initiates through a set of cold, wet, disgusting trials designed to test their worthiness to enter the king's icy realm, Julie looked askance.

"Jeez Louise. That sounds awful! How do I get out of it?" she asked in trepidation.

Nikolai shook his head. "If you want to keep the respect of anyone on the boat, you must take part. It's all in fun, but on a navy vessel, rituals like this can make or break a man's—or woman's—reputation."

He could see his meaning slowly sink in, and her focus shifted across the room to the two crew members who were doing last-minute checks to the torpedo tube. "And since by now everyone on the boat knows we're lovers," she said levelly, "my actions reflect on you." She didn't sound particularly pleased at that revelation.

"Are we?" he asked. "Still lovers?" Despite their conflict, he didn't want to give that up.

She looked down at her sneakers. "The crew thinks we are."

Not what he'd wanted to hear. But at least she hadn't said no.

He reached out to brush a stray lock of hair from her cheek, glad when she didn't move away from his touch. "The trials aren't for days yet. You'll do fine. Tonight I gather it's just some kind of mock interrogation." He dropped his hand and smiled. "To add a little spice to the barbecue."

"Interrogation about what?" she asked with a frown.

His smile turned sardonic. "Trumped-up charges, supposed infractions against the God of the Northern Realm. Whatever's most embarrassing for each pollywog, would be my guess."

She closed her eyes briefly, looking pained. "Swell. You know what that means."

Da, he knew. He was prepared to face the inevitable ribald comments. He just hoped she wouldn't be too uncomfortable. Though he was ready to step in if things went too far.

"What if I can't or won't answer?" she asked.

"That's where the bathing suit comes in."

Her eyes popped, scandalized. "You can't be serious."

"Just be happy it's not winter. You haven't lived until you've run naked across an icy submarine deck in a blizzard."

Her worried expression froze, wide-eyed.

"Don't worry. No nakedness in mixed company," he reassured her with a wink.

"It wasn't the nudity I was worried about," she muttered.

"Oh?" he said, his interest piquing.

She rolled her eyes. "Stop."

She looked so cutely perturbed and irritated with him he wanted to lean over and kiss her. He was sorely tempted.

But she must have sensed his thoughts, for she turned away. "Don't," she whispered.

"Dorogaya—"

She pointedly moved her laptop over her breasts, as though setting up a shield between them. "I still don't get what all that has to do with blue noses," she said, refusing to discuss anything more personal.

He reluctantly accepted her boundaries and didn't push. "If you pass your tests," he explained, "the tip of your nose is painted blue to signify acceptance into the order. You'll also get a certificate. Suitable for framing."

She swore softly and rubbed the end of her nose, but didn't get a chance to comment before Walker interrupted again.

"Okay." Walker pulled his headphones out from his ears and held them there. "I've got a nice variety of useful and annoying sound signatures uploaded, and the simulator is programmed. Ready to input course and coordinates when you are, Skipper."

"All right, then," Nikolai said. With a long exhale, he switched gears. "Let's go harass these bastards."

18

〜〜〜〜〜〜〜〜

Miraculously, the Chinese Shang-class 093 gave up and slunk off into the depths of the Pacific. Victory!

It took a few hours, but Nikolai's strategy worked like a charm. Walker had programmed the simulator to lower the decibel level of the noise by increments as the distance grew between *Ostrov* and the 093, and that had served as a kind of positive reinforcement toward the desired end. The further the enemy sub backed off, the less raucous the music and sounds were blasted at it. The Shang class slowed, then veered, and finally turned to steam off *Ostrov*'s sonar screen for good.

Or so Julie heard. She'd left the boys and their toys after a half hour or so of observation, filled with a whole new understanding of the kind of man who became a submariner: one with patience, cunning, nerves of steel . . . and a very perverse sense of humor.

She had watched the initial launch with interest, feeling the fine hairs on her arms rise when the 093 reacted to the first burst of noise by turning hard and flooding its torpedo tubes to defend against an unexpected attack, then, when the commander finally realized what was going on, maneuvering like an elephant stalking a mouse to try and rid itself of the persistent annoyance. But the much smaller UUV was quick and agile, Nikolai's command of battle maneuvers impressive, and Walker was a veritable pinball wizard on the joystick.

The huge nuclear submarine didn't stand a chance.

The whole story quickly sped through *Ostrov* from man to man, embellished more and more each time it was retold, and was the main topic of conversation at every watch station before and after the Chinese made their ignominious retreat.

As Julie made her way along the main deck a few hours later, the entire crew were still laughing and joking at the nose thumbing their clever captain had given his enemy counterpart. She was on her way to the mess hall, planning to sit at a table until lunch and bang out a couple more articles while her laptop processed the latest batch of photos she'd taken in her quest for the SD card. How she would send it all to her boss without a phone, she had no idea. But she needed to take a break from the search. She was going cross-eyed, and the crew was starting to wonder what she found so fascinating about pipes and fixtures. The artist friend excuse went only so far.

A little while before lunch started, Nikolai strode in, heading for the coffee urn.

"Congratulations on the sound defeat," she told him as she joined him for a top-up to her own mug.

He made a face at her unintended pun. "Thanks."

"I am truly astounded it worked."

His answering smile held the satisfaction of victory, with a hint of amusement thrown in. "Don't tell anyone, but me, too." He put his mug under the spigot and filled it with the strongly aromatic coffee. "But they'll be back soon enough."

"You think?"

"Oh, yeah. They're just humoring us." He slanted her a glance. "We both know why they're here. They won't give up quite so easily."

A wave of apprehension purled through her. "No. I suppose not. I just wish I knew what they're planning."

"Watch and wait is my guess. Not much else they can do without causing a huge international incident." Looking grim, he took a sip of the coffee.

She wondered if he was thinking about his own unfortunate international incident . . . wishing things had gone differently. It was incredibly brave of him to risk further criticism from his superiors by striking out at the Chinese sub as he had. Or incredibly stupid. Or maybe just his way of fiddling while Rome was burning.

He met her gaze. Earlier, she'd been too busy avoiding looking at him to notice, but now she saw his eyes were lined with fatigue and smudged with shadows.

"You look tired," she said. "Have you gotten any sleep at all?"

His lashes dipped languorously. "Not really." His lips curved slightly. "I got distracted by someone last night."

Her cheeks warmed at the way he looked at her. It was a gaze not filled with thoughts of cold collisions, but redolent with the heated memory of what they had done together in his bed just hours before. *Before being reminded how impossible it all was.*

"Nikolai . . ." But her warning died on her tongue as her body flushed with a sudden, powerful awareness of him as her lover. She looked down and gripped her empty coffee cup, feeling the emptiness between her legs. Damn, she missed him. How was that possible?

But the truth was, she was tired, too. Of keeping her feelings in check and holding him at bay because of politics. Politics had nothing to do with them as people. As lovers.

As though sensing the longing that sifted through her, he stepped closer. "Come with me to the stateroom," he urged softly, his voice deep and seductive.

She rallied and allowed herself a little smile. "If I do, I doubt you'll get much sleep."

"Sleep is highly overrated," he said, beginning to lift his coffee cup to his lips again.

A feeling of overwhelming need swept over her, paralyzing her good sense. Without considering the consequences, she put out her hand and covered the cup with her fingers. His gaze jerked up.

Her heartbeat sped at the folly of what she was about to do.

"You go," she whispered. She swallowed heavily. "I'll come to you later. After you get some rest."

His eyes captured hers. Wary. Hopeful. "You're not still angry with me?"

She was. But in the end it didn't matter. His heated exchange with Clint Walker reverberated in her mind like the toll of a wakeup call.

I'm trying to protect her.

Betrayal works both ways. . . .

She was probably making the worst decision of her life. But she needed him to understand she would never betray him, either. That wasn't what this mission was about.

And, oh, how she simply wanted him!

She wanted to feel his arms around her again, his lips moving over her aching flesh. She wanted to banish the loneliness, if only for a few moments of reckless abandon, even though she knew it could never last.

She met his drowning gaze. "Anger's highly overrated, too," she said softly.

She was such a fool.

Slowly he lowered his cup. "All right," he said, still searching her face for possible misunderstanding. There was none to find. "When will you come?"

As soon as you touch me.

"In a few hours," she said. "You need to sleep first."

She felt his fingers touch her cheek as he bent down to brush his lips over hers. "Make it soon, *dorogaya.* I'll be waiting," he murmured.

And then he was gone.

"Mmm-mmm-mmm." The envious hum of approval came from the open passageway, snapping Julie out of the spell of Nikolai's tender kiss. "I'm surprised I didn't vaporize from the heat in here. And trust me, it wasn't coming from the galley stove."

Julie smiled in embarrassment as Josh strolled into the compartment, maple leaf–decorated mug in hand, laptop tucked under his armpit, and a knowing grin gracing his elfin face.

"How is it you always manage to witness my greatest moments of weakness?" she asked him.

His grin spread. "Damn. The drama unfolding on this sub is better than Tolstoy."

"Hopefully with a better ending," she said ruefully.

He just raised a dubious eyebrow.

"Oh, hell," she half groaned. How could one so young be so damned perceptive? "I am *so* screwed."

Thankfully, she was spared further disheartening insights into her future when Dr. Lautenen hurried into the mess. "Oh, good," she said when she spotted Julie. "There you are, Miss Severin."

Josh gave Julie a salute with his mug and sauntered off, back in the direction he'd come.

"Hi, Dr. Lautenen. Can I help you with something?" Julie asked.

The Finnish scientist was plain and a shade heavy, but her face had very nice bone structure and there was a youthful sparkle in her pretty blue eyes.

"Oh, no. I just came to— Here." The other woman held out what looked like a pair of shorts to Julie. "I hear from *Praporshchik* Selnikov you don't have a bathing suit with you," she said. "Borrow these if you want. They are terribly old and ratty, and probably not the best fit, but better than trying to peel off wet jeans. I'm not too old to remember what that's like." She smiled mischievously.

Julie blinked. It took her a second of mental scrambling, but then she remembered. The ceremony. They'd be crossing the international date line in just a few hours.

"Oh! Thank you. Very much. I think." She took the shorts and smiled uncertainly, noting that the older woman was considerably less plain today. She was wearing eye makeup and lipstick.

"I can see you're worried about tonight," Dr. Lautenen said. "Don't be. It'll be great fun. You'll see." She glanced at the galley and lifted her nose in the air. "My goodness, don't those ribs smell wonderful?"

"They do," Julie admitted. Her mouth had started watering shortly after she'd arrived in the mess, when the enticing odors of slow Southern cooking had started wafting out from the galley, accompanied by the cheerful sound of Rufus Edwards whistling. "*That* part I'm very much looking forward to."

Dr. Lautenen laughed cheerfully. "And the beer." She winked. "Well, I'll see you later. Work to do before pleasure."

Julie thanked her again for the shorts and gave her a wave,

tamping down a spark of anticipation at the reminder of the pleasures that awaited her in the stateroom.

A vision of Nikolai's hard body and intense lovemaking shivered through her. Lord, she could hardly wait.

But she must. He needed some sleep. And she also had things to do before she could enjoy the pleasures of his bed.

Nikolai was catching up on his paperwork when Julie came to him. He'd been waiting impatiently, too restless and aroused to sleep more than a couple of hours. He kept dreaming about her.

He wanted her here in the flesh.

The door finally opened and she stepped in, looking first over at the empty bunk, then peeking around to see him sitting at his desk.

"Come in." He beckoned, a rush of gratification filling him that she'd actually come. He hadn't been totally certain she would. "Lock the door," he ordered.

"What are you doing out of bed?" she asked as she obeyed.

His body stirred. "Waiting for you to join me there." He tossed down his pen and closed the log he'd been working on, then turned the chair so he was facing her. "Come here," he said and patted his knee.

She smiled enticingly and walked slowly over to him. He took the things she was carrying and set them on the desk, then guided her to straddle his legs, face-to-face. "What took you so long?"

"I wanted you rested." She sank onto his lap and melted into his embrace, her thighs hugging his, her arms lining his shoulders, her warm breasts nestling against the wall of his chest.

He pulled her close, feeling like he'd landed somewhere just this side of heaven.

He needed to taste her. He put his mouth to hers and she moaned softly, opening to him, whispering his name with a needy sigh. "Nikolai."

He loved to hear the sound of it on her lips, her soft American accent making the common name sound arousingly exotic. And deeply personal. Like he was the only man in the world who could answer her whispered call.

God, he wanted to be that man.

"Liesha," he murmured into her mouth as he deepened the kiss, pretending, for a while at least, that it was true. That he would be able to kiss her and hold her like this whenever he wanted, beyond the few stolen hours they could spend together on *Ostrov*.

With another soft groan of pleasure, she tightened her arms around his neck. As though she never wanted to let him go, either.

Frustration roared through him, and he pressed his lips to hers, hard and demanding. He pulled her closer still, kissing her rougher, more urgently. He kissed her senseless, kissed himself witless, kissed and kissed her until the only thought in his head was how hot and good she tasted and felt in his arms. He wanted to consume her, to fill his senses with the taste and feel and smell of her. To touch her everywhere, to rock himself in the cradle of her warm, welcoming body.

But he held back, feeding his overwhelming need on the sweet succor of her mouth. To make it last . . . a lifetime. His hand fisted in her silky hair, and he held her fast as he plumbed her velvety depths.

Her response was dazzling. Her body writhed against his with every wet dip of his tongue. Her fingers pulled his hair and dug into the back of his neck, kneading his flesh to the rhythm of his strokes.

Finally he could take it no longer. He wound her long auburn hair around his hand and bent her backward. And began to lick his way down to her breasts, losing himself in the warm, fragrant taste of her soft flesh.

Her T-shirt was in the way.

"Take it off," he ordered, reaching for the hem and dragging it up her torso. He was momentarily arrested by the sight of her, lush, naked, and unbound, so beautiful she took his breath away.

As she eased the T-shirt from his fingers and drew it off, he cupped her full breasts in his hands, rubbing over her nipples so they peaked against his palms.

A noise of pure need came from her throat, and she reached for the buttons of his uniform shirt.

"*Nyet,*" he said, stopping her. She'd had the advantage

their first time; he'd been nude well before she'd shed her clothes. Which had been exciting in its own way, but—

"This is my turn. I want you naked."

He lifted her up and she quickly removed her jeans.

Her body quivered when he tugged her back and positioned her body over his. He reveled at the feel of her gliding over the hard ridge where his body ached to join hers. He met her lips and his hands explored her bare shoulders, her ribs, the curve of her waist.

He brushed his palms over the satin skin of her bottom, then parted his legs and slid his fingers through the moist heat of her feminine folds. A moan escaped her as he found her center.

He touched her.

"Nikolai," she panted, arching her back as he circled her need. "Oh, yes."

Arousal poured through him seeing her like this, in the throes of her passion for him. Helpless against the strength of their ardor. He brought her higher and higher, watching the emotions play across her face, until she shattered in his arms, crying out his name in a breathless plea.

She shuddered so sweetly, held him so tightly, driving his own need to the breaking point.

"You," she moaned when she opened her heavy-lidded eyes at last. She fumbled with his trouser buttons, urging him to remove the last physical barrier between them. "Hurry."

He hurried.

He lifted her and lowered her slick velvet heat onto his aching cock.

He groaned. From pleasure. From need. From the knowledge that this . . . this explosive thing between them couldn't last longer than a few short weeks. How wrong was that?

"Julie," he groaned, thrusting up into her. Her name tasted good on his tongue. It tasted so right. Like the taste of her lips and the salt of her skin. Real. Honest. Like the feel of her flesh surrounding his, like her arms clinging to him as she rode him to their mutual pleasure.

"Я буду держать вас," he said, low and urgent, and felt the words sink deep into his soul. *I would keep you.*

But how?

Their situation had them trapped, captive in separate, opposing worlds, just as the Arctic ice kept the sea from touching the sky in winter. An impenetrable barrier. Dangerous to all who attempted to break free.

Finding a way through the obstacles could well prove impossible. Or even deadly.

But as they reached their explosive climax and came together in every sense of the word, in his heart, Nikolai knew he must try.

19

〟〟〟〝〟〝〟〟〟〟

Julie did not want to move.

She was draped over Nikolai's chest, his arms loosely slung around her, the fingers of his hand twirling absently in the ends of her hair. Lord, her body felt like a limp noodle.

But, oh, so very good.

They'd made love again, this time using every square inch of the narrow bunk, sometimes spilling out onto the hard floor amid groans and laughter, kisses and shivers. The man was an irresistible mix of sensuality, sensitivity, powerful masculinity, and an uncontainable free spirit.

"Woman, you take my breath away," Nikolai said, his voice deep and lulling in the aftermath of their loving. His eyes were closed with a peaceful look gracing his strong features.

She kissed his square jaw. "The feeling is mutual," she murmured.

God, he made her happy. So happy she didn't know it was possible to be this happy. She wanted to stay right here and feel this way forever. To let him wrap his arms around her and hold her close and keep her safe from all the unexpected pain and anguish that life could bring. Because she knew he would. He was that kind of man.

She sighed in a mix of longing and contentment. "You must come and visit me in the States. Often." The words were out before she realized she was wishing aloud.

"Sure," he responded lazily, then made a sound in his throat. "If you want me to be arrested."

"Don't even say that!" The protest pierced her heart. "By which side?"

"Take your pick," he returned evenly. "Neither side is going to believe we just want to spend time together. Preferably in bed," he added with a wicked smile.

She gave him a playful smack. "Hey!"

He pursed his curved lips. "Okay. I'd like to see the cherry trees, too. And the new statue of Alexander Pushkin at GWU."

Both tributes to peace between countries. How much proof did she need that he was a good man whose involvement in this spy mess was beyond his control?

"I'll take you to see them," she said, resolutely ignoring the shade of indulgence she detected in his tone. Was his skepticism because he didn't really believe it would happen? Or because he didn't really want it to . . . ?

"I'd like to meet your family, too," he said thoughtfully. "Tell me about them."

She drew in a deep breath and let it out. Not exactly the direction she'd wanted this conversation to go in.

"I mean," he clarified, seeming to feel her reluctance, "you told me what happened with your father, but what about your mother? Do you have sisters, brothers?"

Okay, that she could deal with. She laid her cheek back down on his chest. "No brothers or sisters. Just my mom. And a bunch of aunts and uncles and cousins, but they all live in other states now, so I don't see them much. Mom lives in Maryland, pretty close to D.C."

"So you see her often?" He sounded wistful, and she remembered how much he missed his own mother.

"Not as often as I should," she confessed, feeling vaguely guilty for having a mother alive and well, and not making more of an effort to have a real relationship with her. But it was problematical. . . .

He was silent for several moments, then said, "It must have been very hard on you to lose your father."

She felt her insides still, waiting for him to say something about her mother, too. How devastated she must have been, how brave she was, how difficult it must have been to work two jobs and raise a child on her own. All the things everyone always said because over the years her mother had nearly fallen apart at the seams emotionally, while Julie had held it together like a trouper, excelled in school, and never once needed the help of a shrink to make it through the dark nights.

But he didn't. Instead he said, "They all assumed you were fine, didn't they." More of a statement than a question.

"I *was* fine," she stated automatically.

But suddenly her eyes began to sting. From the pain of the memory, yes . . . but also because from that simple statement she realized at long last she'd found someone who possibly understood what she'd gone through. He saw straight through the façade of strength and well-being to the isolation and anguish she'd kept buried for so many years.

He pressed a kiss to the top of her head and tightened his arms around her. The silence stretched, but comfortably, bringing them somehow closer in unspoken empathy. Then he murmured, "I wish we'd at least been pen pals. We could have compared notes on how fine we both were."

She smiled through her misty eyes. "Except you're a Russian. I would have blamed you for everything that happened to my father. Damn pinko Ruskie."

"Yeah," he said in a matching rueful tone, "and you're American. *My* father would have torn up your letters and burned them before letting you contaminate his only son. Corrupting imperialist Yank."

They both chuckled, though she could hear the truth lurking under the humor on both sides. Sins of the fathers . . .

She sighed. "God. What are we going to do, Nikolai?"

"About what?" he asked, though they both knew exactly what she meant. And it wasn't about solving the legacy of their pasts.

Or maybe it was.

A perverse stubbornness made her say, "About us. You and me."

Again he was mute for several minutes. "Pen pals?" he suggested at length.

"Mmm," she hummed, a dull spiral of disappointment

plowing a swath through her chest. Not that she had a better answer to her own question. She had just hoped . . .

Well. Never mind what she'd hoped. It was useless to think about.

"Guess you'll have to set up that Facebook page after all," she murmured. Then frowned. "But no other women friends. Only me."

This time he didn't chuckle. "That's a promise," he said, his voice quiet and gravel deep.

As they lay there, around them the sounds of the submarine subtly changed, and the ever-present up-and-down heave and roll shifted speed.

Nikolai's body tensed to listen. He said, "The boat's slowing."

"Why?" she asked.

"We must be approaching the date line." He sat up and urged her up as well. He ran a hand through his hopelessly mussed-up hair, then kissed her. "We better get ourselves dressed and out of this stateroom before *Kvartirmyeister* Kresney comes to fetch us again."

She let out a moan. "Already?"

He tapped the end of her nose. "Don't want to be late for the crossing."

He had to remind her.

She was *so* not ready for this.

Nevertheless, they got dressed, left their private cocoon, and reluctantly parted with a lingering kiss at the bottom of the ladder. Nikolai would be heading up to the central post and she over to the mess hall, where the pollywogs were supposed to gather for the impending ceremony.

"Thank you, Liesha," Nikolai said, gently cradling her face in his large hand as he gave her one last kiss. "That was a wonderful way to spend the afternoon."

She sighed in complete agreement. "The pleasure was all mine, *Kapitan*."

His lips curved up. "To be continued," he murmured.

"Yes," she said, doing her best to keep the sadness from her smile as he disappeared up the ladder. How she wished it would never end!

She stood there for several minutes before going up. Not

because she thought they'd be fooling anyone by separating their arrivals, but because she needed to get herself into the right frame of mind to face all those people and the festivities. The time alone with Nikolai had been so intense, so intimate, so personal, she had to take a giant mental step back and try to resurrect that cheerfully objective, professional persona everyone expected to see from her.

She was finding it more and more difficult on this journey to maintain the fiction of her façade, as well as the fiction of her own life, in the face of what she was learning about herself and the world around her.

Suddenly she felt a tingle between her shoulder blades.

Someone was watching her.

She turned around and found Trent Griff standing in the passageway regarding her. His expression was not without sympathy. "Think maybe you're getting a bit out of your depth there?" he questioned.

"Ya think?" She sighed and crossed her arms, feeling exposed at her transparency and uncomfortable because she'd left her laptop in the stateroom, so she had nothing to do with her hands, and nowhere to hide. Despite the shorts she'd put on, she felt naked more because she was without her habitual shield than from her bare legs.

"For what it's worth, looks like he is, too," Griff said, tipping his chin in the direction of the ladder.

"And loads of good that'll do either of us," she returned bleakly.

"The Cold War *is* over," Griff observed philosophically, strolling closer. "You could pack up and move to Russia. Become a foreign correspondent."

If only he knew.

"Yeah," she said, forcing a wry laugh. "Because Petropavlovsk-Kamchatskiya is such a fascinating hotbed of international news."

Though admittedly, it *was* a hotbed of international intrigue. No doubt CIA already had a case officer or two working the Kamchatka Peninsula and wouldn't mind another. The problem being, of course, that the FSB knew exactly who she was and would never let her live within a thousand miles of the place. Even if she and Nikolai were to marry—which, good Lord, was not even on the radar—access to the strategic military region was highly restricted. With her background, even marriage to a Russian citizen wouldn't gain her a residency permit there.

"Well," Griff said with a shrug, leaning his butt against the ladder, "he could move to the States, then. You've got tons of subs over there he could sign on to drive, yeah?"

She smiled sardonically. "Uh-huh. I'm sure the U.S. Navy would be thrilled to have a Russian national apply to command one of their nuclear submarines." Her lips twisted. "I can see their faces now."

"I'm just saying," Griff said with a chortle. "This isn't the fifties. Shouldn't be too hard to be together, if that's what you really want."

She swallowed a sigh. "Yeah," she said.

"Unless that's *not* what you really want." He peered questioningly at her from under a fringe of shaggy, sun-streaked hair.

The million-dollar question.

"Jeez, Griff. How could I possibly know that? I only met the guy a few days ago."

He grinned. "Ever hear of love at first sight?"

"Are you *trying* to mess with my head?" she asked with a groan. If it weren't so close to the mark it would be funny. As it was . . .

He winked. "Just playing devil's advocate, that's all."

Over their heads, the PA system boomed out something unintelligible. After a few seconds of static, someone came on and announced in heavily accented English, "Attention, please. All uncertified warm bodies seeking to enter realm of King Boreas, Supreme Ruler of Frozen North, please report to mess hall immediately."

"That would be you," Griff said, his voice betraying vast amusement.

"Not you?"

"Nah. I've been over the Arctic Circle a half dozen times. And I practically live on the date line."

"Lucky you."

When she got to the mess, several men from the Russian crew, including *Starpom* Varnas and the man she recognized as *Lyeïtenant* Danya Petrov, the radio guy, were in the process of being herded into an untidy line along the forward bulk-head. They were all dressed in swim trunks and nothing else, but because of the diesel engines and the warm day above, the air in the sub was nice and toasty. Most of the men looked keyed up and animated, if not downright excited.

Julie glanced around, but didn't see Nikolai anywhere. She was almost relieved. She didn't relish him seeing her being humiliated, which she had a feeling was about to happen.

"Ah! Miz Severin," called the man in charge. Despite his wearing the most outrageous costume she'd seen since last Halloween, she recognized *Kvartirmyeister* Misha Kresney.

Misha wore a grass skirt and several leis around his neck . . . all made from tacky strings of neon green plastic seaweed and decorated with a veritable school of colorful plastic fish that had been randomly fastened to the strands. In his hand he carried a golden and bejeweled scroll, and on his head he wore what looked suspiciously like a Packers cheese-head, but it had been whittled along the edges and painted white to look like . . . an iceberg?

Okay, then.

"You come," Misha urged, waving the big scroll at her in a beckoning motion.

Fun, she told herself firmly. *This is meant to be fun.*

Steeling her swiftly failing nerves, she walked past a small group of spectators who'd gathered to watch. When she'd taken her place in line, Misha raised his gold-decorated scroll in the air for silence. Its cut-glass jewels sparkled in the flash of a handful of pocket-sized cameras. Great. Her embarrass-ment would be recorded for all posterity.

He made an announcement in Russian, which *Starpom* Varnas, standing next to her, quickly translated. "We go to stern trunk hatch," he said. "Just to follow others." He lifted a hand to indicate she should go before him, so she fell into line.

"Who is he supposed to be dressed as?" she asked Varnas, indicating Misha.

"Davy Jones. The sea devil."

She smiled. "Not a very devilish costume. I love the plastic fish."

Stefan Varnas chuckled. "Plastic not break. Small box to

store many costumes." He used his hands to indicate a size of about one foot by two feet.

"Wow, that is small." She glanced around. "There are other costumes?"

"We see up on deck. But more next week at Arctic crossing. Royal court of King Boreas and Queen Amphitrite and also color guard. Today not so many."

The line headed aft in a single file with Misha at the head calling loudly to one and all to join them on deck for the interrogation and feast. Most of the grinning crew members made humorous comments as they passed. She waved Stefan Varnas off when he offered to translate—she could imagine well enough. Several of the men whistled at her borrowed shorts, which were thankfully too large rather than too small, and ugly as hell. She sent the jokers a "give me a break" look and kept walking.

They reached the ladder, and Misha ushered the line of "warm bodies" topside, where most of the off-duty crew and the scientists were already waiting, packed onto the aft deck like sardines and crowded onto the sail high above it. The sun was dipping toward the horizon and there was a considerable chill in the air, but the wind was calm and *Ostrov* bobbed peacefully on the gentle waves, having cut the engines to allow all but a skeleton crew to enjoy the festivities on deck.

The deck itself had been decorated, festooned with dancing strings of blue and white fairy lights and paper streamers. It looked enchanting.

The delicious smell of barbecue scented the salt air and made Julie's stomach growl as Misha led the pollywogs through the crush, past the fairwater, past where a happily grinning Rufus Edwards stood tending the ribs at a smoking grill, and directed them to stand at the very front of the foredeck.

"Come, stand here," *Starpom* Varnas said, guiding her to the middle of the group. "Not to fall off."

"Thanks," Julie said gratefully.

It was getting easier for her to look out at the vast ocean surrounding them without feeling panic, especially since the daylight was fading and much of the sea was cloaked in orange and robin's egg blue. Nevertheless, she wished there was a bigger buffer of bodies between her and a watery grave. Not to mention the added body heat. In just shorts and a T-shirt she was getting cold. A couple of the men wearing only swimming trunks were starting to shiver.

Nikolai finally appeared, taking up a casual stance at the front wall of the fairwater. His eyes met hers and he smiled warmly. From the knowing looks being cast at them both from the crowd, she was pretty sure that being the captain's lover would prove to be the biggest source of torment for her in the coming ordeal.

She was glad he was there to support her and hoped he didn't leave her twisting in the wind.

"Now hear this!" Misha announced with a dramatic flair. "We have just crossed international date line! Welcome to yesterday!"

There was a big cheer.

"If there is anything you regret, or anything you forget to do today— er, tomorrow, you now have a chance to do it all over again!"

The cheer was even bigger.

She sought Nikolai's eyes. There wasn't a damn thing she regretted. And she couldn't wait to do it all again, exactly the same way. The look he returned said he agreed completely.

Suddenly someone bumped her and she felt herself falling backward. She yelped, and instantly several pairs of hands caught her arms, hauling her upright. Her pulse went into outer space as she steadied herself.

Nikolai had already taken two steps toward her, but she shook her head at him as she murmured her thanks to the men around her who had righted her. Two of them stepped behind her as a fence so she couldn't fall again. *Thank goodness.* Her legs felt like jelly. But his crew had closed in around her and she didn't want to draw any more attention to herself.

"Are you okay?" he mouthed across the deck, concern coloring his expression. He looked like he was ready to shut down the ceremony.

She nodded, sending him a wobbly smile of reassurance. Her heart was still speeding. But there was no need for alarm. She was sure it had been an accident.

At least she was pretty sure it had. . . .

The distinctive sound of a boatswain's pipe suddenly split

the air, the old-school announcement of a dignitary arriving on board.

"Here we go," muttered *Starpom* Varnas, breaking into her silent communication with Nikolai.

"Attention on deck!" Misha cried in his heraldic Davy Jones voice. "Hail to the great and beneficent Lord Ægir, Ruler of the Northern Seas, and his consort, the magnificent and the fearsome Lady Ran!"

"I thought you said King Boreas and Queen Amphitrite," Julie whispered to Varnas, bringing her attention back to the ceremony.

"Not today. They come next week."

"Oh, right."

His lordship, a.k.a. *Praporshchik* Selnikov, rose from the hatch and walked with exaggerated dignity onto the deck, followed, to Julie's surprise, by Dr. Lautenen playing his consort. The spectators greeted the costumed duo with hoots and raucous applause.

Lord Ægir was clad in a brown togalike outfit and leather-laced sandals that might have been borrowed from the set of *Spartacus*. Well. Except for the accessories—a shiny metallic blue cape and a plastic Viking helmet complete with horns. Dr. Lautenen looked very fetching draped in more elegant Greek fashion, her torso knotted in a white bedsheet on which elaborate wave designs had been drawn in multihued blue felt pen. She also wore a Viking helmet, this one adorned with no horns but long plaited braids the color of ripe carrots.

Julie laughed and clapped enthusiastically along with the rest of the crowd. They made quite the eye-catching couple.

"Viking helmets?" she asked Varas.

The *starpom* grinned. "Nordic gods. Frightening, *da*?"

It was. But not in the scary way. She laughed.

The aristocratic pair advanced to stand regally before the line of chilly pollywogs and peered down their noses at them one by one. Julie swallowed her laughter. She wasn't sure if being the only woman, the only non-Russian-speaker, and the only non-crew-member was going to be an advantage or a disadvantage in this mock interrogation. But she feared she was about to find out.

After a thorough visual examination, Lord Ægir turned and spoke to the audience in booming Russian, followed immediately by Dr. Lautenen's equally booming translation, a pattern that continued throughout the proceedings, so everyone present understood everything that was said.

"We have never before seen such a sorry, pathetic group of warm bodies attempting to sneak unnoticed into the Frozen Realm of the great King Boreas! Where is the commanding officer of this offending vessel?" they demanded.

Oh, dear.

Nikolai did not look the least perturbed at being singled out. Perhaps it was part of the usual drill.

He stepped forward and greeted the Lord and Lady of the North with a surprisingly courtly bow. A few of the men snickered, but were soundly hushed by their neighbors.

"Your Grace, my lady," Nikolai said with more humility than Julie had ever heard in his speech before. He explained first in Russian, then in English, "Our valiant and illustrious vessel, *Ostrov*"—at this there were more snickers—"has traversed Your Lordship's seas many times before, always with humbleness and respect. We wouldn't dream of crossing into your realm now with unworthy subjects on board. To that end I have personally ordered all warm bodies to stand before you today, well in advance of our Arctic crossing, so Your Lordship might judge for yourself if they are cold-blooded enough to become proper Bluenoses." He gave another bow with a flourish and stepped back again.

Lord Ægir harrumphed, then turned to Misha. "Davy Jones! The list of names and charges against them, please!"

The *kvartirmyeister* bowed low, one hand flourishing his cheesehead, and handed over his glittering scroll. Lord Ægir made a big show of unrolling it, then scowled as he read down the list. "These are grave infractions indeed. I must interrogate you all very carefully today"—he glared at the small group of pollywogs—"and decide suitable ways for King Boreas to test your true cold-bloodedness when you reach the Frozen North."

Speaking of frozen. Julie shifted nervously and rubbed her arms. She was starting to get cold. The temperature on deck was dropping fast.

"*Starpom* Stefan Mikhailovich Varnas!" Ægir called out his first victim. "Front and center!"

Julie felt a modicum of relief that he hadn't chosen her first. Of course, that just prolonged the agony.

Starpom Varnas grimaced unhappily. Reluctantly he stepped forward and mumbled something, making a stab at a bow but only succeeding at appearing stiff and awkward.

Ægir looked disgusted. "It says here you've been sending unauthorized e-mails from the radio room!" he accused. Varnas blanched like he'd been caught sending state secrets. "To a *woman!*" Ægir said this last as if that were the worst offense of all.

"N-no, s-sir," Varnas actually stammered. "I would never—"

"Lies! Master-at-Arms!" Lord Ægir barked out.

From out of nowhere a bucket of water was thrown at the XO. It splashed onto his face and bare chest, spraying streams of cold, salty seawater onto the other pollywogs as well. Julie yelped as Varnas cried out in shocked protest.

"Quiet!" Lord Ægir cut him off and made much of writing down notes on the scroll with an oversized feather pen. He looked up. "Now, *Starpom* Varnas, I ask you again, did you . . ."

For five more minutes the XO's interrogation continued, with the most ridiculous accusations imaginable. Lord Ægir finished by asking, "Are you claustrophobic, Stefan Mikhailovich?"

"No, er, yes, sir!" the *starpom* answered warily, dripping with seawater and shaking noticeably from the cold.

Ægir's forehead creased as he wrote that down. "Too bad," he muttered. "Very well, you may step back, comrade *starpom*."

Then he went on to the next initiate. And the next. And the next. Until they were all soaking wet and shivering, and only Julie was left.

Lord Ægir's piercing blue eyes drilled into hers in warning. She felt her pulse leap to her throat. Slowly he raised his hand and pointed a menacing finger straight at her.

"You!" he boomed, and even though she'd known it was coming, she jumped. "It is time this lowly female steps forward to face the inquisition of the Great God of the North Sea!"

She swallowed convulsively. *God help her. Here goes nothing.*

20

¬¬¬¬¬¬¬¬/////////

Nikolai sent up a silent prayer on Julie's behalf. He had a hunch this wouldn't go easily for her. Yasha had laid it on thick with every one of the pollywog crew, and she did not seem to be earning any dispensation from the ordeal. But then again, that's what everyone expected. Maximum absurdity, embarrassment, and humiliation mixed with a small dose of reality was the order of the day for this kind of ceremony. That, and turning the supposedly warm-blooded pollywogs to human icicles.

To her credit, Julie stepped gamely out of the line, flashing Nikolai only the briefest of beseeching glances. Not that he could—or would—do anything to help her. Unlike her fear of the ocean, to retain the respect she had earned, and deserved, from everyone so far on the patrol, she must face this trial on her own.

Totally into his role as Lord Ægir, Yasha stuck his face close to Julie's, shouting, "*Ostrov* is being sabotaged! By *you!*"

What the *hell* . . . ?

Snapping to attention, Nikolai barely restrained himself from interfering. *This was going too far.* He and Yasha had agreed to keep the sabotage happening on the boat strictly under wraps!

Julie went pale. "N-no!" she stammered immediately. "Why would I—"

"Silence!" Yasha shouted as a bucket of icy water hit Julie square in the chest. Nikolai winced. He'd reached the conclusion that the only way to avoid the worst of the buckets was to answer yes to anything and everything that was asked, regardless of its truthfulness.

Julie gasped, holding out her T-shirt as the water streamed off her. Thank God the shirt was black, not white. Even so, Nikolai could clearly see her nipples peak from the cold. He stifled a growl as the crew noticed, too.

Yasha paced back and forth in front of her. "So you *deny* attempting to seduce the captain of this vessel?"

At that, the crowd went so quiet you could hear the waves lap along the length of *Ostrov*'s hull. Everyone leaned in to hear her answer.

Nikolai clenched his teeth. Really? Yasha was really going there? He shouldn't be surprised. Their affair was naturally a topic of avid interest. He'd just hoped for a little discretion on Yasha's part.

Julie blinked, obviously taken aback by the rude question. She'd expected to be teased, not accused. Droplets sparkled on her eyelashes. "*What?* No! I—"

Yasha loomed over her. "So you claim you *aren't* sharing the captain's stateroom?"

As pale as her face had been, it now went just as red. "Well, um . . ." She swallowed and rubbed the goose flesh on her wet arms. "Yes, technically, but—"

"Aha!" Yasha cried triumphantly. "So you *admit* to seducing him!"

She licked at a sparkling drop that trickled down her cheek onto her lips, making a quick face at the salt taste. She hesitated, then seemed to come to a decision. "Okay, yes," she said and lifted her chin. "I admit it. I seduced Captain Romanov." Her lips curved in a saucy smile. "And I'd do it again given half a chance."

The crowd erupted in rowdy hoots and catcalls.

Nikolai felt a spurt of relief and couldn't help grinning as the men around him punched his arm and slapped him on the back as they cheered. He had to admit, the woman had balls. *His*, it seemed.

Yasha was momentarily nonplussed at her unexpected turnaround. But he quickly recovered. "So! You're in love with the captain!" he exclaimed triumphantly.

Julie's mouth dropped open. Her eyes widened, then darted to Nikolai's. His heart stopped at what he saw in them.

Слава богу. *No.*

She swallowed, paused for a taut second, then blurted, "Yes!" her voice clear and high above a sudden burst of surprised chatter. She straightened and did her best to put on an amused face. "As a matter of fact, I *do* love him."

Nikolai froze, his heart stalling as again the crowd erupted in whoops and shouts, pleased with her wit and bravery under fire, and her flattery to their commanding officer. It was clear they assumed she was playing along for the drama of the game and didn't really mean it.

But he knew better. For that split second of stark vulnerability, in her eyes he'd seen the truth.

As incredible as it seemed, Julie Severin *had* fallen in love with him.

Ни хуя себе.

Fucking, fucking hell. What the *hell* was he supposed to do with *that*?

Stunned, Nikolai tuned out the conclusion of the interrogation and studiously avoided Julie's nervous gaze as the pollywogs were dismissed and led back to the aft hatch so they could go down and change out of their icy wet clothes.

He couldn't face her.

This was not good. Not good at all. She couldn't be in love with him. She *couldn't*! And he definitely couldn't be in love with her. It could not happen. *They* could not happen. Not in a million years. Devil take it, they weren't ordinary citizens with ordinary jobs! Neither of their governments would allow a real relationship between a spy and a high-ranking naval officer. Not unless one of them defected—or whatever they were calling a change of allegiance these days.

And *that* was about as likely with either of them as seeing wild toucans in the Arctic.

Julie loved her country. And she hated his. She'd made her feelings about Russia crystal clear. No way would she move to the place she felt was responsible for her father's death. Not even to be with Nikolai.

He rubbed his hands across his eyes. Hell, he loved his country, too. True, he was going through a rough patch with those in power at the moment. And yes, okay, he'd thoroughly enjoyed the time he'd spent attending high school in the suburbs of Washington, D.C., and theoretically he wouldn't mind living there. But that didn't mean he wanted to chuck his life and everything he knew and had worked so hard for in order to . . . what? Sweep floors? Flip burgers? For surely the Americans would never allow him to do the job he loved and had trained for his entire life.

No. The whole thing was utterly impossible. Julie had to see that. She must understand their situation was irresolvable.

Or maybe he'd been wrong just now, and he'd only imagined that plaintive, almost guilty look in her eyes. . . . He could only hope.

"Nikolai?"

He was jerked out of his chaotic thoughts by her uncertain greeting. He whipped around and saw she'd changed into coveralls again. *His* coveralls. Inwardly he wanted to cringe. *So* not good.

"Oh. Hi," he said, and even he could hear the distance layering his voice as coolly as a new-fallen snow in the wilderness of their relationship.

Her face fell almost imperceptibly. Almost. "Hi," she returned, then glanced around. Nearly everyone on the forward deck was watching them with keen curiosity. She shifted uneasily. "Guess I, um, went too far. Sorry." She looked back at him earnestly. "That thing about—"

She cleared her throat. "Anyway . . . it was just for show. To go along with the game. You get that, right?"

He pretended to believe her. "Sure," he said and pasted a wry smile on his face. "It certainly did the trick. You even managed to shock Yasha. Not an easy feat."

"Yeah, well. Sorry I made you squirm."

"Are you kidding?" he said. "A beautiful woman announcing she's in love with me? What's to squirm about?"

But they both knew.

"Anyway," she said, looking away. "I'm starving. Think I'll get some of those ribs before they're all gone."

He nodded. "I'll join you in a minute."

"Okay."

But he could tell she didn't believe him.

With good reason.

Love?

"Squirm" didn't even come close.

If he had half a brain, he'd go down that ladder to the central post and stay there for the entire duration of the patrol. Avoid her completely.

Love?

Still, he felt like a complete bastard for leaving her all alone and adrift in the waters of emotional uncertainty like a boat without a paddle. Like when she'd asked him earlier, in bed, what they should do about their relationship, and he'd made that inane remark about being pen pals. God, he was such an unfeeling ass.

But he didn't know what else to do. This was *not* going to end well.

If nothing else he was a realist. And as much as he might wish things were different, as angry as it made him deep inside, they both had to accept reality. At the end of this expedition, they'd be forced to part, and would probably never see each other again.

The thought razored through him, leaving a stinging distress in its wake. It was as if he was stuck in some depressing classic Russian novel, rushing headlong toward a fated tragic ending everyone could see except the two main characters.

Это просто пиздец.

Now was not the time for this. This steel picnic was supposed to be a celebration. The passengers and crew expected a jovial captain, proud of his romantic conquest and ready to jump into the festivities with both feet.

So, giving himself a firm mental kick, he got himself together, put on a pleasant face, and threaded through the crowd to find Julie. At least he could keep up appearances and not be a jerk.

His pulse went up when he spotted her standing with Clint Walker, pressed so close together they were practically in each other's pockets. The two were talking as they ate from paper plates filled with the barbecued ribs, potato salad, and roasted corn on the cob prepared by Chief Edwards. Between their feet on the deck sat two foaming mugs of beer.

Nikolai frowned and halted before he reached them, stifling the immediate urge to wedge himself between their bodies and put a halt to the conversation. He didn't like her talking to Walker. Hell, he didn't like Walker. He felt threatened by the man. Somehow the tight-lipped UUV pilot knew about Nikolai's secrets. Obviously Walker had secrets, too. Big ones. And he didn't even try to hide that fact. Nikolai didn't appreciate the other man inveigling himself into Julie's business. Or worse, her personal life.

Not that Nikolai had anything to say about that. Not after what he'd just done to her.

He ground his jaw. Чертов ад. *Fuck it.*

He stalked through the crowd and went up to her, bending to give her a kiss on the temple while he cast a challenging glare at Walker over her head.

"How are the ribs?" he asked.

She looked up, startled. "Um. Good." She darted a quick look between them. "You should get some before they're gone."

"Yep." He took a rib from her plate and ripped the meat from it with his teeth, chewed, and swallowed. He lifted the napkin from her fingers, ignoring her put-upon expression. "What are you two talking about?"

Walker tilted his head, a half smile curving the corner of his lip. "I was just offering Julie the use of my satellite phone. I managed to fix mine this afternoon." Nikolai couldn't miss the challenging glint in Walker's eye.

He mirrored it right back. "That was fast. Of course we only have your word that it was ever damaged."

"And your chief engineer's. I borrowed his tools."

Walker patted a leather case fastened to his belt next to the orange IDA pouch. It matched the woven leather thong around his wrist. "From now on, I'm keeping it with me at all times."

"Probably smart," Nikolai said grudgingly.

"I'm doing the same when I get mine back," Julie mumbled around a bite of corn. "I haven't called my boss since yesterday. He's probably having a cow."

"You can always use the boat's SATCOM," Nikolai offered.

Julie gave him a "you must be crazy" look. "Yeah. Your Naval Command would love that."

They probably would. The FSB would, anyway.

"In the meantime, you're welcome to borrow mine. Just say the word," Walker told her.

Of course, God only knew who'd be listening in on Walker's phone, either. His loyalties had yet to be determined.

"Thanks," she said. "Maybe later tonight, when it thins out up here?"

"Sure," Walker said. "And there's always tomorrow when we're ashore on Attu. We'll have all day together." He smiled tauntingly over her head at Nikolai.

Мудак. "Won't you have work to do?" Nikolai asked him through clenched teeth. He'd like to take that stupid leather bracelet and strangle him with it.

"Not much to do on the island without the UUVs. I'd planned to take a hike, look around at the scenery and the old Coast Guard station. I was hoping Julie would join me."

"Sure, I'd love to," she said, ignoring Nikolai's glare.

"Is that wise?" he asked pointedly. The man could well be the saboteur. The same one who'd disabled her IDA. What havoc could he wreak alone with her on an island?

"Why not? It'll be great to stretch my legs after being cooped up on this sardine can for three days."

Reminding himself angrily he had no right to object, Nikolai glanced longingly at the beer keg that was flowing freely at the food table. Damn, he could really use a brew. But he never touched alcohol on patrol, not even on port calls.

Abruptly he turned. Hell, if she wasn't worried about Walker, he shouldn't be, either. He couldn't deal with this charade any longer. There was no solution. No winning. And no protecting someone who didn't want protecting.

He tossed the rib bone in a nearby trash bin and wiped his fingers on the napkin. "I need to get back to work," he said, tossing that, too. "Enjoy the party." Then he strode off, slipping through the rowdy crowd, heading for the stern hatch.

Leaving Julie to Walker.

And telling himself that Julie Severin could take care of herself. That little voice of concern in the back of his mind did not matter.

Nor did it matter that his heart was tearing in two.

21

\\\\\\\\//////

It was like an Arctic front had suddenly swept across the deck; that was the kind of chill Julie felt pouring off Nikolai as he strode away. *Brrr.*

She didn't know what he had been more upset by, her unfortunate declaration of love or her tête-à-tête and outing tomorrow with Clint Walker.

Either way, Nikolai had shut down all systems between them.

She sighed. So much for the cherry trees in D.C.

She noticed Walker regarding her. "Sure you wouldn't like to make that phone call now?" he asked neutrally.

She glanced down at her paper plate. Luckily it was nearly empty. Her appetite had vanished. "How's the battery on it?" she asked.

"Just charged this afternoon."

"In that case, yeah," she said. "I probably should." She blew out a misty breath and muttered under it, "Before I freeze solid."

She still hadn't reported the Chinese sub incident to Thurman. She also had three articles to file and about a zillion photographs to send him. And there was something else she remembered when she thought about their last phone call. Even though she couldn't for the life of her think how it could be relevant—especially now—she was still curious to know what he had been about to tell her about Nikolai's mother.

Clint took her plate and pitched it along with his own, then handed her the sat phone and picked up their untouched beers. He jerked his chin toward the front of the deck. "Why don't we move forward a bit? There are fewer people up there to listen in on your conversation."

"Not that I have anything to hide," she said evenly. All the coded stuff was on her own phone's micro storage card, which she had started carrying in her pocket after misplacing it for half the day yesterday. Besides, she'd been ordered not to transmit anything potentially sensitive over anyone else's unsecure phone line. So it would just be a carefully worded conversation to see if Thurman had any updates or new intel for her.

Walker nodded. "Don't forget to keep your cover solid," he reminded her needlessly. "God knows, our Chinese shadow is undoubtedly listening in on every transmission originating from anywhere near us."

She straightened and glanced in surprise past the strings of sparkling party lights lining the deck, out to the glittering blueberry meringue of the ocean. "But I thought you and Nikolai chased off the 093 this morning."

His eyes scanned the dimly lit horizon. "Yeah, and that probably lasted for about five minutes. They're out there all right. Count on it."

She frowned. "Wouldn't Gavrikov pick up a lurking submarine on sonar?"

Walker shook his head. "Not if they're far enough out. The sonar equipment on *Ostrov* is pretty dated. And we've pulled in the towed array."

"Why?" She knew that without the sensitive sonar receptors normally towed behind the sub in a mile-long tail, *Ostrov*'s ability to "see" into the impenetrable waters around them was severely limited.

"Because we're stopped," he answered. "And we'll be transiting with a short array from here on out because we're passing over the Emperor Trough and Seamount Chain into the Bering Sea. The geography for the next couple of days will be unpredictable, full of shallows and mounts and canyons. A lot of it hasn't even been mapped yet. Wouldn't want to have our leash yanked by getting it caught on something."

She peered nervously at the surrounding dark void of water and stifled a shiver. "No. I guess not. Still, it's kind of creepy not knowing what's out there."

He grinned. "Nah. That's what makes it fun."

God. These navy men. "If you say so."

They moved forward and found an open spot at the very tip of the deck. At Walker's urging, she clipped her safety harness to the toe-rail, then punched the CIA contact number for James Thurman into the sat phone's keypad.

While she waited to acquire a signal and for the call to go through, Walker handed her the plastic mug of beer she'd completely forgotten about. He clicked it with his. "Happy Midsummer's Eve."

She knew Nikolai didn't like or trust Walker, but the man was growing on her. Despite the obvious reasons she shouldn't, she had also started to trust him. A little, anyway. "Thanks. You, too," she replied and clicked his mug back. They both drank a few sips.

"So. Ever read *Miss Julie,* the Strindberg play?" he asked with a straight face.

She gave him a dry look. "Ha-ha. You are so very funny."

Just then James Thurman answered. "Still haven't gotten your own phone fixed?" his tinny voice asked, echoing from the satellite bounce in a two-second delay. "What phone are you using this time? I was worried about you when we got cut off yesterday."

"I'm fine," she said, refocusing. "So far, anyway. This phone belongs to Clint Walker. The ex-navy guy. I'm pretty sure he's some kind of military spook. He knows too much not to be."

Walker's brows rose at that as he took another swallow of his beer. But he didn't comment. Nor did Thurman.

"Nice of him to let you borrow his phone," her boss said.

"Yeah. There's a sudden acute shortage of sat phones on board. Six of them were out of commission as of this morning."

Thurman whistled. "Mice?" he asked, but his tone conveyed he understood what she was saying.

"A rat, I think. A big one. I think it's time to set a trap."

"Careful," he warned. "Rats are dangerous when cornered." A sudden burst of laughter from some of the crew standing nearby caused him to ask incredulously, "What on earth is going on out there? Some kind of party?"

"Line-crossing ceremony," she drawled.

"Ah." Then, "Wait. You're at the Arctic Circle already? How is that possible?" He sounded genuinely surprised, and she could hear the rustle of papers on his desk.

"No," she said. "International date line. Sort of a preparty for the real thing that's happening in a few days. By the way, thanks for the warning. I am *so* looking forward to being turned into a human icicle again."

Thurman chortled. "Uh-oh. Guess I forgot about that quaint naval tradition."

"Accidentally, I'm sure. Anyway. I have three more articles and pictures for the paper, but the SD card doesn't fit into this phone. You'll have to wait till next time to get them."

His voice perked up. "So you found it?"

Oops. "Sorry, no. I meant my own . . . the one for my phone."

"I see." Disappointment rang clearly through the receiver. "Please tell me you've at least figured out the, uh, crossword clue we talked about."

She thought about the mysterious "crown" clue and felt more frustrated than ever. She'd had no headway at all deciphering its meaning. "I think it must be a bad translation or something. No one has any idea what I'm talking about when I ask."

"Well, keep at it. And get your damn phone fixed ASAP," he ordered. "I need those articles and photos. They are stirring up some solid environmental interest on this end. What else have you got for me?"

"The captain thinks *Ostrov* is being followed," she said bluntly, not wanting to risk the phone cutting off again before she told him.

She could almost hear Thurman sit up. "By . . . ?"

"A PRC Shang-class 093, according to both sonar operators on board. Which is very strange, since the Chinese deny it. According to Russian Naval Command, the Chinese government insists their two Shangs are in the Atlantic."

"But you disagree?"

"The captain believes the sonar. And so does Walker."

There was a short pause. "You're sure about this?"

"One hundred percent. Check with our China correspondent. I assume he has a source that can confirm." By that she meant her section chief on CIA's China desk.

"I will. Should I be worried about your safety?" Thurman asked, concern coloring his voice.

It was her turn to hesitate. "I don't think so. But I'd appreciate a little extra coverage." Hopefully he could arrange some backup. A navy destroyer or a boomer to scare off the bad guys, maybe. Hell, even an American fishing boat tagging along their route would make her feel less alone out here. But his next words dashed any hope.

"Unfortunately that would mean getting the military involved. You know how they feel about us," he said, "even when we're helping them on important stuff. And I doubt shadowing this kind of scientific expedition would be a high priority for them."

Which was spook code for no way in hell would the U.S. Navy brass ever authorize aid for a CIA op, even if they would ultimately benefit from the resulting intel.

"The Russian Naval Command is pretty much ignoring us, too," she acknowledged with a sigh. "According to Captain Romanov, daily weather reports are about the extent of their support. They're in total denial about this Chinese sub following us."

"I'm shocked," Thurman muttered. "Speaking of Romanov, how are things going otherwise with the captain?"

She turned away from Walker and the merrymakers on deck and faced toward the front of the submarine. On the far-off horizon, the glowing sliver of the midnight sun rested on the sea like a blob of liquid quicksilver on an indigo field. She cleared her throat. "It's all good. Listen, before we were cut off yesterday, you were going to tell me something about his mother?"

"Oh. Right. Hell of a story." He paused. "Turns out she was American."

Julie blinked. Stunned. Wait. "*What?* No. That's not possible."

"It is possible, and she was," Thurman said without a shred of doubt in his voice. "From central New York."

"But . . . how? When? She would have had to be . . ." Julie's words skittered momentarily to a halt. Then, "A defector? A communist?"

She could hear Thurman push out a breath. "Not exactly."

A pregnant silence descended as the implication of that "not exactly" hit Julie square in the chest. She huddled the phone close against her body and whispered so Walker couldn't hear, "She was *sent* there? As a . . . a foreign correspondent?"

"Yes."

Yes. Just yes. No further explanation. And Julie couldn't ask because they couldn't talk freely.

She slammed her eyes shut. Oh, *shit.* Nikolai's mother was a *spy*? Sent to, what, infiltrate the local Russian political scene to which his father belonged?

Good Lord.

"No interviews about this," Thurman warned her firmly. "You cannot tell him."

Oh. Wow. Seriously? "Why not?"

"It's classified. Our source would be compromised."

Source? What was that supposed to mean? She was floundering in the doublespeak and yearned to just come out and ask him the hundred questions doing the Indy 500 through her mind.

"So you want me to lie to him?" she asked, again speaking so no one else could hear. Walker must be getting suspicious by now, but screw it. This was too important.

"Miss Severin," Thurman said with patient but firm formality, "may I remind you, prevarication is part of your job description . . . as a reporter?"

But no! She *couldn't* lie. Not to Nikolai! Not about this.

And that was when it hit her. She was starting to feel more loyalty to her Russian lover than to her job!

And *that* was after he'd made it clear he didn't have any more than superficial feelings for her. She didn't want to think about what might happen if he ever decided he had the kind of feelings she did.

As she mumbled her reluctant assent and ended the call, she

thought about Nikolai's mother. An American spy married to a
Soviet hard-line politician! Good Lord! How had she landed in
such a position? Had she just been following orders all along? Or
had she gone over to the Soviet Union on an unrelated assignment
and somehow fallen in love with Nikolai's father? Then given up
everything—her job, her family, her ties to her own country, her
very political beliefs—so she could be with him forever?

Lord. What a sacrifice!

Goose bumps broke out on Julie's arms. She took a long
drink from her beer.

Yes, thank goodness Nikolai *didn't* return her feelings. Because, really and truly, that was one choice she would never,
ever want to be forced to make.

That night, Nikolai didn't return to their stateroom.

Lying alone in bed Julie sighed, and for the dozenth time
counted the knotholes in the wood paneling above the bunk—
there were still fifteen—and told herself it was because he
was too busy pushing the sub at top speed toward the Aleutians to come and be with her. The Midsummer's Eve party
had lasted until midnight, when they'd toasted the midnight
sun and the beginning of the waning of the light, and then
Ostrov had gotten under way again and they'd officially
chugged off the date line . . . and back into yesterday.

Damn, she really wished that meant she had an actual do-
over of the day, and the previous version wiped out.

She thought about that appealing prospect. What would she
do if she could do yesterday—today—differently than last time?

Would she still sleep with Nikolai . . . again?

God, yes. She couldn't imagine missing those amazing
hours with him.

Would she still confide her secret mission to him?

Yes, she'd do that, too. She desperately needed his help to
find the elusive hidden SD card. Which was even more urgent now that they knew someone else on board was after it,
too.

Would she still stupidly, stupidly, unbe*liev*ably stupidly
blurt out that she loved him in front of the entire crew and
team of scientists?

Yeah, probably not that part. *That's* when everything had started to go downhill between her and Nikolai.

And what about that last fateful phone call to her boss? Would she still bring up the subject of Nikolai's mother to James Thurman? And learn the shocking secret even Nikolai didn't know? A secret that could easily crush him emotionally, calling into question the very foundation of everything he believed in?

Yeah. Probably not that, either. She wished like hell she'd never found out that particular secret.

After hours of internal debate, she finally fell asleep. But it was not a peaceful sleep. For the first time in many years, she had the drowning nightmare. But tonight the setting was not the usual one, the familiar lake back home in Maryland. This time she fell headlong into the vast, icy Bering Sea. She broke the surface freezing and screaming and floundering in the water among a flotilla of sea ice. In the murky depths below floated the lifeless figure of Misha, dressed in his Davy Jones outfit. Pale as death. As she looked on in horror, his cheesehead dislodged and slowly floated up toward her. She grabbed at it, missed, grabbed at it again, finally catching it on the third try, and grasped it to her chest to use as a terrifyingly inadequate life preserver.

Propelling herself to the surface, shivering and coughing, she looked up to see the distinctive black silhouette of a submarine, huge and menacing, gliding away. Leaving her alone and stranded . . . doomed to join Davy Jones in a watery death.

In desperation, she screamed for the submarine not to leave her there. And that was when she saw him.

Far up atop the looming sail a lone figure stood, impassively watching her drown.

Captain Nikolai Kirillovich Romanov.

Just a nightmare.

When Julie awoke, panting and sweating, the sheets in a tangle, she sat up and shivered for several awful minutes while she calmed herself down. Then, with a long exhale, she determinedly shook it off, rose, and gave herself a stern look in the mirror over his desk.

"Get a grip, girl."

It didn't take Freud to be able to interpret *that* dream. And it had nothing to do with hydrophobia.

Good freaking grief.

Well. At least she wouldn't have to spend an awkward day running into Nikolai around every corner. Today, all of the passengers were to disembark and spend the day on Attu Island while *Ostrov* went through some kind of deep submersion drill. Onshore, the scientists had a full agenda of sample and measurement taking to conduct, and she and Clint Walker had planned to do some exploring and picture taking around the abandoned Coast Guard LORAN station. She knew Nikolai didn't approve, but she had come to trust Walker—as much as she trusted anyone in this complicated mess—and felt safe enough accompanying him.

Dressing in her dry jeans and a fresh T-shirt Misha had scrounged for her last night after her other one had been drenched, Julie grabbed her laptop and jacket and made her way to the mess hall. The compartment was nearly empty, but she ran into Dr. Josh, who was just putting his breakfast dishes in the galley's dirty dish bin.

"Hey, girl, ready for shore leave?" he asked cheerfully.

"Am I ever," she said with a smile.

He waggled his eyebrows. "Won't you miss your handsome captain?"

"Oh, I think I'll live," she returned in a drawl.

Josh's eyes widened dramatically. "Uh-oh, do I detect trouble in paradise?"

"Seriously?" She glanced around at their surroundings. "You call *this* paradise?"

His lips twisted in amusement. "Point taken." He glanced around, too. "I'm definitely glad I won't be on board when they submerge this tub of rust under the surface." He shuddered dramatically. "I have these horrible visions of *Das Boot* when all those rivets started popping and the seawater started shooting into the German sub like exploding fire hydrants. Did you hear what happened on board last year?"

She held up her hand. "No. And I'd rather not, thankyouverymuch."

"Oh! Sorry. I forgot." He tried unsuccessfully to look contrite. "Maybe when we're back home on dry land."

She gave him a look.

"Or not." He checked his watch with a flair. "Oh, look what time it is. We're supposed to be assembled at the stern hatch in half an hour to disembark. They're bringing out kayaks to fetch us, or something bizarre like that."

Her jaw dropped. *"Kayaks?"*

"Kayaks, canoes, motorboats, whatev." He waved his hand as if the differences were inconsequential. "There's no harbor on Attu, so that's the only way for us to get onto the island. The institute has hired some Inuit villagers from a nearby island to ferry us."

Suddenly that drowning nightmare was looking a lot more realistic.

"Anyway," he said when she was too dumbstruck to respond, "guess I'd better go get my gear together. How about you?"

She tapped the notebook computer under her arm. "This is all I've got." Which reminded her of her lost suitcase. "Say, I don't suppose there are any stores on this island?" She held out a leg to showcase her ill-fitting jeans. "I could use some new clothes. And shoes." She turned her foot, modeling the clunky borrowed man's sneaker. "Not that these aren't *very* attractive."

Josh laughed. "Sorry. The island has been completely abandoned since the Coast Guard station closed down. But even if there was a village, I doubt you'd find any Jimmy Choos," he said ruefully.

She gave an exaggerated sigh. "Just as well. I've discovered that submarines and high heels don't really mix."

He chuckled again. "That, sweetie, is definitely a matter of opinion." He lifted his hand and waggled his fingers as he headed for the ladder down to the main berthing compartment, where he was quartered. "See you in a few."

"Yep."

She grabbed a coffee mug, filled it, and sat down at one of the tables, debating with herself whether or not to go look for Nikolai. He was probably busy steering the boat to their drop-off spot in Massacre Bay. Griff had told her the waters around these western Aleutian islands were notorious for shallow reefs and swiftly changeable currents.

Right. That was the real reason she was arguing with herself.

Coward, she chided herself.

The truth was, she was too scared to see him. Too chicken-shit to confront him with how she was feeling. Too afraid her new secret about his mother might slip out of her mouth before she could stop it.

Too terrified, now she'd told him what her mission was all about, that he no longer had any interest in her personally. That he had played her like James Bond, and she'd fallen for him like a naïve schoolgirl.

That he'd never really wanted her . . . for her.

The thought of that made her literally sick to her stomach. *Damn.*

She really should just go and ask him outright. Gauge his reaction. She may be naïve, but she wanted to believe he'd tell her the truth if confronted. After all, why continue to lie? He'd already gotten what he wanted. There was no reason to keep up the ruse, if that was what it was.

Was *that* what her nightmare had been all about?

A warning? About Nikolai? Her subconscious warning her that he was bound to cast her aside to sink or swim on her own . . . either metaphorically or literally.

Except . . . in the dream she *hadn't* been on her own. Misha's cheesehead had saved her. Of all the bizarre things. What could *that* mean? To be saved by a crown of cheese, cut to look like an iceberg?

Suddenly it hit her. Oh, my God.

Crown!

The one-word clue to completing her mission blazed through her mind like an avalanche.

Crown.

The part of the submarine no one had ever heard of. Because it *wasn't* part of a submarine. But part of a *costume.*

Could *that* be what the clue meant? Something as ridiculously simple as that?

She leapt up, spilling her coffee. It just might be!

Excitement surged through her. There was only one way to find out.

She had to find that cheesehead!

22

~~~~~\\\\\\\/////~~~~~

"Misha! Where's Misha? *Kvartirmyeister* Kresney?" Julie asked a rating who was helping the scientists bring their equipment up the trunk ladder in order to be transported to Attu Island.

The man answered a few words in Russian, gesturing up the ladder. Misha must be up on deck.

No time to lose. If she hurried, she could grab the cheese-head and take it with her off the submarine and examine it on dry land. If she found the SD card hidden within it, which she was more and more certain she would, she could hide it somewhere on the island and call her boss to come pick it up. And her.

Her mission would be over. And she could go home.

But she wouldn't think about *that* part.

Tucking her small computer uncomfortably into the back of her jeans waistband, she climbed up in a rush. Misha was on the opposite side of the deck, lowering a portable pilot's ladder over the side to reach the motorboats coming to fetch them. One was approaching the submarine, and another two could be seen just taking off from the island, tiny as ants from this distance. She managed to make her way across the deck to Misha without falling overboard. The ocean waves were bigger today, capped with white, making the sub pitch and heave. Big chunks of sea ice surrounded the hull, just like in her nightmare. But good grief. She'd gotten so used to the sound of the ice randomly banging against the metal hull that she hadn't even noticed it this morning.

Or maybe she'd had too many other things on her mind.

"Julie! Ready to go to shore?" Misha called to her above the sound of the wind and waves and grinding ice.

"Yes, almost. Just one thing. Misha, can I borrow your cheesehead?" she asked, coming up to him. Her hair was whipping across her face.

He blinked uncomprehendingly. "Cheese?"

"From last night." She made a triangle shape with her hands around her head.

A grin popped onto his wind-reddened face. "Oh! Cheese hat! To borrow? Why?" He looked charmingly puzzled.

She scrambled for a logical reason, but luckily she was spared explaining when a small motorboat pulled up by the hull and the pilot hailed them.

"Is boat to island. Forget hat. Come, ladies," Misha said, beckoning to her and the two women scientists who were standing next to the fairwater, waiting with their boxes of equipment.

"I'll get the next boat," Julie said quickly. "Where is your cheesehead kept?"

He frowned but didn't argue. "Is in compartment where many men have bunks. In cupboard behind first rack with all decorations. Just ask. Everyone on crew knows where is."

"Thanks, Misha. I'll be back in a flash."

"When you come, you see Borovsky. I go on duty below in few minutes."

She nodded and started back to the hatch, but saw at once that going down this way would be like swimming upstream. She decided to try the forward loading hatch instead. She knew that one, along with the hatch leading down from the bridge, was always open during nice weather while they were on the surface. It led down into the torpedo room.

Turning forward, for the first time she realized she'd been in such a hurry she'd forgotten to put on her safety harness before coming up on deck.

Damn!

But she had no choice. She had to risk traversing the length of the submarine without it. And quickly at that, if she wanted to get down and back before the last boat left for shore. Which she absolutely must.

Inching along in a crouch against the brisk wind, plastering herself against the side of the sail, she managed to get herself forward to the far hatch without incident, fall to her knees, and grab the rim.

Thank *God*.

She slid down the ladder by the rails—mentally applauding herself for pulling off the tricky maneuver for the first time ever—and practically dove through the watertight doors to reach the ladder that went down into the general berthing compartment.

When she got there, except for one sleeping man turned toward the bulkhead, the room was deserted.

Good. She didn't want to have to explain her actions to random crew members who happened by. She sprinted silently to the cupboard behind the first set of bunk beds as Misha had instructed, and quietly opened it up, careful not to wake the sleeping man. She peered inside the locker. It was tall and narrow like the one in Nikolai's stateroom but larger, and packed floor to ceiling with a conglomeration of lidded plastic storage bins and equipment, strings of lights, bags of extra clothes, and even a blue wetsuit.

She grabbed the top bin, hoping it was the box Misha meant since it would have been used last. She opened it up, wincing when it made a loud burp.

Yes! There were the grass skirt and plastic fish of his costume. Under them the white-painted cheesehead had been squashed into a corner of the bin. She lifted it out. She should just take it and go, and not chance being discovered rooting through things that didn't belong to her.

But no, she had to make sure the SD card was hidden somewhere in the iceberg-shaped block of foam. Hiding such a thin, small object wouldn't have been difficult. Just use a knife to cut a tiny slice into the foam and slip the microcard into it. Genius. It shouldn't be hard to find, either.

But it wasn't there.

Julie searched the entire cheesehead three times, top, bottom, and sides, each examination more frantic than the last. Still she found nothing. Not even an empty slot where it might have been.

"Shit," she muttered under her breath. "Shit, shit, shit. Where *is* it?"

Desperation seeped through her. She'd been so certain it would be here!

Okay. Maybe the crown thing was just a clue to finding the storage box itself. Maybe the SD card was hidden in something else. Another costume, maybe.

Using as much caution as possible, she dumped the contents of the bin gingerly onto the nearest bunk.

And that's when she found it. Or rather, them.

Two silver crowns.

Well. Two long, flat, obviously handmade cardboard cut-outs covered in tinfoil that could be joined at the ends to make a circlet, like those hamburger chain crowns for kids.

"Oh, my God, finally!" She wanted to shout it out at the top of her lungs.

But the sleeping man stirred just then.

Adrenaline surged through her veins. But he didn't awaken.

She returned her attention to the silver cardboard. This *must* be what the CIA asset had meant by the crown clue. *Please, let the SD card be hidden somewhere on one of these two crowns.* She paused for a few seconds, battling the urge to just rip the things apart to find it. But that would not be wise. Better not leave any suspicious evidence for the enemy saboteur to find.

So she laid the pieces flat on the bunk and pressed her fingers to the foil of one side, running them lightly down the length of it.

Nothing.

She flipped it over and searched the other side.

Again, she felt nothing. *Damn it!*

By now her pulse was going at a gallop. It *had* to be here! She laid the second crown onto the bunk. And carefully felt across the top.

There!

Her excitement leapt as a small, square lump resolved itself to her touch.

Yes!

With trembling fingers, she gently unfolded the tinfoil where it had been wrapped around the cardboard and eased a finger underneath. She extracted the lump.

It was the micro storage card.

She'd found it!

A huge weight lifted from her shoulders. She'd actually done it! She'd fulfilled her mission and . . .

Okay, not quite. She still had to get the SD card and its critical information safely back to Langley. Which meant she'd better hightail it back up on deck so she could catch the last boat to Attu, call her boss immediately, and arrange to be extracted.

They were in American waters. Thurman would no doubt have a plan in place to have her picked up and flown home as soon as she had the data card in her possession.

Carefully she pushed the tiny card deep into the coin pocket of her jeans, as far as it would go. It should be okay there for now.

After hurriedly repacking and replacing the storage box, she started back to the stern hatch where the scientists had gathered to be transported to the island. No need to go to the stateroom. All she had on board was her mini laptop, and she still had that with her, tucked into the waistband of her jeans. As big a pain as it was to carry around all the time, she wasn't about to have it sabotaged, too.

But then a clot of mixed emotions punched into her belly.

What about Nikolai?

What should she do about him? Even with her doubts about their relationship, could she really just leave him like this, after what they'd shared, without a word of good-bye?

Would he be hurt? Angry? Would he even care that she'd left?

She thought he would. She wished she knew for sure.

She squeezed her eyes shut for a moment, then rose to her feet. Yes, he *would* care. She had to believe that. Had to believe that the feelings she had for him were returned at least in some small measure.

That he'd truly miss her when she was gone. She couldn't bear to think otherwise. Because she would miss him terribly.

How different she was now from when she'd first seen him at that hotel bar in Petropavlovsk! She'd been a terrified, lonely, uncertain woman then. Now she was courageous, decisive, and filled with a need for love. His love.

She realized now what it was about Nikolai that spoke to her so profoundly. That made him so different from the other men she'd met. The thing that made her yearn to be with him. The need deep within her that he alone filled, and no one else in her life had ever touched.

He believed in her.

When he looked at her, all their outward differences and conflicts melted away, and they connected on a soul-deep emotional level. Whether it was their similar upbringing or just an instinctual recognition of like hearts and minds, he got her. He really *saw* her. And he believed in what he saw.

It killed her to let him go. But she had to accept that she and Nikolai had no future together.

Even so, she couldn't imagine leaving *Ostrov* without saying good-bye to him. Without seeing him one last time. Without holding him in her arms and telling him how much she'd grown to like him over the past few days.

How much she'd grown to love him.

She sighed. Okay, maybe not that last part.

But perhaps there was one other thing she should tell him before she left—the secret James Thurman had confided about his mother.

Her loyalties whispered she shouldn't go against her boss's orders. But her heart told her she must. Nikolai had a right to know about his own family. She would want to know if it were her mother . . . or father.

Resolved, Julie climbed up the ladder, ducked through the watertight door, and walked into the central post. Because of the departure of the scientists, the usual watch section of duty officers and ratings was considerably thinner than usual. It always surprised her how few people it actually took to run a submarine on the surface. Now, only the helmsman, a warrant officer, and the JOOD were manning the controls here in the central post. The rest of the watch must be up in the conning tower manning the flying bridge and up in the cockpit on lookout duty.

"*Kapitan* Romanov?" she asked the JOOD, whom she recognized from yesterday—she had an indelible vision of him drinking beer while being held upside down by his ankles at the party last night. He gestured to the ladder up to the bridge.

She climbed to the landing halfway up the conning tower. Past the trio of metal periscope and radar columns she could see several men crowded into the small flying bridge compartment, all glued to the view of Attu Island beyond the open windows.

But no Nikolai. He must be up in the cockpit.

She was about to grab the ladder and continue up when she heard her name in a low, muffled call.

"Julie. I'm in here." The muted voice came from the other side of the open steel door leading to the stern side of the landing deck, where the wet storerooms were located.

The most private spot on the boat, other than their stateroom.

She smiled wistfully. She must have been wrong. Nikolai must want to see her off for the day in a place where prying eyes couldn't watch.

He just didn't know yet that this good-bye would be forever.

Steeling herself to keep her wavering emotions in check, and her tears firmly behind her eyelids, she pushed open the door. "Nikolai?"

"Back here."

She stepped in, eased the door closed, and walked around a corner into a hidden space behind a metal storage unit. "Gee, do you think this is—"

But she never got the chance to finish.

A blinding pain exploded in the back of her head.

Everything went very cold.

And she sank into a void of blackness.

23

~~~~~~~~~~

Nikolai strode into the central post.

"Captain on deck," the OOD, *Praporshchik* Zubkin, announced loudly.

"I have the conn," Nikolai returned. It was time to take command so they could get going on the planned deep-dive evolution. It would be good to have his mind on something other than Julie. Last night and this morning he'd thought of nothing else but rushing down to the stateroom and pulling her into his arms, kissing her to within an inch of her life, and begging her forgiveness for breaking things off so abruptly.

But he couldn't do that.

It wasn't going to work between them. How could it? So he had to be strong.

For both their sakes.

At Nikolai's order, the OOD and the watch section engineer acknowledged the shift of command. "Captain has the conn," they echoed.

"Are all the passengers safely ashore?" he asked the *starpom*.

"Aye, *Kapitan*," Stefan Mikhailovich said. "*Lyeĭtenant* Petrov received word a few minutes ago letting us know all three transports had arrived at Pyramid Cove on Attu in good order."

"Very good."

As he gave the crew orders to secure the boat and make ready to get under way, weighing anchor and directing *Ostrov* away from the shallow waters around the island, Nikolai had to work hard to keep his disappointment at bay.

Julie had not come to find him before leaving, as he'd hoped she would. Just before the passengers' departure he'd been with Yasha in engineering, making sure no other mechanical problems had come to light that might disrupt the morning's exercise. When he and his chief engineer had finished going over everything, Nikolai had gone to search for her. Too late he'd learned from Borovsky that the women had been the first to be helped onto the three small motorboats heading for shore, and Julie was gone. Not that he blamed her.

He knew he had no right to be aggravated that she'd left without so much as a word, let alone a kiss good-bye. Or two, or three. After all, he'd been the one to walk away and stay away from her last night.

Still, it hurt. Just a little.

He'd hoped she might fight him on his unilateral decision. Just a little . . .

But apparently she agreed they had no business being together.

Or perhaps she had decided to abandon him in favor of Clint Walker. He decided he didn't want to ponder that possibility.

But thinking of the scientists going ashore reminded him vividly of another worry. In spite of his frustration over their personal relationship, he was concerned about Julie's safety on this jaunt. Especially being on her own on the island. Correction: being with Walker.

Would the other man protect her if it came right down to it?

And who would protect her from Walker?

Hell, the enemy saboteur could be anyone, including the UUV pilot or one of the scientists. Julie had pooh-poohed that whole idea when he'd brought it up yesterday during their après-sex conversation, saying the team members had all been vetted for political and terrorist agendas before being accepted to the expedition. It couldn't be one of them.

To which he'd blithely replied that *she'd* gotten on board, hadn't she?

She hadn't had a comeback for that.

Nevertheless, when he found out she'd already gone ashore, he'd pulled aside the skinny Canadian genius who kept ogling him and asked if he would keep an eye on her. To which Dr. Stedman had replied he'd be happy to do so. The kid had then made moon eyes at him and said he was even nicer than he was good-looking, and if he ever wanted to take a walk on the wild side to let him know. Which might have annoyed Nikolai even more, except that now he knew he had one less thing to worry about with Julie out of his sight.

Too bad Clint Walker wasn't gay, too.

Nikolai's attention was jerked back to the present by a loud, metallic clang reverberating through the central post. Probably an especially large chunk of drift ice hitting the hull. Although he could swear it had sounded like it came from above, not from the waterline. A couple of the other men were glancing upward, also.

"Deck officer, are all hatches secure?" Nikolai asked, though he'd just gotten the report that they were.

"Yes, sir," Zubkin promptly repeated. "I checked the conning tower trunk hatch myself, sir. Topside is rigged for dive, last man down, and all hatches secure. Watches all present and on post."

"Very well," Nikolai said and put it from his mind. By now they'd run on the surface several miles out to sea to get beyond the shallow reefs. It was time to submerge and see what *Ostrov* was really made of. He crossed his arms over his chest and looked in turn at each man on the central post watch, gauging their mettle for the upcoming drill. Today he planned to separate the men from the boys.

"So," he announced somberly, "are we ready to put this tin can through her paces, and take her down so deep her rivets start to pop?"

"Yes, sir!" they all responded in loud unison. He could feel their excitement mount, the air of anticipation grabbing hold of every member of the crew. These were men used to action, not leisurely scientific patrols. They might be outlaws in the eyes of the brass, but they loved being submariners—and the adrenaline rush of danger that went with that job.

Just as he did.

Nikolai pulled off his well-worn cap and tugged it back on so it sat securely on his head. This could be a bumpy ride.

"Okay, men!" he declared. "Let's see what she can do! Submerge the boat, Mr. Zubkin, and take us to oh-three-zero meters. Steady on course zero-two-seven, and increase speed to—"

Just then another muffled clang interrupted him, vibrating through the central post, yanking everyone's attention like a cry of "fire!" in the relative silence of listening to his orders.

какого чёрта бля!

"What the fucking *hell* is that?" he demanded hotly. Good God, was the damn submarine *already* falling apart? They weren't even submerged yet! "Belay those orders and find out!"

Zubkin snapped an order and a rating scurried up the ladder to check the bridge trunk hatch yet again. "All secure, sir!" he yelled down.

Immediately, there was another clang, this one even louder.

"Sir, one of the conning tower door latches must have come loose," the rating called down. "Shall I go up and secure it, sir?"

For the love of— "Yes!" Nikolai yelled back up, and he waited impatiently for the man to return so they could proceed.

But instead, a few seconds later the rating gave a cry of surprise. "*Kapitan!* Come quickly!"

Now what? "What is it, man?" Nikolai asked, heading in irritation for the ladder.

"It's . . . it's the woman reporter! She's hurt!" came the man's dismayed reply.

"*What?*" Nikolai roared, instantly launching himself up, climbing two rungs at a time. *Julie?* How the hell had she gotten up there? She was supposed to be—

He burst through the flapping metal door. "Where? *Where is she?*"

"Here!" The rating was crouched on the floor, his eyes

wide and frightened. He was cradling Julie's head and shoulders in his arms. There was blood on the floor and caked on the side of her head. Her eyes were closed.

Nikolai's heart stalled.

He dropped to his knees next to her. Fear knifed through him, razor sharp. "Is she breathing?" he asked, resisting the urge to grab her away from the man and cradle her in his own arms.

"Yes," the rating said. "She was awake when I found her. I think she just fainted."

By now several other men had rushed up to join them in the small space. They gathered around, muttering in shocked speculation over how she could have gotten there and what might have happened had they started to submerge.

Nikolai wanted to kill someone. One thing was for damn certain. When he found out who'd done this, he *would* kill the bastard. And damn the consequences!

With terrified fingers, Nikolai felt carefully over her head wound. She moaned and her eyes fluttered open.

When she saw him bending over her, a profound light of relief went through them. "Nikolai. Oh, thank God." Her whisper was strangled as she threw her arms around his neck.

He didn't care what he'd said last night. Didn't care if the whole damn crew saw the way he felt about her. He was so shaken he needed to hold her and feel for himself that she was alive and breathing.

"It's okay," he soothed, drawing her up into his arms and embracing her as tightly as he dared without knowing the extent of her injuries. "You're safe now. I have you."

He rocked her against his chest for an intense moment, absorbing her fear and the trembling of her body into his. When she'd calmed a little, he tried to pull back to look at her.

She clung to him even harder. "Don't let go. Not yet. Please."

At her plea, he turned to kiss her temple. And saw the bloodstains on her face up close. He almost came apart at the seams. "Who did this to you, Liesha? Tell me!"

She shook her head, her hair tickling his jaw. "I don't know."

He could feel deep tremors working up and down her body. His rage threatened to boil over. "How did it happen?"

The men around them shifted closer to hear.

"I don't know," she said, her tone hoarse with residual shock. "Whoever it was hit me from behind. At first I thought it was . . ." Her words halted abruptly and she swallowed. "I'm sorry. I didn't see who it was."

He hadn't missed the swift left turn in her statement.

"Who did you think it was?" he demanded, ready to tear the man limb from limb. When her eyes glided away from him and she didn't answer right away, he almost lost it. "*Me?* By God! You thought it was *me*?" he exclaimed. "Why the hell would you think—"

"Your voice . . ." she said.

He scowled fiercely. "What about my voice?"

"I thought you were on the bridge, so I came up to see you before I disembarked. To . . . say good-bye."

"And?" he asked, mentally kicking himself up one side and down the other for not seeking her out himself, but putting her in danger with his damn stubbornness.

"Someone called to me, from in here. By name. It sounded like you."

Distress raced through him. "I was in engineering, with Yasha, seeing to the—"

"Oh, Nikolai, I believe you. It was just for a second that I thought . . ." She buried her face against his chest. "I know you'd never hurt me. Truly I do."

A murmur went through the men as their conversation was translated. Several of them made noises of assent and support for their commander.

Nikolai jetted out a breath. And glanced up at the circle of faces above him. These were men that, until now, he would have sworn he could trust with his very life, as well as with the lives of the other crew and passengers.

Had one of his own men done this horrible thing to Julie? And was now berating himself for not getting the job done properly?

Nikolai's stomach knotted. Maybe. Maybe not. The small group of men watching them was just a handful of his crew. The culprit could be anyone, here observing, or still belowdecks.

Or ashore, among the scientists, he reminded himself.

How could he possibly figure out who was guilty? He was a sub driver, not a damn police detective!

He gently set Julie away from him, and this time she didn't resist. "We'll return immediately to the island," he said. "You need to see a doctor, and Professor Sundesvall is a licensed—"

"No!" Julie said quickly, gingerly touching her blood-matted hair with still-shaking fingers. "Please don't do that. I'm okay. Really."

He gaped at her, incredulous. She didn't *look* okay. Far from it. She was still white as a sheet, and he could see her struggling to keep her teeth from chattering.

"You can't mean that. Leisha, someone just tried to *kill* you!"

She swiped a trembling hand over her brow. "Believe me, I get that. But the blow only knocked me out for a few minutes. Just now when I passed out? It was from pure relief at being found in time." She grimaced at the fresh blood that now covered her fingers. "Scalp wounds always look a lot worse than they are. I'll be fine."

He shook his head. The blow must have knocked the sense out of her. "Even if I accept that—which I don't—attempted murder is a serious crime. We must contact the closest authorities to investigate."

She blinked up at him. "Nikolai, stop for a minute and think." She shook her head, then winced at the motion. "We're in U.S. waters and the closest authorities are American. *Ostrov* is a Russian submarine. There are passengers on board from five other countries. What happens to the scientific expedition? What if the press gets hold of this? Or rather, *when* it does? Can you imagine the political fallout from all of that?"

Inwardly he steeled himself against a flood of bitterness. Yes, as a matter of fact, he could very well imagine the fallout. In fact, he was intimately acquainted with the entire Technicolor spectrum of shit that would descend upon him. *Again.* But just as last time, he was willing to deal with it, and the consequences. It was the right thing to do.

"I don't care," he said. "I need to get you off this boat and away from—"

"No!" she said more vehemently, her voice getting stronger. "I'm okay. And I am *not* letting this monster, whoever it is, win. I have a job to do on this expedition, and I intend to finish it, come hell or high water." She made a sound of consternation at the unintended but very apt pun.

He scowled down at her, his heart pounding with fear for her safety. But the stubborn look in her eyes told him if he wanted her off this boat, he'd have to physically overpower her, tie her up, and carry her off himself.

Which he would go ahead and do, if he had half a brain.

But as his actions over the past year, and especially during the past few days, proved, the jury was still out as to whether he actually did have half a brain.

His men were smiling grimly and nodding as her words were translated, admiration for her pluck shining in their eyes.

Nikolai ground his jaw. "Fine. You can stay aboard. But you will do exactly as I say. And until this bastard is caught, you don't leave my sight. *Ever.* Agreed?"

She nodded somberly. "Agreed."

Suddenly one of the men gave a shout from behind a storage bin. It was Danya Petrov.

"*Kapitan!* Look what I found!" He came forward and stretched out his hand. Lying on his outstretched palm was an ivory charm in the shape of a bear claw.

The one from Clint Walker's leather bracelet.

"Well," Nikolai said in a deadly growl, "I guess we now know who's the saboteur."

And why was he not surprised?

24

///////////////

Nikolai wanted to carry Julie down the ladder himself, but she insisted on descending back into the interior of the submarine under her own steam. He had to hand it to her, she was being a lot braver than he'd have given her credit for.

And a lot more foolish.

"This proves nothing," she insisted upon seeing the ivory bear claw. "It could have been planted."

"Sure it could," he said agreeably, while silently planning Clint Walker's painful demise.

"He had no reason to kill me!" Julie persisted. "He helped you get rid of the 093. Why would he have done that?"

"To throw us off? Look, this changes everything. We must call the authorities. Have him arrested."

"No," she said. "Not until we know for sure it's really him. You need to question him first."

He'd give a lot to get the man alone in a room and extract some answers, he grudgingly admitted. But—

"What if he runs? Bribes one of the transport boats to take him off Attu and he disappears?"

"Then we'll know. And we'll be rid of him for now. I can tell my boss to sic the FBI on him. But in the meantime, you should proceed today as though it wasn't him. Just in case he's innocent. We need to find the *real* guilty party. Please. No law enforcement. Not yet."

Nikolai, being in command, could easily overrule her. But she was right. Even if they had Walker on board and in custody—which they didn't—the fallout would be a nightmare: A Russian submarine—however outdated—delivered straight into the hands of the American authorities. The brass all over him for letting it happen. And for knowing about a saboteur on board but not finding and dealing with him quietly and immediately, using any means necessary. The press crucifying him for getting an important international scientific expedition shut down on his watch.

And once again Nikolai would no doubt not be allowed to say a word in his own defense to any of them. Let alone if Julie was right and it turned out not to be Walker after all. Then he'd truly be screwed. For the second time in as many years, he'd be the Russian Naval Command's whipping boy and sacrificial lamb, and this time his career most certainly would be over before the sun set on the accusations. He'd be out of the submarine service, out of the entire military, out on his ass. Definitively and permanently. No more uniform. No more command. No more life he loved.

And after all the negative publicity, another job would be tough, if not impossible, for him to find. He'd probably end up forced to submit to Cherenkov's pressuring and work for the FSB.

Чёрт возьми. And that was the very *last* thing he wanted to do.

Nikolai was just anxious enough to hang on to the last thread of his quickly eclipsing career to accede to Julie's wishes. Though he had the distinct and bitter feeling he would live to regret that decision.

"Okay, no law enforcement. Yet," he conceded. "We'll wait until we can question Walker." And Nikolai would involve the boat's security officer, whether Julie liked it or not.

Ostrov was too small to have a sick bay, and since Professor Sundesvall possessed a medical degree, a navy doctor had not been assigned to this patrol. "But you are seeing the crew medic, and don't even think about fighting me on that."

She didn't.

So Nikolai summoned the medic from his watch post and looked on anxiously while he examined Julie.

She perched calmly on a table in the mess hall as the man ran his fingers over her skull, shone a flashlight in her eyes, and haltingly asked her a series of questions in broken English. Finally he pronounced her fit, but gave her the usual warnings and instructions for those with head injuries.

"She should go to the hospital," the medic told Nikolai afterward in Russian. "And be seen by a real physician."

"You tell her that," Nikolai grumbled. "I tried. She won't listen."

"Of course, the closest medical facility is on Atka Island. Over eight hundred kilometers away," the medic said. "She'd need to be airlifted."

Nikolai squeezed the bridge of his nose. "She has refused to leave the boat. Will she be all right?" he asked, drilling the man with his most commanding gaze. "Tell me the truth."

The medic gathered up his instruments. "Probably, but it's impossible to say for sure yet. Watch her closely. Wake her every few hours when she sleeps. Let me know immediately if any unusual symptoms occur."

Nikolai nodded. "You can be sure I will."

The other man turned to Julie and switched back to English. "Go ahead to wash hair. Wound is not deep for stitchings, but here is butterfly bandage. To keep together to stop bleeding. Get plenty rest. No exertions for twenty-four hours."

"Thanks, doc," she said, and the medic smiled and left them there. They were finally alone.

She slid off the table to her feet, and he caught her when she wobbled. "Good thing the party was last night," she said ruefully.

Nikolai broke down and put his arms around her. "Are you sure about this?" he asked, holding her tight. "I swear if anything happens to you . . ."

After a microsecond of hesitation, she hugged him back. "Don't worry. I'm tougher than I look."

He let out a long sigh. "I'm beginning to see that."

"Liesha—," he said at the exact moment she said, "Nikolai—"

He slid his hand up to the back of her neck, caressed her soft skin. "You first."

She gazed at him for a long moment, then gingerly shook her head and said, "Nothing. Just wondering what happened to my laptop." She pulled away. "Did anyone find it in the storage area?"

Okay, so she didn't want to delve into their personal issues now. He stifled the urge to pull her back to him. To explain his actions last night. To tell her how much he was hurting.

Devil take it.

Probably not the best time for that anyway.

He shook his head. "No, sorry. I didn't even think to have someone look. I was too upset over you."

She nodded, looking disappointed but resigned. "Yeah. Okay. I think I'll take that shower now."

They started walking. "Your attacker could have taken it. Would that be a problem?" he asked.

"There's nothing on it that matters." She didn't sound too worried.

"That's good."

"Will you be in the central post?" she asked when they reached the stateroom door.

"Remember what I said about not leaving my sight?" he reminded her.

She glanced down the passageway to where the officers' shower was located, then back at him, and her lips parted. He could tell exactly what she was thinking.

A fierce stab of longing hit him deep in his belly. He wanted nothing more than to join her in the shower. To touch her and renew their relationship under the soothing hot spray and warm suds. To lovingly wash the memory of the attack from her hair and her body.

But he forced himself to say instead, "I'll wait right outside the door."

She regarded him for a few endless seconds, said, "Okay. I'll get my towel," then turned and disappeared into his stateroom, snicking the door shut behind her.

He was doing the right thing, he told himself. Then he closed his eyes and softly cursed.

And never felt more alone in his life.

Half an hour later Nikolai was back at the central command post. Brooking no arguments with Julie regarding his watch over her, he'd tucked her off to one side in one of the console chairs that went unused because of the abbreviated crew. Misha had found her a clean coverall somewhere—and knew his captain well enough to choose one with no crew member's name sewn onto it—and she sat there wrapped in a blanket Nikolai himself had fetched for her, quietly observing the bustle of activity as they once again prepared to dive the boat.

He'd also asked the chop to bring her a glass of hot, fragrant tea with lots of sugar to help stave off shock, even though she kept saying said she was fine.

She was putting on a brave front, but one look at her ashen face and shadowed eyes, and he knew better. She was *not* fine.

Who could blame her for being afraid? Walker, or whoever the saboteur was, had upped the ante, using deadly force to try and ensure she would not find the hidden SD card. After taking such a huge risk, the would-be killer would not stop until the card was in his possession. Which meant Julie would be in constant danger until they figured out for sure who it was and dealt with him.

The crew was also agitated, rumors flying wildly about Walker, and why the man would possibly attack Julie—why anyone would do such an awful thing to the captain's lady.

Nikolai was growing just uncertain enough of Walker's guilt that he gave in and launched a full-out investigation of everyone on board. Upon returning to the central post, Nikolai took his senior officers aside and ordered *Starpom* Varnas, *Praporshchik* Zubkin, and *Kvartirmyeister* Kresney to carry out the questioning of the crew, under the leadership of the security officer.

"But what about the depth drill?" Zubkin protested. "We should be at our posts for that."

"This investigation takes precedence," Nikolai told him forcefully. "I want to know who is guilty of this atrocity!"

"How would you like us to proceed?" asked the security officer, ignoring the *praporshchik*'s scowl.

"Interrogate every man on board as to their movements

before, during, and after the departure of the scientists,"
Nikolai ordered, pacing back and forth. He whirled back to
them. "And then you're to corroborate all the statements with
at least two witnesses."

"But sir—"

"No exceptions!" he snapped. "I want a list of anyone who
can't verify their whereabouts with absolute certainty. And I
want to know where Walker was for every damn minute until
he left the boat!"

"What about the other scientists?" Varnas interjected.

Nikolai scowled. "By the time we return to Attu and pick
them up tonight, we should know if the guilty party is one of
the crew. If not, I will interrogate Walker and the scientists
personally." The others nodded. "Now get going. I want this
bastard found. *Today*."

"Da, Kapitan," they all responded, coming to attention.

While the three officers turned over their watches, Nikolai
stepped into the radio room and gave *Lyeĭtenant* Petrov a
message to encrypt and send to Naval Command informing
them of the latest developments and requesting they do an
investigation of Walker plus a careful background on everyone on the crew, and be ready to relay the results as soon as
Ostrov surfaced again. He figured if the saboteur wasn't
Walker but someone officially working for his own side, that
request should flush out the truth.

He also sent a short message to Comrade Cherenkov, giving the FSB word of the attack on Julie, as well as a one-sen-
tence statement of her mission as he'd learned it.

He tried not to feel like he was betraying her, informing on
her like that. But it was best this way. If anything else happened and he wasn't around to defend her, at least the FSB
would know she hadn't been spying on Russia and she
wouldn't end up in a Moscow prison.

Or worse.

When he emerged from the radio room along with Danya
Petrov, his three senior officers headed off to formulate a plan
and start questioning the crew.

Nothing else for it. Time to get back to the business of the
day.

Nikolai glanced around at the new faces manning the

watch posts, including the two planesmen who hadn't been needed while transiting on the surface. They all followed his movements expectantly. Everyone seemed tense and on edge. His own nerves were strung tight as an anchor chain.

Just then, Gavrikov called over the circuit from the sonar shack, "Conn, sonar. *Kapitan*, I have a contact."

"Sonar, conn. What kind of vessel?" His stomach tightened even more. Like he needed to ask.

"It's the Chinese 093, sir," Gavrikov replied.

Nikolai's day was complete.

Although . . .

Hell, they could all use a good, solid distraction. Nothing like a real-time game of cat and mouse to get the men's attention back where it should be. Not to mention his own.

"Bearing?" he asked.

He narrowed his eyes as Gavrikov rattled off the bearing, checking the repeater on the control console monitor as he listened.

"Very well, *Starshina*," he said. The blip was barely visible in the waterfall; the enemy sub was keeping to the outer fringes of their sonar range. Every man in the central post knew what the bearing meant. The Shang class was taunting *Ostrov*. Daring Nikolai to pull another stunt like yesterday's.

The tension in the space was suddenly electric. The men all swung around to look at him questioningly.

Nikolai smiled with satisfaction.

"They want to play?" he said, then turned to the OOD. "Very well. Mr. Borovsky, submerge the boat and take us to oh-four-zero meters. Steady on course zero-two-five."

Borovsky snapped to. "Submerge the boat to oh-four-zero meters, steady on course zero-two-five, aye, sir!"

As the OOD passed his orders on to the diving officer, Nikolai glanced over to make sure Julie was still okay and upright in her seat.

Overhead, the klaxon sounded and 1MC blared out its warning, "Dive! Dive!"

Their eyes met. Hers were wide and anxious. He smiled reassuringly, trying to let her know she'd be okay. He'd keep her safe, come what may.

He just hoped to hell he could make it true.

25

〰〰〰〰〰

"Dive! Dive!"

Julie's heart stalled when she heard the loud squawk from the overhead speaker. The words were in Russian, but she didn't need a translator to know what the urgent syllables meant.

This was when she was supposed to have died. All alone in the dark as the icy waters swept through the storage room in the sail, dragging her down into the depths of the fathomless ocean with no way of saving herself.

God.

Had it really been Clint who did this to her? She didn't believe it. If for no other reason than that he'd had ample opportunity last night, as she'd made her phone call, to push her off the edge of the deck. He'd clipped her safety harness to the toe-rail; he could have left it unfastened and merely tipped her off. In the confusion of the celebration no one would even have noticed. No. It wasn't him. Which meant whoever it was, was still out there. *And still able to get to her.*

She squeezed her eyes shut and took several deep breaths to calm her racing heartbeat.

No. It was okay. *She was okay.* No one was going to get to her. She wouldn't drown.

She *hadn't* drowned. Nikolai had saved her in time.

And she wasn't going to drown now, either. *Ostrov* was *not* going to implode, or sink, or whatever submarines did when they sprang a leak. Nikolai would never take the crew on this exercise if he had a single doubt that they'd be able to come up again from the frigid black abyss below.

The steaming liquid in her tea glass tilted off kilter and she felt the subtle shift of the deck under her as the vessel slipped below the ocean surface. She grabbed the edge of the console, but no one else in the busy command center even seemed to notice the slight change in the angle of their upright stances.

The blare from the overhead speakers cut off and, as if a switch had been flipped, the compartment went eerily silent. After days of running full tilt under the power of the smelly, noisy diesel engines, the intense quiet of the submarine using its electric motors was almost unnerving. It was like going from the cacophonous streets of summer Manhattan to the winter silence of a snowy Vermont wood.

She popped her ears at the increasing heaviness of the atmospheric pressure—or maybe she was just feeling the marked jump in tension in the cramped space. Was it her imagination, or was it getting darker, too?

Even the voices of the men were abnormally hushed as they concentrated with almost palpable intensity on their instrument panels and monitors. She'd never seen them so focused on task. Or were they all just avoiding her gaze? Did they think she was bringing the boat bad luck?

Was it one of them who'd tried to kill her . . . ?

She forced her thoughts away from the harrowing incident and watched Nikolai as he strode from station to station, checking everything, having short exchanges with his men. His expression seemed to vacillate between forbidding and . . . oddly, almost eager.

It was as though he and the crew were all waiting for something to happen. Something other than preparing for a routine dive. . . .

Abruptly Julie sat straight up in her chair, at once suspicious. She shot a glance over at the sonar repeater screen. Her heartbeat slammed.

There, on one edge of the cascading image, she recognized the snowy blip of a contact.

A ship? A whale? The Chinese sub returning . . . ?

She set down her tea, peeled off her blanket, and caught Nikolai's arm as he strode past on his way to the navigation table. "Nikolai, what's going on?"

He stopped, hesitated a beat, then said, "We just passed the twelve-mile limit, leaving American waters. And the 093 is back."

She worried her lower lip. Great. So Clint was right. It *hadn't* gone away. But . . . "Surely they won't try anything, will they?"

"You mean besides harassing us?" Nikolai shook his head. "That would be pretty damn stupid."

"Yeah. I guess. . . ." But she still felt doubtful. As did Nikolai, obviously.

Especially after what had just happened to her. She desperately wished she could talk with James Thurman at Langley. Get his opinion. *Get some help.*

"The Chinese are anything but stupid," she added in a murmur, hoping to convince herself they really *weren't* planning anything.

Thank God the SD card was still in her possession, wrapped in a tissue and transferred safely after her shower to her coverall pocket. If her assailant had searched her for it, he hadn't checked her jeans coin pocket. Which, to her—though she could be wrong—pointed to a non-American as the culprit, since she'd noticed foreign jeans seldom had that convenient feature. But it would be the first place an American would look.

Her boss was going to be thrilled at the news she'd succeeded. But even before finding the micro data card, she'd planned to borrow Clint's phone on Attu and ask Thurman if he'd learned anything about the Chinese sub situation, from one of their assets in China perhaps.

It was weird, but this whole thing was beginning to feel like a setup to her. An elaborate trap of some kind.

And yet, that made no sense.

Could it be the SD card was a plant? A fake? But then why try to kill her? She needed to get a look at what was on it. But how could she read the thing with neither her laptop nor her sat phone?

"Why do you think the 093 is back?" she asked Nikolai, returning to the present.

"Obviously," he said stonily, fiddling with a dial on a neighboring console, "the captain is a slow learner."

Something about his tone made alarm zip through her. Oh, *hell*. She sprang to her feet and grasped his other arm. "Nikolai. What are you planning?"

But just then a commotion broke out in the passageway just outside the central post, and she never got an answer.

"Kapitan!"

The call was shouted over a string of angry protests ground out in English. A furious spate of Russian cut the protester off.

Julie and Nikolai swung to the sounds at the same time. Both their mouths dropped open when they saw who was being dragged into the compartment by the fuming *starpom* and an irate *kvartirmyeister*.

Clint Walker.

Julie couldn't believe her eyes.

But . . . how? Clint was supposed to be on Attu Island with the scientists!

"Clint!" she exclaimed in surprise. "What are you doing still on board?"

Nikolai's hand came down on her shoulder and squeezed off her questions. Then he barked out something in Russian, which produced a storm of scowls and exclamations from Misha and *Starpom* Varnas.

She wished to hell she could understand what they were saying.

The half dozen crewmen in the room were all glancing from Varnas to Walker to Julie and back again. Their expressions grew more thunderous by the second.

She didn't need a translation for this, either. They believed he was the one who'd tried to kill her.

Doubt suddenly assailed her. Had she been wrong about him? Had he been her attacker, after all? Was her judgment so off?

Her body, still humming with dread from the morning's ordeal, felt weightless and unreal. She was tempted to creep behind Nikolai and simply hide from the uproar. To give up and just let him protect her.

She wasn't cut out for this deadly brand of deception! She couldn't take much more of it.

But then Clint's eyes captured hers. They were also filled with questions. "Julie," he said below the ongoing Russian debate, "what the hell is happening?"

He seemed genuinely clueless. Then again, how could she possibly know what was real and what was lies with him any more than with Nikolai?

She swallowed. And asked, "Clint, did you just try to kill me?"

He froze in what looked like pure shock. Then he pressed his lips together, shook his head, and said, "No. I didn't."

Just that. No arguments, no indignation, no panicked explanations.

And that, more than anything, convinced her he was telling the truth. All at once she noticed his disheveled appearance, as though he'd been rousted out of bed in the middle of the night. Except it was nearly eleven o'clock in the morning. Come to think of it, she hadn't seen him all day. . . .

As if reading her gaze and the doubts behind it, he said, "I overslept. Like I was dead. I *never* oversleep." He gave her a penetrating look.

She realized Nikolai was standing with his feet apart, fists on his hips, staring down at her.

"What?" she asked.

"*I'll* conduct this interview, if you don't mind."

"He didn't do it," she stated.

Nikolai's eyebrows rose. "Excuse me?"

"He didn't try to . . . kill me."

"And you know this how?"

She could have gone into all the reasons, but she only shook her head. "I just know."

Nikolai jetted out a short breath, then looked around at his men. He clipped out an order and they all reluctantly turned back to their instruments and monitors. Then he turned to face Clint. "If it wasn't you, how do you explain this?" He dug in his pocket and held up the ivory bear claw.

Clint instinctively checked his wrist. A murderous expression crept across his face. The woven leather thong he always wore there was gone. "Find my band and you'll find your attacker," was all he said.

Nikolai studied him closely, then put the ivory totem back in his pocket. With a gesture, he indicated that the *starpom* and Misha should let Walker go.

Varnas immediately objected, which Nikolai shut down with a harsh word.

They let Walker go.

Nikolai jerked his head toward the watertight door. "*Starpom*, continue questioning the crew. *Kvartirmyeister*, you may resume your regular duties."

"Aye, sir."

Stefan Mikhailovich gave Walker a death look before grudgingly stalking out of the central post, muttering.

Bruises were already starting to show on Clint's bronze skin, but he didn't rub his arms as Julie would have done. He just crossed them over his chest, mirroring Nikolai's belligerent stance. "Thank you, Captain Romanov," he said nonetheless. "Now if someone will please tell me what the hell this is all about?"

All at once, Gavrikov's urgent voice sounded over the circuit from the sonar shack. Whatever he said made everyone in the central post turn to look at the sonar repeater. Julie did, too.

The spidery blip that was the Chinese 093 had gotten a lot closer to the center of the screen—and to *Ostrov*.

With a curse, Nikolai pulled off his cap, slashed a hand through his hair, and tugged it back on again. Then he pointed at the empty console chair in front of the sonar repeater and turned to Clint. "Sit," he ordered. "If you move out of that damn chair I'll have you put in irons until we get back to Attu and I can throw you off this boat for good, which is really what I'd like to do right now. Is that clear, Mr. Walker?"

Clint gave a curt, angry nod, strode over to the chair, and sat.

Misha gave him a menacing glare.

Julie opened her mouth, but Nikolai beat her to it. "You

trust him? Fine. You watch him. He moves an inch off that chair, I want to know about it."

She nodded. She didn't really blame Nikolai for his anger and suspicion. She was angry, too. Just not at Clint. At least not yet. Not until someone proved to her he'd done it. "Can I tell him what happened to me?"

Nikolai considered for a second. "Just the basics. No details. But before you do"—he reached for a pad of paper on the console and glanced at Clint—"I want a written account of how you spent the morning and exactly why you are still on board." He tossed him the pad. "Get writing."

"Whatever," Clint said, looking distinctly annoyed. "I don't suppose your medic can take a blood sample for me? From myself," he added.

Nikolai frowned. "Why?"

"I was drugged. I'd like to be able to prove it."

"What?" Julie exclaimed.

"Like I said, I *never* oversleep."

Nikolai's frown deepened. "I'll see what I can do." Then he turned his back to the man and strode over to the navigation table.

Julie's head was spinning. *Drugged.* Good Lord. If Clint was telling the truth, that meant . . . what? *Both* of them were targets of the saboteur?

But for the same reason? Was it a simple frame job—maneuvering an innocent man to be accused of assaulting her—or was Clint aboard *Ostrov* for the same reason she was, and that was why he was also targeted? Or was the mysterious UUV driver's role in all this more nefarious than that?

Clint picked up a pen from the console. "If I were you," he said without looking at her, "I'd double-check my IDA. Just to make sure no one's been messing with it while I slept."

Jerking out of her thoughts, she instinctively touched the bright orange pouch hanging from her belt, which Nikolai still insisted everyone on board keep with them at all times. She hadn't thought much about it since the night of the drill. What was Clint trying to say? That the entire sub was in danger?

A sick feeling blossomed in the pit of her stomach at the implication of his advice. And at the direction of her welling suspicions.

Oh, God.

Things were bad enough already. But somehow, she had a sinking feeling that Clint knew more than he was saying, and things were about to get a whole lot worse.

The Chinese 093 was closing in on *Ostrov.*

Nikolai wasn't exactly alarmed, but he sure didn't like it. What the devil was the enemy sub playing at? He had made his displeasure very clear the day before . . . and still the 093 pursued them. Was this an egotistical commander's inappropriate challenge? A tactical learning opportunity being exploited to an annoying degree? Or the prelude to an outright attack, either to retrieve or to sink and destroy the SD card with their stolen technology, and *Ostrov* along with it?

Whichever way, Nikolai figured they were in big trouble.

Admittedly, the enemy's maneuvering had gotten his adrenaline pumping at the possibilities, both good and bad. The question was, how should he steer *Ostrov* to react? Defense or offense?

Somehow he needed to lure the 093's commander into revealing his plan. Difficult, but not impossible.

For hundreds of miles around them, the ocean floor was riddled with high seamounts and deepwater trenches, peaks, troughs, and canyons. In other words, perfect for what Nikolai had in mind. A submarine could play a mean game of hide-and-seek within the mazelike features of the undersea landscape. How—and if—the enemy followed them would reveal much about their intent.

And if they wanted to take things further than a game, he and *Ostrov* would be ready.

Nikolai turned to his navigator, *Praporshchik* Zubkin. "Nav, how close are we to the nearest deep canyon?"

Zubkin pursed his lips, spread out a chart, and pointed to their position. "Do you want to go north or south, *Kapitan*? There's the Bowers Ridge area curving around up here. And down here are Agattu and Abraham canyons. They are the closest. How deep do you want to go?"

The maximum depth for a Kilo-class 636 in top condition was around three hundred meters. The Aleutian Trench went down to more than seven thousand. But the comblike network of faults and troughs that led from the island chain down into the ocean trench varied wildly in every aspect, from the bottom depths to the actual geological formations—some shallow and sandy, some steep and rocky.

Exactly what they needed. It would be hard to run. But easy to hide. Hell, they didn't call the Kilo-class 636 "the black hole" for nothing. When *Ostrov* went silent, there wasn't a nuclear sub on the planet that could detect her. Not without the nuke's sonar going active and aggressive against the unarmed scientific vessel—which could easily be construed as an act of war.

Either way, the Chinese sub would be forced to show her true colors.

But first, he really did need to test *Ostrov*'s fitness at depth.

"Turn west," Nikolai told the nav. They'd already cruised south to within striking distance of the Aleutian Trench. No sense backtracking. "Plot a course for . . ." The curved network of deepening canyons beckoned. He pinpointed a spot in one of the two that Zubkin had pointed out, which also happened to be the two biggest canyons and filled with a cornucopia of natural formations they could use as shields and blinds if it should come to that. "Let's head for Agattu Canyon first. Do a few angles and dangles. See if the 093 tags along."

Zubkin grinned. *"Da, Kapitan."* He made some swift calculations and slid the charted figures over for his approval.

Nikolai nodded. "Steady on course two-three-zero, Mr. Zubkin, and make your speed four knots," he commanded, his blood humming. He was so ready for this hunt. "Ease us down to one-zero-zero meters."

The men snapped to and his orders were repeated down through the chain of command. Seconds later, *Ostrov* nimbly changed bearing, slipped over the edge of the ridge, and descended into the abyss.

26

▧▨▨▨▨▨▨▨▨▨▨

The big Chinese nuke slowly turned and glided along in *Ostrov*'s baffles, like a giant menacing shark following their scent. For half an hour Nikolai had done a series of circles and turns as they descended into Agattu Canyon. Not exactly a crazy Ivan, more like strolling around the block a few times to see what shook out. The Shang class stayed with them the whole way, a long lurking shadow, not aggressive but keeping steady pace.

There was no mistaking it, *Ostrov* was being deliberately pursued.

In the central post, the navigation table was covered with both their Russian charts as well as the American ones brought along by the scientific team. Because so much of the seabed in this area hadn't been mapped yet, there were whole blank sections on all of them. It was folly to rely on just one navigational chart. Or on any of them, really.

Which was what Nikolai planned to take advantage of.

"Slow to three knots," he ordered. "Watch your depth, nav," he called as they inched their way further down into unknown territory. He turned to *Starpom* Varnas, who had finished questioning the crew and returned to the central post to take over OOD duties. "Announce every twenty meters we mark, and have each watch report in as we go deeper. I want to know immediately if any problems develop."

"*Da, Kapitan,*" Stefan Mikhailovich said in curt tones. Even though he and Misha had confirmed Walker's story of being asleep during Julie's attack, the *starpom* was still convinced of the American's guilt and was angry Nikolai not only refused to put the man under arrest but had allowed Walker to remain free in the central post.

The better to keep an eye on both of them, Nikolai figured. He had a feeling if they found themselves alone in a compartment, only one would emerge alive.

He strode across the space to check the sonar repeater over *Lyeĭtenant* Petrov's shoulder. He'd wanted his best men front and center on this evolution, and since the radio was basically useless under the surface anyway, he'd assigned Danya as conning officer and phone talker. Aside from watching all the repeaters, the radioman would keep up a running commentary on everything that came over the circuits, acting as the hub of communications coming from the various watch posts around the boat.

As the sub descended, the digital images on the sonar monitor were getting harder to interpret. In his mind's eye, Nikolai converted the snowy patterns into a mental picture of the sea bottom, the cliffs and mounds, the slopes and bommies, and the fathomless trench below.

He narrowed his eyes. "Sonar, conn. Keep a sharp lookout on the geography," he said, and Danya repeated it over the circuit. "We'll want to find some nice confusing features down there to shield us if we're to play hide-and-seek with these clowns."

After a second, Julie's voice piped up in English. "What do you mean, hide-and-seek? You aren't actually planning to provoke them, are you?"

Nikolai swiveled his head to her, blinked, and suddenly realized Walker must have been translating what was being said. How had he not known the man spoke Russian . . . ? Nikolai's suspicions about the tight-lipped UUV pilot rose even higher. He might not have been responsible for Julie's attack, but Nikolai still didn't trust the man.

"No," he told her. "Not provoke. Draw them out. They're tailing us and I want to know their intentions."

"Yeah." She made a face. "If that's even possible. The Chinese tend to be pretty subtle in their military strategy."

Nikolai regarded her, recalling that China was her specialty at CIA. "So you agree their intentions are military."

"What else could they be?"

"Indeed." He shot her the shadow of a smile. "Then we shall be disciplined and calm, and await the appearance of disorder among the enemy," he quoted.

Her lips parted in momentary astonishment.

Was she really so surprised a Russian naval captain had read *The Art of War*?

Apparently not. She gave him an odd smile. "And thus the enemy shall provide us with the direction of his own defeat."

For a moment their smiles and gazes held. Damn. A woman who could quote Sun Tzu. He was definitely in love.

"Unless, of course," Walker said dryly, shattering the moment, "they decide to launch a torpedo or two and just blow us out of the water."

Julie went pale. "Not funny."

Nikolai punched a finger toward him. "Don't press your luck, mister."

The other man shrugged. "You think I'm kidding. I'm not."

"I guess we'll find out soon enough," Nikolai said darkly.

At this point he didn't know what to believe. About the Chinese or about Walker. Walker hadn't lied about his alibi for the time of the attack. Nikolai had believed him to the extent of allowing his blood to be drawn as he'd requested. Although it couldn't be tested, and thus proved or disproved, until the scientists came back on board, after what happened to Julie, Nikolai would believe the saboteur capable of just about anything, including drugging the man. But Walker *was* lying about something. Nikolai could feel it in his bones.

Unfortunately he didn't have time to think about that right now.

"One-zero-zero meters," Danya reported. "Passing over the Aleutian Bench. No problems reported, sir."

"Very well." Nikolai consulted the nav, adjusted the course, and ordered them out of the canyon and down over the steep cliffs to two hundred meters—two-thirds of the way to *Ostrov*'s maximum depth.

Still the 093 shadowed them.

Nikolai glanced back at Julie. Her face held a look of intense concentration. "What are you thinking about?" he asked, vaguely surprised she wasn't getting more panicked about being submerged this deep.

"Dissimulation," she said.

"Pardon me?"

"Our Chinese tail." Her brow beetled. "They strive to appear harmless, therefore they must be dangerous. They seem to be following us, so they must surely be leading us. They let themselves be seen, thus they must be hiding something we aren't supposed to see." She met his gaze. "Something that will achieve their true purpose."

More Sun Tzu.

"But we're in front of them," he said. "How can they be leading us?"

Her gaze shadowed. "You said yourself it's a game of cat and mouse."

Nikolai regarded her. "And you think we're the mouse?"

"Aren't we?"

He allowed himself the hint of a smile. "I sure as hell hope not." However, she did seem to possess an innate understanding of the subtleties of their stalker's actions. He would do well to pay attention to her instincts. This was her area of expertise, after all. His smile faded. "So, if your theory is correct, what *is* their true purpose?"

She wasn't going to say it aloud, but the objective for the Chinese wasn't so difficult to guess.

To stop the SD card from falling into the hands of their enemies—namely, Russia and the United States.

That must be the ultimate goal of this exercise for the 093. There was really no other possible reason for their behavior—as inscrutable as it was. And at least one other person knew it— the person working for them aboard *Ostrov*. Nikolai just wished he knew if that traitor was still actually on board at the moment, or off on Attu Island.

"Is there scuba gear on the boat?" Walker asked, breaking into their contemplative silence.

Nikolai frowned. "Yes, of course." He glanced at *Starpom* Varnas, who had actually brought his own gear along.

"Scuba is standard equipment," Varnas said, who had been listening with one ear to the conversation. "In case repairs are needed below the surface."

"Perhaps that's your answer," Walker said.

Nikolai scrutinized his bland expression. "You're saying you think someone is—what? Planning to jump ship using scuba gear, and . . . and then what? Get plucked up by the Chinese sub?"

Varnas snorted.

Walker's head tilted, ignoring the *starpom*. "You have a scenario that fits the facts better?"

Nikolai sighed inwardly. Well, no. Not really. But that one seemed . . .

Чертов ад.

Okay. Just improbable enough to be correct.

An Arctic-weight wetsuit would protect a person against the near freezing temperature of the sea easily long enough to be fished up. But one would have to be equipped with more than a wetsuit to survive a swim to the ocean surface from a hundred meters down. Aside from the difficulty of getting off the hermetically sealed vessel, the outside pressure alone would crush a man to a pulp.

Nikolai turned back to the sonar monitor and considered it. "If you're right," he mused, "we're safe as long as *Ostrov* remains below safe human dive limits."

Julie peered at him nervously. "Safe from what?"

He thinned his lips. He'd noticed that the 093 was creeping closer. And Walker's offhanded comment about torpedoes had definitely gotten his attention. "That's the question, isn't it? I just have a feeling our friends out there are planning something far less obvious than plucking an agent from the water."

Walker studied him thoughtfully. "Such as?" he asked.

Nikolai wished he knew.

"One hundred sixty meters," Danya announced, then came to sudden attention and touched his earphones. "Sir! The COB reports flooding in the engine room!"

Nikolai strode over and grabbed a headset. Over the static he could hear shouting and the distinctive sound of water spraying in the background.

"Engine room, conn. Status report!"

Seconds later came Yasha's calm reply. "Nothing to worry about, *Kapitan*. Looks like a faulty weld in one of the pipes. We're fitting it with a bandit patch."

"That's the only leak?" Nikolai asked.

"Looks like it," the COB came back. "I'll report immediately if the situation changes."

Nikolai checked the fathometer. Just one hundred seventy-five meters. *The devil*. The boat was showing its age a lot sooner than he'd expected.

Nevertheless, when Stefan Mikhailovich shot him a questioning glance, he nodded. "Continue as ordered, *Starpom* Varnas."

He noticed Julie gripping the arms of her chair. "Are we going to sink?" she asked, eyes wide as teacups.

Nikolai gave her a crooked smile. "It'll take more than one faulty pipe weld to sink us," he assured her.

Everyone was a bit jumpy today—including him—but the fact was, occasional leaks were a way of life on an old boat. Nothing to worry about. Much, anyway.

She looked around and when she saw nobody else panicking, her shoulders notched down a fraction. "Sorry. Still a little shaky."

"You're entitled," he said. "How about if I let you know when you need to be scared? Otherwise, just assume you don't have to worry. Okay?"

She eased out a breath. "Okay."

"One-eight-zero meters," Danya announced.

Nikolai gave her another reassuring smile, then turned back to the instruments. He could hear the ubiquitous creak and groan of *Ostrov*'s double metal hulls as the sub slipped farther down toward the bottom. By now they'd glided free of the canyon and into the open water above the trench. They were entering some very deep territory. The increased pressure felt heavy in Nikolai's blood and his lungs, and his legs felt leaden.

"Sir! Another leak," Danya called out moments later. "This one's in the forward battery compartment."

The compartment just below his stateroom. Nikolai glanced at the fathometer and ordered the diving officer, "Dive, steady on two-zero-zero!" as he brought his headset up over his ears again. "Forward mechanics, conn. Status!"

"Another pipe weld, *Kapitan*. Working to clamp it," came the report.

"Are the batteries in danger of compromise?" he quickly asked.

One of the worst potential dangers on board a diesel-electric submarine was the possibility of battery acid somehow mixing with seawater. The result was a release of deadly chlorine gas. Fatal if breathed for longer than a few moments.

"Not as far as we can tell, sir. The waterproof wells should protect the batteries until we can get the weld repaired."

Even so, he was beginning to get a bad feeling. And it didn't help that the Chinese sub kept moving closer.

He gave orders for the batteries to be thoroughly examined, just to make sure they'd get no nasty surprises from that quarter later on. He'd dearly like to go down and check them himself. But he was needed here. And that would also mean leaving Julie, which he wouldn't do.

However, his face must have shown his growing worry.

"Nikolai, go if you need to. I'll be fine here," she told him.

"No," he said. "My men can take care of it." And he knew they could. He just . . . had a niggling feeling.

"Shall we continue on our present course, Commander?" the navigator asked.

Nikolai pursed his lips. One leak was routine, two was bad luck. Should he risk three . . . or more?

They'd reached a depth of two hundred meters. The Arctic Sea where they were headed was sixty meters at its deepest. There was no reason to push the depth any farther.

But it was high time to address their other concern.

"Nyet," he told the nav. "How about those geographical features I asked you to look out for? Anything good within striking distance?"

The navigator grinned in relief, along with every man on the watch. They knew what was coming. *"Da, Komandir,"* he said, reaching for his charts. "Would you like us to disappear, to turn the tables on the 093, or to make the whole Chinese navy tell ghost stories of *Ostrov* for generations to come?"

Nikolai laughed, then turned to the other crew members. "Well, men? What say you? Shall we become ghosts?"

But before anyone could respond, Danya Petrov launched out of his seat, eyes wide, hands pressing his headphones to his ears. "Sir!" he exclaimed. "They're flooding their torpedo tubes!"

27

\\\\\\\\\///////

Julie saw Nikolai and the rest of the crew stop in their tracks as though suddenly frozen solid. Tension surged through the room like a bolt of lightning.

"What's going on?" she asked in alarm, cursing for the hundredth time today that she'd never learned the Russian language. She spun. "Clint?"

Nikolai barked an order and the room exploded into action. Overhead, the klaxon went off and the speakers blared something in Russian that made everyone jump. No one paid the slightest attention to her question. Even Clint had popped up, an astonished frown on his face.

"Clint!" she exclaimed, coming to her feet as well. "What on earth is happening?"

He shot her a distracted glance. "The 093 seems to be preparing to launch torpedoes."

She stared at him in horror. "Are you serious? But why? What did we do?"

"Not a damn thing," Nikolai interjected from where he stood at the main console, scowling. Everyone was poised over their instruments as though teetering on a dime, ready to act on a word from their captain.

"This is crazy. They have to know we're unarmed!" she exclaimed hoarsely.

"They don't appear to care."

Abruptly, she sat back down. Goose bumps crawled over her arms like giant spiders.

Shit, shit, shit.

What were the Chinese doing? Were they planning to sink *Ostrov*? Would they really risk starting a world war over the UUV plans contained on the data card that was currently burning a hole in her coverall pocket? Could those plans possibly be so important to them?

Once again she wondered if there might be something on the storage card other than what she'd been told. . . .

"Look," Clint said, lowering his voice so only the two of them could hear, "I know you found the SD card. Have you told anyone? Could the Chinese have somehow found out that you have it now?"

She gaped at him, wide-eyed. "How did you know?"

The corner of his lip curved. "You just told me."

She stood up abruptly, furious with herself for falling for the oldest trick in the book. "Who the hell *are* you?" she demanded in a low but intense voice. "What are you doing on this boat? You'd better tell me right now or I swear to God I'll have Nikolai slap you back in—"

He held up his hands. "No need for dramatics. We're on the same side. Honest!"

"Julie! Are you all right?" Nikolai called, having sliced them a glance when she'd jumped up.

"If you want answers," Clint said impassively, "tell him to back off. And keep your voice down."

"I don't like being told what to do," she retorted. But quietly.

"Yeah, I got that," he said.

Nevertheless, she nodded her head and smiled Nikolai off. She *did* want answers. And Clint was right. The real saboteur could be listening to their conversation even now.

"Now, about that SD card. Does anyone else know?"

She shook her head. "No."

He shot a glance at Nikolai. "No one?"

Again she shook her head. "I just found it this morning. I was going to tell him, but I"—she gave an involuntary shiver—"never got the chance."

"You still have it? The attacker didn't take it off you?"

Her hand strayed to her pocket. "No. I checked it when I changed clothes."

"And you're sure it's the same SD card?"

She nodded. "I drew a small Chinese symbol onto the label after I found it. It hasn't been switched."

"Well," he said, "the good news is the attacker must not know you have it, or it would be gone."

Small favors.

"And the bad news?"

All at once a loud noise reverberated through the hull, sending a physical jolt through her bones. Her hands flew up to steady herself as she gasped.

"Christ," Clint said. "They're going active."

Fear gripped her. "What does that mean?"

Nikolai shouted an order and no one moved a muscle. She could see sweat pop out on brows all around.

"Sonar. We just got targeted," Clint told her, frown deepening.

"They're *shooting* at us?" she squeaked.

Nikolai's eyes narrowed, looking more calculating than afraid. "My guess is they're trying to scare the pants off us," he said from where he stood. "In retaliation for yesterday."

"Well, it's working," she croaked.

Still, as Nikolai exchanged terse words with his men she felt somewhat relieved. She should have thought of that. Of course the 093 would try to get back at *Ostrov* for the embarrassing musical UUV maneuver Nikolai and Clint had pulled with their decoy sounds. Maybe that was all this was. Saving face. Not starting World War III.

"Still no torpedoes launched," Clint said, watching the instruments like a hawk.

She met Nikolai's gaze. "Should I be worried yet?" she asked shakily, recalling his promise.

"Not quite yet." Calm as the center of a storm, he looked at her evenly. "So," he asked, "how do they expect us to react to this blatant intimidation?"

After her initial surprise over being consulted again, she warmed inwardly at his trust in her judgment. He really *did* believe in her.

Her eyes went back to the sonar monitor, where she could see the Chinese sub getting closer and closer. She nibbled her lip. How *should* they react?

If this was simple retaliation, a show of fear by *Ostrov*'s captain would satisfy their honor. But things were seldom quite so simple with the Chinese. They were unparalleled strategists and masters of subtlety. If this was them lulling *Ostrov* into complacency, or into an unknown trap, it would behoove Nikolai to be thinking several moves ahead.

"They'll expect us to act frightened. If not in reality, then in pretense, to allow them to save face. I suggest you do so. But let it be the first chess move of your own plan. Be the queen, not a pawn."

Nikolai smiled. "Or perhaps a knight. I've always fancied learning to ride a horse."

She tilted her head, momentarily distracted. "You've never ridden?"

He shook his head. "Not even a seahorse."

She smiled. "My aunt has horses on her farm in Oklahoma." She opened her mouth to tell him she'd take him riding when he came to visit. Except he wasn't going to visit. So she closed it again.

The pain of knowing that stabbed through her. How she wished . . .

Clint cleared his throat. "Whatever you do, Skipper, I think you should be quick about it."

Another active sonar ping hammered *Ostrov*'s hull, emphasizing his words. Once again all eyes went to Nikolai, who whipped back to his instruments, calling out orders. Then he grabbed a headset, strode over to Julie, and thrust it into her hands.

"What's this for?" she asked in surprise.

"My secret weapon," he said, a hint of satisfaction in his voice.

"Which is?"

He lifted her hands with his and urged her to put on the headset. "You."

Julie's jaw dropped in shock. *"What?"*

Nikolai couldn't believe he hadn't thought of this sooner. "You speak Mandarin, right?"

"Well, yes, but—"

"Good. Then you can speak with that Chinese captain and find out what the hell he's up to."

Her eyes widened. He had to be kidding. "You realize it won't be that easy. First of all, I doubt he'll talk to me."

"Oh, he'll talk to you, all right."

"But is that wise?" Walker interjected.

Nikolai was getting a little tired of the man's interference. Everywhere he turned, Clint Walker was sticking his nose in. One more and he'd get out the duct tape.

"If they know about the SD card, they have to know CIA sent someone to retrieve it. It won't be too hard for them to guess it's Julie," Walker warned, his voice lowered.

"That's what I'm counting on," Nikolai said through his teeth, sliding on his own circuit earphones. Ship-to-ship communication underwater was tenuous at best, but at this close range it was just possible. "Mr. Petrov, get the captain of the 093 on the growler, and patch in Miss Severin," he ordered his radioman, who glanced at him in surprise, then scrambled to obey.

"What am I supposed to say?" Julie asked nervously.

"Ask him what he's planning to do," Nikolai returned. "And when he refuses to say, tell him point-blank you found the stolen data card days ago and have already transmitted all the information on it to your employer, so anything they might have in mind in the way of a plan to retrieve—or destroy—it will be too late."

She blinked owlishly. "I'm pretty sure they've been monitoring our communications, including satellite phone calls. They'll know that's a lie. Even if I weren't a terrible liar. Which I am." At that her eyes dipped away, looking guilty for a brief second.

His attention snagged. A suspicion niggled at him. Was she hiding something from him?

"Granted," he replied, "but hopefully it will produce a cloud of confusion long enough for us to slip away." Not to mention the fact that it was a civilian woman speaking to the vessel's commanding officer—the very woman they were hunting—and not *Ostrov*'s captain. That should buy Nikolai time as the enemy tried to analyze the unorthodox and totally unexpected move.

"Yeah, okay," Julie said doubtfully.

Unconsciously, her fingers touched the pocket of her coverall, again drawing his attention. She *was* hiding something! Something small.

Nikolai wasn't the only one who saw the movement. Walker's gaze darted speculatively to his. Nikolai kept his expression carefully neutral, pretending he hadn't noticed.

What the hell? Had Julie actually found the SD card? Sometime between when he'd walked away from her last night and the attempt on her life this morning?

But just then his headset came to life, static echoing in his ears, and a tinny, faraway voice came on speaking Chinese. Julie jerked up in her seat and said something in reply, whereupon there was more static. Finally a man whose clipped, authoritative voice could only be that of the 093's CO came on. Nikolai could clearly hear the restrained outrage in his tone, but could only guess at what he might be saying to Julie.

While they spoke, Nikolai ordered *Ostrov* about, so they were facing the enemy nose to nose. That should give the enemy commander another unexpected move to think about as he lied through his teeth to Julie.

Who was impressing the hell out of Nikolai. Though he couldn't understand the conversation, a serene expression had settled over her face and she spoke with elegant dignity as she and the Chinese captain conducted their short, excruciatingly polite exchange. She didn't let his curt answers ruffle her, and when nothing further was forthcoming, she politely thanked him—at least it sounded that way to Nikolai—and with a *click* the earphones filled with static once more.

She slid off the headset. "Well. That was fun. Not."

"What did he say?" Walker asked.

Nikolai glared at him in irritation. The other man raised his palms in conciliation. "Sorry."

Julie's expression turned wry. "He said he had no idea what I was talking about."

"I'm shocked," Walker muttered.

"Conn, sonar. More tubes flooding!" Gavrikov announced from the sonar shack.

It was all Nikolai needed to hear. He smiled grimly. It didn't matter what the 093 had in mind, he wasn't sticking around to find out.

"Bring battle stations to full alert, OOD. Prepare to dive the boat, Mr. Zubkin!" he ordered briskly. "Nav! Plot a course for those canyons. I think it's high time we became a ghost ship."

He just hoped it was only metaphorically.

One of the principal advantages of a diesel-electric submarine over a nuclear-powered one was the ability to dive and surface quickly. *Ostrov* moved in the water like a whale, large but swift and decisive. The 093 was more ponderous, like an ungainly water buffalo—once going it was formidable, but gearing up and turning about, it took its sweet time.

Nikolai used every precious minute of that time to disappear.

"*Kvartirmyeister* Kresney reports a leak in the galley, sir!" Danya called out just before they hit the two-one-five mark.

Хуйня. The old tub was leaking like a goddamn sieve.

"How bad?" Nikolai demanded over the circuit. "Can we make it?" They were diving hell-bent for leather under the big nuke, and he planned to sprint for the uneven shelter of the canyons as soon as they were clear of the hull, before the enemy could turn around and pursue them.

"It's bad, *Kapitan*," came Misha's report, shouted over the sound of gushing water. "Don't dive any deeper or we risk the whole damn boat coming apart!"

No way could they come up yet without risking shearing off the sail on the bottom of the Chinese sub, gutting it like a trout in the process. Fatal for both boats.

He noticed that Walker had stopped translating for Julie. Her gaze was darting around the central post with a look of growing panic. Her fingers clutched the arms of her chair in a death grip.

He paused to send her a reassuring smile. "Don't get worried yet," he said, knowing exactly what she was thinking. "We'll be fine."

He turned back to his monitors. The second they cleared the 093, he ordered, "All ahead full, Mr. Zubkin. Full rise on bow and stern planes! Bring her up to one-five-zero and make it fast."

He felt the surge of buoyancy as pressurized air was blown into the ballast tanks and *Ostrov* cut up like a dolphin through the water toward the surface. His own adrenaline surged along with it, feeling the force of the pressure pressing his feet into the deck.

"Conn, sonar. The 093 is starting to turn."

Good luck with that, he thought. By the time the nuke came about, *Ostrov* would already be swallowed up by the recesses of the feature-rich canyon the nav had discovered.

"Fucking hell!" Gavrikov's voice burst over the circuit. "Conn, sonar! Torpedo has been launched! Repeat, torpedo in the water!"

28

⫸⫸⫷⫷

Julie knew immediately that something was very, very wrong. This time there was no frozen pause before the entire central post watch launched into a chaos of shouts and action.

She didn't need a translation. The Russian word *torpeda* was not so different from the English.

Terror ripped through her veins, but she ruthlessly tamped it down. Falling apart now would serve nothing, and it would not save her or the lives of the others if *Ostrov* was about to be blown up.

God help them all!

At the helm, Nikolai held the tense crew together, assuming control with an iron will, calming the tumult that swept through the space, urging the men back into military efficiency, launching countermeasures, snapping commands, and ordering *Ostrov* into a diving sprint so fast Julie could feel the grind of the main propeller shaft as it bit into the water. He was magnificent, every inch the hero, and despite her terror Julie felt a huge admiration for the man she'd come to love.

Clint had jumped up at the first sign of trouble and was now peering intently at the sonar repeater. For the moment, the small blip that had shot out from the still-turning 093 was heading away from *Ostrov*, being forced to boomerang around in a semicircle after being launched in the wrong direction due to the 093's position.

"It's not a torpedo," Clint announced loudly, bringing Nikolai whipping around. "It's a UUV."

Relief seared through Julie. *Oh, thank God.*

It took Nikolai about two seconds to digest this information and bark a few words into his headset. He listened, then said, "Gavrikov agrees."

"We're too close for a torpedo attack," Clint said, probably for her benefit.

Nikolai nodded at the sonar blip, in the zenith of its U-turn but still closer to the Chinese sub than to *Ostrov*. "They'd risk damaging their own boat in the explosion."

"Nothing worse than getting sunk by your own fish," Clint observed.

Julie shivered at the thought. "Other than being sunk by someone else's."

Nikolai scowled. "So what's its purpose?"

Clint pursed his lips. "Too many possibilities even to guess."

"Could it be carrying explosives?" he asked.

Clint's shoulder lifted. "If they wanted to blow us up, they're carrying plenty of real torpedoes. They didn't *have* to get so close."

Nikolai glanced over at her. "Julie? Any suggestions?"

She peeled her horrified attention from the blinking dot and forced herself to think. Her heart pounded painfully. "The Chinese have been testing several new kinds of ASW technologies. I guess it would depend on whether they want to follow us, disable us, sink us, or . . ." She let her suggestions trail off. She honestly didn't want to come up with any more scenarios.

He didn't press her. "Well, I'm not about to stick around to find out." He paced back to the main console, calling out orders as he went.

Seconds later the sub made a deep turn, and Julie grabbed hold of her chair, hanging on for dear life while the seasoned submariners simply leaned their bodies with the motion.

She squeezed her eyes shut, listening to Nikolai's com-

manding voice as he guided them away from danger, trying to
absorb his calm strength through osmosis. He knew what he
was doing. He'd get them out of there safely. He had to!

She couldn't believe it had come to this. This insane mission had changed her life in ways she hadn't ever imagined.
And now it might take it away completely.

No. She mustn't think that way. That *wasn't* going to
happen.

She opened her eyes again, watching and listening in
white-knuckled fear as Nikolai drove *Ostrov* at full tilt up
through the steep underwater canyon, searching for a hiding
place. The pit of her stomach lurched at every change of depth
and turn of the rudder as the sub dashed over ridges and
around seamounts to shake their pursuer. She knew their
speed wasn't more than a couple of knots at most, but it felt
like a high-speed car chase at ninety miles per hour. The staccato Russian exchanges between Nikolai and his men and the
urgent bleat of the overhead speakers made a taut soundtrack
to the indecipherable snowstorm of the sonar monitor's visu-
als. Cutting through it all was the loud, intermittent ping of
the 093's active sonar blasts, each new one making her jump
out of her skin.

Just when she thought she couldn't take the tension any
longer, the chase came to an abrupt halt. The sub slowed like
it had hit a solid wall of molasses. Nikolai gave one last
clipped command and immediately every sound on the submarine ceased. She opened her mouth to ask what had happened, but he quickly put a finger to his lips, signaling for
absolute silence.

She held her breath. They'd gone ultraquiet, hiding in the
uneven geography of the canyon, hoping to disappear completely.

Adrenaline surged through her veins as she held her breath.
She was certain the Chinese sonar operator must be able to
hear the timpani of her heartbeat.

Long, tense moments passed, everyone standing at attention, listening intently, eyes cutting from the sonar monitor to
the hull of the boat as though trying to see through the steel
walls out to the cold, black water beyond.

All at once a high, metallic ping bounced through the

space. Not the familiar hammer jolt, but a thinner, smaller sound.

Nikolai gave a harsh curse at the same time Walker muttered disgustedly, "Damn little fucker!"

"What is it?" Julie asked in alarm.

"The UUV. It pinged us. Jesus. I can't believe the fucking thing found us."

Nikolai stalked back and forth, mouth set in an angry line. "I guess that answers our question about what it's doing," he said tersely, then switched back to Russian and clipped out more orders.

The crew snapped back into action and instantly she was hanging on to the console again, clenching her stomach against the force of the submarine lurching into a sprint and continuing its uneven run through the obstacle course of the undersea features.

All the while their small shadow followed.

"Isn't there anything you can do?" she asked Walker minutes later, her voice hoarse with apprehension for what might happen next. "I mean with one of your UUVs? Like chase it off? Or ram it to pieces or something?"

They both glanced at the repeater. The small blip hovered behind them, taking on an air of menace, like one of those creepy little flesh-eating creatures in a horror movie.

"I believe you've been reading my mind," he said, and he jerked his chin at Nikolai. "Think he'd trust me out of his sight?"

She blew out an uneven breath. "Hell, Clint. I still don't know if *I'd* trust you."

His lips quirked. "I'm hurt."

"Yeah, yeah. Give me a reason to," she said. "Tell me who you're working for."

His jaw tightened as the sub went into another steep turn, and he seemed to come to a decision. To her surprise, he said, "All right. I guess it's time you knew." He glanced around, assessing who might be within earshot. Everyone was busy at their controls. When he was satisfied they weren't being eavesdropped upon, he leveled her a look and said in barely a murmur, "I'm with Naval Intelligence."

Relief mingled with surprise. Even though it made perfect

sense given his background, she hadn't expected that particular agency. At least he wasn't CIA as she'd suspected. *If* he was telling the truth.

"*U.S.* Naval Intelligence?" she clarified.

He chuckled softly. "Yes. I work for the U.S. military."

She swallowed. She needed to know. "Tell me why you're here on *Ostrov.*"

To his credit, he didn't lie. "Same reason you are. To retrieve the SD card."

That was what she was afraid of. "Then we're going to have a problem," she said, wondering how the navy had found out about it. She'd thought that intel had been exclusively CIA property.

The sub was hit by another high-pitched ping, and Clint's eyes went to the repeater, to the enemy UUV stalking them. It was getting closer. The larger mother ship had also reappeared on the screen, hovering at the edge. "Woman, in case you hadn't noticed, we already have a problem."

No freaking kidding. But he was avoiding the issue. "I'm not letting you take the SD card from me," she told him determinedly. "Nikolai won't—"

"Captain Romanov is a Russian military officer," he said impatiently, "who works as an asset for the FSB. You really think he'll let you hold on to something this important?"

"He promised—"

"Trust me, he'd promise anything and do even more to get his hands on the intelligence stored on that card. It's his ticket to saving his career. You know that as well as I do."

She shook her head in denial. It wasn't true. Nikolai wouldn't betray her. She wanted to tell Clint, to shout it out loud at him, but her words stuck in her throat. "It doesn't matter. The point is he won't let *you* take it from me."

Clint looked smug. "He can only stop me if he knows you found the SD card. When were you planning to tell him? Or were you going to . . . ?"

Her fingers held the edge of her seat with white knuckles. But this time it wasn't because of the erratic movement of the boat. It was to keep herself from reaching over and wringing Clint Walker's neck.

"I'll tell him right now," she ground out, just to prove to the insolent jerk—and possibly to herself—that she would. She stood up.

Nikolai looked over.

Already on his feet, Clint put a hand on her arm, urging her back down. "Julie, there's no need to—"

Just then the sub made another sharp turn, throwing her off balance. She landed in Clint's arms.

Instantly Nikolai was there, yanking her away from him. "Do *not* touch her," he growled.

Walker raised his hands, palms out. "Then stop doing goddamn loop-de-loops. *Ostrov*'s a submarine, not a goddamn Spitfire."

The force of *Ostrov* slicing through the water made all their bodies tilt precariously. Nikolai put his arm around her waist and held her tighter.

"Why did you stand up?" he asked her without shifting his glare off the other man. "Is there a problem here? Is he—"

"No," she assured him, then turned in Nikolai's arms and rushed on before the conversation took a nosedive. "I just wanted to tell you . . ." She regrouped. "You know that thing I've been looking for?"

Releasing her, he took a step back to look down at her, his expression wary. "Yeah?"

"I found it. This morning."

He froze for a millisecond, then his icy gaze razored back to Clint. "He knows?"

She nodded. "I'm sorry. He guessed. Just now." She leaned in closer and whispered, "He's with U.S. Naval Intelligence."

Nikolai's breath jetted out angrily. "Really. Anything else I should know?"

She hesitated, then plowed on. "We were thinking he could try to do something about the Chinese UUV out there, using one of ours."

Nikolai's scowl eased fractionally. She had his attention. "Such as?"

Clint leaned back on his heels. "Well. I've got an interesting little device I developed that can magnetically wipe any and all electronics software it's aimed at. That should annoy them to no end."

An unwilling smile crossed Nikolai's face. "It should, indeed." He studied Walker for a moment. "What would it take to set that up?"

"I'll need to work from the UUV console in the torpedo room," Walker said. "And I'll need some help."

Nikolai considered him with a steely regard. Julie knew he was weighing how far Clint could be trusted. But he had already been cleared of her attack, and he couldn't really make his UUV do anything bad to *Ostrov* without dooming himself along with everyone else. And why would he? He was after the SD card. Not out for sabotage. He wasn't the enemy. Not the saboteur.

"Are you on board with this?" he asked Julie.

She gave him a wobbly smile. "Yeah," she said.

"Very well," Nikolai said at length. "Do it," he told Clint. "I'll assign *Kvartirmyeister* Kresney to accompany you, and one of the weps techs to help. Will that do?"

Clint smiled. "Perfect."

Nikolai nodded and started to walk away, then hesitated and turned back to Julie. "Is it in a safe place?" he asked.

Despite the sharp shift in subject, there was little doubt what he was talking about. When his gaze dropped briefly to her coverall pocket, she also knew he knew exactly where she was keeping it.

"It's as safe as I am," she said.

"Then let's keep it that way," he said tightly and strode away, back to the main command console.

As she watched him go, her heart fluttered. It was ridiculous how huge a crush she had on that man. Absurd how crazy in lust, and absolutely in awe of him, she was. Total insanity how she'd managed to fall in love with Nikolai Kirillovich Romanov so thoroughly in such a short time. But how could she not have? He was the most powerful, intelligent, and thoughtful man she'd ever met, as well as being the sexiest man alive.

It broke her heart completely that she would have to give him up soon. *Too* soon. Now that she'd found the SD card, as soon as she was able to contact Thurman she'd be recalled home immediately.

As though reading her thoughts, Clint's expression turned serious. "What'll you do when they order you to leave him behind, and never allow you to see him again . . . ?"

Pain cut through her. She didn't want to think about that. And she sure as hell didn't want Clint Walker reminding her of it. "That's none of your damn business," she snapped.

He leaned in. "Julie. I can *make* it my business. I can help you be together."

She threw him a skeptical look. "You? How?"

"My agency, and the navy, could learn a lot from a cooperative Russian naval commander of Nikolai's rank and status. I'm sure they'd be willing to pave the way for him to come to the States in exchange for the opportunity to question him."

She leveled him a gaze. "I doubt he'd agree to betray his country."

"It's not like they deserve his loyalty. They've pretty much thrown him to the wolves."

It was true. But Julie knew how honorable Nikolai was.

"You don't know until you ask him," Clint persisted.

"I suppose."

"The thing is . . ."

She'd known there would be a catch. "Yes?"

"We'd need something from you in return."

She set her jaw. "Me?"

"It would only be fair. For bringing Romanov over for you."

Yeah, like *she* would be the one benefiting most from any of that. And gee, one guess what they'd want from her in exchange. "You're kidding, right?" she ground out. "You must think I'm a complete idiot."

"No," he said. "I think you're a woman in love."

"Same thing," she muttered and dropped back onto her chair. "But you can forget it. I have every intention of fulfilling my mission."

"The plans on that storage card are critical to our nation's defense," Clint said earnestly. "Believe me, CIA isn't going to keep them secret from the navy."

"I realize that," she conceded.

"So what difference does it make who actually brings it in? I'll make sure you get credit for finding and retrieving it, and Nikolai for his cooperation."

Her brain couldn't help but fantasize. She had to admit the offer was tempting. Very tempting.

Well. Except for one thing.

"The whole question is moot," she said, tamping down the hurt that swirled inside her at the bitter reality. "Nikolai isn't interested in a long-term relationship. No way will he want to move to the States. Not for me, anyway."

Clint shot her a look of incredulity. "What universe are you living in?"

"The real one," she said, a pang of regret cramping her insides. "Spies working for opposing sides only live happily ever after in the movies."

Just ask her father.

Or Nikolai's mother.

Clint's brows flicked up at Julie. "Anyone ever mention to you that the Cold War is over?"

"Yeah, as a matter of fact," Julie murmured, a chill tinkling down her spine like out-of-tune piano keys. "Nikolai said exactly the same thing the first day we met." The day he'd gotten orders from the FSB to seduce her into giving up her mission.

Was Clint doing the same thing, just using different bait? Oh, wait. The same bait, just in a different way.

Wow. Did these men think *all* women were so damn gullible, or just her?

Hell. The Cold War might be over, but sexpionage was alive and well. And it always seemed to be women who paid the price.

Just then *Kvartirmyeister* Kresney ducked through the watertight door and reported to the captain, then frowned when he received his instructions. Apparently he still wasn't convinced of Clint's innocence.

Misha gave Clint a curt signal to get moving. Clint tossed her a wry smile and said over his shoulder as he followed the quartermaster out of the central post, "There, you see? Great minds think alike."

Yeah, if you were a Neanderthal.

"Sorry, Walker. No deal," she called after him. "So go do something useful with yourself and kill that goddamn UUV."

29

||||||\\\////||||||

"Yes, ma'am." Clint's voice floated back after he'd disappeared from view.

Nikolai suppressed his irritation as he walked over to Julie. "What was that all about?" he asked. She and Walker had been having an intense conversation in hushed tones and he wanted to know the subject.

"Nothing."

"Really." He didn't even try to hide the sarcasm.

Her lips thinned in a nose sigh. "Fine. He offered to have the navy invite you to move to the United States if I gave him the SD card in exchange. I told him you wouldn't be interested."

Nikolai was momentarily stiff with shock. Yes, about her denial, but mostly about Walker's offer in the first place. *The U.S. Navy would bring him to America?* "What makes you think I wouldn't be interested?" he asked, recovering.

She glanced up at him in patent disbelief. "Are you saying you would?"

He was still too taken aback to know how he would feel about that, other than his initial knee-jerk inner dialogue—*No way in hell*—followed swiftly by *Jesus, I wouldn't have to give her up.*

Aloud he said, "What I would have liked is to answer for myself."

Her cheeks flushed lightly. "Sorry. I just assumed—"

He needed to change the subject before he said something stupid. Something like, "Yes! Yes! Yes!"

"You seem to be confiding in Walker a lot." He did his best not to sound petulant. Not sure he succeeded.

Her tongue peeked out and swiped over her lower lip. "Nikolai," she began, but thankfully she was interrupted when Walker appeared back at the door.

"Skipper," Walker called from the door, "it occurred to me that you might try to scrape that sucker off our butt by going too deep for it. The max depth on most UUVs of this type is either two or three hundred meters, or somewhere in between. You could try diving below two hundred and see if it can follow."

Now there was an interesting idea. Nikolai considered. And now that he thought about it, the Chinese had only launched their UUV after *Ostrov* had come up from the deep submersion drill. Afterthought . . . or necessity?

"What's the max depth of your UUVs?" he asked Walker.

Walker grinned. "Four hundred meters." With that, he disappeared again.

Nikolai strode over to Danya Petrov, raising the circuit headphones to his ears. "Get me *Praporshchik* Selnikov."

"*Da*, *Kapitan*."

When Yasha came on the line, Nikolai asked, "How are the leaks holding up?"

"Well, we haven't drowned yet," his chief engineer responded. "But we're getting mighty low on chewing gum and duct tape."

Nikolai smiled despite himself. "Let me know when you run out. Meanwhile, can we push her down to three hundred meters?"

Yasha started to cough loudly. "You got a death wish, boy?"

Nikolai told him what Walker had suggested.

"Shit, we barely made it down to *two* hundred before the welds started splitting," Yasha reminded him gruffly. "Three hundred will pop the rivets for sure."

"Hell, let's give it a shot, *Praporshchik*. We can come right up again if things get hairy."

"That's pretty much a guarantee," Yasha grumbled.

"Do your best, Yasha." Nikolai tore off the headphones. "Nav! Find me a blasted canyon!"

Twenty minutes later, they were hovering just under the lip of the Aleutian Trench at two hundred thirty-five meters, hiding from the 093's aggressive sonar in a narrow natural depression between three boxy seamounts.

They hadn't lost the UUV at two hundred meters as they'd hoped. They could still hear it swimming around, pinging away at the seabed playing hunt and peck. It was, however, only making quick forays below that depth, so Nikolai figured they were very close to its limit.

"Two-four-zero meters," Borovsky announced from the fathometer.

Nikolai planned to go as deep as he dared and hunker down for the time it would take for Walker to launch one of his UUVs and rid them for good of the persistent pest.

So far, *Ostrov*'s integrity had held up fairly well. Just two new leaks, both quickly sealed. Only the old weld break above the battery compartment was giving Yasha trouble, springing open anew no matter what kind of repairs and mechanical wizardry the chief engineer threw at it.

"It's like someone used fucking toothpaste to weld it," Yasha complained bitterly. "The whole fucking space is awash in sea spray. The men are working in fucking foul weather gear."

"Just make sure the batteries are protected," Nikolai said unnecessarily. "Can your men hold out for another hour or so?"

"We'll give it our best, *Kapitan*."

He figured that was about how long it would be before Walker could make good on his plan.

Assuming he intended to do so. Nikolai was still not one hundred percent convinced of Walker's intentions. With his idea he'd effectively driven *Ostrov* back into the deep, where at any second the ill-maintained sub could conceivably fall apart and implode. But Nikolai had to trust him, because, as Julie pointed out, Walker would also suffer any bad consequences. The American didn't seem ready to die just yet.

"Two-five-zero meters," Borovsky announced, sweating nervously forty-five minutes later.

Julie joined Nikolai at the repeater and looked on breathlessly as Walker finally launched the UUV. The entire central post watch stood behind them, glued to the sight of the tiny blip as it shot away from *Ostrov*'s torpedo tube.

"Here goes nothing," she murmured.

The moment the tubes were flooded, their hiding place had been exposed, of course. But Nikolai and the nav had already mapped out their escape route, through a feature-filled side canyon at two hundred sixty meters that cut back toward Attu Island.

He waited impatiently until the UUV was well away, then called to the OOD, "Get us out of here, Mr. Zubkin."

He took the sub into a slow downward dive, heading for the canyon. Holding his breath as they went.

Moments later Danya called out, "Sir! We have a contact. Not the 093. A different signature. Something above the surface." Nikolai spun his attention to the radioman, who listened intently for a moment on the headphones. "Sonar says it's a Chinese Y-8MPA aircraft. Flying a loose pattern over the area. Range closing fast."

Чертов ад.

"This is crazy," he muttered. "Now they're throwing *aircraft* at us?"

Julie's worried gaze shot to his. "Is that bad?"

It could be. Very bad. "Usually there's only one reason aircraft get involved in enemy sub hunts: to drop nasty things in the water. Things like sonobuoys, explosive locators, or depth charges."

"Depth charges?" Her eyes rounded.

He rubbed a hand over his mouth. "It's undoubtedly just another tease. We have to believe this is still a peaceful encounter," he reassured her. Though he was beginning to wonder. "But they're playing real dirty."

That was when all hell broke loose below.

"Kapitan!" Danya shouted. "Mr. Walker reports flooding in the torpedo room! And *Praporshchik* Selnikov is yelling they can't control the leaking over the battery compartment.

It's getting worse. He politely suggests we get ourselves up to a less precarious depth."

Nikolai slammed on his earphones. "Torpedo room, conn. Walker, will the flooding effect the UUV sortie?"

"No, we're good, Skipper," came the reply over the sound of shouting and spraying water. "The crew is getting it under control."

"How long before the enemy UUV is neutralized?"

There was static and more shouts and cursing in the background. "The fucker's hightailing it," Walker said over the noise. "It could be a while if I have to chase him down."

Nikolai swore under his breath. "The boat's starting to fall apart, Walker. I'll need to bring her depth up. Fast. What's your operating range?"

"Do what you have to do. I'll manage somehow."

"Keep me informed." He switched circuits. "Engineering, conn. Yasha, what's going on down there?"

"We're wading in half a meter of water, *Kapitan*. I'm afraid the—" Suddenly alarms started to wail both in the central post and over the circuit. The overhead lights and the control monitors all went out, leaving them in darkness for a few seconds before the red battle lanterns flickered on. Yasha let loose a string of obscenities. "We have a battery short, sir! I have to—"

"Go."

Nikolai made the emergency announcement over the 1MC and glanced over at Julie. When things erupted, she'd backed away from the main console, returning to her seat. She stood gripping the back of it, looking pale even in the red glow. He fought the instinct to go to her and fold her in his arms. "Don't worry," he called to her. "Just a glitch with the batteries."

He didn't think she believed him, but she nodded and stayed put.

Yasha's harried voice came over the sound-powered phones. "Sir, we managed to stop the sparking before it caught fire."

Thank God. "Damage report?"

"We're still assessing, but we've lost the forward batteries until we can isolate the affected circuits and get the short repaired."

Losing the batteries was bad, but a fire would have been far worse. Fire on a submarine was one of the worst disasters imaginable. There was nowhere for the heat, smoke, and toxic gases to go other than straight into everyone's lungs.

"How long?" Nikolai asked, his gaze running over the darkened monitors.

"A couple of hours at least."

So much for playing games with the 093.

With only the after battery array intact, all nonessential equipment would have to be shut off. They still had power, but it wasn't enough to drive the ship through the water. Not at any speed.

And if the rest of the batteries failed . . .

Nyet. Best not even go there.

Luckily, they didn't need full power to reach the surface. Once there, they'd have the diesels to run on. He turned to Borovsky. "Dive, take us up to periscope depth. Slow and steady. Bearing zero-six-five."

"Attu Island, *Kapitan*?"

"As fun as this party's been, it's time to bail." He had a feeling they'd be late picking up the scientists.

Assuming they made it back in one piece.

Julie was still watching him anxiously. As he strode over to her, the regular lights came back on. Yasha was a miracle worker.

"Are we in trouble yet?" Julie asked, fear sanding her voice as she looked around at the men's faces.

"We've lost some of the battery power," Nikolai told her. "Yasha is fixing them now. We're heading for the surface so we can use the diesel engines. We'll be fine."

"What about the aircraft?"

"Still out there." He gripped her shoulders and urged her down into the seat. "Liesha, my men are all busy. Can you do something for me?"

"Of course."

"I need you to sit here and watch the UUVs on the repeater. Let me know the instant one of them disappears. Preferably theirs, if you can arrange it."

"Okay, but—"

"We're heading back to Attu now, *milaya moya*, but I won't lie, it could be a bumpy ride."

She swallowed heavily, her pretty face drawn with worry. "Isn't there anything else I can do to help?"

He smiled dryly before slipping on his headset again. "You might practice saying 'We surrender' in Mandarin."

He was kidding.

Julie knew Nikolai was making a joke, trying to lighten things up so she wouldn't worry. But she understood misdirection when she heard it. The entire crew had gone all grim and deadly serious. The tension in the central post was so thick you'd need a buzz saw to cut it.

She'd picked up enough Russian words over the past few days to be able to recognize a few, especially the submarine lingo, since it was often similar to the English words. So she knew the hull was leaking like a sieve and there was something bad happening with the batteries. Nikolai had ordered *Starpom* Varnas to the lower deck to help *Praporshchik* Selnikov, and the rest of the crew was rushing back and forth between compartments dealing with a bevy of emergencies.

It was worse than a nightmare. On the outside Julie was determinedly putting on a brave face, but inside she was barely holding herself together. She couldn't get Josh's vivid image of rivets popping all over the sub out of her mind. Lord, she couldn't believe the crew could function so well under such insane pressure. When the lights had gone out earlier, she'd nearly fainted, but they'd barely paused in their work.

She was a complete wreck. Which was probably why Nikolai had assigned her the obviously unnecessary duty of UUV lookout.

Nevertheless, she was grateful. The task gave her something to focus on besides her own growing terror.

Anxiously, she watched the two gnatlike blips chase and circle each other around the monitor, suddenly terribly unsure of whether killing the Chinese UUV was such a great idea. It was no doubt a very expensive piece of equipment. It might make the 093 angry. Angry enough for reprisals? In its present state, she didn't know if *Ostrov* could take much more punishment.

She also wondered if any of the disasters on board were the work of the enemy agent.

Honestly? She didn't think so. The leaks were happening because of long-term neglect on the part of the Russian navy, and the electrical shorts had been caused by the leaks. Still. Something just didn't feel right about all this happening at once.

On the monitor, suddenly one of the blips winked off. It didn't come back on.

She blinked, then jumped up excitedly. "Nikolai, he got it! Walker zapped the UUV! It's gone!"

A few seconds later, Walker's triumphant voice came over the 1MC and announced, "*Ostrov* scores one, Shang class zero. Sortie complete."

After a moment's delay for translation, a cheer went up all along the boat.

Nikolai came over and gave her a quick hug, kissing the top of her head. "Okay. So I may not like the guy, but I'm getting more convinced he's on our side."

The cosmic and personal irony of that "our" didn't escape her. How far she'd come in a few short days. And him, as well.

"Told you," she said with a weak smile. "Okay, now what do we do?"

"I think in a situation like this it's again best to follow the advice of the sage Sun Tzu."

She sifted through her mind for which quote he might be referring to. But there were too many to choose from. "Which is . . . ?" she asked.

He returned her smile confidently and said, "When in doubt, run like hell."

30

███▌▌▌▌▌▌▌▞▞▞▞▞▞

That earned Nikolai a smile from Julie. Though he wasn't actually kidding.

Unfortunately, though, they couldn't run with no battery power. And they definitely couldn't stay in the canyon and hide with the boat falling apart around them. Heading for the surface was the best they could do.

"Two-five-zero meters," reported Borovsky.

"Conn, sonar. We've reacquired the 093," Gavrikov reported.

Nikolai checked the display. Sure enough, the Chinese nuclear sub had reappeared, hovering above the far rim of the deep canyon *Ostrov* had just left behind. Probably searching for their missing UUV.

Good luck with that.

"Conn, engineering. Damage assessed," Yasha called up moments later.

Nikolai switched circuits. "Engineering, conn. Talk to me."

"It's not as bad as we thought, *Kapitan*," Yasha said. "We should have her up to full power in an hour."

"Excellent." Not that they'd be running under battery power anytime soon. If Nikolai had his way—which he would—they'd be transiting on the surface for the rest of this ill-fated patrol. "What's the status of the flooding?" he asked.

"Damn thing's still leaking, *Kapitan*. But we've managed to slow it down. Once we're on the roof and can blow this swimming pool, I suggest we do a complete new weld."

"We'll put in to Attu for as long as it takes," Nikolai said. He didn't want to bring passengers aboard with the boat in this condition.

Of course, that opened up a whole new can of worms.

The investigation into Julie's attack had not yielded a suspect. Walker had been cleared. Everyone else on board had accounted for their movements to *Starpom* Varnas, *Praporshchik* Zubkin, and *Kvartirmyeister* Kresney, and his chief of security. No crew member had jumped out to them as being remotely suspicious. Which meant either this was a consummate pro who knew how to cover his tracks well, or the saboteur was among the scientists on Attu.

Nikolai didn't want to think about what might happen while the boat was crippled, the crew preoccupied with repairs, and the scientists at loose ends and disgruntled over the delay.

"Send *Starpom* Varnas back up to me. I'll have him put together the repair plan."

"The *starpom* isn't here," Yasha informed him. "He went to check that the after batteries are secure."

"Very well." Nikolai switched off and called over to Zubkin, who'd assumed his OOD duties. "Find the *starpom*. I need him here ASAP."

"Two-zero-zero meters," Borovsky said.

Meanwhile, Nikolai paced up and down the upward-tilted deck, scanning the scores of monitors, scouting for signs of trouble as the control party blew the ballast in steady blasts and the helmsman took *Ostrov* in a contained ascent up through the canyonlands to the roof.

"Conn, sonar!" Gavrikov called apprehensively. "The Y-8MPA is dropping a sonobuoy! Bearing three-four-two."

Nikolai halted in disbelief. "You can't be serious." Why the hell would they be doing *that*?

Of course, as far as the Chinese were concerned the two subs were still engaged in war games. It would be impossible for them not to be hearing *Ostrov*'s ascent to the surface. But the 093 had no way of knowing about their emergencies. And to be fair, Walker had just killed one of their expensive toys.

Хуйня.

"And I have a second contact," Gavrikov said, even more uneasily. "A big one. Surface vessel. Bearing two-three-five. Give me a minute to analyze . . ."

"One-five-zero meters," Borovsky announced.

Seconds later Gavrikov came back with, "Identified as . . . a fishing trawler. And we've got nets, sir."

A fishing trawler. Okay. Fishing was the main industry in these parts. They'd already passed by a dozen or more commercial fishing boats along the way. They could be a nuisance for subs because these days nets could reach down as far as six or seven hundred meters. Something to be avoided. But not particularly dangerous.

Nikolai's shoulders notched down a fraction. This could be good news. At least they'd have a witness if anything untoward went down with the 093. And possible rescuers nearby if they didn't get that damn leak fixed, and went down literally.

"Another sonobuoy dropped, sir!" Gavrikov called, his voice going up an octave. "Bearing one-one-three."

"Ignore it. Ignore them all," Nikolai admonished the men. "The Chinese wouldn't dare—"

All at once the sound of an explosion pulsed through the walls of the sub. Not a big one. Maybe the size of a hand grenade.

Everyone froze for an instant.

Suddenly the sonobuoys made sense. They were echo ranging. Lay a field of sonobuoys, then drop a small explosion into the middle of it, and sonar will pick up that sound, but also the echoes as they bounce off anything solid blocking the sound's path. Like a submarine. The Russians had perfected the technique. He had no idea the Chinese also used it.

Clever. At least it would have been, before *Ostrov* had started dumping ballast. Which could probably be heard clear to Hawaii.

"Was that an explosion?" Julie cried in alarm.

He turned to her. "Just a small one. Nothing to worry about."

"Ex-*cuse* me?" She looked alarmed and scandalized.

"It's called echo ranging. The underwater equivalent of triangulation," he explained. "Though God knows why. Not like they couldn't find us now even if they were deaf, dumb, and blind."

She stared at him. "Why would they do it, then?"

"One-zero-zero meters," said Borovsky.

"Damn good question. No reason I can think of. Not now, anyway."

"Prearranged plan?" she offered. "Didn't you say there was no way to communicate other than at close range when a sub is underwater? Maybe the plane doesn't know we're surfacing."

"They've got sonar, too."

"All right. Maybe they really are practicing on us and don't really care if they already know where we are."

"I suppose it's possible," he said. "Though again: why? They can practice this stuff on their own subs. Why us, and why now?"

She looked thoughtful. "So they appear to be searching for us, but they already know where we are. . . ." She thought some more. "You're right. This has to be part of their strategy."

She was back to Sun Tzu.

He nodded. "Their actions must have another, hidden purpose."

They gazed silently at each other, both mentally sifting through the possibilities.

"A diversion?" she suggested.

The sound of another distant explosion pounded through the hull. This time, the men barely glanced up from their controls.

"Not a very good one," Nikolai said doubtfully, surveying the uninterrupted activity of his crew. "Unless . . ." He glanced at the sonar repeater, then called to Zubkin, "Keep a sharp ear on that fishing trawler. I want to know if anyone so much as farts on it."

Zubkin looked doubtful, but said, *"Da, Kapitan."*

Nikolai turned back impatiently to the repeater.

"The fishing trawler?" Julie asked, following the direction of his focus.

Nikolai frowned. "It's the only other thing out there, other than the 093. Okay, what else could those explosions mean . . . ?"

She worried her lip with her teeth then looked up, her eyes clearing. "How about a signal?"

The idea stabbed through him, causing a visceral reaction. Every one of his instincts came to attention.

A signal!

"That's it," he growled, straightening like a shot. Everything fit.

But a signal to whom? Someone on board *Ostrov*? Or someone out there in—or on—the Bering Sea? One thing seemed certain, whoever it was wasn't on Attu Island.

He swung around and scrutinized each of the central post watch standers. No furtive looks. No changed posture. Everyone was acting completely as expected.

So a signal for someone else, then.

"And for what?" he whispered.

He needed a clue.

Think.

There had been two explosions. One, two . . .

But in triangulation they always came in sets of three.

His pulse kicked up.

What would happen on three?

His sudden grim certainty must have shown on his face. Julie looked at him, her color growing paler still.

"Zero-five-zero meters," Borovsky announced. They were nearly to the surface.

"I'm sensing," she murmured, "it's time for me to get scared." Her voice wavered slightly.

He leaned down and kissed her, full on the lips. "Do you believe in prayer?" In truth, he hadn't done much of it himself. Especially lately.

She nodded. "Yes."

The third explosion hit. It was closer to them this time, jolting the deck beneath their feet.

He met her widening eyes. "In that case, now would be a good time to start."

Nikolai held his breath, waiting for something to happen.

Seconds ticked by.

Nothing did.

Not that they knew about.

But the hair was rising on the back of his neck.

He strode to the periscope stand, ready to send up P1 as soon as the sub leveled off at depth. The sound of clinking sea ice dotted the sonar display. A short distance away from *Ostrov*, the fishing trawler blinked. Farther away, the 093 seemed to have slowed, as if lying in wait. But for what?

"Zero-one-zero," Borovsky announced and looked over at Nikolai.

He nodded. "Steady on course zero-six-seven," he ordered. "Rig for diesel, Mr. Zubkin."

While the OOD called out orders and the control party made ready for the switch in power, Nikolai ordered the periscope up. He peered through it, doing a slow 360° scan to check out the situation on the surface. Every eye in the central post turned to the TV repeater, which transmitted the picture he was seeing.

In the distance to the northeast he could see the low hills of Attu Island, swathed as it usually was in a gossamer coat of mist. He kept turning, but chunks of ice bobbing on the low waves blocked part of the view, so he raised the scope a bit higher.

Sure enough, situated about two kilometers to the south he spotted the distinct silhouette of a trawler with its nets splayed out behind. He focused in tighter.

In the bright afternoon sun, he could see the Canadian flag fluttering above the ship's stern; a trio of men stood on deck. One of them had binoculars to his eyes and seemed to be returning Nikolai's intense scrutiny. He raised a hand.

Nikolai blinked. A greeting? Or . . .

Not. He watched as the two other men approached the first, each carrying a long, cylindrical object. Which they lifted to their shoulders. And pointed right at *Ostrov*. Twin laser beams burned into the periscope eye.

Слава богу! Holy mother of—

"Man battle stations! Incoming RPGs! Crash dive! Dive! Dive!" he yelled, bringing down the periscope. A handheld antitank Bastion could probably not pierce the double steel hull of a submarine, but Nikolai wasn't taking any chances.

A shocked Zubkin relayed his orders, and the entire stupefied central post sprang into action as the emergency warnings were blared over the 1MC to the rest of the sub. The command watch had seen the same thing as he had on the P1 monitor.

"Where the *fuck* is *Starpom* Varnas?" he shouted over the controlled chaos of the crash dive.

The alarm screamed and the 1MC announcements ripped through the air. The deck tipped sharply as *Ostrov* bit into the dive to escape.

But it was too late.

The high-pitched whine of the approaching missiles made everyone look up in horror.

"Brace for impact!" Nikolai yelled.

He whirled to find Julie on her feet, a look of terror slashed across her face. "Down!" he shouted at her. "Get down!" And he dove to cover her with his body.

31

\\\\\\\\\//////////

Julie screamed as the first missile hit.

It exploded above the central post with a huge metallic *bang!* and a sharp jolt that shook the deck and smacked the submarine into a quick sideways roll. Pain rang through her head like the peal of a thousand bells. Things flew through the air—cups, clipboards, pencils, maps. Men grabbed for consoles to avoid being thrown from their seats.

Nikolai's heavy body crushed hers into the hard metal deck. She grabbed hold of him and clung desperately.

The second rocket exploded a heartbeat later right above their heads with a gut-jarring slam and the scream of splitting metal. Nikolai cursed. Julie was too terrified to scream. Her vocal cords refused to work. She was sure a giant hole had been ripped in the submarine and any second water would pour down on them and it would be the end.

Her ears sang and her head pounded. She fought not to burst into tears. She didn't want to die!

"It's okay, we'll be fine." Nikolai's deep voice penetrated the cacophony in her skull.

She didn't want to die without telling Nikolai how she felt about him.

"They just hit the sail above the hatch. I doubt the explosions penetrated the hull."

She opened her mouth, trying to get her voice to work, but before she could speak, he told her, "Stay here, Liesha." He gave her a quick kiss, then leapt to his feet and was back in the fray.

She managed to sit up and scooted against the nearest console, pressing her back into its solid, comforting bulk. She sat there for several minutes with her knees pressed under her chin, shaking like a leaf. The deck leveled off, so they must have ceased to dive, which was a good thing considering the state of the submarine. She didn't want to be too far from the surface. But how could they get away from their attackers with the batteries not fully functional?

The men were tense, the younger ones clearly frightened, but no one was panicking. Which told her Nikolai must be right and damage to the sub not too bad, that everything was under control.

She squeezed her eyes tightly shut and again just listened to Nikolai's voice, seeking the comfort of its firm, commanding tones as he received damage reports and gave orders. She'd just managed to convince herself that they really *weren't* going to sink into oblivion, and had moved gingerly up into her chair, when he received a message that made the quality of his voice change sharply.

She peered over at him. His furious gaze met hers.

"What is it?" she asked, fear rising anew.

"One of my men is dead."

She sucked in a breath of dismay. "Oh, my God. From the explosion?"

"No," he said, his eyes going flat. "His neck was broken. The man was murdered."

Julie covered her mouth with shaking hands to keep from crying out.

Dismay rushed through her. She realized what this meant. *The saboteur, her attacker, must still be on board.*

"Who is it? Why was he killed?"

"They believe the dead man is *Starpom* Varnas," Nikolai

said. "I don't know why yet, but I have a suspicion. He was found in the aft mechanical compartment on the lower deck, where the atmospheric equipment is located." Nikolai looked distinctly unhappy. "Liesha, I must go down there and see what happened."

She wanted to tell him no! It's too dangerous! But she saved her breath. She reluctantly got to her feet, remembering his earlier admonition not to leave his sight. "Okay. I'll go with you."

He shook his head. "No," he said, "it's too dangerous," and she nearly let out a hysterical laugh.

"But you made me promise—"

"I know. But things have changed. You'll be safer here in the central post. Think about it. None of the men here could have done this. They've all been with us the whole time."

Tears stung her eyes. "But what if they shoot at us again? What if we start to sink? Please, Nikolai. I want to stay with you."

"We're too deep now for RPGs to reach us. I won't risk your safety with this maniac on the loose." His expression was firm. He gave her a quick, tight hug and kissed her temple. "Stay here. My men will guard you with their lives. This I swear."

She bit her lip and nodded, doing her best to bottle up her fear. The last thing he needed to deal with right now was a scared, clingy female. "Please be careful," she admonished.

"I will. I'll only be gone for a few minutes."

He set her away and she watched with trepidation as he strode off toward the watertight door.

"Mr. Zubkin, you have the conn."

And felt like she'd just lost her anchor.

Nikolai met *Praporshchik* Selnikov at the foot of the ladder to the second mechanical compartment. The chief engineer looked like he'd aged twenty years in one day.

"Well?" Nikolai asked him as they hurried aft together. "Is it as we feared?"

After the body was discovered, he'd had Yasha get out his homemade chemical "sniffer" and test the atmospheric pro-

duction equipment that had been sabotaged at the beginning
of the patrol. It had been too big a coincidence that the death
had occurred there.

"Nyet," Yasha said to his surprise as they ducked through
the watertight door. "Carbon dioxide levels are normal. The
equipment has not been sabotaged again."

"Thank God. But then, why was Varnas killed?"

Yasha shook his head. "The dead man is not the *starpom.*"
He gave the name of a young rating.

Nikolai frowned as they entered the compartment, joining
the medic and the security officer who were standing by. "He
was misidentified?"

"He had the same hair and body type as *Starpom* Varnas
and was lying facedown. No one wanted to touch him until
the medic arrived."

Nikolai halted at the dead man's feet and looked down at
him, filled with sorrow and regret. So young. His death so
unnecessary.

He sighed, then looked at the security officer. "So then
where is *Starpom* Varnas?" Nikolai was getting concerned.
And a little suspicious. Stefan Mikhailovich had been MIA
for too long.

"With all the leaks and the batteries, things have been hectic," Yasha said. "I'm sure he'll turn up any minute to deny the
rumors of his demise."

Nikolai was beginning to wonder. Would they also find the
starpom's body murdered and hidden away somewhere? He
didn't want to think about the alternative. He spoke to the security officer. "Have the men search every inch of this boat. I
want Varnas found. And document the crime scene here carefully. I want nothing missed, do you hear me?"

"Da, Kapitan."

He turned to head back to the central post, then stopped
abruptly and said to the medic, gesturing to the dead rating,
"Do me a favor, and empty his pockets."

The medic did so respectfully but thoroughly, dropping
everything into a paper bag supplied by the security officer.
He handed it over.

Nikolai used a pen to sift through the items. Coins, a pair
of dice, a candy bar, and a few other unremarkable things.

But no leather bracelet.

"Thank you," he said and signaled Yasha to follow him out of the compartment. "What is the damage from the RPG attack?" he asked.

His chief engineer shook his head in obvious frustration. "One of the periscopes is gone, as well as the communications array, *Kapitan*. We'll be unable to use the radio until they have been repaired. Which requires getting up to the bridge."

Which required being on the surface.

Nikolai swore roundly. They were effectively being forced to go up and expose themselves to the crazies with the RPGs. Without battery power it would be impossible to outrun them. And without weapons they were unable to fight back. They'd be sitting ducks.

Which was undoubtedly the saboteur's plan.

He swore again. And wondered furiously what role the 093 would take in this deadly play.

He gave Yasha's shoulder an encouraging squeeze. "I know you'll do your best, *Praporshchik*. I have every faith you'll see us through this in one piece."

"As do I you, *Kapitan*," Yasha replied as they parted ways.

Nikolai started to hurry back to the central post, but changed his mind and headed instead for officer country, where the trapdoor down to the forward battery compartment was located in an out-of-the-way corner behind the staterooms.

He had a hunch he wanted to check out. He just hoped to hell he was wrong.

He wasn't.

Nikolai found *Starpom* Varnas in the narrow crawl space between the lower deck and the tightly packed batteries. Stefan Mikhailovich was lying facedown across the top of the bank.

Unfortunately he wasn't dead.

He was setting the detonator on a thumb-sized ball of C-4 he'd attached to one of the batteries. Using a strip of woven leather for support.

The fucking bastard.

Nikolai had been very quiet in his descent into the claustrophobically narrow space so the traitor didn't hear him drop down. The lights were on, so he had no trouble seeing what the saboteur was doing. Or what he was wearing. One leg of Varnas's coveralls had ridden up to reveal a blue wetsuit under it. Around his neck hung an IDA-59, with two more hanging from his belt.

Never more had Nikolai regretted not having his sidearm on this patrol.

Or perhaps it was a good thing. He knew when he stopped seeing red he'd think better of spending the rest of his life in prison for killing the man.

Not that the act of murder seemed to bother Stefan Mikhailovich any. He was using just enough C-4 to break through the housings of several of the batteries. But that was plenty to kill everyone on board in a matter of minutes. Deadly chlorine gas was the inevitable result of seawater coming in contact with exposed battery acid. A virtual certainty, considering the floor of the space was awash with seawater from the leak in the torpedo room above.

The fucking, *fucking* bastard.

Varnas finished placing the detonator and flipped over, sitting up. Which was when he saw Nikolai crouching under the trapdoor, ready to spring.

Stefan Mikhailovich froze for a beat, then smiled wryly. "I was wondering when you'd be on to me," he said. "When did you figure it out?"

Nikolai regarded him coldly. "I started to suspect during the Midsummer ceremony. I didn't want to believe it though."

"Ah, yes." He nodded, making himself more comfortable on the batteries. "My bad reaction to Lord Ægir's revelation of my e-mails."

Nikolai didn't move. "Communications not with a woman, but with the enemy, I assume. Too bad I ignored my gut instincts. A good man is dead because I didn't want to believe you were the traitor."

"I am sorry about that. He came looking for me. Saw what I was doing. I had no choice."

"And Julie? She wasn't looking for you when you tried to drown her this morning."

Varnas's lips twisted downward. "I truly regretted having to kill her. I know you care for her. But when I realized she works for CIA, well, she couldn't be allowed to find that SD card."

Nikolai almost said, "Too late," but stopped himself.

Varnas frowned and glanced down at the C-4 explosive charge. "Her survival has complicated matters. That, and *Praporshchik* Selnikov finding the malfunction in the atmospheric production equipment when he did. No one else was supposed to have gotten hurt."

"Sorry to have spoiled your plans," Nikolai said in a seething drawl.

The *starpom* pulled a Makarov PMM with silencer from his pocket and pointed it at him. "Oh, but you haven't. In fact, you've played right into them." He waggled the gun at the trapdoor. "Now, please climb up. And don't try anything, *Kapitan*. You must know I won't hesitate to shoot you."

Anger boiled in Nikolai's blood, but he complied. "Why?" he asked through clenched teeth as he hoisted himself through the trapdoor. "Why are you doing this?"

"I already told you earlier," Varnas said, coming up after him, pistol raised. "In our first conversation on the bridge. For love."

Nikolai dredged his memory as they got to their feet. "You said you fell in love with the wrong woman, an admiral's daughter. As I recall, you were hoping to impress her father on this patrol, to make a worthy son-in-law. I hardly think this is the way to do that, Stefan Mikhailovich."

The *starpom* chuckled. "You assume he is a Russian admiral."

Nikolai stared. Чертов ад!

He wanted to kick himself. "The wrong woman. Meaning the daughter of a *Chinese* admiral," he ground out, slapping his fist against the bulkhead. Why hadn't he probed deeper?

Varnas pressed the Makarov's silencer into his ribs. "Exactly. And he is over on the 093 as we speak, waiting for me to come and claim his daughter's hand. But first I must furnish the proof of my worthiness."

"Which is?" Not that Nikolai believed for a minute the old goat would give his daughter to a filthy Russian.

"To sink *Ostrov* and deliver Julie Severin into his hands."

Fury shot through Nikolai. "If you hurt her, or—"

Varnas raised his free hand. "Strictly a rescue operation. The 093 will pluck up *Ostrov*'s crew after toxic gas is released, caused by a malicious attack by terrorists. The Canadian fishing trawler was a nice touch, I thought."

"And I'll have no choice but to accept the Chinese offer of help because you've destroyed every means of communication on board so we can't call in the Russians or the Americans." Which also explained the satellite phone sabotage.

The plan was well thought out, he had to give them that. They'd won by removing all other possibilities. Classic strategy. He should have paid more attention to the details.

"I assume the plan is to send *Ostrov* to the bottom, with me on it."

"I seriously doubt anyone will miss *Ostrov*. As for you, unless you push me, there is no need for your death. We only wish to retrieve or destroy those guidance system plans."

Nikolai looked at Varnas incredulously. "You think I won't tell anyone who'll listen exactly what happened here? Who you are? Who did this?"

The *starpom* smiled. "Honestly, Nikolai. Do you really think the Russian Naval Command will actually listen? Who will they believe, an already disgraced captain who's lost yet another submarine, or the Chinese government? Besides, it won't matter who they believe. They'll need someone to take the blame, and I'll give you one guess who that will be."

Nikolai's anger roiled. The fact that it was true only made him more furious.

"Besides," Varnas added, "we'll have Miss Severin to ensure your cooperation."

His temper jumped into the danger zone. "What are you planning to do to her?" he demanded.

"Up to you, *Kapitan*. Tell the world this was a random terrorist attack, and she'll be sent home safe and sound. If," he qualified, "she doesn't have the SD card in her possession when rescued."

Nikolai clenched his jaw. "And if she does?"

Varnas shrugged. "Anyone found holding stolen Chinese military intelligence will be arrested and tried for espionage. It's out of my hands."

But it wasn't out of Nikolai's. He'd heard enough.

He whirled, throwing his body full against Varnas, knocking him off balance. The gun flew up, but not before Varnas had pressed the trigger.

A loud *pop* echoed through the passageway and a searing fireball burned through Nikolai's side.

He grunted in excruciating pain, steadied himself, and grabbed for the gun, trying to wrench it from Varnas's hand. It went off again. This time Varnas cried out; he crumpled to the floor, blood pouring from his belly.

Nikolai staggered from his own wound, falling against the bulkhead, and watched in horror as the *starpom* pulled a small remote control from his coverall pocket and held it in a shaky hand.

Stefan Mikhailovich's breath was shallow, his face bathed in pain and sweat. "I shall be worthy, Nikolai," he said, his voice strangled but his eyes triumphant as he put his thumb to the button of the remote.

"Nyet!" Nikolai cried, as he lunged for it amid a shower of crimson. He stumbled to his hands and knees, weakened from loss of blood. His head spun, and his grab missed.

Varnas pressed the button. Then his eyes fluttered closed.

Below, Nikolai heard the dull rumble of an explosion. It would be a miracle if bilgewater did not get into the batteries after that.

Пиздец!

His heart raced. *Julie!* He had to warn her and the crew!

He glanced up to get his bearings. He was right around the corner from his own stateroom door. There was a comm in there. He tried to rise to his feet, but couldn't manage it. So he crawled. Using one hand to stanch his wound from bleeding, he forced himself to stay conscious while he dragged himself to the door. Somehow he reached the handle, turned it, and fell into the stateroom in a bloody heap.

The edges of his vision dimmed. Black spots flickered and grew bigger. With a monumental effort, he put his back to the bulkhead, slid himself up it, and groped for the comm receiver hanging next to the door.

"Conn, this is the captain," he wheezed when he finally had it clutched in his hand. "Don IDAs and abandon ship!

Chlorine gas leak in forward battery compartment. Say again, chlorine gas, abandon ship!"

With his last spurt of tremulous consciousness, he reached down for his IDA and pulled out the mask. But before he could tug it on completely, the dancing black spots in his vision blurred together into a single dizzying whirlpool.

And, falling back against the door, he slid to the floor, unconscious.

32

〟〟〟〟〟〟〟〟〟〟〟

"No! I'm not going anywhere without Captain Romanov!"

"But Miss—"

"*No.*"

Julie backed away from Misha, who was urging her toward the torpedo room, where the crew was rushing to pile up onto the deck after surfacing just moments ago. It had been almost five minutes since Nikolai's urgent call came over the circuit warning of the deadly chlorine gas. So far none had been detected in the air, thank God. But Nikolai had not returned to the central post, either.

She knew he wouldn't leave her here terrified like this. And he sure as hell wouldn't abandon ship without her. Therefore, something must have happened to him. Something very bad.

"Is dangerous!" Misha protested. "You must come!"

"I need to find Nikolai!" she said, shaking him off when he would have grabbed her arm.

"*Kapitan* is fine. He call us, *da*? He busy with helping, then come to deck, I am sure."

"Sorry, I need to see that for myself." She jerked away and ran for the watertight door.

He could be lying hurt somewhere, or the traitor could be holding him hostage. She just prayed he had on his IDA. She felt for hers, and brought it out of the pouch, and started to pull it over her head. The filter would last between ten and thirty minutes before she needed to get to fresh air. *Please, let that be enough time.*

She collided with Clint Walker.

"Julie? Hey, where are you going?" he asked when she attempted a quarterback sneak around him. "This gas is fatal in, like, five minutes! You need to get up on deck ASAP."

"Not without Nikolai," she ground out like a broken record, still fumbling with the straps of her mask as she hurried.

"He's not here?" Clint called after her with a frown, his own mask dangling in his hand.

"No! I haven't seen him. He has to be in trouble, Clint. I'm going to find him." She spotted Misha coming after her and took off at a trot before he could catch up.

Clint's lips thinned and he muttered a curse. But he waved Misha off. "Julie! Wait up. I'm coming with you."

"Thank you," she said as they got to the ladder. "I appreciate the help."

"Stop," Clint said. "Tighten your mask properly. Chlorine gas is heavy, so the danger is much greater on the lower deck."

As they both adjusted their masks, an announcement blared out from the overhead speakers. Clint paused to listen.

"What is it?"

"Interesting," he said through his respirator, sounding like Darth Vader. The Chinese sub is on its way to pick us up, passengers and crew, and transport us all to safety. They claim it's a rescue."

They stared at each other apprehensively through their IDAs' buglike eyeholes. "Crap," she said.

That was a twist she hadn't seen coming.

"No fucking kidding." He blew out a breath and the respirator wheezed. "We need to find the skipper pronto. Where should we start?"

She turned back to the ladder. "The gas alert is for the forward battery compartment. He must have been there to give the alarm."

"Yep."

She grabbed the rails of the ladder and slid down to the lower deck. "I'm just not exactly sure where it is."

"This way," Clint said, taking the lead. They dove through the watertight door to the officers' staterooms and ran along the passageway. "The opening's down to the—"

His words cut off abruptly and they skidded to a halt when they rounded the corner. They nearly tripped over the prone, bloody body of *Starpom* Varnas.

Julie gasped, biting off a scream. "My God! Is he—"

Clint nodded, kneeling to feel the pulse at the side of the *starpom*'s neck. "Dead."

A gaping hole split the body's midsection and a pool of blood surrounded him on the deck, but the expression on his face was surprisingly peaceful. In one hand he held a small box.

"Shot, by the looks of it," Clint said.

"But . . . I didn't think there were any weapons on board," Julie said, looking around for Nikolai. The sight of Varnas sprawled out dead was making her sick. Her heart pounded in her throat. What had *happened* here? "Nikolai!" she called, more worried than ever.

"I'll check the battery compartment," Clint said, and he started to climb down through a trapdoor in the floor.

"Clint, be careful!" she cried. "That's where the gas is supposed to—"

But he had already disappeared.

While he was gone, there was another announcement over the loudspeaker. Another warning to come up on deck, she assumed. *They needed to hurry.*

Clint came back up less than thirty seconds later and quickly hoisted himself out. "He's not down there. But there's been some kind of explosion. The gas is right up to the top of the space." He slammed the trapdoor shut with a racking cough. "We need to find Romanov. Any second now, the gas'll be seeping up through the deck. If he doesn't have his mask on . . ."

He didn't need to finish. As they watched, the first shimmers of yellow-green curled up through the seams of the trapdoor, spreading out across the deck.

"Nikolai!" she called again, the desperation in her mind rising. "Where *are* you?"

From the other compartments she could hear the sounds of IDA-muffled shouting and things being tossed around as crewmen hastily grabbed some of their belongings to take with them.

But there was no answering call from Nikolai.

"Look," Clint said, pointing to a pair of bloody hand smears on the bulkhead. "Only one of Varnas's hands has blood on it. These must have been made by someone else."

Julie's heart stalled. "No!" she said past the lump of fear growing in her throat. She glanced around, searching for more signs, a blood trail to follow. Anything.

"Here!" she called, following a thin line of reddish brown drops on the deck. They led around the corner and stopped at a stateroom door. *Nikolai's stateroom.* More bloody smears were around the door handle. "He must be inside!"

She tried to open the door. Something was blocking it.

"Nikolai! Answer me!" she cried, pushing hard against the door. It wouldn't budge.

"Here, let me," Clint said, and used his shoulder and full weight to force his way into the dark stateroom, moving an inert body out of the way.

The light snapped on.

"Nikolai!" she gasped and rushed in, throwing herself to her knees by him. His limp hand was clutching at a wound in his side. He was soaked in blood, though not as badly as Varnas. "He's been shot!"

"Get his mask on," Clint ordered as he checked his neck for a pulse. "He's still alive."

"Thank God, oh, thank God," she murmured as she grabbed the mask and started to pull it down over Nikolai's face.

He moaned, and his other hand moved, reaching up to keep the mask off. *"Nyet,"* he groaned. "Julie."

Her heart leapt. He was waking up! That had to be a good sign. "I'm here, *dorogoy.* You're going to be okay."

He muttered something unintelligible, but his lips curved up slightly.

"Shhh. You have to put your mask on. The gas—"

He rolled his head away. *"Nyet."* He murmured something that was more recognizably Russian.

"He's saying something about the SD card," Clint said, wrapping a sheet around Nikolai's middle to bind the wound. "We have to get him up on deck. I'm no doctor, but the bullet seems to have missed the vital organs. He may have cracked a rib though. Either way, he should get to a hospital. He's lost a lot of blood." Clint tied off the sheet and Nikolai moaned again.

She tugged the IDA mask all the way down over his face. "Sweetheart, we've got to go. Can you hear me?"

Under the bug eyes of the mask, his lashes fluttered up and he looked at her. They softened. "Julie? Is that you?"

"I'm right here," she said and smiled, though she knew he couldn't see it under her respirator. "Clint, too. We've come to get you out of here."

He swallowed and winced with pain. "Varnas?"

"He's dead," she told him gently. "I'm so sorry."

His eyes closed briefly. "I'm not."

"It was him?" Clint asked when she was too surprised to respond right away. *Varnas?*

"Da," Nikolai said. "Everything."

Clint nodded. "Understood. All right. Let's get you on your feet, Skipper."

Once he was up, he limped to the desk, gathered up a few things, and put them in a leather satchel. She took it from him to carry.

"My papers," he said, and she nodded.

As slowly and gently as possible, with one on each side supporting him, they walked him to the ladder. At the bottom they stopped to let him rest.

He leaned his back against it and groaned. "Damn, this hurts." His breath came in gasps, his hands were clammy, and there was a fresh ring of scarlet blooming in the white of the makeshift bandage.

She couldn't look at his pain-drawn face without wanting to let him lie down until he felt better, so she checked her watch. Time was running out. It had been ten minutes already. Hopefully their IDA filters would last until they got on deck.

She sensed something was different around them. She

cocked her head and listened. And realized what it was. The submarine was eerily quiet. No engines. No voices. No mechanical noises. Even the sound of the air filtration had ceased. Everyone must be up on deck already, awaiting rescue, all systems shut down for the abandonment.

For one frightening moment, she imagined they'd all left without the three of them. *Her nightmare come true.* But then the overhead speakers squawked out another announcement, and she breathed a little easier.

"Hell. We need to hurry," Clint said. He pointed down. Yellow-green tendrils were licking at their shoes.

Nikolai straightened away from the ladder, putting his hand on her arm to steady himself. "Liesha, do you have the SD card?"

"Yes. Don't worry, I won't lose it."

He grasped the handrail. "No. You don't understand. You must get rid of it."

"What? Nikolai, no way. It's what I came to—"

"Varnas said"—he winced against a wave of pain as he lifted himself onto the first rung—"they know it's you. They'll arrest you if you have it in your possession."

She watched his difficult climb, her mind in a whirl. She knew very well what that meant. "Okay," she said, following him up. "We can decide what to do with it when we get up on deck."

He grunted again, but didn't argue.

It must have been excruciating for Nikolai to climb the ladder, but somehow he managed it.

"You go up," he told her when they got as far as the central post. They were headed for the closest access to the outside deck, the forward torpedo room hatch. "I'll be there in a minute."

"Hell, no," she said. "I'm not going anywhere without you."

She knew as captain he must have a certain protocol to follow when abandoning ship. He had to get the boat's official logbook, for instance, and add it to the notebooks in the satchel she was carrying for him. Who knew what else.

"You are one damn stubborn woman," he muttered, and she couldn't help smiling as she helped him over to the cupboard where the ship's logs were kept.

"Yeah, and that's why you love me," she said jokingly.

But there was no joke in Nikolai's gaze when he turned back to her, logbook in hand. He gazed down at her through the ridiculous orange insect mask, his own eyes dark like the midnight sea. Behind the many shadows she saw in them—the pain of his wound, and the anger at Varnas's betrayal, the frustration of losing his boat, and the powerlessness over his career—she saw something else, as well.

Something meltingly warm and wonderfully good and absolutely right.

"Yes, Julie Yelizaveta Severina," he said in his deep, incredibly romantic voice, "that is why I love you. One of the many reasons."

"Oh, Nikolai," she whispered, her heart turning over in a drowning ache. "I love you, too. So much."

She desperately wanted to throw her arms around him and hold him close, but she didn't dare for fear of hurting his wound. She couldn't hug him. She couldn't even kiss him, because of the stupid respirators covering their faces.

This was not how she'd imagined declaring her true love for the man of her dreams.

But somehow she knew he was smiling.

"We should go up," he said, but suddenly she didn't want to. In minutes they'd be torn apart, and God knew if they'd ever see each other again.

"Yes," she said. And fervently wished they hadn't wasted so much of their time being suspicious of each other . . . when they could have been making love.

33

~~~~~~~\\\\\\\\\//////////

"Julie." It was Clint, striding into the central post. Hell. She'd forgotten all about him.

"We're ready," she said and reluctantly turned away from Nikolai.

To her amazement, Clint was wearing a thick, black wetsuit and carrying a mask, flippers, snorkel, and a small dry bag. With his IDA still on, he looked like a space alien straight from Roswell.

Wide-eyed, she took him in. "Clint. What the heck?"

He cleared his throat. For the first time in her memory his stance was uncertain, for all his broad, muscular height. "Julie, I know I haven't been all that forthcoming with you on this trip. But I've told you what I could, and it's all been the truth."

She nodded, wondering where this was going. "Okay. I believe you." She looked at Nikolai and after a hesitation, he nodded, too.

"I can't get on that Chinese submarine," Clint said simply, with no other explanation. "So I'm going to jump off here."

She sucked in a breath of shock. "And do what? *Swim?*"

He made a face and shrugged. "Fresh out of helicopters."

"Are you freaking *insane*? That water's freezing! And it's got to be twenty miles to Attu Island!"

He lifted a shoulder. "I've faced worse. I used to be a SEAL, you know. And this Russian Arctic gear is aces. I like my chances. Better than on that Chinese sub, anyway."

She was appalled. "Hello! I'm a spy, too. What can they do to you that they can't do to me?" She didn't actually want to think about what they might do to her. "Hell, you don't even have the SD card." She grasped Nikolai's arm. "Nikolai, tell him he's crazy. He can't possibly—"

"Milaya," Nikolai interrupted, leaning his butt against a console with a tight groan, "I think you're missing his point."

She blinked, looking from him to Clint. "I am?"

Clint's respirator sighed. "Let me have the card, Julie. I'll take it safely back to D.C. and make sure Langley gets a copy."

She stared at him, speechless. Was he *kidding*?

"Help me out, here, Skipper."

Nikolai gave a soft grunt and said, "It's that or throw it into the sea, Liesha. You'll never get it past the Chinese. It's not worth your life to try."

"The captain's right," Clint said somberly. "Trust me, they're going to put you under a microscope before they let you go. You don't want to be caught within a mile of that data card. I'm the only shot we have of saving the intel on it for our side."

Her chest squeezed with the dismal knowledge that after going through all this, after having the damn thing in her freaking *pocket*, she was going to fail in her mission after all.

Unbelievable.

But she also realized his assessment of the situation was probably correct.

The question was, did she trust him to keep his word?

Hell, did it actually matter?

No, not really.

At least if she gave the SD card to Clint, the information on it would be used to keep her country safe. That was the most important thing. Not who brought it home to which agency.

With a resigned sigh, she dug deep in her pocket and pulled out the thumb-sized card. After holding it in her hand for a short moment, she handed it to him.

"Please, just do me a favor and steer clear of sharks and polar bears while you're out there," she said.

His eyes smiled back at her. "That's a promise." He tucked it into his dry bag and slung it over his shoulder. "Now, let's get you both up on deck before you miss your ride."

"Right." Suddenly she remembered something. "Hang on. Give me thirty seconds."

She ran to the locker where the foul weather gear was kept and flung it open. She grabbed Nikolai's greatcoat off its usual hook, and also the coat he'd given her. Then she reached for his mother's wolf fur hat. She wasn't about to let him leave this boat without that.

She helped him on with his coat and slipped on hers, but when she went to put the fur *ushanka* on his head, he pressed it back into her hands.

"You keep it, *milaya moya.*"

"Nikolai, no, I couldn't . . ."

"I want you to have it," he insisted, and his voice went soft. "To remember me by."

Tears stung her eyes as she held the fur hat she knew meant the world to him. "Thank you," she whispered. "I'll treasure it always. But Nikolai, even without this beautiful gift, there is no chance I will ever forget you."

"Come help me with Captain Romanov!" Julie called as she helped Nikolai climb painfully from the hatch.

She ripped both their IDAs from their heads and he breathed in big gulps of clean, fresh air. It smelled wonderful and tasted better, all salty and chilly. It was good to be out in the wind and the sun.

It was good to be alive at all.

He was so exhausted he could barely drag himself up onto the deck. As they'd previously arranged, she made an embarrassing fuss over him, and he moaned and groaned loudly—mostly as a diversion so Walker could pop up from the hatch in his scuba gear and tank and sprint over behind the sail out of sight. But for Nikolai's part, the groans were real enough.

"I still can't believe he's doing that," she murmured after

Walker had slipped over the side and dropped into the tin gray sea. "The man is out of his mind."

At the moment, Nikolai would gladly have traded places. His side throbbed like the devil, his head was spinning like a whirligig, and it felt like a giant hole was being carved from his chest.

Because it was.

Julie had given him a heartbreakingly lovely smile when she'd put on his mother's *ushanka* just now, but she would be taking so much more than a wolf fur hat away with her when they parted.

She'd be taking his heart, as well.

"*Kapitan!* Thank goodness you're all right." It was Yasha hurrying over to help them. "*Kvartirmyeister* Kresney has been frantic with worry about Miss Severin ever since she went to find you. But our gracious Chinese hosts refused to permit anyone to go down to search for either of you. The gas was too dangerous, they said." He scowled and said something so rude that Nikolai grinned despite his pain, inside and out.

"I'll live," Nikolai assured him. "Though admittedly I've felt better."

And it only got worse.

The rubber raft was already full to overflowing, the last of his crew barely fitting into it. So Nikolai and Julie had to wait for them to be deposited on the 093 and the dinghy to come back. The Chinese sailors wouldn't let any of his men stay behind with them.

Nikolai had a very bad feeling about this.

Julie was reading his mind. "I wonder if they'll drive off and leave us here," she mused.

He refrained from an ironic laugh because it would hurt too much. "Wouldn't be surprised." He took her hand. "Good thing Walker called in the cavalry."

She whipped him a surprised look. "When did he do that?"

Nikolai closed his eyes and smiled. He was lying on his back on the cold, wet deck, but it actually felt better than standing up, and better by far than sitting. He could feel her penetrating stare. "He had Danya send a signal via radio to his people moments before the communications array got hit by that RPG. Apparently he informed them of *Ostrov*'s condition and his suspicions that we'd be targeted. Killer instincts, that guy." He hated to admit it.

A scowl creased her forehead. "So wait. You're saying the Americans know about all this? That someone is coming for us?"

"It was before the attack, and he didn't request extraction specifically. But they'll surely send the Coast Guard to do a flyby to check on our condition. Possibly the Russians, too, since the scientists are probably screaming bloody murder by now because we haven't picked them up yet. The Chinese will be forced to report the attack and the rescue. And therefore not leave us stranded."

Unless, of course, they planned to kill him and Julie and dump their bodies into the ocean.

He opened his eyes and found her staring at him intently. "And when did he tell you about this?"

"Just before we came up on deck."

"Why, the little bastard," she muttered.

"Not so little," Nikolai said.

"So he *knew* there's a good chance we'll be picked up by the Americans and the SD card would have been safe with me! All we'd have to do is stall until they show up and wave a white flag or something!"

He took her hand. She was sitting cross-legged on the wet deck next to him, bundled up in the oversized coat and his mother's hat down to her eyebrows. Her cheeks were red from the wind . . . or perhaps from anger. She'd never looked so beautiful.

"We can't be sure of that," he said, kissing her fingers. "I'm glad you gave it to him. If anything happened to you . . ." The thought frightened him as nothing else ever had. "I would be forced to do things to that Chinese captain I'm presently in no condition to do."

Her gaze met his, and she smiled softly. "Oh, Nikolai," she murmured. "What's going to happen to us?"

"I don't know," he said truthfully. "Come here."

He tugged on her hand and she lay down next to him, curled up against his good side. He turned his head and they kissed. An achingly tender, bittersweet kiss.

"Come with me," she whispered. "When they come to get me, come with me to America."

"*Dorogaya*, you know I—"

"No, listen. Walker promised if I gave him the SD card he'd have the navy bring you over. Well, I gave him the card, didn't I?"

"Yes, but—"

She looked so damn crestfallen his heart squeezed more painfully than his wound.

"Don't you want to come? To be with me? I know we've only known each other a few days, but—"

"Of course I want to be with you," he assured her, hanging on to her hand, wishing all his feelings would flow through that connection so she'd know how deep his emotions went. "I don't care how little time we've had. The few minutes I've spent with you have been the happiest in my life. I love you, Liesha, and I'd give anything to spend every day I have left on earth with you."

Her fingers touched his cheek with the warmth of a lover. "Then come. Please? Think of the cherry trees, and the Pushkin statue."

God, how he wanted to say yes!

But how would it be possible?

"The Main Naval Command, and the FSB, they'll never allow me to leave Russia. You have to know that."

"Then don't go back. When the Americans come for me in their ship or their helicopter, I'll tell them to take you, too. That I won't leave without you." She smiled, her fingers trailing over the stubble on his jaw. "You know I can do it."

He didn't doubt it for a second. He gazed at her, a crazy hope blossoming in his chest. Cherenkov would probably send someone to assassinate him, but being with her for even a little while might just be worth it.

"You can meet my mother, and your American family, too. We could—"

He frowned. "What?"

Her face froze. Consternation swept across it. "Oh, my God! I totally forgot!" Her voice cracked on the last word. She yanked her hand back, curled her fingers into a ball, and pressed it to her mouth.

His pulse kicked up. "Forgot what? Liesha, what did you mean, my family?"

"Oh, Nikolai." Her eyes suddenly blazed with tears. "I'm so sorry I—" And distress. "I only found out last night, after you . . . after I . . . spoke with my boss. He told me, and I—"

Nikolai stilled, his whole body becoming weightless. What could her boss possibly have told her about *his* family?

Except he already knew.

"Told you what?" he quietly asked.

She rushed on. "I was coming to find you this morning, to tell you, I swear. But that's when I was— And after that, there was never a—"

"Tell me *what?*"

The blur of words halted. A tear crested her lashes. "About your mother."

He grasped her shoulder, wincing at the pain it caused him to cant his body toward her. His fingers dug into her flesh. "What about my mother?" he asked, his voice bordering on a low growl.

"She was American. She worked for CIA."

Jesus, God. So it was true.

"And you have family in New York."

For an endless, stunned moment he couldn't move. Then he fell back onto the deck, his spine hitting the hard metal ribs of the deck, but he barely noticed the impact.

Family.

"I was ordered not to tell you. But I thought you deserved to know the truth."

He didn't know whether to laugh or cry. To be furious, or more grateful for anything in his life. To yell at the woman next to him for waiting so long to tell him, or to kiss her to within an inch of her life for telling him at all.

His mother had been a spy.

Shot down on a street in Moscow.

He stared up at the blue sky, only just beginning to dim with the approaching evening twilight, and watched a flock of gulls wheel and cry overhead. They swam out of focus.

He had family in America. People who'd known her. People whose blood ran in his veins.

People who might give a damn about him.

If they'd known he existed.

His life might have been so different. If only he'd known *they* existed.

Anger filled him to the very brim of his soul. Because there was no doubt in his mind who *did* know they existed. Who had known all along about his mother, and had threatened and manipulated him with that knowledge. Had kept Nikolai in the dark about his heritage for his own twisted political purposes.

Comrade Leonid Cherenkov.

Сволочь!

Псина чертова.

"Nikolai?" Julie whispered. "What are you thinking?"

Too much. Nothing good. What to do? What not to do?

"I'm thinking," he said at length, "that this changes everything."

"What about us?" she asked, her voice trembling with emotion. "Does it change us?"

"Oh, yes," he said.

She waited for a long time for him to say something more. But he couldn't. His mind was too busy with the task of reordering his life. Of pulling puzzle pieces apart and putting them together in a whole new way.

So busy sorting through the chaos that he didn't hear the *whop-whop-whop* of helicopter rotors in the distance.

"Nikolai," Julie said with quiet urgency, "they're coming! They're coming to pick me up!" She grabbed his hand again and pressed it to her heart. "Come with me. Please."

He gazed at her, meeting her beautiful, desperate eyes. Her auburn hair whipped around her face, lit up by the golden rays of the evening summer sun, making her look like an angel.

The helicopter was getting closer. Louder.

"Liesha," he whispered. His heart and soul filled with conflicting emotions.

"*Please*, Nikolai."

He wanted to. God knew he loved her. But—

She leaned down to kiss him. A sweet, pleading kiss filled with sincerity and hope for a wonderful future together. "I love you, Nikolai Kirillovich Romanov," she whispered, her eyes brimming over with tears.

The helicopter swept over *Ostrov*, its blades whipping the air around them into a frenzy.

"I love you, too, Liesha. To my very soul," he said, though he knew she couldn't hear his words over the roar of the helo. "But I—"

He looked up, and his heart sank to the pit of his stomach.

"I can't," he said.

Because it wasn't the Americans coming for Julie at all.

The helicopter was Russian.

34

///////////////

Julie strolled into the Four Seasons Hotel Lounge in George-
town, paused just inside the door to readjust her black silk suit
jacket and her red Christian Louboutins, took a deep breath,
and breezed over to the bar.

"Tequila this time, straight up," she said to the bartender
with a smile that didn't even feel forced. *Progress.* He nodded
and smiled, and she turned toward her table. Then stopped
and turned back again. "Make that vodka instead," she said.

The bartender smiled wider and nodded again. He already
had the bottle of Russian Standard in his hand. "Sure thing,
Julie," he said, plunking seven shot glasses on a small round
tray.

She looked from him to the bottle and deflated. "That obvious, eh?"

"Over a week since you started coming in. Not once have
you ordered anything but vodka," he said affably, starting to
pour.

She grimaced, weaving a tad in her high heels. Every once
in a while the deck rolled under her feet, as though she were
still at sea. And it had nothing to do with the vodka. *Fucking
Russian sub driver.* This was what he'd done to her.

She glanced up at the TV set mounted in the wood paneling. The news was playing with the sound muted. Some poor, hapless cargo ship had been hijacked by pirates and the incident had been all over the news for days. *Naturally* it had happened off the coast of Alaska in—wait for it—the Aleutian Islands. Like she *ever*—in real life *or* on TV—wanted to see *that* place again. Or another damn chunk of sea ice. *Or another freaking submarine or its goddamn captain.*

But she digressed.

She took another deep breath. "I can take those. Just put them on my tab, Kev."

"Sure thing, Julie."

She picked up the round tray.

"He set up his Facebook page yet?" he asked conversationally, leaving the bottle conspicuously on the counter.

She clamped her teeth. "Haven't checked," she said evenly and walked back to the table, doing her best not to weave. She probably shouldn't have this third shot, but she found it easier to get to sleep at night after two or three. And she didn't dream as much.

"Last round's on me!" she announced as she slid into her seat next to Dr. Josh with a flourish.

"Dang, girl. We thought you fell in," Josh said, distributing the shot glasses to a rousing cheer from the four others around the table.

"You know how I feel about bodies of water," she said with a wry grin. Hell, sometimes a girl just needed to excuse herself for a good cry. But she was all better now.

Really.

She lifted her shot glass and they all yelled, *"Za lyublov!"* Well, everyone but her. The last thing *she* wanted to toast to was love. Especially not in Russian. *Thank you, Dr. Josh.*

"Don't worry, Julie," her friend Linda said with a wink when she saw her shut her mouth at the toast. "There's more than one fish in the sea. If you like navy guys, I know this amazingly hunky—"

Julie held up her hands. "*Hell*, no. But thanks." Who knew the mousy blond in the next cubicle had such an extensive little black book? This was the fourth guy Linda had offered to hook her up with. And that was just tonight.

Josh leaned over and gave Julie a hug. "Forget him, honey. I knew that man was trouble the first time I laid eyes on him."

Julie kissed him on the cheek. "You're sweet. I'm so glad you decided to stop over on your way back to Toronto and say hi."

"Yes, well," he said, eyeing a cute young congressional type who'd been flirting with him outrageously all evening, "I do love the Fourth of July. I can't *wait* for the fireworks." He waggled his eyebrows.

She choked on her beer chaser. "Looks like they might be happening a day early."

Josh grinned and lifted up a napkin with a room number written on it. "Got this delivered under a dirty martini while you were powdering your nose."

She laughed through a stab of envy. "Wow. Go for it."

"You think?"

"Absolutely. Don't let a chance for happiness slip through your fingers. You never know who'll turn out to be Mr. Right."

He gazed back at her with far too much understanding in those youthful blue eyes. "You got that right. Life's too short for missed opportunities."

Amen.

She took a sip of beer to keep her smile intact. "Anyway. I was glad the expedition didn't get canceled after the *Ostrov* fiasco." See? She could even say the name without bursting into tears. *More* progress.

He nodded, instantly cheerful again. "Yeah. Who'd have thought the U.S. Coast Guard would come through with a cutter so we could carry on with our work?"

"They got some great publicity out of it when you scientists were stranded and they came to your aid. I'll bet their recruitment jumps by twenty percent this year."

"Unlike the Russian navy," he said with a snort. "Cripes. I'm shocked that rust bucket submarine didn't sink years ago. Not surprised they scuttled it on the spot."

"Yeah," she agreed, a wistful lump forming in her throat. She'd had the best days of her life on that rust bucket. *And the worst,* she reminded herself.

"That Coast Guard cutter was insane," Josh said dreamily. "Although, the captain wasn't nearly as hot as—"

She turned her head and gave him a look.

He winced. "Sorry." He sighed. "Jules, he probably just hasn't been able to—"

"Josh. Stop," she said. "The American helicopter got there *two minutes* after the Russians. I begged him to come with me. *Begged* him.

She closed her eyes at the gut-wrenching memory. "I even offered to go with him, Josh. To Russia. Can you imagine how pathetic I felt when he told me no?"

That was what had hurt the most. She'd been willing to give up everything to be with him. *Everything.* Give up her country and her family, just as his mother had done years before. But this time for love.

He hadn't even hesitated before saying no, he didn't want her in Russia, that she must go back to the States without him.

Seeing her in distress now, Josh gave her a hug. "Oh, hon. The man was about to have his career taken away, and God knows what else happen to him. He was probably just thinking of you, getting stuck there and—"

"No," she interrupted. She couldn't listen to the straws Josh was grasping at. She'd done it all herself. "I found out through channels that after he got out of the hospital he *didn't* get fired by the navy. In fact, they've sent him on some special posh assignment."

"I still say they must have threatened him so he couldn't get in touch with you," Josh insisted. "Or tortured him with bamboo splinters under his—"

She shook her head firmly, pushing back with all her might the tears that stung anew. If only she'd told Nikolai sooner about his mother. That was what he hadn't been able to forgive her for.

Or . . . maybe that hadn't mattered at all.

"No," she told herself as well as Josh. "Nikolai got what he wanted all along. He never made any secret his career was the most important thing in his life. Trust me, he flew off in that helicopter and when they offered it back to him, he forgot all about me."

Her own fault for not listening.

She stared very hard across at the TV on the wall and took a steadying breath. The pirate story was still going on. There must have been some big development. They were showing previous footage of the captured ship. But now a photo of a man was superimposed over it.

"My God," Josh exclaimed, "is that Clint Walker?"

She blinked in surprise and looked closer. "Good Lord. I think you're right." What the heck was he—

But before they could speculate, a cultured masculine voice sounded behind her.

"Excuse me," it said. Her heart leapt. *Nikolai?*

She jerked her gaze away from the TV and up to his face. But it wasn't him. *Again.* It was the cute young congressional type. And he wasn't looking at her.

"Did you, by any chance, lose this?" he asked Josh, holding up a Four Seasons key card.

Josh's mouth parted, and he darted a nonplussed look at her. She shifted gears.

"It *is* yours!" she said without missing a beat. "Dr. Stedman, you need to be more careful with your room key. No telling what you might find when you go up there."

He blinked. And smiled shyly. "You're right. Gosh, maybe I'd better go up and check."

"Oh, I definitely think you should," she agreed.

"You'll be all right?" He looked at her earnestly. She nodded, and, after a slight hesitation, he kissed her cheek. "Okay. See you tomorrow."

"Sleep in. It's a holiday."

She watched him go, then Linda said something to her and she was drawn back into the lively conversation around the table.

It was good to have friends. She supposed that was the silver lining in the whole disaster with Nikolai. After being with him, she'd changed. She realized she didn't like her isolated life anymore and had started reaching out to her friends at work, and also to her family. She and her mother talked on the phone nearly every day now. She was really glad about that. Both of them were.

She had Nikolai to thank for that. In a sort of freakish, backward way. She missed him so much it took two dozen friends and family to fill the void.

Ho-boy. *Not* what she should be thinking about.

It was getting late, nearly midnight, and the others started drifting off home. She'd better, too. But since she was taking a taxi back to her apartment anyway, she decided to have one more for the road. For some reason she still felt completely clearheaded and able to think. And remember. Which she'd just as soon not.

She sauntered up to the bar and took a seat on one of the stools, peeling off her jacket and dropping it onto the open seat next to her so she could say she was waiting for someone if she needed to. She really didn't feel like dealing with drunken come-ons tonight. Or sober ones, either, for that matter. Tonight, or for the rest of her life.

"One more, Kev," she told the bartender.

"Make that two, Kev," said a deep, accented voice behind her. *A Russian accent.*

God, it sounded so much like Nikolai that she had to grip the edge of the bar to keep from crumbling.

Just what she needed. *Not.*

"Fuck off, sailor," she told him in perfect Russian. The only whole Russian phrase she knew, but, oh, so appropriate. She'd learned it from one of her colleagues before . . . Well, before.

She didn't bother to look at the man as she said it. She didn't want to be disappointed.

For the hundredth time in less than two weeks.

The man tutted. And said something back to her in Russian. What. Ever.

The drinks arrived. A twenty floated onto the table. A strong, masculine hand reached out and lifted the shot glass. The fingers were long and tan and calloused. Something stirred deep within her. She forced herself not to look at their owner, but her pulse quickened anyway.

A moment later the glass came back down empty.

Then a room key card clattered lightly onto the bar beside it.

Her heart took off at a gallop. No. Freaking. Way.

The hand grasped the other shot glass and raised it, too.

"Hey!" she exclaimed. The man had some nerve!

"Sorry, but—"

She spun to accuse the jerk of—

She froze.

"—one is just never enough. Don't you agree?"

And then he smiled at her. A blindingly sensual, heat-filled smile.

"Nikolai!"

"Except," he said, "when it comes to lovers. Then one is exactly right." He tilted his head at her questioningly. *"Da . . . ?"*

He looked amazing. Fit and healthy, and handsome as sin in his black Russian captain's uniform with all its gold braid and colorful ribbons and medals pinned across his chest. Even that goofy wide hat tucked under his arm was agonizingly sexy.

So not fair.

She managed to recover her voice, but not her composure. She'd started to tremble. She wanted to hit him. Hard. She wanted to hug him. Desperately. She wanted to know where the *hell* he'd been and why he hadn't contacted her for all this time.

What was he doing here?

She shouldn't care. He'd made his choice.

"Sometimes," she said, turning away, "one is too many." She couldn't look at him. Not and keep herself from falling apart.

His finger toyed with the edge of the key card. "Would you like to test that theory?" he quietly asked.

She got to her feet and grabbed her jacket, then turned to look him straight in the eyes. "No," she said and walked away.

God, that felt good.

So why did her heart feel like it was in a meat grinder?

He followed her out of the bar. "At least talk to me, Leisha. Let me explain."

"No!"

"Why not?" he asked, his voice so earnest she wanted to shake him until his teeth rattled.

She rounded on him, fists clenched.

"You *left* me, Nikolai. You left me standing there on the deck of that goddamn submarine all by myself, like a fool, pleading with you to forgive me, to choose me and let me be with you no matter what I had to give up to do it. And crying my eyes out when you heartlessly said no and climbed onto that goddamn helicopter and flew away without another word."

"Hoisted."

"What?"

"I was hoisted. In a harness. Like a sack of potatoes."

She snorted. "Yeah, well, so was I. That's beside the point."

"I was crying, too," he said.

She stared at him and weakened for a moment. Then remembered he'd been shot. "I hope it hurt like hell." She whirled and headed for the door. He couldn't have hurt even half as much as she had. Did. Still did.

"It did hurt," he said, and he caught her arm, bringing her to a halt in the hall next to the elevators. "It hurt a lot. But not my wound. It was my heart that hurt."

"Join the club," she muttered, and to her mortification she started to cry. Again.

Damn.

"Liesha. *Dorogaya*," he murmured and pulled her into his arms. His hat fell to the floor. She tried to push him away, but he wouldn't let her. He pressed his cheek to the top of her head and held her as she cried, whispering all the things she needed to hear.

"You have no idea how much I wanted to go with you. And when you offered to come with me . . . Ah, Liesha, my heart nearly shattered with joy."

She swiped at her cheeks. "Then why? Why did you turn me away?"

"What you told me," he murmured softly, "about my mother, you surprised me. I had suspected it for a long time, but had never expected to hear the truth. When I did . . ." He put his lips to hers. "Forgive me, my love. There was no time to explain. And there was no way I could let you come with me. Because I knew there was something I must do, or it would haunt me for the rest of my life."

She sniffed. "What was it?"

"Kill a man."

She sucked in a breath. "Nikolai!"

He kissed her again. "I didn't do it. I couldn't. Because I realized that if I did, I could never see you again. But, oh, I was sorely tempted."

"Who? Who was it?" she asked.

He shook his head. "He's not important. Not anymore. The

only thing that's important is you and me, Liesha. And your forgiveness. I love you, Julie. Please. Give me a chance to show you how much."

She stood there in his arms, feeling her heart slowly swell to bursting. Was it true? Was it really true that he loved her? That he wanted her?

"But how?" she asked. "I'm still with CIA and you're still a Russian officer."

"Yes, but as of Monday morning, I'm a Russian officer who's a guest senior lecturer at the U.S. Naval Submarine School. I've been transferred to the States."

Stunned, she peered up at him. "Really? They can do that?"

"A new exchange program, in the spirit of friendship and transparency between our nations. They offered it to me last week when I went in to resign."

Her heart melted even more. "You resigned?"

"How could you doubt it? My only thought was to settle my affairs and come to you. When I handed in my papers, my commander tore them up. He said that, considering my background and experience, I'd be perfect for this job. Frankly, I just think Naval Command would rather have me sinking American subs than any more Russian ones," he said dryly.

She hiccuped and risked a small smile. "Their new secret weapon. Diabolical."

He skimmed his knuckles down her cheek, gathering the moisture there and gently wiping it away. "As for CIA, that's up to you to arrange. If you want to. But my mother did work for them. That should count for something."

"They still might not approve," she said.

But in her heart she knew it didn't matter. If they didn't approve of her relationship with Nikolai, she'd quit the Agency. She could always go back to being a journalist. *He* was what she wanted. More than anything else in the world.

He cupped her chin. "So you want to?" he asked, and she didn't miss the hope mirrored in his eyes. "You want to give us a try?"

She wound her arms around him, holding him tight. "Yes. Oh, yes, Nikolai. I do."

He kissed her. A long, warm, adoring kiss, filled with the

promise of sweet, loving days and sizzling hot nights. "Then come with me," he murmured. "Up to my room. And fill my life with joy. I don't ever want to let you go again."

She melted into his embrace as he led her into the elevator after swiping up his hat, and she whispered, "I'll hold you to that," as she kissed him again.

"God, I hope so," he returned.

They tumbled into his room and shut the door behind them, touching and kissing and falling into an endless sea of passion. She slid off his uniform jacket and tossed it onto a chair as they stumbled past.

Lights glowed brightly in the room. "Wait," he said, unbuttoning his shirt and going for the lamps, throwing her heated looks as he switched them off one by one.

She watched him, as she had done so many times on *Ostrov*. Her heart was so full of love it made her dizzy. The sight of him made her limp in the knees. But there was something she needed to know.

"How long?" she asked.

"How long what?" The last lamp dimmed, leaving the room bathed in a soft, romantic glow.

"The lectureship? How long do we have to be together this time?"

He turned to face her. His expression was dark and intensely sensual, filled with emotion . . . and something else she'd never seen in him before. Uncertainty?

"How long do you want?" he asked, pausing with a hand on his belt.

She took him in, the man she loved with every breath in her body. The man who saw her for who she was, and believed in her as no other person on earth had ever done. And she knew the answer in her heart.

"Forever," she said. "I want forever."

The uncertain slant of his lips slowly curved into a smile. "Forever sounds good. Not that I was ever going to let you go again."

She took a step toward him. "No?"

"Not a chance. There's a ring in my jacket pocket. I was going to propose later. After we make love."

She smiled back. She didn't think it was possible to be this happy. "Yeah? You mean, as in marriage?"

"As in Mr. and Mrs. Nikolai Romanov." He started to tug off his belt, a devilish look of temptation filling his eyes. "So you might want to prepare your answer."

She nodded, oh, so tempted to run to his jacket and get the ring right now, put it on and never take it off. But no, she wanted the words, the bended knee, the whole nine yards. "Oh, I think I know what my answer will be. But . . . is it really possible? What will our bosses say?"

He gave her a look that said he didn't give a damn, she was *his*. She shivered with the thrilling knowledge that he wanted to be with her that badly. Because she did, too.

His pants hit the floor. "Do you really care what they say?" He cocked a brow.

He was still wearing his hat. But nothing else.

"Hell, no," she said.

He was tall and broad and muscled masculine perfection, standing next to the biggest bed she'd ever seen.

And he was all hers. Forever.

Turn the page for a sneak peek at the next novel
in Nina Bruhns's Men in Uniform series

WHITE HOT

Available winter 2012 from Berkley Sensation!

For a man on the run, the fog was both a blessing and a curse.

For the past week, U.S. Navy Lieutenant Commander Clint Walker had been grateful for the recurring blanket of mist as he'd scrambled to stay two steps ahead of his pursuers, island-hopping his way along the Aleutians toward mainland Alaska. So far he'd managed to evade the enemy hot on his trail—Chinese operatives determined to retrieve the stolen military plans in his possession . . . and no doubt kill him for their trouble.

It was after midnight. A severe storm had left a thick shroud of gray that blotted out the pale midsummer sun lingering on the horizon, and cast the surrounding landscape in an eerie, impenetrable glow.

The hair on the back of Clint's neck prickled, every sense attuned to the danger lurking in the mist. The enemy was out there. Close by. *Stalking him.* He could feel their presence down to his marrow.

It wouldn't take a rocket scientist to guess where he was heading. The biggest airport in the Aleutians was in Dutch Harbor. The agents tracking him might already be hiding there, lying in wait for him to show up. But he'd have to risk it. He needed to get the microdisc containing the stolen plans back to D.C. ASAP.

If he could find the damned airport.

It seemed like he'd been jogging for miles. After four days of hell on a fishing trawler working his passage to get this far—hell, it had seemed like a good idea at the time, but *damn*, that job was a backbreaker—Clint was dead on his feet. All he wanted was to find a way back to D.C. and his apartment, grab a steaming hot shower, and sleep for twenty-four hours straight.

But that wasn't going to happen unless he made it to the airport and onto a plane. Preferably alive.

He stopped jogging long enough to catch his breath. And listen. He could hear the shallow waves of Iliuliuk Bay sucking at the nearby shore, so he knew he was still on the right road. In the distance, a foghorn's low, mournful moan did a duet with the distinct metallic clank of chains from a dozen or more ships moored in the harbor. The sharp smell of raw fish filled the air, but gave no clue as to whether he was closer to the airport or to cannery row. Of course, with just one change of clothes it might be himself he was smelling.

Hell. He couldn't see a goddamn thing in this fucking pea soup. He must have missed the turnoff for the airport.

Being the middle of the night, the runway lights had been turned off, and there were no other visual or auditory clues. The entire island seemed to be closed up tight as a clam. Rather than risk running into the bad guys, he'd hunker down for the night, and first thing in the morning scout out a plane to hitch a ride on to Anchorage or Seattle.

Unless they found him first . . .

Was that footsteps behind him?

No. Just the rustle of leaves.

He'd spotted his pursuers back on Adak Island. There'd been three of them, moving in concert to hunt him down, a stealthy, efficient killing unit. The Chinese *really* wanted those plans back. That was when Clint had decided he'd rather face the wrath of a fishing trawler captain as a stowaway and work off his unplanned passage. He couldn't lose that disc.

Pulling down a deep breath, he started to jog again.

Hell. He was getting too old for this shit. If he managed to make it back to D.C. in one piece, maybe he'd actually accept

that Pentagon job the commander had been dangling in front
of his nose for a few years now.

Suddenly the faint whisper of hushed human voices floated
out from the fog.

Again Clint halted in his tracks and listened. *One, two,
three speakers.* He couldn't hear the language they were
speaking, but it didn't sound English. It sounded Chinese.
And they didn't sound happy.

Clint swore silently and veered off the road. Folding himself into a patch of low juniper, he waited. Moments later,
three soundless black silhouettes glided stealthily past.

He swore again. *So much for the airport.*

He assessed his options. There was only one road off
Amaknak Island. The sea lapped at one side of it, and when
the fog lifted, the stunted tundra shrubs on the other wouldn't
hide a large cat. In front of him, an ambush awaited.

Nowhere to run. Nowhere to hide.

Fucking hell.

There was only one thing left to do.

He turned and started to sprint, heading back the way he'd
come.

Time for plan B.

Captain Samantha Richardson heaved the last insanely heavy
box into place on top of the endless rows of crates and car-
tons. She and most of her ship's crew had spent the past three
hours restacking. Who knew biscuits weighed so damn
much?

A freak summer storm had swept across the Bering Sea
yesterday, pounding *Île de Cœur* with fifteen-foot waves and
wreaking havoc in three of the seven cargo holds of the old
tramp freighter, which were only three-quarters full. Anything not nailed down had been tossed about like confetti.

Samantha had already fired and booted off the chief mate,
the officer who'd been responsible for overseeing the loading
and securing of the cargo in Japan. Or rather, *not* securing it.
The crew was now a man down, but she'd manage. She'd actually been glad for the excuse. The guy'd had a real attitude
problem. Especially about serving under a woman.

And if this was a sample of his work, good riddance.

"Finally," she muttered, surveying the evenly distributed stacks of boxes that she and the crew were standing on top of. She wiped the sweat from her brow with a sleeve. "I thought we'd *never* finish."

Luckily, she'd spent three years as a chief mate en route to her captain's license, and her second mate was taking the captain's exam this fall, so together they'd known how to expertly redistribute the load so it wouldn't shift again.

A chorus of amens came back at her from the five men and one woman heading for the ladder up to the lower deck. Lars Bolun was second mate, Carin Tornarsuk was the oiler, there were four able seamen: Johnny Dorn, Frank Tennyson, Jeeter Pond, and old salt Spiros Tsanaka. If they all managed to climb out of the cargo hold, grab a bite to eat, and fall into their bunks without losing consciousness from exhaustion first, it would be a pure damn miracle.

They had to shove off by oh-six-hundred. Sam absolutely, unequivocally, had to get this cargo to Nome before noon on the Fourth of July. In hold two was the precious order of special fireworks she'd managed by hook, crook, and more than a few shady side deals to scrounge together last week for the new mayor of Nome and his self-aggrandizing election celebration. The new mayor was founder and owner of Bravo Logging Corp, Richardson Shipping's biggest client, with eyes on the Alaska governor's mansion. Her father had promised the mayor his fireworks even though at this late date every firework in Japan and China had been spoken for and shipped out long ago. Then he'd given Sam the assignment of fulfilling the order, knowing she'd fail.

But failure wasn't in Sam's vocabulary. Bringing in this cargo, on time, would ensure that her father would have to end her infuriating "trial contract" and hire her on permanently. Effectively robbing those who wanted her gone from the family business of the ammunition they needed to convince her father to fire her.

And she knew better than to think he wouldn't.

Seaman Johnny Dorn's expressive moan brought her out of her frustrating thoughts. "I am never, ever, *ever* going to eat another White Lover as long as I live," Johnny declared, collapsing back against the steel bulkhead to wait for her. "Even after drinking a *hundred* gallons of beer."

Everyone was too wiped out to laugh. The inevitable ribald jokes about the unfortunately named Japanese biscuits had kept them amused for the first fifteen minutes. After that the humor had fizzled under the weight of the task.

She started up the ladder. The cargo holds were below the lower deck where the roll-on roll-off cargo was tied down. Above that was the main deck, where the big containers and the deck crane were out in the weather.

"Hey, how 'bout someone up there giving me a hand up?" she called, reaching for the rim of the hatch.

Second Mate Lars Bolun knelt and reached down, trying to slip his arm around her torso as she popped her head up. "Relax, Skipper," he said with a grin. "I'll pull you the rest of the way up."

She snorted, and batted him away. "In your dreams, Mate." She did, however, grab his hand to steady herself as she hauled herself up onto the lower deck. She wobbled a bit and he put a hand to her waist to keep her from toppling.

She straightened away from him, forcing her rubbery legs to carry her weight whether they wanted to or not. "Thanks. I'm good."

He gave her an amused look. "One of these days, Captain, you'll fall willingly into my arms."

At that, everyone else snorted.

She rolled her eyes. "Wouldn't hold my breath, Mr. Bolun." They all knew he didn't stand a chance.

Not that he wasn't a good-looking guy. Tall and muscular, with silver blond hair, and smart to boot. But she was his boss. It just wasn't going to happen.

Besides, he was steady, earnest, and determined. In other words, the kind of man who'd be looking for a commitment from a woman. And Samantha Richardson didn't do commitment. Not anymore.

Suddenly, there was a shout from the top of the narrow metal stairway leading up to the main deck. "Captain Richardson! You need to come up here!"

It was Smitty, the wiper—the young greenhorn seaman who got all the dirty maintenance and gofer jobs on board.

"What's going on, Mr. Shijagurumayum?" she called back. The others called him Smitty for obvious reasons. She'd had to practice for a half hour before she'd gotten her tongue wrapped around his ridiculously long name.

"Ginger saw a guy climbing up the aft mooring line!" he said excitedly. "He must be trying to stow away!"

"What?" She stared for a second in surprise. Then she whirled and made a beeline for the stairs. A *stowaway*? *Hell*, no. That was not going to happen either. "You didn't let him get on board, did you?"

"No, ma'am. Shandy's waiting at the top of the line to grab him."

"Good." She bounded up the stairs two at a time. She hadn't thought to post a guard on the dock. She hadn't thought she needed one. With the threat of terrorism and piracy, port security was tight as a drum. No unauthorized persons should be able to get in.

How had this guy gotten past?

She burst up onto the main deck, followed closely by the others. They all ran aft across the mist-shrouded deck where Shandy stood at the rail peering down at the dock twenty feet below. His gaze swept from side to side searching the thick black void between the ship and the cement dock, where the mooring line cut through the fog up to the hull. But no one was clinging to it.

"Where is he? Did you get him?" Sam asked breathlessly, scanning the dockside. It was impossible to see anything but the ghostly silhouettes of buildings and equipment in the fog. Even the streetlights were just glowing spheres of yellow in a shroud of shimmering gray.

Shandy looked up disgustedly. "Gone. He must have heard Ginger shout to me and taken off."

Sam's shoulders and anxiety notched down a fraction. "You're sure?"

"Trust me, Captain, nobody got past me." Shandy lifted a hand. It was clutching an oily wrench. A big one.

Sam winced a little, but was grateful for his vigilance. "Okay. Good. But let's set up a watch tonight, yeah? I'll call the harbor cops and report an intruder."

"I'll take the watch," Lars Bolun volunteered. "I can sleep tomorrow."

"Thanks," she said with a smile. She could always count on the second mate to step up. "I'll send Ginger out with a plate of food and some coffee." Sam turned to the others. "Hit the hay, everyone. We sail at high tide." Which was at six a.m.

They all groaned as she started for the bridge.

"Maybe we should just let the fucker come on board and work him like a dog," Frank grumbled. "We *are* a man short . . ."

She laughed and kept walking. "Right. Because we really want a desperate criminal or a terrorist working side-by-side with us."

She made her way to the wheelhouse and placed the call, then retired to her stateroom for a quick shower. At last she sank onto her bunk and closed her eyes with a tired sigh. She was so exhausted her head was spinning.

Despite that, sleep refused to come. She just couldn't put the intruder out of her mind. Who was he? An escaped prisoner? A terrorist? Or just some poor schmuck who didn't have money for passage to Seattle? Was he still out there? She shivered and pulled her blanket up tight under her chin. Of all the ships in Dutch Harbor, why had he chosen *Île de Cœur* to try and stow away on?

She pushed out a breath. And thought about her side arm. A brand-new Glock 23. It was stored in the safe in her wall and, thank goodness, had so far only come out for cleanings.

Finally she gave up, slid out of bed, and got the Glock out of the safe. She even loaded the clip. But she drew the line at racking it. Setting the gun on the tiny nightstand next to her bunk, she got back into bed and firmly closed her eyes. She was going to get some sleep if it killed her.

She'd just sunk into that floaty twilight zone between waking and sleeping, her body relaxed and her lids heavy as lead, when there was a soft knock at her stateroom door.

She forced her eyelids up and frowned. "Who is it?"

No one answered.

"Who is it?" she repeated, alarm creeping through her muzzy mind. She sat up and reached for the Glock.

"It— It's me," a deep voice said softly.

She blinked, her hand hovering above the weapon. Who the hell would be— "Bolun, is that you?"

"Open the door," he said, his voice muffled, but more cajoling than demanding. "I, um, need to . . ."

Oh, for God's sake. She rose from the bunk and grabbed her robe, wrapping it tightly around herself. At the last second she picked up the Glock. Padding to the door, she unlocked it, cracked it open, and carefully peeked out.

"What is it?" she asked. "I thought you were on watch."

He was standing a few feet back. In the total darkness of the passageway she couldn't see more than the outline of his large body.

Except there was something wrong. His hair . . . it should have been blond and pale even in the dark. Instead it was black as the midnight sky.

Not Bolun.

She gasped and slammed the door.

Too late.

The man moved like lightning. He slapped his palm against the door, preventing it from closing, then pushed his huge body into it so it flung open and she flew backward onto the bunk.

Suddenly she remembered the Glock in her hand. She whipped it up and started to aim.

"Don't," he warned.

Her heart slammed to her throat.

A large black pistol was pointing right back at her.